Real studies 15

REAL Studies Editors

Josef Schmied
Christoph Haase
Matthias Hofmann

Series Advisors

Marina Bondi
Gabriela Miššíková
Renata Povolná
Andrew Tollet
Andrew Wilson

Previous Titles

Academic Writing for Africa: The Journal Article

Edited by

Josef Schmied
Matthias Hofmann
Alexandra Esimaje

Cuvillier Verlag

Bibliographical information held by the German National Library
The German National Library has listed this book in the Deutsche Nationalbibliografie (German national bibliography); detailed bibliographic information is available online at http://dnb.d-nb.de.
1st edition - Göttingen: Cuvillier, 2018

This book has been published with funding from the Volkswagen Foundation.

  ISBN 978-3-7369-9937-4
  eISBN 978-3-7369-8937-5

Preface

The contributions in this volume are the result of the intensive workshop that was organised in Benin City with the generous support of the Volkswagen Foundation in Germany. The workshop and the corresponding Volkswagen Application was a result of the discussions that were held during a previous visit by Professor Alexandra Esimaje in Chemnitz, where she had had the opportunity to participate in our PhD Symposium and a small conference, in which Chemnitz PhD students discussed their PhD topics including related conference presentations and journal articles.

The workshop in Benin City provided a new format of intensive training by experienced researchers from different parts of Africa and two specialists from Chemnitz in Germany. The workshop consisted mainly of plenary presentations and intensive guidance by mentors. The mentors had received the participants' first drafts well before the first meeting and had made suggestions for improvement, which the participants in the workshop were able to study before the workshop in Benin City started.

Despite the excellent preparation of the workshop by the local organisers in Benin City, the whole project faced several unexpected problems:

a) Three of the mentors were not able to attend the workshop at short notice because of health and security problems. Thus, others who were not so familiar with the entire project had to take over and managed to complete all their assignments and guidance successfully.

b) The post-workshop preparation for journal articles proved more difficult than expected. This can be put down partly to the usual workload of African scholars at the home universities and partly to the general difficulty in academic communication. It was just difficult for African scholars to provide more up-to-date references and include them into their writings, because internet downloads can still be difficult.

c) This may be related to the pervasive problem of plagiarism by African scholars, which made it difficult for the editors of the final volume, since not only the participants, but even some mentors obviously included passages that were too close to originals. Whereas European scholars can retrieve on the internet rapidly, African scholars find it difficult to verify whether they had used their own words in their drafts and not copied from what they had previously read and appreciated.

Since it is obviously the authors' responsibility to decide on the final versions of their papers, the editors did not insist on all their queries being answered in detail, but decided in the end in many cases to accept the final versions with minor inconsistencies, in particular in quoting and tracking ideas and in their presentation in the oral discussions and final publication.

This volume includes two types of presentation: At the beginning, we present meta-articles that can be taken as guidelines by other young scholars who could not participate in the Benin City Workshop or who wish to read to prepare for similar workshops in future. The style in these contributions is somewhat collo-quial and persuasive, so that they require no previous knowledge and understand-ing. The remaining articles are selected contributions that derive from the work-shop in Benin City, which may be of interest to many scholars. Although they are far from perfect and may reveal many traces of African English and African re-search specificity, they may be seen as a reward for the young participants and as a useful stepping stone to further improvement until similar writing projects are completed and can be submitted to the international journals which all scholars aim for.

The individual contributions show, also in their domestic styles, the different research and style traditions in African universities. We particularly observed that African authors tend towards declarative style, where European authors might have preferred the conventionalized share of hedging in academic writing, and that conclusions are often shorter and weaker than introductions. The emphasis on practical approaches in teaching academic writing to novice African researchers allows us to take theoretical backgrounds into consideration wherever needed while maintaining the accessibility of this project and this volume to young re-searchers. Author-specific idiomaticity and some grammatical special features were left untouched, when the general understanding was not affected. Even for-matting of references was only harmonized when functional necessities appeared prominent (e.g. to distinguish independent publications like books from independ-ent publications like articles). It has to be emphasized at the very beginning of this volume that this is not intended as a model that has to be followed by graduates in various parts of Africa and/or Europe, but that is a documentation of the different conventions and practices of academic writing in different parts of Africa. Gradu-ates in this field must be aware of these conventions and practices, so that they can make their own decisions about which conventions to follow and which to neglect in their own writings. Thus they may find a good compromise between the neces-sities of the field and their own identity as independent scholars.

In the opening section of this volume, Schmied introduces 'a global view' on the project and the theme of the 'journal article'. His understanding of global is two-fold: On the one hand, principles and practices of high-quality research arti-cles are similar in most English Departments; on the other hand, the conceptuali-sation of the writing process should start at the structural level, before the planning reaches the sub-levels of sequencing paragraphs and individual sentences. Unlike the other contributions, he concentrates on the whole writing process which covers the development of topics and research questions, the identification of appropriate journals, the planning of the writing process, and editing the first draft before the submission. Schmied's contribution thus has an introductory character for this spe-cial volume, which is why it serves as the opening section.

His section is followed by Hofmann's methodological contribution to research designs in general and quantitative studies in particular. He focusses on the link between the journal articles' proposed research questions/hypotheses and their subsequent systematized answering process, by outlining rules and recommendations for the operationalisation of variables that are necessary to answer the research questions and falsify the research hypotheses, respectively. He further illustrates the different types of variables by examples that enable young, novice scholars to access such notions more easily.

In section 3, Ochieng & Ekundayo meticulously outline the various components of the peer reviewing process of the journal article. They focus on a review of previous literature on this process and provide advice on self-editing a paper by the novice author before its submission as well as on coping strategies for reviewers' comments. They illustrate these by examples outlined by experienced authors taken from the literature.

The three contributions above are placed on a metalevel to reflect on conventions, best practice examples, and illustrations of conducting and documenting research on such a level that novice scholars at the beginning of their careers have access to a substantial resource they can consult before the submission of their manuscripts to an academic journal. The contributions that follow are examples for studies that have been conceptualised and conducted by African scholars in the different fields linguistics has to offer. The next four contributions are discourse-analytical studies, which exemplify a qualitative analysis of language use in religious, institutional, and political contexts.

The first of these contributions, section 4, is Muo's study on religious ambivalence as a behavioural response to multiculturalism in two literary texts. The emphasis is placed on a contrastive analysis of two Igbo societies, one at home and one in the diaspora, and their reconstruction of religious experiences that promote division. Religious belief and doubt are comprehended as consequence of anxiety and social dominance, which influences individuals, families, and societies. The study concludes that the two communities are closely connected.

In section 5, Dada argues for the power of religion in citizenship education, using church programme handbills as data. By taking a systemic functional perspective, Dada analyses the semantic meaning of religious discourse exemplified in verbal and visual elements of the handbills, using Kress & Van Leeuwen's (2006) visual grammar approach. The results of this study show that synergetic effects can be expected in religious discourse when both elements, verbal and visual, are used to convey the ideological power of the discourse.

Using print media news, Ogungbemi analyses the discourse of terrorism in Nigeria in section 6. More specifically, he concentrates on the representation of social actors during the Boko Haram insurgency between 2009 and 2014 in five private Nigerian newspapers, using Critical Discourse Analysis (Wodak 1995) and Halliday's (2004) ideational meta-function. The results show that Nigerian print media accuses the government of having politicised the crisis and that the ideologies of radical Islamism and of an us-versus-them dichotomy dominate the news discourse while moderate Muslims are praised.

Finally, Adam-Moses and Marfo investigate the role of power in university admission letters in section 7, using van Dijk's (1989) framework of social power and discourse control. The manifestation of power in these letters was found to be overtly expressed through threats and commands on the one hand, but also concealed through passives, declaratives, and abstract rhetors on the other hand.

The next contribution adds a quantitative corpus-linguistic perspective to the analysis of authorial stance in political discourse and thus constitutes a link between the discourse analytical studies before it and the two corpus-linguistic studies that follow. Using Biber's (2006) Frame of Grammatically Marked Stance, Ugah investigates a self-compiled, specialized news corpus on a Nigerian political party's agenda to identify the linguistic features that convey the journalists' stance towards the party and its electorate. Her results confirm those of previous studies that news reporting is not objective as it should be, but rather linguistically marked by the authors' stance.

In section 9, Esimaje engages a well-researched topic in corpus linguistic studies, using a self-compiled corpus and employing a systemic functional perspective (Halliday 1978). In a 257,000-word corpus of journal articles, she investigates the frequencies of some hedges such as modals, verbs, and adverbials in Nigerian senior academic writing. Her results confirm hedging in academic writing and show high frequencies for the verbs *notes* and *argue* and the adverbial *according to*.

In a self-compiled corpus of research article introductions, Amuzie analyses the structural conformity in these introductions of advanced academics to the Create-a-Research-Space (CARS) model in section 10. The model of rhetorical moves in introductions was postulated by Swales (1990) within the linguistic subdiscipline of academic writing. The specialized corpus contains 31 research article introductions, covering the disciplines of Linguistics, Teaching English to Speakers of Other Languages (TESOL), and Literature. Her results show that most Nigerian introductions are cyclic in their structure which does not conform to the linearity proposed in the CARS model.

The next four contributions form a new thematic complex that is unconnected to the previous studies' topics. While the topic changes to Second Language Acquisition/TESOL, linguistic theory, methods, and concepts are as crucial for the upcoming studies as they were for the studies mentioned above. In section 11, Okumo investigates the notion of transfer in the pronunciation of tertiary second-language English speaking students in Southern Nigeria. In a descriptive approach, she identifies significant features of sound substitution, insertion, stress, and intonation and observes that English sounds are adjusted to sounds which are part of the learners' first language when a gap in English phonology is encountered. Further, Okumo finds that similar forms in the first and second languages are typically mixed in second-language performance. From these findings, she formulates suggestions for teaching English in the classroom.

In section 12, Akindele investigates 200 university undergraduates' stress patterns in 15 English compounds in formal style, using the *Speech Filing System* and a laptop for recording. The speakers of English as a second language (ESL) only showed conformity to Received Pronunciation stress patterns in 3.3% of the cases. Instead, the ESL undergraduates preferred to realize stress on both syllables of two-syllable compounds.

Gbenedio and Osa-Omoregie's study concentrates on the effects of cooperative language learning on student writing in English in section 13. The research design is a quasi-experimental study in which 40 secondary school students in the experimental group were taught writing using Cooperative Language Learning and 40 students in the control group were taught writing using the traditional product approach. Results of two *t-tests* showed that students of the experimental group outperform those of the control group, which call for a change in teaching policies at secondary schools.

The last study in this thematic complex is Nnamani's investigation of reading choices in tertiary education in section 14. The theoretical position for the study is the researcher's experience that students either do not read their assignments or that they are not efficient in reading. Methodologically, the study relies on interviews and questionnaires to assess whether the offer of reading choices increases the success of learning English grammar. The study concludes that under teacher supervision reading choices increase the motivation for reading and the performance in mechanical accuracy.

The remaining two contributions constitute the end of this edited volume for their contents. In section 15, Esimaje and Gbenedio analyse the role of reviewers' comments as feedback in the development of academic writing skills. Data were derived from the reviews of 20 draft journal articles as well as a questionnaire and yielded results that attest success to learning writing skills from feedback.

The last section is concerned with paralinguistic features of Igbo and Yoruba. By using Saussure's semiotic theory, Akujobi seeks similarities and differences between the two languages that help to evaluate the potential of conflict versus communication. Participant observation and interviews are used as means of data collection, which show more similarities than differences in paralinguistic features between the two ethnicities.

December 2018   Josef Schmied & Matthias Hofmann

References

Biber, D. (2006). Stance in Spoken and Written University Registers. *Journal of English for Academic Purpose* 5, 97-116.

Halliday, M.A.K. (1978). *Language as Social Semiotic*. London: Arnold.

Halliday, M.A.K. (2004). *An Introduction to Functional Grammar*. 3rd ed. Rev. Mathiessen C. London: Edward Arnold.

Kress, G. and van Leeuwen, T. (2006). *Reading Images – The Grammar of Visual Design*. 2nd ed. London: Routledge.

Swales, J. (1990). *Genre Analysis*. Cambridge: Cambridge University Press.

van Dijk, T. A. (1989). How "They" Hit the Headlines: Ethnic Minorities in the Press. In G. Smitherman-Donaldson & T. A. van Dijk. (Eds.) *Discourse and Discrimination*. Detroit: Wayne State University Press, 18-59.

Wodak, R. (1995). Critical Linguistics and Critical Discourse Analysis. In J. Verschueren, J.-O. Östman, J. Blommaert and C. Bulcaen (Eds.). *Handbook of Pragmatics*. Amsterdam: John Benjamins, 204-201.

Contents

A Global View on Writing Research Articles for International Journals: Principles & Practices[1]

Josef Schmied

Chemnitz University of Technology

Abstract

This contribution provides a global view in two senses: first, it claims that the principles and practices of good research articles in English are similar in most English Departments world-wide, and second, it emphasizes that the planning and writing of journal articles should start from a global perspective, i.e. the sequence of chapters should be planned first, the sequence of paragraphs in the sections second, and the individual sentences last. It is particularly addressed to young scholars and thus discusses how to find an appropriate topic, an appropriate journal, an appropriate title. It starts with modern key issues like finding a research question or a research hypothesis and key concepts like academic discourses, metalanguage, and genres, with journal conventions in the centre. The focus of this contribution is on global thinking and editing: The writer starts at the macro-level, the global paradigm, the sequence of chapters and headlines, and concrete examples are taken from current articles in journals that are easily accessible and recommended to African scholars. At the meso-level, managing the information and argumentation flow within and beyond paragraphs is particularly important for effective communication. Finally, at the micro-level, the controversial issues of intertextuality and plagiarism and of idiomaticity and transparency are discussed. All this is summarized in the conclusion, which gives advice to young African academics who wish to start a career within the English research community.

Keywords: Academic writing, global perspective, structure, plagiarism

1. Global views on Writing

1.1. Meanings of "global"

By "global" view, I mean something like a bird's eye view, a top-down or holistic approach to journal articles and research articles. I distinguish between a macro-, meso- and micro-level: By macro-level I mean a chapter or a section, by meso-level I mean a paragraph and by micro-level I mean a sentence – and I think it is

---

[1] The journal article is a broader and more neutral term. It is not so strict in its format (IMRaD), as explained. It can also be more theoretical and then it may also require more experience, if it is a good journal article. Therefore, I have focussed on the research article which may be difficult, but in the end easier for a young scholar. A research paper can be relatively restricted, and if it is data-based, it will also be accepted more easily.

really unfortunate that most writers or most style guide books concentrate on the micro-level only. I think that planning a project and a piece of writing (Buckingham 2016) should start from the highest level and result in a draft, after which a considerable amount of work still remains to edit the text. I usually tell my students: "Don't hand in your first draft." Students do not spend enough time on editing – and on planning. So I tell them that they should spend at least 20% of the time on the planning instead of writing immediately. They often just manage a first draft and I tell them: "This is only half of it, you still need to invest a lot of time and hard work – at least 30% of the whole work is on editing."

Another global perspective is the writing of a journal article focussing on the result, and here a bird's eye view should mean some 20% introduction, 60% main part but also 20% conclusion; from experience, I can say that in many texts the conclusions are often too short and do not really wind up enough what should be the main focus of the text.

1.2. Meanings of "writing"

When I say writing here, I want to emphasize that today we have all types of literacy, not only the traditional literacy or the now well-known multimedia literacy. I also mean the literacy of (reading and writing) academic texts, which includes the collection of information, the processing of information and the presentation of information in a new context. This literacy is an advanced skill – much more advanced than the usual four or five skills that we teach in practical language classes. I see the presentation of academic knowledge from a constructivist perspective, and I would like to emphasize two main points: the first is discourse community, the academic readership/audience in our field; the second is genre, the text type conventions expected in our discourse community (Swales 1990, Swales/Feak 2012). These expectations are partly in contrast to the writers' personal identity, because writers always say something about their background, their academic training, etc. and they have their own way of liaising with their academic discourse community (Hyland 2012). And all this needs to be learned; writers cannot wait for a "spontaneous overflow of powerful feelings", as Wordsworth wrote. Academic writing is a craft and hard work - partly also, because academic writing includes a complete set of metalanguage, which is expected in the discourse community and enshrined in the conventions of the discipline.

2. First steps: From pre-writing activities to first draft

2.1. Finding a topic

Before writing, there is reading. This is partly because there are two approaches to finding a topic: first, top-down, from theory to practice, through reading. Theoretically, young scholars read "the literature" on the topic, find a gap and say "this gap needs to be filled". If it is a large gap, the topic has be narrowed down, so that it is manageable, operational (Buckingham 2016: 5-10, with examples). The problem is that this is a really difficult approach because we can never be sure whether there is really a gap or whether we just have not read enough. A lot of students thus postpone their writing, because they have the feeling that maybe it is only them who see the gap. A better approach through reading is to find a model article in the research literature and say "I would like to do something like this, hopefully with my own new data". The second approach is a bottom-up approach: from data to analysis, i.e. when I see some striking or at least interesting feature in the data, I can say "this must be worth exploring" or maybe even more difficult "I can do some statistical analyses or maybe even find the patterns in the data that I did not see with my own eyes". And then in the data, beyond the purely statistical, I can "see a rationale", maybe a functional reason why the language is used in this way. These two different approaches are possible; in the end, finding a model article is probably the easiest way for a young scholar, but that depends on the accessibility of journals.

2.2. Finding a journal

Although in many developing countries researchers and PhD students are given lists of accepted journals (of course, international, peer-reviewed, with high impact factor), it seems more advisable to follow the advice (or only the footsteps) of peers and colleagues, who have successfully published in journals. Alternatively, you could approach journals that you know from reading in your field and that have published useful model articles (cf. 4.3. below); they may be interested in continuing the academic discourse in the same field.

2.3. Finding a research hypothesis

One of the most challenging tasks for young scholars is to set up a working hypothesis (Buckingham 2016: 9). It does not have to be a final one, hypotheses are provisionally set up on the basis of reading and accepted as a basis for further research. Many hypotheses cannot be tested convincingly and many cannot be confirmed but this can still be a good academic result. Actually, a clever strategy is a null hypothesis, e.g. "there is no difference between two groups of people interacting or two types of language usage for us", and if you can reject a null hypothesis, which says there is no difference, then you can prove that there is a, maybe text linguistic, maybe sociolinguistic difference between your datasets. It is easier to falsify a hypothesis by finding just one case that does not fit. Research hypotheses and research questions are much more important in English studies today than 50 years ago, as they were taken over from natural and social sciences. They serve three purposes at the beginning of an academic discourse: to determine what kind of research the writer will be doing, to raise expectations in the readers, and to identify the specific objectives the study will focus on. Formulating a good research hypothesis is a methodologically central issue in advanced writing and has to be practiced in the context of advanced empirical research methodologies (Hofmann 2018).

2.4. Finding a research question

For young researchers, it may be easier to formulate research questions than research hypotheses, bearing in mind that many research questions may be asked, but few can be answered satisfactorily with the tools available (cf. section 2.5. below). I can give you two examples of my own research questions, although I have to admit that in this case the research questions are not written down explicitly in these two texts: the first one is my PhD thesis, which was on "English in Tanzania", and the research question there is "Is Tanzania a second language country or an international language country (which is sometimes called a foreign language country today)?". Because in contrast to Nigeria, the biggest and prototypical second language country in Africa, the situation in Tanzania then and even today is not so clear because they have Kiswahili as a nation-wide accepted national language. In my postdoctoral thesis, I compared British and Indian English using an established corpus with different text types or genres and here the research question was "Is the variation in relative constructions greater between the varieties [i.e. British and Indian English] than between different genres within these varieties?", and the result was, in a nutshell, there is more variation within varieties than between British and Indian English. But of course, grammatical constructions – like relative constructions – are never observed as distinguishing varieties of English as much as pronunciation and the lexicon, for instance (cf. Quirk et al. 1985). But these would be typical research questions, which are expected today, but were not expected 30 years ago when I wrote these texts.

2.5. Critical issues: access to infrastructure, equipment, etc.

Finally, I also want to mention that it is not always easy to answer research questions adequately, and you have to ask yourself critically: "Is, what I can do, sufficient to answer this research question in an academic way?", for instance "Can I collect recordings that are good enough for differentiating patterns in phonetics?" or "Can I collect 'representative' samples of social media discourse in Nigeria as a basis for an analysis of Nigerian usages of 'democrat*'?".

Nowadays, questions of technical equipment seem negligible, but not in all African universities: everyone has a smartphone, but of course recordings in a conference hall are not good enough for linguistic analyses – at least phonetic ones. Or African scholars have to ask themselves: "Is my internet connection stable enough, so that I can use HTTrack to download (huge amounts of messy) newspaper texts over night?" "Do I have at least access to an eye-tracker to do reading research seriously? ... so that I can see how readers process language, where they stop, when a word is unclear or where they drift off, when they have their own idea related to what they hear or read?" (cf. Schmied & Hofmann 2018).

Unfortunately, many interesting research questions cannot be answered satisfactorily, because they cannot be transformed into an operational research strategy, at least today, by a poor individual researcher in a specific (unfavourable) research environment – and this applies to African scholars more than to others.

2.6. Finding a title and subtitle

Another way of focussing, and marketing an article for a journal, is an attractive title and often subtitle. I can suggest three paradigms of finding an appropriate title: for instance, you could have a "sexy" quotation which is striking, provocative or at least interesting, and then after a colon explain the topic and the method if possible; or one could indicate a broad research area in the title and then add a more specific research question; or, one can have a research question first and then explain what that means in context. The choice is between a more sexy, journalistic title and a more descriptive one, between a striking quotation and more academic phrases indicating data (*MA theses*), methodology (*corpus-linguistic*), theoretical framework (*systemic functional grammar*) or context of application (*education, teaching*).

Here are some examples from texts written by participants in the Benin workshop. A title can include a strong statement like "Religious Bigots or Extremists?", which is, of course, provocative in a university context, but maybe not in social media; or, "PDP Administration Actively Sustained a Crisis Profiteering from it", a clear attack on a political party, but easily found in social media. A much more serious article would be "Constructing Religion and Politics in Nigerian Terrorism News". Of course, the same article can be used with a different, more journalistic title, like "Nigerian Terrorism News" – a broad area, so you might want to specify: "Who Blames Whom and How?" This is basically the same as "Religion or Politics? Linguistic Devises Used in Nigerian Terrorism News". The writer has to decide which of these possible titles is appropriate for which journal.

Another interesting case is a nice African language exercise in one of the workshop articles entitled "Bokyi noun class system", where I noticed that, like in most drafts, the headlines or the titles could be made much better. One possibility is "A New Analysis of Bokyi Noun Phrases: Noun Classes, Agreement, and Valency". The "new" promises something, the three linguistic details make it sound scholarly. You can also ask explicitly the research questions "Is Bokyi a Bantu Language? A New Analysis of Noun Phrases", and of course, noun phrases include Classes, Agreement, and Valency. Both of these articles are quite attractive and still linguistically specific enough. The question of which one is better depends on the journal, where you want to "sell" this article.

In more general terms: What is an effective title? It is effective, if it fulfils one or more of the following functions: A title has to indicate the theoretical, regional or academic discourse context in which the text should be understood. It orients the reader towards the topic research area. In form, it strikes the balance between brevity and clarity. It must be really understandable, so it should indicate enough, but not reveal too much: it should not pre-empt your conclusion and the main point:

It should make further reading beyond the title, beyond the abstract, interesting, attractive, maybe useful (cf. Hannay & Mackenzie 2017: 51).

I can illustrate this here with four examples of complex titles again from my own writing. One is the book we have edited recently called "Working with Media Texts. Deconstructing and Constructing Crises in Europe". Another one is an article entitled "Complexity and Coherence in English Student Writing, Specifically in Hypertext Learning Systems" which I wrote almost 20 years ago at the beginning of the world-wide web when hypertext was relatively new. Or "Where the grass is greener? Colour terms in East African English". Many African languages have relatively few colour terms and then questions can be asked like: "How many colour terms are used by African writers?" or "Is *rose* or *pink* in the second or third circle of colours?" The fourth title is, similarly, a wide area plus a specific case: "Corpus-Based Contrastive Lexicology: the Case of English *with* and its German Translation Equivalents". These are examples of what I think could be effective titles in the sense that they may make the reader curious and they may convince the journal editor to accept the contribution.

2.7. Abstract?

Whether an abstract should be written before or after the journal article is an old question. In any case, the abstract must be revised after the article is completed, especially if the writer feels that he/she has not be able to completely deliver what he/she had promised at the beginning of the writing project. This distinguishes a journal abstract from a conference abstract, which is more a promise of something that may be delivered by the time the conference takes place and is (usually) not altered even if the presenter cannot keep all the promises and may not be able to fulfil the expectations. In our discussion of pre-writing activities, an abstract may help the writer to focus his/her ideas and is thus for many a good exercise before the actual writing of the article.

2.8. Scaffolded writing

Finally, we have to start writing. In many writing classes today, scaffolded writing is practised. As the metaphor suggests, this approach assumes that this is a process of enculturation into social practices with supported interaction with people who have already mastered the discourse, as is the case in an academic writing workshop. For individual writers, this is less easy, but generally it may help the writer to complete the big global task, when a complex text like a journal paper is broken down into smaller fixed structures like the IMRaD paradigm discussed below (4.1. – 4.2.). Then many small steps or obligatory and optional moves (Swales 1990) steadily take the writer further and further. Good practice examples may also serve as models, which make the task less daunting than a complete individual start from Introduction to Conclusion. Of course, this approach also can only lead to a first draft, which has to be revised constantly to bring it closer to the ideal set up by the self-critical writer and, in some cases, the constant interventions of experienced mentors that guide young scholars from academic novice to research discourse (Fig. 1).

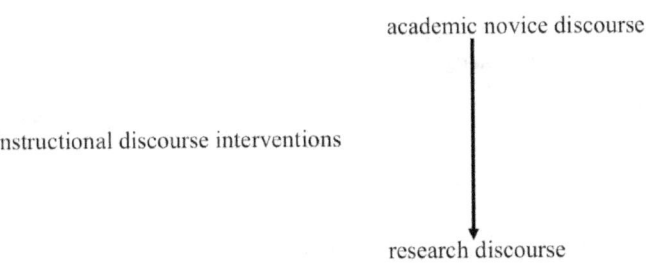

Figure 1:   Through instructional discourse from novice to research discourse.

3. Key concepts

3.1. Discourses in academic communication

Over the last few years, European universities have developed not only writing centres (even for writing in the mother-tongue), but also academic writing classes. Whereas previous student generations seem to have acquired academic reading and writing skills independently (and on the basis of a traditional secondary school education), the "digital natives" seem to need more help. This may also be the case because the rules have become stricter and the genre conventions are more established today in many types of academic communication.

The complexities, functions and features of academic genres have been discussed elsewhere (e.g. Schmied 2015). Although some key concepts are used in all types of academic discourse, we can distinguish between popularisation discourse (e.g. press releases), instructional discourse (e.g. lectures) and research discourse (e.g. PhD theses). The focus of young researchers must be on the research discourses in their PhD theses, conference presentations and journal articles. Journal articles are becoming more and more important and have started replacing PhD theses – a key publication for academic careers. Therefore, the Benin workshop tried to use mentors' instructional discourse to guide young researchers from novice to research discourse that may be accepted by international journals (cf. Fig 1).

3.2. The academic research cycle and its key medium – the research article

The research discourse is fully integrated into what is commonly known an academic research cycle (cf. Fig. 2). We first try to identify a gap in the overall knowledge complex, try to create knowledge, to assure that the quality of the knowledge is good enough for publication, and then in our publication we want to disseminate the knowledge so that other people can develop ideas for further continuing this cycle.

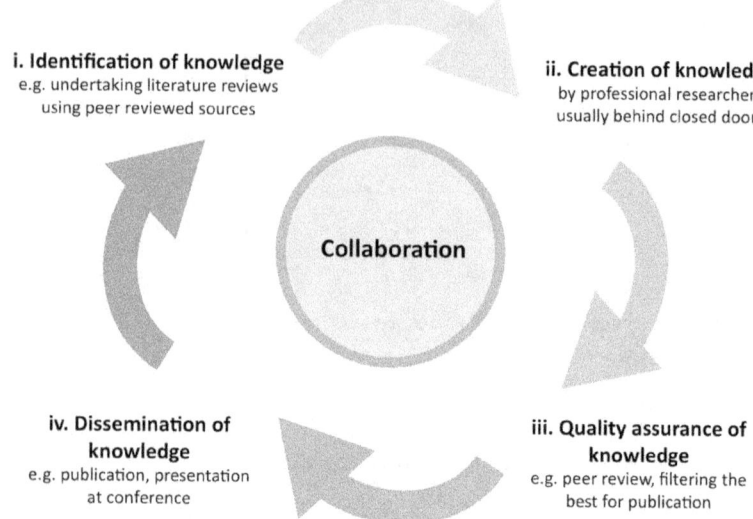

Figure 2: The Academic Research Cycle (Figure taken from Cann, Dimitrou & Hooley 2011: 15).

When we accept a prototype approach to genres and knowledge creation, we can identify the research article today as the central element in the academic research cycle because it ensures the fastest and most reliable dissemination of academic knowledge. Other research outputs, like writing book reviews, writing project proposals or making conference presentations, are also valid, have to be learned, but they are not as decisive for scholars' recognition in the national and international discourses as a research article. Thus, all other academic genres are peripheral (Schmied 2015: 11).

3.3. Academic metadiscourse, metalanguage

The terms metalanguage and metadiscourse, i.e. language about language, are related to the information management or the reader guidance beyond the plain facts, the proposition. We look at the global text management, the argumentation structure, the sequencing of chapters and sections in an academic article, from the top down to paragraphing, and then to the cohesion between the smallest text passages. Academic words and phrases signal the position of a text passage in the global argumentation structure: *define* in the conceptualisation section, *research question* or *hypothesis* in the initial methodology section, but also in the results section, *conclude, limitations* and *further research* towards the end in the conclusion, etc.

This global text management works in a similar manner to the local text management. All these cohesive devices help to produce cognitive coherence in the mind of the reader, and the writer controls this by giving signposts like *first, second, third* or *thus* or *because*. Similar cohesive devices can be found on all discourse levels, the micro-level of sentences, the meso-level of paragraphs and the macro-level of sections or chapters. All this contributes to the writer-reader interaction, including the direct form of address, for example. It is always a big question whether or not a writer in an academic context is allowed to use *you* or *we*. This is decided on the basis of the disciplinary conventions and the journal conventions.

Another important point is the writer's commitment to the truth value or reliability of what he/she is saying. Many comparative PhD theses on hedging in different writing contexts (Germany, China, and Africa) are written today and, of course, model auxiliaries or model adverbs are the clear signposts that a writer has to use when he/she wants to say "I think this is correct, but I am not completely offended, if you disagree with me". So *maybe* or *arguably* is chosen by writers to distance themselves from their research but still take their research seriously enough. Occasionally, though this is a little culture-specific, you may use boosters like *certainly* or *in fact* or *this is a fact*. But in academic writing usually we find more hedging than boosting. I cannot go into details here, however, a vast amount of secondary literature on meta-language is available today (e.g. Hyland 2005).

4. Focus on the journal article global paradigm (the macro-level)

4.1. The IMRaD/IMAC global paradigm spreading from Natural Sciences into Humanities

A very common global paradigm is spreading from Natural Sciences into Humanities, and that means into Linguistics and even a little into Cultural Studies and Literary Studies. We have several levels, one of which is called the global vs. local planning, and although there are, naturally, different types of planners, global planners are at an advantage: they can take a global strategy as a skeleton, and thus find it easier to demonstrate that they are good writers. Such writing strategies have been revealed by Swales (1990) in his model of moves and steps, the CARS model, which is an acronym for Creating A Research Space, i.e. to identify a gap to fill in the introduction of a research article. We can expand this model to include the complete text of a journal article.

If we look for a global design model for research articles we immediately come across IMRaD, which stands for Introduction, Methodology, Research, And Discussion. However, I want to modify this slightly to Issue, Methodology, Analysis, and Conclusion (IMAC): instead of Introduction I refer to Issue, or "why is this interesting for the reader?". The Methodology is, of course, a major part and expected chapter heading; it cannot be changed. The Analysis may include a Discussion and Interpretation, and finally the Conclusion can often be extended systematically in several sub-sections. The most interesting aspect about this paradigm is that it can be applied to abstracts as well as (empirical) research articles and BA/MA/PhD theses – and the corresponding general academic lexemes and phrases can be taken over from subject- and culture-specific conventions easily.

4.2. Signposting paradigms: the IMRaD/IMAC structure in the lexicon

This global paradigm can be signalled, for instance, by standard CARS or Issue phrases like "*not enough ... research on this topic, yet*". Other such phrases include *it is relevant, it is important* "in the academic discourse", or "for practical applications". Or you say "My short article here is *focussed*, it is *data-based*", although the data will be small, and it is *carefully researched*, and the results are *reliable*, of course, it could be "expanded" or "it is just a small contribution" in a wide mosaic in the wide discussion framework that we know from the literature.

The second major section in this paradigm is the Methodology. Sometimes this includes the literature review, including the evaluation of the literature, in a separate section. Then it depends on the topic whether you find "hypotheses" possible, whether you can think of good "research questions". You may want to introduce the database and the procedures or the tests you are going to use before you actually do these tests in the next chapter and analyse your data, and then you can have different types of proof evidence, you can simply state examples if you have a more qualitative approach; if you have a quantitative approach you need statistic tables as summaries. You can also have figures, because they are better illustrations, visualisation; when you find significance in the appropriate significance tests, then the reader is convinced that what you have done for your data should also be the case for other data that are collected in a similar way.

The final sections are in the Conclusion, and this concluding section is often too short in young writers' articles, which is why I am giving you several suggestions here. One possibility is a summary. If you do not have a summary at the end of the analysis, in this case a summary would start with signal words like "in conclusion" or "we have shown" or, if you want to be more tentative, "we hope to have shown". It can also be an interpretation ("This proves that a small study may have major consequences") or what I call contextualization, which often contains phrases like "in a wider perspective", etc. For young researchers it is often advisable that they themselves indicate the limitations of their studies (before others do it), and then say "More data should be collected" and "Similar analyses on a different database could be carried out". "Further research is necessary" is a little elementary, but if you can specify what type of research seems logical after your contribution in the large research mosaic, then that is always a good ending, whether you want to do it yourself or would prefer someone else to continue.

4.3. Paradigm examples from academic journals

Now we look at a few concrete examples of these global paradigms. I have selected articles from journals which are very accessible also from Africa: *Brno Studies in English* is accessible online, open for African scholars. The example has a good, comprehensive title (according to the principles discussed in section 2.6. above) "Epistemic modal verbs in research articles written by Ghanaian and international

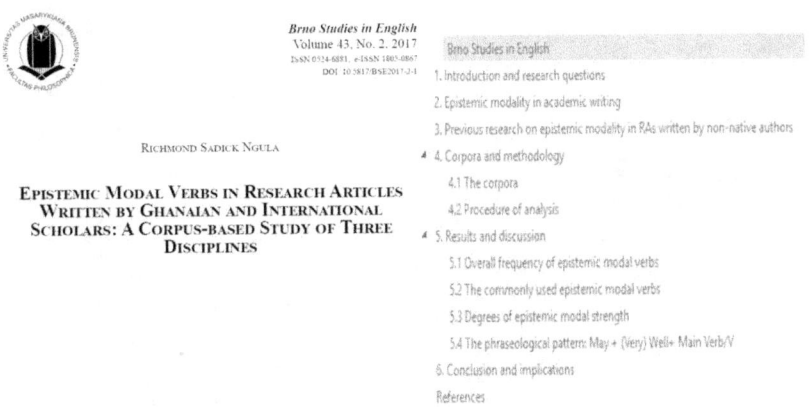

Figure 3:   Journal article with IMRaD structure in *Brno Studies in English*

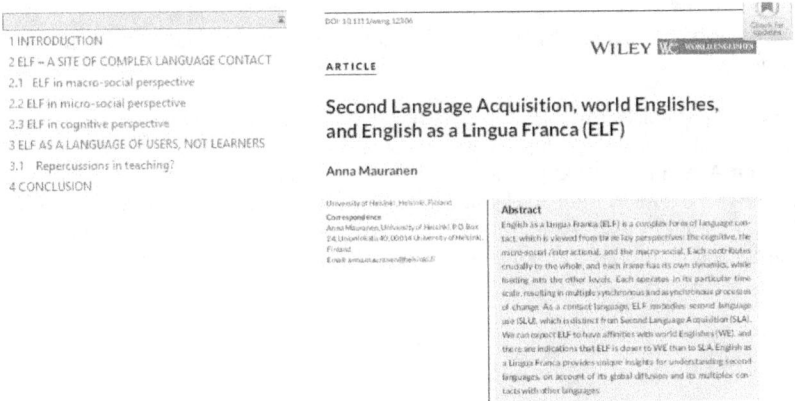

Figure 4:   Journal article with non-IMRaD structure in *World Englishes*

scholars. A corpus-based study of three disciplines" (I have converted the down-loaded pdf-file into a doc-format so that you can see the outline in Fig. 3): it has an Introduction and research questions, epistemic modality in academic writing, i.e. key words or key concept explained, the Literature Review, the Methodology with the data-base, a detailed section on Results and Discussion, and a Conclusion with Implications.

The example in Fig. 4 is from a journal called *World Englishes*. With this type of focus it is not too difficult for Africans to publish in this journal, and here is an article not written in this IMRaD structure, because it is a journal article, not necessarily an empirical research article. In this case, it is perfectly justifiable, it is

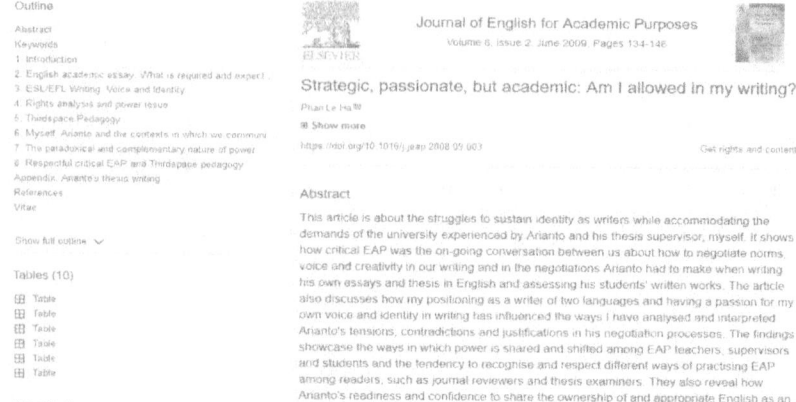

Figure 5:   Journal article with non-IMRaD structure in *Journal of English for Academic Purposes*

even entirely understandable, why this journal article does not have any IMRaD structure.

Another journal that publishes papers relevant to Nigerian young researchers regularly is the *Journal of English for Academic Purposes*. It publishes articles from and on Africa but also allows Africans a global comparison (Fig. 5). Here I have chosen an example from academic writing that does not follow an IMRaD structure, although it also has a clear and detailed set-up, which could be copied, and the academic discourse continued from another university or country experience.

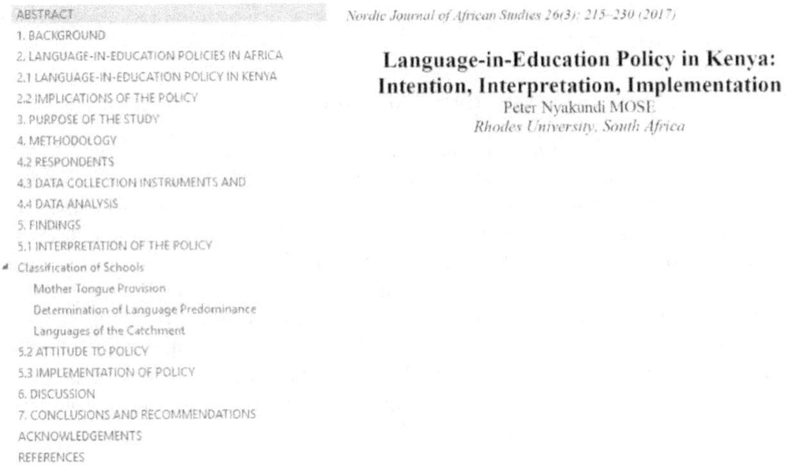
ABSTRACT
1. BACKGROUND
2. LANGUAGE-IN-EDUCATION POLICIES IN AFRICA
2.1 LANGUAGE-IN-EDUCATION POLICY IN KENYA
2.2 IMPLICATIONS OF THE POLICY
3. PURPOSE OF THE STUDY
4. METHODOLOGY
4.2 RESPONDENTS
4.3 DATA COLLECTION INSTRUMENTS AND
4.4 DATA ANALYSIS
5. FINDINGS
5.1 INTERPRETATION OF THE POLICY
Classification of Schools
Mother Tongue Provision
Determination of Language Predominance
Languages of the Catchment
5.2 ATTITUDE TO POLICY
5.3 IMPLEMENTATION OF POLICY
6. DISCUSSION
7. CONCLUSIONS AND RECOMMENDATIONS
ACKNOWLEDGEMENTS
REFERENCES

Nordic Journal of African Studies 26(3): 215–230 (2017)

Language-in-Education Policy in Kenya: Intention, Interpretation, Implementation
Peter Nyakundi MOSE
Rhodes University, South Africa

Figure 6: Journal article with IMRaD structure in *Nordic Journal of African Studies*

Finally, the *Nordic Journal of African Studies* is, of course, open for contributions from Africa (Fig. 6). Here I have chosen an example from Kenya, language and education policy, which is an issue in many African countries, and you can see that to a global extent, it follows a neat IMRaD/IMAC structure, so language and education in Nigeria or in only parts of Nigeria, in one state, could be an interesting topic for this journal. In this article on Kenya, we have sections on the Purpose of the study, the Methodology with respondents, data collection, data analysis etc. etc. This is a clear structure, which could be copied, and, to some extent, replicated.

5. Editing paragraphs from a global perspective (the meso level)

5.1. An introductory paragraph and opening sentence

The second level in a global perspective is the meso-level, where the argumentative flow within and beyond paragraphs is managed to ensure effective communication. An introductory paragraph in a journal article is maybe not as important as in creative writing, but it provides a context for the argument that expresses your perspective on the issue that you will be dealing with. It can be explicit or implicit to attract the reader to continue reading, and has forward dynamics presenting a coherent development of the topic sentence and involving the reader in this argument. So, the introductory paragraph is crucial to the whole section, and the same applies to the introductory sentence in the paragraph. Such an opening sentence does not depend on the previous title for its understanding, it is a fresh start: it should be uncontroversial, not too provocative and not linked directly to the time of writing. Often it is a more global statement so that the paragraph continues with a *now* in a certain contrast, like “For centuries, increasing meat consumption has been an indicator of increasing prosperity. But today, a new trend vegan, ..." (Hannay & Mackenzie 2017: 54).

5.2. Climax introduction: thesis statement

The paragraph structure may then be developed over several sentences until finally the thesis statement is the climax of the introduction: it expresses the central concern, it must be recognisable by its paragraph final positioning, and it must be recognisable without any cumbersome signposting. Basically, you should not have to give too many clues that this is important. The final position in the paragraph must make it clear in the paragraph that this is the big point now. It can be rather neutral or suggestive of the line to be followed. So, we would look at that in more detail. And it is formulated in such a way as to end the paragraph in a strong and confident crescendo, so that it sticks in the mind, or at least the short-term memory of the reader. Let me give you two examples (from Hannay & Mackenzie 2017: 59) and state whether this is good or bad:

(1) The thesis to be examined in the following paragraphs is whether grandparents should once again be given a place in the family home.

(2) Any decision to place restrictions on what is broadcast should follow on a careful consideration of the pros and cons of television censorship.

"The thesis to be examined" includes clear signposting and thus is not a good thesis statement. One issue worth consideration is whether it is too clearly signposted and does not indicate by itself that this is the focus, the climax. The second is much better, ending in "television censorship".

5.3. Structure and linking of paragraphs

The global view on paragraph structures can be clearly seen in Table 1, which shows that the three parts follow each other logically. They do so, because they have different functions and orientation links: the topic sentence links back and the climax sentence forward.

structure	function	orientation link
topic sentence	setting the scene, defining the scope	back to issue or theoretical context
elaboration	developing the argumentation	
climax sentence	stating the point	forward to evidence or references

Table 1:   Paragraph structure as the meso-level in a global perspective (adapted from Hannay & Mackenzie 2017: 68)

Thus everything should be linked to the previous text, but ideally also linked to the following text. This similarly means that you cannot have, for instance, one-sentence paragraphs, for instance: sometimes I notice that young scholars have relatively short paragraphs, but the argumentation suggested here means that we need at least three moves in a paragraph, so the paragraph cannot be too short.

This can be seen in the theoretical context of the theme and focus from a functional linguistic point of view, either, from the Prague School or, in Halliday's Systemic Functional Grammar. You have a theme topic or the background of the presupposition, if you prefer. You have a focus that was called in the Prague School called the rheme, nowadays often refered to as the new or the comment. And the theme may depend on the previous focus of the previous theme. So, all the themes and the focuses can be related. All these cohesions may be signalled explicitly throughout the text by a wide range of cohesive devices that create or construe the text, conjunctions, references, substitution/ellipsis, and lexical cohesion (Halliday & Matthiessen 2014: 593-658).

A final word of warning is in place here for the 'experienced' writer who has attended academic writing classes, for instance: all explicit cohesion, whether temporal or causal, for instance, has to be supported by the inner logical; just adding causal conjuncts regularly is not enough – if they are not justified and may even be considered overdone or non-native (cf. section 6.2.). So, the advice to academic novices must be to add cohesive devices consciously and systematically, whereas the warning to advanced scholars may be not to do it for its own sake.

5.4. Cohesive devices: linking, connectors, etc., e.g. clause adverbials

A small example for cohesive devices, sometimes called linking, sometimes called connectors, can be illustrated by analysing conjuncts or adverbials in corpora of academic writing (cf. Schmied 2015). I find this interesting, because many students think that *unfortunately* is not used in academic writing, but in a corpus of academic writing, *unfortunately* is quite often used (Fig. 7). This is a clear cohesion and unexpected cohesion marker and the coherence that is built up in your brain here is basically that *unfortunately* means *contrary to expectations, contrary to what I have read in the secondary literature and thus expected etc.* You can also see clearly that these "*unfortunatelys*" are often used as a sentence adverbial, that means at the beginning of a sentence and even marked off by a comma. This is thoughtful of the writer to help the reader by putting commas after sentence adverbs or adverbials.

1 It is unfortunately not the case that knowledge of the mechanical	0002AX
2 Unfortunately, an instantaneous comparison was not possible	0003AX1
3 Unfortunately, exact information on gas usage is unavailable	0003AX1
4 Unfortunately, one has no a priori way of predicting	0003AX1
5 Unfortunately, neither easily works.	0003AX1
6 Unfortunately, there are as yet no reliable calculations that	0004AX1
7 Unfortunately our experience is confined to an equilibrium ...	0004AX2
8 Unfortunately, the energy resolution of a neutrino telescope is ...	0015AX
9 ... technique to obtain black hole masses which, unfortunately, is unfeasible	0018AX
10 Unfortunately, lack of information about the collective ...	0021AX
11 Unfortunately, the complexity of each subprocess also grows ...	0025AX
12 Unfortunately these theorems tell us practically nothing about ...	0032AX
13 Unfortunately there are very few analytic results available	0040AX
14 Unfortunately, all recent experiments are, in principle,	0043AX
15 Unfortunately, all those exciting recent experiments are	0043AX
16 Unfortunately, those prior art solutions require daunting experiments	0043AX
17 Unfortunately, the NID is uncomputable since the constituent ...	0045AX
18 Unfortunately, in many places such information is getting harder ...	0056NS
19 it's a good protective barrier," says Hildebrand, "unfortunately."	0069NS
20 Unfortunately, because of the rarity of plant data from this ...	0100PN

Figure 7:   Usage of *unfortunately* as clause-initial sentence adverbial in academic writing

6. Digesting information and construing meaning at the local level (micro-level)

6.1. Intertextuality and plagiarism

Finally, at the micro-level of our journal article revision, we can discuss the controversial issues of intertextuality and plagiarism. Well before the global availability of the internet, Pennycook (1996) argued that "borrowing others' words" should not be directly connected to threats or admonitions, as in most Western traditions, as a challenge to the moral foundations on which student-teacher relationships are built. He pleaded for accepting patch-writing "as positive and non-transgressive because it is an attempt on the part of the writer to engage with the linguistic and discursive forms of particular disciplinary fields, as opposed to wholesale coping of entire paragraphs or texts without modification" (Chandrasoma, Thompson & Pennycook 2004: 176). Here copying is actually an important part of learning and not "a crime".

In this thinking, many cases of such intertextuality can be interpreted as lack of conscious editing or digesting of information in text, which is clearly the work of the writer at the local, the micro-level. At this level, writers have to decide whether excerpts from previous texts are so important in their argumentation that they should be cited literally or whether it is enough to summarise them and integrate them into a new argumentation structure. Intertextuality can then be seen as something positive in a wider academic discourse, which writers use to add more weight to their argumentation (cf. Schmied 2018). This has to be discussed and practiced intensively in writing classes (cf. Buckingham 2016: 128-132), maybe particularly in Africa, where some young scholars seem to think that after changing a few phrases the original passages cannot be found or the reference can be omitted, because it is common knowledge.

6.2. Idiomaticity and transparency

In this local context, issues of idiomaticity and transparency can be discussed. Of course, all technical devices and (internet) resources should be used to check whether language patterns are consistent with regular, unmarked usage in the discourse community. This discourse community today often includes more non-native than native users. Thus, a certain simplicity and transparency may be appropriate, if the writer has the readers' text-processing ability and effectiveness in mind. A nice example of this is structured parallelism (cf. Biber et al. 1991: 897), where even long sentences may become processible more easily when their syntactic embedding is clear.

Finally, we have to consider what Halliday calls the 'discourse flow' (Halliday & Matthiessen 2014: 114), which goes far beyond the cohesive devices discussed above (in section 5.3.). This is really an argument for practice, practice, practice. It is not the native speaker, it is the conscious diligent editor that produces the best texts in the end, because everyone can develop a feel for academic conventions, but it is a long way from novice to expert – and some guidance may help to make it shorter or less winding.

7. Conclusion: advice to young academics

I would like to conclude by summarising the advice to young academics from Africa again. I have said that writing and in particular editing your own draft is a craft, it can be learned, and it determines the success of academic careers. My main focus is from global to local, at every level macro-, meso- and micro-level, and I would like to emphasize that it is worth bearing these considerations in mind during the entire writing process from first draft to final proof-reading. The global planning is important and it should be helpful to have a sort of skeleton with this IMRaD structure, for instance. If you have a writing block, you fill in parts of the skeleton and hope that your model will be complete at some point. It is important to start from a global perspective, from sections to subsections to paragraph, and then finish diligently the details on the local level: the right words, the right idiomaticity, in particular the prepositions, the standard grammar, in particular definite articles, and also the right punctuation, regular commas, but also reader-friendly colons and semicolons.

Finally, for young scholars it should also be clear that all academic resources like spell, style, and grammar checkers should be used, and the last piece of advice for today is this: it is always worth looking for good research articles in your area of research and interest, and then trying to imitate them in this sense, and enriching them with your own data. Of course, by imitating I do not mean copying without using the options of non-transgressive intertextuality to gain support for our argumentation from (recognised authorities and writers of) older texts. But the sources have to be indicated, and in academic discourse young scholars should not be afraid of stepping in the footsteps of older scholars. If you have your own data, you can always apply the thinking of other people to these new data and produce your own almost perfect articles. I keep my fingers crossed that you find the right advice to have them published in the end, for the benefit of your academic career.

References

Biber, D., S. Johansson, G. Leech, S. Conrad & E. Finegan (1999). *Longman Grammar of Spoken and Written English*. Harlow: Longman.
Buckingham, L. (2016). *Doing a Research Project in English Studies*. London: Routledge.
Cann, A., K. Dimitriou & T. Hooley (2011). *Social Media: A Guide for Researchers*. London: Research Information Network.
Chandrasoma, R., C. Thompson & A. Pennycook (2004). Beyond Plagiarism: Transgressive and Nontransgressive Intertextuality. *Journal of Language, Identity, and Education 3*, 3, 171-193.
Halliday, M.A.K. & C. Matthiesen (2014). *An Introduction to Functional Grammar*. 4th ed. London: Edward Arnold.
Hannay, M. & J. L. Mackenzie (2017). *Effective Writing in English. A Sourcebook*. Bussum: Coutinho.
Hofmann, M. (2018). *Operationalising Variables: Objectivity, Reliability, and Validity* (this volume).
Huddleston, R. & G. Pullum (2002). *The Cambridge Grammar of the English Language*. Cambridge: Cambridge University Press.
Hyland, K. (2005). *Metadiscourse*. London: Continuum.
Hyland, K. (2012). *Disciplinary Identities: Individuality and Community in Academic Writing*. Cambridge: Cambridge University Press.
Pennycook, A. (1996). Borrowing others' words: text, ownership, memory, and Plagiarism. *TESOLQuarterly 30,2*, 201-230
Pérez-Llantada, C. (2012). *Scientific Discourse and the Rhetoric of Globalization*. London: Continuum.
Quirk, R., S. Greenbaum, G. Leech & J. Svartvik (1985). *A Comprehensive Grammar of the English Language*. Harlow: Longman.
Schmied, J. (2011). Academic Writing in Europe: A Survey of Approaches and Problems. In Schmied, J. (ed. 2011), 1-22.
Schmied, J. ed. (2011). *Academic Writing in Europe: Empirical Perspectives*. Göttingen: Cuvillier.
Schmied, J. (2015). Graduate Academic Writing in Europe in Comparison: A Research-based Approach to Metalanguage and Genre. In Schmied, J. (ed. 2015), 1-24.
Schmied, J. ed. (2015). *Academic Writing for South Eastern Europe: Practical and Theoretical Perspectives*. Göttingen: Cuvillier.
Schmied, J. (2018). Credibility in academic and journalistic writing and beyond. In Schmied, J. (Ed.). *Credibility, Honesty, Ethics, and Politeness in Academic and Journalistic Writing*. Göttingen: Cuvillier, 1-12
Schmied, J. & M. Hofmann (2018). New Digital Methodologies for Old Grammar Problems: Corpus Analyses and Eye-Tracking to Discover Non-native English Article Usage Preferences. In Zwierlein, A.-J., J. Petzold, K. Boehm & M. Decker (Eds.) *Anglistentag 2017. Proceedings*. Trier: Wissenschaftlicher Verlag, 103-116.
Schmied, J., I. van der Bom eds. (2017). *Working with Media Texts: Deconstructing and Constructing Crises in Europe*. Göttingen: Cuvillier.
Siepmann D., J. D. Gallagher, M. Hannay, J. L. Mackenzie (2011). *Writing in English: A Guide for Advanced Learners*. Tübingen: A. Francke.
Swales, J. M. (1990). *Genre Analysis. English in Academic and Research Settings*. Cambridge: Cambridge University Press.
Swales, J. M., Ch. B. Feak (2012). *Academic Writing for Graduate Students: Essential Tasks and Skills*. 3rd ed. Ann Arbor: University of Michigan Press.

Operationalising Variables: Objectivity, Reliability, and Validity

Matthias Hofmann

Chemnitz University of Technology

Abstract

Empirical research is quite varied in terms of being scientific in nature on the one hand and of being of high quality on the other hand. Depending on the methodology, different criteria have been established in the academic literature for measuring and assuring the quality of research in general. These criteria are embedded in the larger framework of operationalising variables and illustrated in detail using linguistic examples in this contribution. Its focus lies on quantitative studies. The objective is to arrive at a rather general description and illustration of the methodological criteria of objectivity, reliability, and validity as well as to incorporate these notions into the operationalisation of variables by using linguistic examples as well. Operationalisation is crucial for every empirical study to arrive at meaningful results and excellence in research. It places much responsibility on the shoulders of the novice researcher, which can be addressed by a thorough review of existing academic literature on the object of investigation. Although operationalisation is a key factor in quantitative studies, it is usually not explicitly addressed in advanced research. This contribution explains the implicit requirements for a scientific study of excellent quality.

Keywords: academic writing, methodology, rigour, structure

1. Introduction

This contribution aims at shedding light on methodological criteria in empirical research that enhance the quality of a study. Most empirical research follows a structure, which is usually comprised of an introduction, a literature review, a methodology, a results and discussion section, and a conclusion. This structure is particularly conventionalized in journal articles, and may be complemented further by several sub-level headings in monographs or similar works. Following the epistemological research-theoretical position, a thorough literature review provides a sound basis for an overview of previous work on the phenomenon one is interested in, which in turn provides the basis for a potential identification of research gaps or follow-up work.

After such gaps or work have been identified, scientific hypotheses or research questions are formulated – according to Popper's ([1934] 1989) critical rationalism – which need suitable methods that help falsifying the hypotheses or that help answering the research questions. Between these steps – the formulation of hypotheses and their falsification – the variables invoked in these hypotheses have to be operationalised, i.e. one has to determine how these variables are investigated.

In such determination, the scientific quality criterion of validity becomes the central objective to be reached in the process, alongside the scientific quality indicators of objectivity and reliability. The terminology used here readily implies that these criteria and the above-mentioned structure are relevant only for quantitative research designs. While this is certainly true, I would argue that they are equally relevant for qualitative studies, albeit to a lesser degree, if not at least reduced to credibility (which translates into validity) when hermeneutics is the desired methodological take on a qualitative endeavour. For an overview of additional scientific quality standards in qualitative research designs see, for instance, Döring and Bortz (2016).

In the next part, I will define crucial terminology such as the above-mentioned criteria using questionnaires as a means of measurement to illustrate them, as well as the concept of a variable and of a hypothesis. In part 3, I briefly summarize the work necessary to identify the variables that might influence the object of investigation. In part 4, I will argue why an operationalisation of variables is of crucial importance for empirical studies in general, focusing on linguistic examples to describe and elucidate how variables can be investigated, what types of variables can be differentiated, and what role they are assigned in the hypotheses.

2. Definitions and key concepts

2.1. Objectivity, reliability, and validity

2.1.1. *Criteria for research quality*

For a study to be considered a scientific study, it must (1) gear towards an object of investigation that is recognized as scientific by the academic community; (2) use suitable scientific methods; (3) follow the principles of research ethics; and (4) report in detail the design of the research and its results. After a study has met the standards of being scientific in nature, the supra-disciplinary criteria of rigour and relevance determine the quality of empirical research, by differentiating weak scientific studies from average and excellent ones. While relevance determines the quality of (1), methodological rigour determines the quality of (2), which is the focus of this contribution. The criteria for (3) is ethical rigour, and for (4) it is the quality of the presentation of the research to the target audience (cf. Schmied 2018).

Although rigour and relevance are supra-disciplinary criteria, they have to be specified in each academic discipline such as linguistics as well as in each paradigm within an academic discipline such as the focus on investigating Chomsky's language performance or Saussure's *parole* rather than Chomsky's language competence or Saussure's *langue*. Within the paradigm of investigating language in use rigour and relevance have to specified further in terms of using qualitative methods, quantitative methods, or both.

2.1.2. Methodological rigour

Methodological rigour is high in any discipline, if a study uses challenging or sound methods and methodologies and follows them stringently. Methodological rigour is a purely research-immanent criterion and differentiates several sub-categories, which are defined quite differently in qualitative, quantitative, and mixed-methods approaches. These sub-categories are heavily intertwined and typically understood as a multidimensional continuum: if, for example, mistakes are made during data collection, or if the data cleaning process is imprecise and/or inaccurate, the quality of the data can be reduced or the results of the analysis can be distorted; at the same time, however, the quality of the analysis itself can be excellent through, for example, the use of suitable statistical tests. Multidimensionality thus means, that despite the interconnectedness of the sub-categories, a study can be of high scientific quality in one sub-category and of low scientific quality in another sub-category at the same time.

2.1.3. Types of validity

In quantitative research designs, methodological rigour is measured through the criterion of validity, which means the degree to which a scientific statement is true. Although validity is a property of statements, it can also refer to the methodologies and the methods used in an empirical study. Research in Psychology has differentiated four types of validity (cf. Campbell 1957; Shadish, Cook, and Campbell 2002), which can be simplified and reduced to two types: internal validity and external validity. Internal validity is high, if the relations between the variables investigated in a study are cause-and-effect relations, i.e. the independent variables can be doubtlessly interpreted as cause of the dependent variables. These relations are typically established through the research design of a study, which can be experimental, quasi-experimental or pre-experimental and non-experimental, respectively, in psychological research (cf. Döring and Bortz 2016).

In empirical linguistic research, experimental and quasi-experimental designs are typically not accepted by the scientific community, because the object of investigation often is natural language use, i.e. language use that would be rated as authentic in perceptual studies. In acoustic phonetic research, however, experimental and quasi-experimental designs are the norm, because of the infrastructural conditions that are necessary to do this kind of research. Such studies also allow for causal interpretations of variable relations with high internal validity. One aspect of internal validity is statistical validity that is typically achieved in the data analysis part of such a study through use of suitable, hypothesis-based statistical tests. Pre-experimental or non-experimental study designs can only describe relations between variables without empirical evidence for a cause of these relations. Internal validity is thus low in such designs.

External validity is high when the results of a study can be generalised to other communities, times, operationalisations of dependent and independent variables or respondents than the ones investigated or used. Field work typically has higher external validity than experimental designs. Real-time studies (i.e. longitudinal research) also typically have higher external validity than apparent-time studies. Triangulation of the results of a study, i.e. multiple parallel operationalisations, through the use of several different methods also increase the external validity. Like internal validity, external validity is predominantly increased through the design of the study (cf. Döring and Bortz 2016). Unlike internal validity, external validity also depends on a representative sample and the representativeness and balance of a corpus. Empirical sociolinguistic and corpus linguistic research are typically comprised of field work and apparent-time studies, in which linguistic variation is investigated and confounding or distorting external effects are controlled for (which increases internal validity).

The most important aspect of external validity is construct validity, which is high when the theorems, concepts, and theories to be investigated in a study are accurately defined on the basis of the theoretical framework and the existing literature. During the operationalisation of the study in the methodology section, it has to be shown how the selected, standardised methods are able to measure observable features of the respective theorem, concept or theory under investigation. The construct validity of the method, i.e. how well can the collected data and the conclusions drawn from these data be justified theoretically and empirically, is crucial for the quality of a study. A method can only yield correct and valid measurements, if it is objective and if its reliability is high (cf. Döring and Bortz 2016).

2.1.4. *The quality criteria exemplified*

In order to illustrate objectivity, reliability, and validity of a method, the use of a questionnaire might serve as a good example that many novice linguists can relate to. A questionnaire is objective, when it can be used by different researchers and always yields identical results. That is, the questionnaire is independent of the researcher. This independence can be reached, for instance, through the use of standardized instructions that are as literal possible and that use examples from the questionnaire for illustrative purposes. Without such an independence, the use of online questionnaires would be seriously stalled, as no researcher is present that would be able to explain the questionnaire or to answer potential questions participants might have. If more than one researcher evaluates the responses to the questionnaire, independence can be reached by a coding scheme for the responses in case of multiple-choice questions and by standardized interpretations of responses in case of open questions.

Reliability refers to the accuracy of measuring with a questionnaire and is high when the errors of a measurement are small. That is, in a questionnaire, each item (i.e. question) should be clear, unambiguous, and accessible to the target audience to avoid misunderstandings and guesses, which potentially introduce errors. The types of questions used should be suitable regarding the limits of the questions. For instance, yes/no questions collect responses that arrive at a distribution, but cannot provide information on *who?*, *where?*, *when?*, and *why?* aspects in the data. Open questions are the least preferable type of question, because they pose many potential threats. For most respondents, they are a hassle to answer. They potentially gather irrelevant/unnecessary data or their responses bear the potential of ambiguity, which can be very difficult to code during the evaluation process of the study. Depending on the level of education of the respondents, open questions can remain unanswered when respondents fear making spelling mistakes or revealing their stylistic insufficiencies. Multiple choice questions are probably the most well-known type of questionnaire item, but they are difficult to design, because the order of the responses affects the respondents' choices. If the response options do not include all potential options, an alternative, usually a blank, should be offered to avoid errors. Some concepts such as language attitudes should not be measured with questions, but statements which are captured on scales, such as a five- or seven-point rating scale (not to be confused with Likert, Guttman or Thurstone scales; cf. Döring and Bortz 2016) or semantic differentials. Other means to avoid errors are, for instance, not to hint at a 'preferred response' in items, an intermediate response style (questionnaire items should not be too hard and not too easy to agree to), to avoid quantifying descriptions like *almost* and *barely* in combination with rating scales, and not to expect the respondents to know and remember everything.

Validity assures that a questionnaire measures exactly what it is supposed to measure. That is, the items on a questionnaire must saturate the content of the construct to be measured. No new item must introduce a new aspect. For instance, if a questionnaire is designed to measure attitudes towards a variety of English, every level of that variety must be covered. The questionnaire cannot simply include phonology and syntax, it also must have items on attitudes towards morphology and lexis. This saturation of the investigated concept is solely based on the intuition of the researcher. For novice researchers who lack a professional intuition, it is vital to read existing literature on content and methods, to identify earlier studies that have done similar analyses, and to validate their questionnaire, using, for instance, a variety of English that the attitudes to are already known and well established (cf. 'Known-groups' method in Döring and Bortz 2016). A pre-test or a pilot study can also help reach validity of a questionnaire and should always be striven for, because the analysis of the respondents' comments helps to assess whether all aspects of the construct have been dealt with. These comments might also reveal whether all items have been understood correctly by the respondents, which increases the objectivity of the questionnaire.

2.2. Variables

In the previous sub-section, the term variable, has been mentioned quite frequently without any explanation. It is an important term in quantitative studies and for this contribution, as it constitutes the core of the operationalisation process in any empirical study. The term variable already reveals the core defining criterion of a variable, which is its opposition to a constant. A variable is a measurable feature of a case that is alterable, a feature that can change or acquire different levels or states, which are typically referred to as 'variants' in quantitative linguistics (and

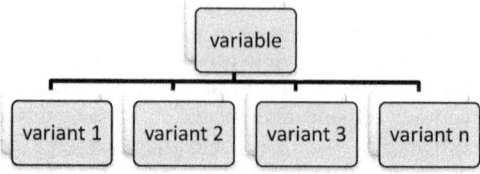

Figure 1: Conceptualisation of a variable and the variable levels.

other disciplines), and as 'factor levels' in conservative variationist-sociolinguistic register (i.e. jargon). More specifically, a variable is defined as a symbol, not a feature, that exhibits at least two different variants to fulfil the criterion of variability (cf. Döring and Bortz 2016: 222; Gries 2013: 8; Johnson 2008: 4; Rasinger 2008: 18). In each observable case, a variable can only show one variant for a particular concept. Linguistic studies usually deal with more than one case in empirical research, so that a variable for several cases also shows several different variants.

Figure 1 shows a schematic of a hypothetical variable and the different states or variants it can take. The last variant in the figure is referred to as 'variant n' which means that the number of variants a variable can have is theoretically infinite for some and limited for others, but by no means restricted to four. The limitation itself, however, is not specified, but naturally depends on the object of investigation. The number of variables necessary to investigate in a quantitative study also depends on the object of investigation. Most linguistic studies deal with several variables and several variants simultaneously, but their number can sometimes be constrained by the statistical modelling process.

Typical linguistic variables are those of 'age' and 'gender'. Age can theoretically vary from zero to indefinitely, if it was not constrained by the end of the natural aging process of the human body. In a group of five or more people, every person can have a different age, so that the variable 'age' in this example would have five different variants, such as 19, 21, 34, 48, and 69. Gender can have more variants than one might assume without further contemplation. The difference between the notions of 'gender' and 'sex' have been discussed exhaustively in the literature of the past decades (e.g., Cheshire 2002; Eckert 1989). Since gender is a social construct, it can have many different variants, whereas sex as a biological condition can have only two in most cases. Since it sounds politically more correct, the variable 'gender' usually means 'sex' in quantitative studies, i.e. it has only two variants regardless of how people feel, although this potentially causes misunderstandings. For that reason, Labov postulated the preference of the use of the term 'sex' over 'gender' especially when the emphasis of quantitative studies is on replicability (1990; also cf. Hofmann 2015). For the variable 'sex', other variants than 'male' and 'female' are not permissible.

2.3. Hypotheses

According to Bortz & Döring (2006: 4), a hypothesis is a general statement that is concerned with more than just one event. The statement needs to be at least implicit and usually has the structure of a conditional sentence: *if..., then...* or *the ... the*. If it does not explicitly follow this structure it should be possible to paraphrase the statement into one. As critical rationalism proposes, hypotheses are potentially falsifiable, that is, the hypothesis is rejected when events or situations are observed that contradict the statement of the hypothesis. Verifiability would mean that a hypothesis is only accepted when it has been verified sufficiently, which is a logic that contradicts critical rationalism. The notion of falsifiability also implies that the event described in the statement must also be testable, which is not true.

(3) If children grow up without any linguistic input, then they will grow up to speak Latin.

Gries' (2013, 11) example shows that while the statement is falsifiable, i.e. children do not grow up to speak Latin, it is not testable without violating ethical standards. Such a violation would render the study to be unscientific. An example of a scientific hypothesis according to the criteria outlined above is the following:

(4) English language training at the age of six years by first-language English teachers in African countries will result in a loss of differences between African varieties of English.

The statement is quite general and not limited to just one situation, one student, one African country, etc. Likewise, it is possible to paraphrase this statement into a conditional sentence as shown in the example below:

(5) If English language training for African children is already offered at the age of six by first-language English teachers in African countries, then all differences between African varieties of English will be lost.

The statement in example (2) is falsifiable, because it is quite likely that the differences between African varieties of English would not going to be lost after American or British teachers or tutors had begun to teach English to African children across the continent at the age of six. If the statement in example (2) would be altered into a statement as in example (4), it would not be a scientific hypothesis.

(6) English language training at the age of six years by first-language English teachers in African countries may result in a loss of differences between African varieties of English.

Although the statement in example (4) fulfils the criteria of being general and of having the potential to be paraphrased in a conditional sentence, it is not falsifiable, because the verb *may* makes this statement always true, regardless of the result a test would yield: if the result shows a loss of differences, the statement is true and if the result shows no loss of differences, the statement is true as well. The result is thus completely irrelevant for the truth value of the statement.

3. Combining theory and linguistic reality

3.1. Identifying variables and variants

Before each study commences, a literature review or at the very least a scouting process should forego any methodological planning or study design attempts. Following Gries (2013: 8), the example of constituent order alternation of transitive phrasal verbs will illustrate the large number of variables that influence particle placement below (also cf. Gries 2003; Gries and Stefanowitsch 2004).

(7)
  a) He picked up [NP the book].
      variable 'Construction': verb - particle - object (VPO)
  b) He picked [NP the book] up.
      variable 'Construction': verb - object - particle (VOP)

Among the many variables that influence constructional choice are (1) 'sentence complexity', (2) 'length' of the direct object, (3) 'directional object', (4) 'animacy' (5) 'concreteness', and (6) 'type'. Each of these variables has several variants, which are outlined in the list below (Gries 2013: 9):

- Complexity (1): is the direct object a
    o simple direct object (DO; e.g. *the book*)
    o phrasally-modified DO (e.g. *the brown book*)
    o clausally-modified DO (e.g. *the book I had bought recently*)
- Length (2): of the DO, measured in letters, syllables, etc.
- Directional object (3):
    o presence of a directional prepositional phrase after the transitive verb (e.g. *He picked to book up from the table*) or
    o absence
- Animacy (4):
    o animate referent of the DO (e.g. *He picked his dad up*) or
    o inanimate referent (e.g. *He picked up the book*)
- Concreteness (5):
    o abstract referent of the DO (e.g. *He brought back peace*) or
    o concrete referent (e.g. *He brought his dad back*)
- Type (6): is the DO's phrasal head a
    o pronoun (e.g. *He picked him up this morning*)
    o semipronoun (e.g. *He picked something up from the floor*)
    o lexical noun (e.g. *He picked people up this morning*)
    o proper name (e.g. *He picked Peter up this morning*)

It can be seen from this list that variables (1) and (6) have three and four variants, respectively, and that the remaining variables have only two variants. In addition to this list, it is also necessary to scan the literature for the preference of each of those variants regarding particle placement, i.e. does a phrasally-modified DO occur more often with the constructional choice of *picked up the brown book* (VPO) or rather of *picked the brown book up* (VOP). This behavior is best summarized in a tabular format, as it eases the overview of the different studies consulted. An example of such a table is Table 1.

The table reveals that not every variant shows a statistical preference for one of the two constructional choices in the literature. However, the findings are detailed enough to see that 'Construction': VPO, i.e. *He picked up the book*, occurs typically with complex DOs that are long, have inanimate and abstract referents, and lack a directional prepositional phrase. The variant 'Construction': VOP occurs with DOs that have a pronominal head, animate and concrete referents, and are normally followed by a directional prepositional phrase.

	Variable level for 'Construction': VPO	Variable level for 'Construction': VOP
'Complexity'	phrasally-modified clausally-modified	
'Length'	long	
'DirectionalPP'	absence	presence
'Animacy'	inanimate	animate
'Concreteness'	abstract	concrete
'Type'		pronoun semipronoun

Table 1:   Overview of the preference of each variant for the constructional choice of VPO and VOP, respectively, according to the literature (Gries 2013: 10).

It is important to keep in mind that the above variables and variants are just examples of influencing factors on particle placement. Their listing is incomplete and too imprecise to be the basis of a real scientific investigation. To continue the example of particle placement, Table 1 will serve as the basis for the formulation of scientific hypotheses.

3.2. Formulating hypotheses

Each of the variables and variants mentioned in the previous section can be paraphrased into conditional sentences, so that they fulfil the defining criteria for scientific hypotheses. For the variable 'Complexity' the hypothesis could be formulated as follows:

(8)   If the direct object of a transitive phrasal verb is syntactically complex, then it will be more often realized after the verb and its particle in native speaker discourse than when the direct object is syntactically simple.

The same *if...*, *then...* pattern can be produced for all the other variables in Table 1. The guiding principle for the formulation of hypotheses is precision. Every notion or concept mentioned in a scientific hypothesis, regardless of how straightforward it may seem, needs to be definable by linguistic theory. If notions such as *formants* or *level of education* are undertheorized in linguistics, they cannot be used in a scientific hypothesis.

The conditional-sentence pattern illustrated above clearly consists of two parts, the *if* part and the *then* part, which both contain a variable each. The *if* part contains the independent variable, abbreviated as *IV*, and the *then* part contains the dependent variable, abbreviated as *DV*. The logic behind the conditional-sentence formulation is to express the relationship between these two variables: The *IV* typically causes (when the internal validity is high, cf. section 2.1.3), affects or influences the *DV*. The *DV* usually has to be explained in terms of its variability or values of distribution. The conditional sentence in example (6), in fact all paraphrased hypotheses, can be paraphrased again, using the notions of *IV* and *DV*. The independent variable is the syntactic complexity of the DOs, referred to as 'Complexity', and includes the variants simple, phrasally-modified, and clausally-modified.

In addition to the identification of dependent and independent variables, the formulation of scientific hypotheses also involves the identification and definition of situations or conditions under which the hypotheses are falsified. These are often realized by turning the content of the formulated hypothesis into the logical opposite. In statistical terms, the hypothesis formulated in text form in example (6) is referred to as *alternative hypothesis* and abbreviated by a capital H (for hypothesis) and a $_1$, as in H_1. The logical opposite is referred to as *null hypothesis* and abbreviated as H_0. The simplest realization of the H_0 for example (6) is shown in example (7):

(9) If the direct object of a transitive phrasal verb is syntactically complex, then it will <u>not</u> be more often realized after the verb and its particle in native speaker discourse than when the direct object is syntactically simple.

The idea behind the formulation of both of these hypotheses is that they have to cover every result that is theoretical possible. Thus, if the H_0 would be phrased as in (8), it would not cover those instances, in which the constructions are equally frequent.

(10) If the direct object of a transitive phrasal verb is syntactically complex, then it will be <u>less</u> often realized after the verb and its particle in native speaker discourse than when the direct object is syntactically simple.

In most cases, the H_0 states that there is no relation between the dependent and the independent variable at all. Even if there was a relation, it would be due to chance and thus not meaningful (cf. Gries 2013).

4. Types of variables

4.1. Translational choices

The text form of the formulated hypotheses as shown in examples (6) and (7) serve the purpose of having summarised the information in the literature and reduced it to the crucial points, and they serve as a starting point for the investigation of each of these hypotheses – or research questions, if under-researched objects of investigation limit the information necessary to formulate hypotheses. Before measurements can be taken – which is the basis of quantitative investigations – the hypotheses need to be translated into numbers; or they must be defined in useful ways. The researcher is responsible for this translation or definition process and has to decide what will be observed, counted, measured and so on when investigating variables. One of the key terms in those decisions is that of *observe*. Only directly observable variables can be measured or counted. Abstract variables like native-speaker competence, success in learning, or the amount of words in a variety of English are very difficult, if not impossible to measure or count.

The variables and variants mentioned in Table 1 above are clearly definable and translatable into numbers or measurements. Although measurements are also numbers, they differ from mere numbers by the fact that they are accompanied by a unit, such as milliseconds and Hertz, which gives them additional meaning. For instance, Variable (2) – length of the direct object – can be defined as characters, graphemes, phonemes, morphemes, lexical items and so on, which then can be counted, as in the direct object is twelve graphemes long. Variable (3) – the presence and absence of a directional prepositional phrase – can take two categorical states: presence or absence. But these could theoretically also be translated into 'mere numbers' such as 0 for absence and 1 for presence. These numbers are not accompanied by a unit such as milliseconds, Hertz or graphemes. They simply signal a difference without the additional meaning of duration, frequency or letters. Variables can thus not only be differentiated according to their role in hypotheses, but also according to their level of measurement (cf. Gries 2013).

4.2. Levels of measurements

4.2.1. *Categorical scale data*

Categorical variables are the 'lowest' type of variables, as they contain the lowest amount of information. They can have two or more distinct or discrete outcomes, which means that each case can only be put in exactly one category. An example to illustrate the distinctiveness of the outcomes is that of a pregnant woman. The variable 'pregnancy' hast two outcomes: either a woman is pregnant (= category one) or she is not pregnant (= category one, or better category zero). There is no woman that can be 75% pregnant or 'a little bit pregnant' (cf. Rasinger 2008: 25). In such instances, where there are only two variable levels or variants possible, the variable is referred to as a nominal variable or a binary variable.

Variable (3) mentioned above is also a nominal variable with only two outcomes and could be coded similarly as the variable 'pregnancy': the absence of a directional PP could be coded with one and the presence with two. The fact that two is twice as large as one does, however, not imply a hierarchy in categorical variables. There is no differentiation that *pregnant* is better or more than *non-pregnant*, just as *absence* of directional PP is not better or more than *presence* of directional PP. Categorical and nominal variables only provide labels to the different variants to differentiate them from one another. Variables (4), (5), and (6) are also nominal and categorical variables (cf. section 2.2).

4.2.2. Ordinal scale data

In addition to labelling the different variants of a variable or to distinguishing entities as members of different groups, ordinal data can be put into an order or a ranking system, i.e. the data allow for a greater-smaller-relation. Typical examples include military ranks (e.g. those of the crew, non-commissioned officers, and officers), customer-ranked places for vacation (e.g. first, second, third, etc. place of tourist destinations), intensity of smoking (e.g. non-smoker, occasional smoker, regular smoker) or the grading system in primary and secondary schools (e.g. grade A with four points, grade C with two points, etc.).

Ordinal scales are ranked such that the dominating variant receives the largest rank number. The difference between ranks is however arbitrary and does not mean *twice as much* or *half as much* than the other rank. As the grading example shows, a grade A student did not necessarily do twice as good as a grade C student did, simply because four is twice as much as two. Depending on the task and the grading system, the A-student may have had three times as many correct answers as the C-student. Variable (1) – syntactic complexity – is also an example of ordinal scale data with rank one for the variant simple, rank two for variant phrasally-modified, and rank three for the variant clausally-modified (cf. Döring and Bortz 2016; Gries 2013; Rasinger 2008).

4.2.3. Interval scale data

Similar to ordinal variables, interval variables allow for labelling the variants and putting them into a meaningful sequence. Unlike ordinal scale data, the difference between the variants is fixed and most importantly equidistant. Interval variables are typically used in sociolinguistic and psycholinguistic research when personality traits such as attitudes, stereotypes, preferences or motives for second language acquisition are measured, using five- or seven-point rating scales. Other examples for interval variables are the temperature in Fahrenheit or Celsius, as the difference between 10°C and 12°C is equal to the difference between 25°C and 27°C (cf. Döring and Bortz 2016; Rasinger 2008).

4.2.4. Ratio scale data

Ratio variables are similar to interval variables as they allow for labelling, sequencing, and an equidistant difference between variants. Ratio variables differ from interval variables in that they have an absolute zero, with zero indicating that there is no measurable amount. The opposite feature of ratio variables is that they can be open-ended or indefinitely. Standard examples for such variables are the number of children, age, body height, body weight or reaction time in a psycholinguistic experiment. In all these examples, the comparison of differences and ratios between values is meaningful. For instance, the duration of a vowel's nucleus in milliseconds is a ratio variable: when one vowel is 70 ms long and another is 140 ms long, then the first vowel is of a different length than the second (the categorical information), the first is longer than the second (the ordinal information), the second is exactly twice as long as the first (cf. Gries 2013), and the vowels could theoretically be zero milliseconds long (no vowel is realized) or indefinitely long (indefinite number of digits after the decimals: 140.1548…ms).

5. Conclusion

Operationalisation of variables is of crucial importance for each empirical study. It not only ensures that it is measured what is intended to be measured, i.e. the validity of a study, it also has the potential to determine the result of an empirical study alone (for a nice illustration of this potential see Gries 2013: 18). Operationalisation can be straight forward and seem obvious to the novice researcher, but at the same time it can be more challenging than first meets the eye. Additionally, abstract concepts and those that are comprised of several variables and sub-concepts can pose serious threats to the validity of the study. Especially personality traits such as attitudes and motivations may require time, effort and a lot of trial and error. In any regard, the key to successful operationalisation for novice researchers is to invest enough time and effort into a thorough literature review. The influence of the theoretical framework of a study, the results and theoretical contributions of earlier studies, and the methodological expertise by experienced researchers cannot be emphasized enough, when attempts are made at operationalising the variables properly.

References

Bortz, J. & N. Döring. (2006). *Forschungsmethoden Und Evaluation in Den Sozial- Und Humanwissenschaften*. 4th ed. Springer-Lehrbuch. Berlin: Springer-Verlag.

Campbell, D. T. (1957). Factors Relevant to the Validity of Experiments in Social Settings. *Psychological Bulletin* 54 (4): 297-311.

Cheshire, J. (2002). Sex and Gender in Variationist Research. In *The Handbook of Language Variation and Change*, 423-43. Oxford: Blackwell.

Döring, N. & J. Bortz. (2016). *Forschungsmethoden und Evaluation in den Sozial- und Humanwissenschaften*. 5th ed. Springer-Lehrbuch. Berlin: Springer-Verlag.

Eckert, P. (1989). The Whole Woman: Sex and Gender Differences in Variation. *Language Variation and Change* 1(3): 245-67.

Gries, S. Th. (2003). *Multifactorial Analysis in Corpus Linguistics: A Study of Particle Placement*. London: Continuum.

Gries, S. Th. (2013). *Statistics for Linguistics with R: A Practical Introduction*. 2nd ed. Berlin: Walter de Gruyter.

Gries, S. Th., & A. Stefanowitsch. (2004). Extending Collostructional Analysis: A Corpus-Based Perspective on "Alternations". *International Journal of Corpus Linguistics* 9(1): 97-129.

Hofmann, M. (2015). 'Mainland Canadian English in Newfoundland: The Canadian Shift in Urban Middle-Class St. John's'. PhD Dissertation, Chemnitz: Technische Universität Chemnitz. http://nbn-resolving.de/urn:nbn:de:bsz:ch1-qucosa-172221.

Johnson, K. (2008). *Quantitative Methods in Linguistics*. Malden, MA: Blackwell.

Labov, W. (1990). The Intersection of Sex and Social Class in the Course of Linguistic Change. *Language Variation and Change* 2(2): 205-54.

Litosseliti, L. (2009). *Research Methods in Linguistics*. London: Continuum.

Paltridge, B. & A. Phakiti (eds). (2015). *Research Methods in Applied Linguistics: A Practical Resource*. Research Methods in Linguistics. London: Bloomsbury.

Podesva, R. & S. Devyani. (2013). *Research Methods in Linguistics*. Cambridge: Cambridge University Press.

Popper, K. ([1934] 1989). *Logik der Forschung*. 9th ed. Tübingen: Mohr Siebeck.

Rasinger, S. M. (2008). *Quantitative Research in Linguistics: An Introduction*. London: Continuum.

Schmied, J. (2018). *A Global View on Writing Research Articles for International Journals: Principles & Practices* (this volume).

Shadish, W. R., T. D. Cook & D. T. Campbell. (2002). *Experimental and Quasi-Experimental Designs for Generalized Causal Inference*. Boston: Houghton Mifflin.

Tackling and Tracking Reviews/Revision and Technical Details of a Journal Paper

Dunlop Ochieng & Steve Bode Ekundayo

Open University of Tanzania & University of Benin

Abstract

This paper examines the processes of tracking reviews, revision and the technical details of a journal paper with a view to equipping the budding scholars with the requisite technical know-how of writing and publishing a brilliant journal article. To teach and illustrate this arduous task in academics, the presenters critically review previous works in the area, explain and illustrate the processes of writing and publishing a good journal article, as well as use some real examples to illustrate the points advanced in the paper. We discovered that many journal papers are rejected because of the incompetence of contributors. Consequently, we explain and demonstrate in this article how writers can avoid the pitfalls that compel editors and reviewers to reject their papers, and how to best respond to arguable comments from peer reviewers in a way that leaves each party satisfied.

Keywords: Peer review, journal article, pre-publication, proofreading, editing, paper publication

1. Introduction

Writing and publishing a good paper in a reputable journal is one of the difficult aspects of academic work. This owes to the fact that the process is long, rigorous, intricate, technical and full of disappointments. According to Matthew (2016), some high-impact journals reject nine out of every ten papers submitted to them for consideration. The rejection is partly attributed to the shortcomings in the manuscript preparation and submission process (Shaikh 2018). Ensom (2011: 12) identifies some reasons journals and publishers reject papers as "fatal flaw in design and/or reporting (e.g., inappropriate methodology and/or analyses), lack of originality no or very little new information to the literature, low impact and/or minimal applicability to other sites, failure to answer the stated research question, failure to meet the standard of practice for the journal, poor organization and/or clarity, inadequate description and interpretation of results, and negligence of journal's submission requirements". To avoid these pitfalls, different stages of the academic article should be approached with special care and attention.

In this paper, we, therefore, focus mainly on the peer review stage of a draft for publication and the processes of standardizing and perfecting a paper before the article is published. The paper sets out to teach the *modus operandi* of writing and publishing scholarly articles in reputable journals. Thus, readers will be able to define and explain peer review, as well as identify its dynamic substages, do self-review, proofread and edit their draft works and fine-tune them, explain the importance of a cover letter and write it appropriately, respond properly to and rationalize blind peer-reviewers' comments and correction, and argue their convictions strongly and convincingly in response to the arguable comments in peer reviews.

The paper draws from previous works in the area of focus, the presenters' knowledge as writers of research articles, peer reviewers for several journals and teachers of academic writing and publishing for many years. Examples used in this paper are extracted from previously peer-reviewed works which later are published in some reputable journals. The method of data analysis and presentation is exploratory and explanatory. Further, appendices of peer-reviewed papers are added for the readers to consult.

2. Peer Reviewing Process

"Peer review is the evaluation of work by one or more people of similar competence to the producers of the work (peers). It constitutes a form of self-regulation by qualified members of a profession within the relevant field" (Academy of IRMBR 2018). Once a manuscript is submitted to a journal, an editor and several reviewers may recommend some changes with a view to improving the submitted article. It is a normal pathway to the publication of the article (Muchenje 2017). The peer review stage comes after passing the gate of journal editors. It is very important for eliciting feedback and gatekeeping in scientific productions. Without peer review, false claims and findings would be published, which might cause a lot of damage in the society. According to Noble (2017: 1), "the reviewing process can significantly improve your manuscript by allowing you to take into account the advice of multiple experts in your field. Indeed, empirical evidence suggests that papers that have undergone multiple rounds of peer review fare better in terms of citation counts than papers that are quickly accepted."

Against this background, peer reviews have been both rewarding and frustrating to both authors and reviewers. To authors, it may be displeasure and frustration, especially where an author has worked very hard on the manuscript, just to receive disparaging reviews of their hard work, some of which may not be genuine. To reviewers, it is time-consuming (mostly unpaid) and annoying, especially when the quality of the work does not measure up to established standards of output or quality. Mostly, the process is quite long and discouraging. Figure 1 from Wiley (2018) illustrates the process:

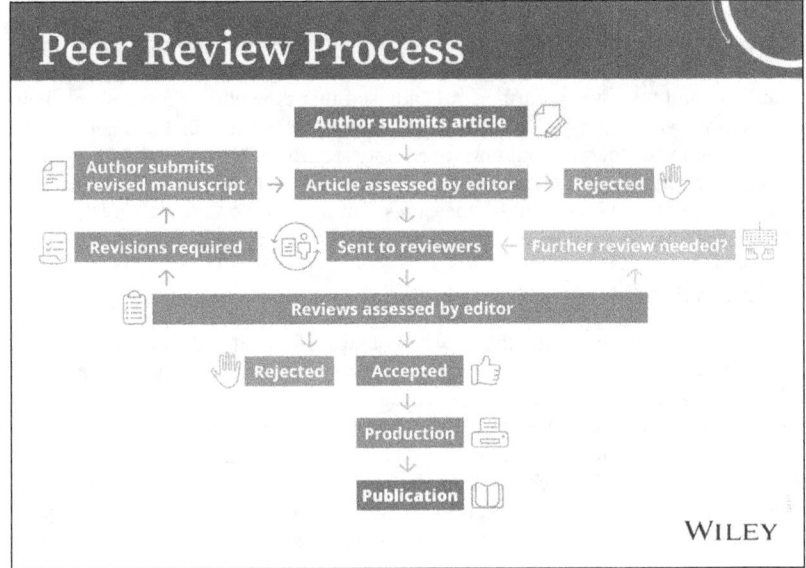

Figure 1:   Peer review process (adopted from Wiley 2018)

As illustrated above, the process involves: (i) submitting a paper (online, by carefully filling some necessary information in a fixed format, or by simply sending it as attachment and email), (ii) assessment by the editorial office, (iii) appraisal by the chief editor, (iv) assignment of the work to an associate editor to monitor the review process, (v) invitation to reviewers, (vi) response to the invitation, (vii) the review process, (viii) journal evaluation of the reviews, (ix) communicating decisions to authors (rejection or further review by authors), (x) receiving author's revision, (xi) assessing author's revision (editor), (xii) rejecting the work or producing and publishing it. We give the details of some of these processes hereunder.

2.1. Pre-review Stage

Authors need to know that articles are normally screened to determine their technical and factual sufficiency for publication. Some of the things checked, even before an article is channeled through a peer review process, involves the originality (plagiarism and duplication), completeness of a paper, conformity to guidelines and scope of the journal, soundness of data analysis, justification of the conclusion, comprehensibility and the 'interestingness' of the paper (Thrower 2012).

On this backdrop, authors are expected to strive to meet all these requirements before submitting them to a journal to be considered for publication. Failure to meet the requirements can constrain the editors and reviewers to reject the paper. One way for authors to meet these requirements is by rereading their works and finding out all weaknesses that they can themselves fix before their works reach editors and reviewers (Shaikh 2018). This proactive approach, efforts and attitude will definitely reduce or even prevent the chances of rejection and disappointment by editors and reviewers. Further, it is advised that the author should share their manuscripts with colleagues or other researchers for feedback that can help to improve weaknesses therein. In doing so, authors are advised to highlight all sections of the manuscripts that they would like their reviewers to concentrate on (Shaikh 2018). We present other specific measures that need to be undertaken before an article is submitted for publication consideration in the subsequent sections.

2.1.1. *Revising/Editing and Proofreading*

Editing is an act of improving the flow and quality of a written document, its structure, data presentation and its analysis, clarity, style and referencing, whereas, proofreading is an act of correcting spelling, punctuation marks, grammatical and typographical errors in a document due to be published. An editor reviews every sentence of a work, identifies fragmented parts and reorganizes them, ensures logical flow of presentations, checks correspondence between headings and contents, sharpens statements, summarizes, removes redundancies, checks grammar, appropriateness of tenses, correctness of graphs and charts, clarity of expressions, truth value of statements, and pays attention to critical turns and junctions of syntactic constructions, for example, concord, boosters and hedgers. The editor also rewrites some parts of the work, deletes and merges sections where necessary.

A proofreader, on the other hand, corrects punctuation errors, wrong formats, tracks the use of punctuation marks, particularly the use of the full stop and the comma. The proof-reader equally tracks the use of schemas, tables, figures, and checks diagrams to ensure that they are well positioned and captioned. Further, the proof-reader should check page numbering, either at the top or bottom corner of the pages, or middle of the bottom. He or she should spell check documents using software or carrying out an eagle-eyed reading of the document. Editing and proofreading also involve tracking the numbering of headings and subsections to ensure that they are well written and have consistent use of small and capital letters specified by the publisher. Consistency in paragraphing format, either the block or the indented form, and even spacing between sentences and paragraphs throughout the document should also be checked.

Authors should self-proofread and edit their work as much as possible. They should, at this stage, use of spelling and grammar checkers that are inbuilt in many word processors, e.g. a spelling and grammar checker in Microsoft Word. Authors can alternatively use online spelling and grammar checkers such as Grammarly – an online spelling and grammar checker which identifies obvious errors and mistakes in written texts and even suggests how to improve sentence structures and avoid monotony. Nonetheless, neither the authors nor these softwares can completely or successfully remove all errors and inadequacies in a draft of an article. Consequently, it is highly recommended that authors should give their works to experienced colleagues to read and give them feedback that can help them to improve their works. Alternatively, they can give their works to professional editors or editing firms if they are financially capable of doing so.

It is highly advised that the work should be thoroughly edited before it is submitted for publication to enhance its chance of acceptance. According to Shaikh (2018), between 30 and 50 percent of articles submitted to Elsevier are rejected before reaching the peer-review stage, mostly because of the evidence of poor language on the documents. The statistics, thus, underscores the significance of editing and proofreading before a work is submitted to a reputable journal for publication. Editing and proofreading should be thoroughly done to correct the simplest and most complex of errors and inadequacies in a paper, particularly mechanics (punctuation and spelling), linguistic infelicities such as concord errors and wrong use of tenses and aspects, syntactic constructions, dangling modifiers and phrases, coherence and cohesion as well as structure, logic, content and sexist use of language.

2.1.2. *Making a Good First Impression with a Title and an Abstract*

Editors tend to focus on title and abstract in deciding to channel the article into a further process or reject it outright. This suggests that more thought and concentration should be put into composing these sections of the paper. The title should indicate the field and reflect the problem and objectives of the paper. Similarly, an abstract should expose the problem, purpose, scope, methodology, findings, conclusion and recommendation. There should not be conspicuous language or punctuation errors in these parts of the document, for they are likely to put off the journal editors and bias their judgement of the paper.

2.1.3. *Writing an Effective Cover Letter*

A journal article is often accompanied with a cover letter to the editor. The letter explains the contents of the article, its significance, identify the target readers and declares the originality of the paper. This rationalizes why it should be written with great care and attention. It is an opportunity for the authors to convince the editor that their papers have publication potential.

In structure, a journal submission letter has the same format as other business letters, except that it is supposed to be shorter and clearer. The letter must begin with the name of the article, the rationale for writing the journal and the major findings of the work. Further, the authors can refer to their other published works to demonstrate that they have been certified by other publishers as capable scholars. In the letter, authors should also explain why their manuscripts would be a good fit for that particular journal and state why it would be of interest to the journal's readers (Mudrak 2018). Further, the author can also mention, in the letter, some "peers and colleagues who read the article and provided feedback before the manuscript's submission" (Shaikh 2018: 5).

2.1.4. *Selecting an Appropriate Journal*

Choosing the right journal is a bit of a challenge to many due to the multiplicity of journals and their variability in requirements such as article lengths, approaches, topic or style and referencing format. The works sent to wrong journals are often rejected right away, which is wastage of time to authors, especially if the rejection comes after a long wait. Similarly, the author who publishes in a wrong journal is likely to miss his target audience.

Authors need to read the home page of journals or introductory information to determine their aims, scope, and target research area. Foremost, they should select a journal that publishes articles that have similar or complementary methodological approach to theirs. For instance, "qualitative work will not necessarily sit well in quantitative data heavy publications" (NHSFT 2014: 1). Further, they should consider other factors such as the rate of accessibility of their articles and its acceptance if they have to use the publications for justifications such as facilitating promotion at an educational institution. They should consider whether to publish in a closed or an open-access journal, low or high-impact journal – considering the fact that each type has its weaknesses and strengths. An open-access journal, for instance, enhances the availability and retrievability of one's paper but may sometimes fail to fetch respect associated with high-impact journals – most of which are closed-access journals. According to Corcos (2017), publishing in high impact journals can be an institutional requirement, but not necessarily the best choice in terms of paper accessibility. Ranking journals by their impact factor is intended to help librarians to determine which journals to buy or subscribe to. That is to say, the higher the impact factor, the more likely the journals are respected and valued by the community. However, publishing in a journal with a high impact is very laborious and time-consuming. It is also noted that most of such journals exalt the technicalities over the substance and the broader purpose of the paper, which cause them to reject even articles with great potential.

However, it should be noted that finding the right journal is not enough in itself; some journals may be right but are such choosy that they may not accommodate your article. In this regard, one rule of thumb to choosing a journal is to find out from colleagues about the most appropriate journal to submit your manuscript to or to check where the colleagues in the workplace have been publishing their works. The author can equally "send an e-mail inquiry to a prospective journal editor to ascertain a particular journal's interest" in receiving your manuscript (Ensom 2011: 389).

Research ethics and policies of all scholarly journals suggest that authors should submit a manuscript to only one journal at a time. Doing otherwise can cause embarrassment and lead to copyright problems for the author, the university employer and the journals involved. The safest way, therefore, is to wait until one journal rejects your paper before sending it to another journal.

2.1.5. *Following Author Guidelines*

Author guidelines are the written statements to inform authors of measures to take before submitting a paper. They inform authors about fonts, requirements for figures, tables, references and margins, just to mention a few. As these measures are mostly technicalities, authors have tended to ignore them, having completed the daunting task of researching and writing a 'masterpiece'. However, authors should know that guidelines are documents to be downloaded and adhered to if they want to increase the chances of their publication in the journal in question. According to Thrower (2012), between 30 and 50 percent of articles do not even make it to the peer review process because of technicalities that could have been corrected if authors conformed to the provided guidelines. If your manuscript is not structured and formatted according to the target journal layout, for instance, the likelihood is that it will receive a desk rejection from the editor without being sent out for peer review, which is quite disheartening to authors, and might lower their enthusiasm to research and publish.

2.1.6. *Compliance with a Submission Checklist*

It is strongly recommended that authors should format their works before sending them out to journals. These include selecting fonts, ensuring right spacing, inserting page numbers, setting pages to the correct location (left or right side pages), and orienting all texts in the right locations on the page. They must also ensure that images used in the text are properly sized and meet the required resolution for the printing of coloured images, normally 300dpi resolution. In addition, authors must ensure that codes, tables and figures are sequentially and logically arranged. Further, they must make sure that the margins, footers, gutters are all properly set and that the reviewers' comments are removed; track changes or any other author automatic formatting programmes used in the preparation of the document are switched off, just to mention a few.

Authors should not assume that their target journals will simply accept the formats they used in preparing their works. This is not possible because each journal has its format requirements. Neglecting format requirements suggests the lack of rigour on the part of the author. So, painstaking editorial work should go into the style and lay out of every article before it is submitted for publication.

2.2. Review stage

Upon receiving reviews from editors, editors-in-chief can reject the paper or ask authors to revise it and resubmit in line with recommendations provided by reviewers. These revisions may be minor (i.e. simple grammatical or typographical errors) or major (i.e. redesigning experiments, additional data and compiling new data or adding a section). It is important to address all the recommended revisions diligently and fully and the following subsections strive to offer some direction.

2.2.1. Responding to Peer-Reviewers' Comments

A peer is a person with a similar competence to authors. They are the persons assigned to evaluate and advise publishers on the suitability of a work submitted for publication consideration. Most of the times, the peer reviewers work voluntarily to read and evaluate the works "blindly" and give 'free and fair' comments on the work in question. Due to the anonymity of the exercise, the reviewers regularly give fair comments on the work. However, the difference of contexts between the author and the reviewer may cause some reviewers to misunderstand some information about the work being assessed and, hence, make comments that may be deemed irrelevant. Some reviewers are personally chock-full of criticism and humour (Hamilton 2014), or "write long-winded comments, which make it difficult to pinpoint the specific aspects you need to address" (Khanam 2013: 1). Consequently, the peer reviewer's feedback is more likely to frustrate budding authors who might have worked so hard to compile "masterpieces" they ultimately submitted to a journal for publication consideration. All the same, peer reviewers' comments are mostly meaningful despite the above-mentioned limitations. Ensom (2011: 390) writes the following from her own experience:

> The reviewers' comments sometimes make me very angry (prompting me to ask, "Didn't they even read my paper?"). However, after taking time to simmer down, I usually realize that if something was unclear to the reviewer, it would likely be equally unclear to a future reader. At the end of the day, addressing the reviewers' comments (whether or not I am in agreement) has always helped me to strengthen my papers.

Due to this experience, it is even advised that authors should take a couple of days to ponder over the overall feedback upon receiving a peer review. This owes to the fact that reviewers' comments can sometimes be overwhelming at first sight. The author may, therefore, fail to identify requirements of reviewers and, thus, fail to address them satisfactorily or feel that the reviewer has not properly understood their study or has made unreasonable demands (Khanam 2013).

After allowing the work to lie fallow for a while, authors are advised to browse the given comments and carefully gather their thoughts on how to address them. Enago Academy (2015) advises that authors should work on the given comments one by one, but starting from a simple to a complex comment. Muchenje (2017: 116) advises that authors should "avoid referring a certain reviewer "A" to another reviewer "B"'s response to any comment, even if they ask the same question. Respond to each reviewer as if his/her comments were the only ones you received". Authors should "identify the major concerns of the reviewers. For example, are most of the comments on the methodology that you used? Did the reviewers question the way you interpreted your results? Do you have additional data that you could include in the manuscript in support of your arguments? Once you identify the reviewers' concern, start framing your responses" (Khanam 2013: 1).

It is permissible also to disagree with the reviewers, but tactfully and respectfully. Authors may present a rebuttal such as "We acknowledge the reviewer's point, but respectfully disagree for the following reasons" (Ensom 2011). According to Noble (2017: 5), if the reviewer failed to understand something, apologize for not making it clear. Even if you are convinced that the text is already clear (i.e., the reviewer simply missed it). This owes to the fact that the fault likely lies, at least in part, with the author for the failure to make his point clear enough. Even when the author feels that the reviewer in question lacked the intellectual capacity to review his/her work, it is advised not to convey this impression to the reviewer. Authors should remember that their level of expertise (or lack thereof) may be a representative of many readers of the journal out there" (Noble 2017: 5).

In a nutshell, authors should better revise with the goal of showing the reviewer that they were carefully read and understood, even if the requested change seems unnecessary. It is also advised that authors should be punctual with the review deadline to demonstrate that they are serious and enthusiastic to publish their documents. If authors need more time, they should notify the Journal immediately, rather than returning the reviewed draft after the deadline for resubmission has passed (Ensom 2011). Even if the paper is rejected, the author is advised to read the reviewers' comments carefully and use them to strengthen their paper for submission to another journal. The danger of ignoring comments is the possibility that "a manuscript submitted to a different journal may end up in the hands of the same reviewer" (Ensom 2011: 390).

2.2.2. The Review Submission Letter

In returning reviews, authors should remember that two documents are required, the revised document and the cover letter. In the revised document, authors should highlight all modifications made in line with recommendations received from the reviewers for editors of the journal to track and appreciate the changes made to the document. In the cover letter, authors should list all responses to concerns raised by reviewers and should persuasively argue their course of action to convince reviewers to accept their points (Enago Academy 2015; Shaikh 2018). They should, for example, thoroughly explain themselves and support their positions with previously published literature (Enago Academy 2015). "Too frequently, authors focus on revising the manuscript itself and spend too little time making the response document clear and compelling. The result can be misunderstandings between the reviewers and the authors and ultimately, the possible rejection of a high-quality manuscript" (Noble 2017: 3).

3. Conclusion

This paper is motivated by the observation that authors tend to put less effort in the final stages of writing articles and in the pre-publication process such as editing, following author guidelines, searching for the appropriate journals and writing effective cover letters, yet these are the key determinants of article acceptance by many academic journals. Consonantly, the article underscores the significance of these stages and proposes effective approaches to handling them for higher chances of publication. In so doing, the article strives to change the outlook and perspectives of the budding scholars on the pre-publication, which might earn them different results in their attempts to publish articles in academic journals. It is expected that the article boosts understanding of contextual dynamics that militate against the successful composition and publication of a research paper that emanate from the author, the standards of the journal publication as well as the competence and/or intellectual inclinations of the peer reviewers. The insights and the new outlook instilled by the article, are, therefore, expected to help scholars who utilize the information herein to realize different results in their process of writing and publishing journal articles.

References

Academy of IRMBR. (2018). *Double blind peer review.* Retrieved on April 10 from http://www.academyirmbr.com/double.php

Corcos, D. (2017). Is it worth publishing your research in a high impact journal? Retrieved on March 23 from https://www.researchgate.net/post/Is_it_worth_publishing_your_research_in_a_high impact_journal.

Enago Academy. (2015). How to respond to reviewer comments and revise your *research paper*. Retrieved on March 22 from https://www.enago.com/academy/responding-to-reviewer-comments-andrevising-your- research-paper/.

Ensom, M. (2011). Improving the chances of manuscript acceptance: How to address peer reviewers' comments. *The Canadian Journal of Hospital Pharmacy* 64 (6): 389 –391.

Hamilton, K. (2014). 12 unimpressed comments from peer reviewers. Retrieved on March 25 from http://www.iflscience.com/editors-blog/my-peer-reviewer-said-what/.

Khanam, S. (2013). Do's and don'ts for responding to peer reviewers' comments. Editage Insights. Retrieved on April 10 from https://www.editage.com/insights/dos-and-donts-for-responding-to-peer-reviewers comments.

Matthew, D. (2016). High rejection rates by journals 'pointless'. Retrieved on March 22 from https://www.timeshighereducation.com/news/high-rejection-rates-by-journals pointless on 3/22/2018.

Muchenje, V. (2017). How to respond to reviewers' comments. *South African Journal of Animal Science* 47 (2): 116-117.

Mudrak, B. (2018). *Writing a cover letter.* Durham: American Journal Experts.

Noble, W. (2017). Ten simple rules for writing a response to reviewers. *PLoS Computational Biology* 13 (10): 1-4.

Norfolk and Suffolk Foundation Trust (NHSFT). (2014). Choosing the right journal for publication. Retrieved from http://www.nsft.nhs.uk/Getinvolved/Documents/Choosing%20the%20Journal%20for%20Publication.pdf/.

Shaikh, A. (2018). 7 steps to publishing in a scientific journal. Retrieved on March 7 from https://www.elsevier.com/connect/7-steps-to-publishing-in-a-scientific-journal/.

Thrower, P. (2012). Eight reasons I rejected your article. Retrieved on March 8 from https://www.elsevier.com/connect/8-reasons-i-rejected-your-article/.

Wiley (2018). The peer review process. Retrieved on March 22 from https://authorservices.wiley.com/Reviewers/journal-reviewers/what-is-peer-review/the-peer-review-process.html on 3/22/2018/.

Appendix

A sample of response to reviewers' comments

1. COMMENT: This is an interesting, well-written paper. I think you bring up some important issues that will spark considerable debate, both in terms of what you have actually found and in terms of the policy implications (tenure, recruiting, pay, etc.). My comments are mainly aimed at tightening up the logic and clarity of what you have communicated and tested. I summarize my comments below based on the order I found them in the paper because these seem to be the points where the issue comes up -- I'd like to see you tackle all of these (very doable) and that is why they are presented in page order as opposed to any other prioritization.

RESPONSE: Thank you very much for your kind words about our paper. We are delighted to hear that you think our work will spark debate in our field. In the following sections, you will find our responses to each of your points and suggestions. We are grateful for the time and energy you expended on our behalf.

2. COMMENT: abstract -- starting with the abstract, and wherever you say there are differences between micro and macro, please say what you actually found, not just that there are differences. This point will make the paper controversial (if defensible) and as such lends to the value of having it published.

RESPONSE: Thank you for this suggestion. In the revision, we attempted to describe differences between the two sub-disciplines in a balanced manner; one that promotes healthy respect and discussion between the sub-disciplines within management. Nonetheless, we do maintain some of these arguments. Per your suggestion, we now include in the abstract how competition in macro is more pronounced than in micro.

3. COMMENT: p. 2 - publication norms - this term is pretty loaded and ambiguous in its meaning. I suggest that you use something like "authorship" or "average productivity of management scholars," in lieu of publication norms since you don't really ever look at what it takes to get an article published. You do talk later in the paper about norms for earning tenure, but this is different.

RESPONSE: You raise a very valid point about the terminology we employed in our original submission. Per your advice, we have eliminated our references to norms and now use "scholarly productivity" instead. We agree that this is a more accurate description of the phenomenon we are exploring. Thank you for this great suggestion.

4. COMMENT: p. 2 - demographic shifts - I don't think you ever connected the dots later in the paper with this early observation. It sounds like your underlying logic is that the number of authors has increased, and so has competition, but unevenly across sub-disciplines - if there will be a radical decrease in authors then does this mean that competition will decrease? You need to help the reader understand this important facet of the landscape.

RESPONSE: You raise an important question regarding competition in our industry. To better assess how competition has changed over time, we performed supplementary analyses. Specifically, we calculated for each year in our sample the number of unique authors publishing an article in the journals in our sample in the previous five years. In 1988, for example, we calculated how many individuals published an article between 1984 and 1988. This approach proxies for competition, because it assesses how many individuals compete for journal space. We found a substantial increase in the number of people publishing over time. In 1988, for example, we found that 1572 individuals published an article between 1984 and 1998. In the last year of our sample, 2008, we found that this number increased to 3158. This is important information, as we are now better able to discuss changes over time. With this addition we do not emphasize demographic shifts until we reach our discussion. We hope that our revised discussion now more clearly develops the linkages to which you refer.

Source: Adapted from ADOC (2018). https://adoc.site/queue/pdf-ebook-general-comments-to-the-referees-and-editor-we-are-a5b31f203c4756?&queue_id=-1&v=1533292137&u=MTk2LjIxNi4yNDcuNDA

'I Belong to None and I Belong to All': Religious Ambivalence in Achebe's *Arrow of God* and John's *Unburnable*

Adaobi Muo

Abstract

The paper examines religious ambivalence as a major behavioural response to multiculturalism in two comparable Igbo societies of Nigeria and Dominica using Chinua Achebe's *Arrow of God* and Marie-Elena John's *Unburnable* as entry points. A significant percentage of critical discourse displays concern with dramatizations of religious interface arising from Western imperialism in non-Western societies, and its consequences, especially in texts written by blacks. However, few pay adequate attention to manifestations of equivocation, its causes and impact in works which reconstruct the religious experiences of the Igbo both at home and in the Diaspora. This crucial aspect needs to be studied more comprehensively, considering what is being done with religion in black societies, and how such distort human relationships by promoting division. Therefore, this paper interprets ambivalent elements of belief and doubt, encapsulated in characters' relationship with Christianity and Indigenous Igbo Religion (IIR), as regulated by anxiety over an unknown future and quest for dominance in a rapidly changing society. The interpretation is chiefly regulated by Freud's Psychoanalytic concept of Fear of Castration. The study further examines the impact and dynamics of such religious attitude on individuals, family and society. Furthermore, it establishes a consensus of imaginative expression and thus a closer connection between Nigeria and Dominica - two seemingly separate regions of the world. The article concludes that both texts provide a basis for understanding religious behaviours in pluri-religious environments and at this period when religion has become susceptible to various interpretations.

Keywords: Religious interface, Western Imperialism, ambivalence

1. Introduction

The pluri-religious condition of African and Caribbean environments has persistently provided abundant materials for creative writers to reconstruct religious conducts. The religious behaviours of some major characters in such texts exhibit loyalty and disloyalty to different gods/God and, thus, proclaim *I belong to no god/God and I belong to all gods/God*. Such texts are Andre Brink's *Praying Mantis*, Yvonne Vera's *Nehanda*, Orlando Patterson's *Children of Sisyphus*, Zee Edgell's *Beka Lamb* and Ahmed Yerimah's *Hard Ground*. In the last text, for instance, a character, Mama, is portrayed as a fervent Catholic and a worshipper of Olokun and her ancestors. Mama's simultaneous allegiance and infidelity to two religions is a precautionary measure against family disintegration. This trend is more lucidly articulated in *Arrow of God* and *Unburnable*.

In Achebe's *Arrow of God*, henceforth *Arrow*, and John's *Unburnable*, ambivalence is best realized in the characters, Ezeulu and Matilda, as they respectively relate with Indigenous Igbo Religion (IIR) and Christianity, both present in their Nigerian and Dominican societies. Indigenous religions, like IIR, on the one hand, existed initially in the pre-colonial Nigeria. Christianity, on the other hand, accompanied colonialism into the country, while IIR was introduced into Dominica by Igbo slaves captured and shipped into the West Indies to work as plantation hands. Thus, Western imperialism facilitated the development of different religions among the Igbo in both environments where the novels are set.

Arrow is primarily set in Umuaro, a fictional federation of six villages which serves as a microcosm of the early 20th century Igbo society under colonialism. Ezeulu, who is constructed as exceptionally comely, is the protagonist and the chief priest of Ulu, the principal deity of Umuaro. Umuaro has other major gods including Idemili, the god of the sky and owner of the sacred python, and Eru – the god of wealth. There are also "minor deities" (Achebe 1964: 202) such as Agwu – the rash brother of madness and Ngene – owner a stream. With Westernization, the foreign Christian God makes a late entrance into the land. As a result, both indigenous and foreign deities are present in the religious consciousness of Umuaro. *Arrow*, more than many other African creative writings, "portrays the relationship between man and god" (Akanbi Olarongbo Afolabi, Noor Hashima Abd Aziz & Rohizaz Halim 2018: 69).

Unburnable, like *Arrow*, is set in colonial Dominica. The text represents the country as mainly populated by descendants of African slaves as it traces the "tribal identity" of most Dominican Blacks to "the slave ship" from West Africa (John 2006: 134). *Unburnable*'s Dominica is a devout Christian society where African religions are still practiced. The relationship between the two religions is encapsulated in the explanation that IIR stands "outside colonial power and Catholicism" and European ideology (Denison 2009: 366-7). African religion is fully expressed in the text's account of Noir. Noir is reconstructed as a pure maroon village on one of Dominica's mountains. The mountain-top rural community is named "black ... after the colour of its people" (John 2006: 262). It was founded by escapee female slaves and headed by the intimidating black Matilda. Matilda, unlike Ezeulu, is not the protagonist of *Unburnable* but she is crafted as a memorable character and contributes extensively to the development of the plot.

In Noir, homes are dotted with shrines where different gods are worshipped with sacrifices. The people relate with their ancestors through masquerades. The masking tradition, more than other cultural images, reveals the community as Igbo. Based on the appearances and activities of the masquerades, the British colonial officer, Mr Drummond, who had previously encountered similar masquerades during his stay in Nigeria declares that "the Igbos were here (in Dominica) for sure" (John 2006: 134). In addition, Noir rural society practices polygamy. *Unburnable*, therefore, reconstructs a typical traditional Igbo village in Noir and the society corresponds with *Arrow*'s Umuaro. Ezeulu and Matilda are separated by region, gender and complexion but united by similar remarkable personalities and leadership positions in their separate Igbo worlds at home and in diaspora. More importantly, both display similar attitudes of 'I belong to none and I belong to all' as they relate with IIR and Christianity. Thus, the representations, in their correspondences and departures, provide a concrete basis for an analysis of religious ambivalence.

The first part of the topic: 'I belong to none and I belong to all' is adopted from Charles de Gaulle's declaration "I am a man who belongs to no-one and who belongs to everyone". De Gaulle was the 18th President of France and led the country from 1958 to1969. The statement is contained in his press conference in France on May 19, 1958 during the political crisis engendered by the Algerian revolution. However, it has been popularized recently by the Nigerian President Muhammadu Buhari who used a slightly modified version of the statement in his inaugural speech on 29th May 2015. The statement is modified for the purpose of this research to encapsulate the occurrence of vacillation in characters' sporadic loyalty to IIR and Christianity, the two religions in the Nigerian and Dominican Igbo societies portrayed in the primary texts. In the following sections, the literature review is presented and this is followed by the presentation of results and analysis before the conclusion and recommendations.

2. Literature Review and Conceptual Framework

The functional value of religion and its principal position within contemporary conversation have been articulated by scholars, represented by Ruano and Soyinka. Ruano (2010: 896) identifies religion as a valuable means of understanding "certain forms of social conduct." Soyinka (2007: 141) classifies it as the "life and death discourse of the 21st century". Moreover, V. Y. Mudimbe (2007: 60), Ngugi wa Thiong'o (2007: 477), and Akinkurolere & Ariyo (2015: 140) respectively, posit that subjects like religious behaviour find amplified articulation in the creative domain. Thus, *Arrow* and *Unburnable*'s engagement with ambiguity can be employed in the comprehension of religious behaviours in multicultural environments.

Literary critics are interested in people's attempt to live out their religious beliefs in pluri-religious societies as portrayed in African and West Indian creative corpora. *Arrow*'s profound attention to ambiguity as an attitudinal response to IIR and Christianity interface in Nigerian society, its effect and underlying forces are tentatively and randomly discussed by scholars across different decades of literary criticism. Such scholars include Irele (2000), Ojinmah (1991), Machila (1981), Abussamen (2018), Afolabi et. al. (2018), Ogwude (2011), Chuma-Ude (2014), and Chukwuma (2016).

First, in a study of cultural memory in *Things Fall Apart, TFA* after here, Irele (2000: 4) observes that Achebe's rural novels are "situated at the point of intersection between two world orders" African and Euro-Christian and both "impinge upon his (Achebe) creative consciousness". In this, Irele (2000) identifies the influence of multiculturalism, which provides the basis for this study, on Achebe's creative consciousness. However, he is hardly concerned with the manifestation of religious ambiguity and its consequences as a reaction to the condition.

Second, Ojinmah (1991: 25-26), in a study of Achebe's imaginative corpus, extends Irele's (2000) scope by identifying the consanguinity between *TFA* and *Arrow* and Achebe's realistic portrayal of Igbo society. Furthermore, the scholar posits that Ezeulu's portrayal as a dual character - human and spirit – "creates interpretative ambiguity" and represents "the dilemma and stresses of a man poised between two worlds" (Ojinmah 1991: 31, 26). Ojinmah's (1991) submissions recognise *Arrow*'s employment of Ezeulu in the dramatization of vacillation and its effects. Moreover, his study notes the complexity woven into the characterization of Ezeulu and its contribution to his religious ambivalence. These views justify the selection of Ezeulu for a study of this nature. Nevertheless, Ojinma's (1991) essay glosses over the intensive representation of ambivalence, using the character.

Third, Chukwuma (2016: 2) examines Ezeulu's characterization as a tragic hero and classifies him "a victim of the cultural, social, political, and metaphysical states of affairs and contradictions of his world". In this, he implies the dynamics which propel the character's religious attitude.

Fourth, Machila (1981: 119) analyses the ambiguities maintained by *Arrow* but from the perspective of how Ezeulu's attitude affects his perception by other characters and his society. The critic observes that Ezeulu is "a complex ... ambiguous character (whose) motives are always mixed" and emanate from his "personal drives" and official duty as a chief priest. Machila (1981) deepens Ojinmah's sparse concern in Ezeulu's vacillation and balances Chukwuma's view by providing the internal dynamics of the character's relationship with the religions of his world. His examination also notes the underlying factor of the attitude, which also forms the concern of this research and guides the choice of its concept. Nonetheless, the study is tangentially interested in religious behaviour, which drives the plot of *Arrow* and rotates the orbit of this study.

Fifth, Abussamen (2018: 5) studies different levels of ambivalence in *Arrow*. He identifies the most potent evidence of Ezeulu's vacillation which is that as the chief priest of Ulu, he sends his son to represent him in the western Christianity but refuses to represent the western culture among his people. Sixth, Afolabi et al. (2018: 71) submit that Ezeulu's "actions depict that the custodian of people's tradition and spiritual powers is accommodating foreign culture". This view implies the import of Ezeulu's romance with Christianity. Furthermore, Ogwude (2011: 2) notes that Ezeulu's indirect acceptance of Christianity is based on "pure pragmatic considerations." Her interpretation tacitly observes the quest for dominance which motivates Ezeulu's romance with Christianity even as the chief priest of the principal deity of Umuaro. Lastly, Ngozi Chuma-Ude (2014: 218) examines Ezeulu's characterization and posits that the unhealthy relationship between indigenous gods and priests results from "stiff rivalry against each other in a context for supremacy". This identifies the impact of religious ambivalence. Again, the reading validates the employment of Freud's concept of fear of castration as an analytical tool in this research, which derives its primary data from *Arrow* and *Unburnable*.

The literature available to this study indicates that in comparison with *Arrow*, *Unburnable* is yet to be extensively examined by literary critics. *Unburnable*'s lucid demonstration of religious vacillation arising from religious interface in multi-cultural Dominica as well as its causes and effects are largely ignored. However, a number of literary critics, arbitrarily and cautiously, observe the relationship between IIR and Christianity in the society. These include scholars like Harrison (2017), Clark (2010), Hillhouse (2006), Bryce (2006), Ali (2010), and Bailey (2013).

First, Harrison (2017: 7) notes the African religious content of the West Indian novel in his submission that *Unburnable* "weaves together West Indian history, West African mythology, and Diasporic sensibility". Second, Roberta (2010: 1) observes that the text takes us back to the circumstances and consequences of "the arrival of Africans in Dominica". Her view explains, albeit remotely, the text's representation of the slave origin of the Igbo in Dominica. This is a major dynamic of religious vacillation. Third, Carol (2013: 42) shows interest in the novel's portrayal of the cultural impact of slavery by observing the "African religious practices" that marked the "plantation society".

Hillhouse (2006) extends the argument by identifying several layers "of duality (and) ... multiplicity of realities and perspectives" in *Unburnable*. She holds that "ideologically, it straddles ... Afro-Caribbean and Euro-Caribbean ways of being – including African spirituality and Judeo-Christian [and specifically Catholic] spirituality" (Hillhouse 2006: 1). These interpretations provide the background to the pluri-religious condition of *Unburnable*'s West-Indian setting which, in turn, engenders vacillation. However, the studies speak in general terms. They hardly recognize the novel's exploitation of Igbo religion and its Nigerian connection. In addition, the readings largely shy away from the major concern of this work.

Bryce (2006: 2) tentatively caters for some of the identified gaps. He notes that the incorporation of a Nigerian priest, Fr. Okeke, and a colonial officer functions as a tool for "decoding African retentions" which are becoming extinct among Black Dominicans. Moreover, Ali (2010: 386, 378, 383) observes the characterization of Matilda as an "Obeah woman ... a customary African female chief ... a powerful tribal leader", who desires the position of an ancestor. Thus, he identifies a potent vessel employed in the dramatization of religious ambiguity but fails to examine it further. Like Ali's (2010), most interpretations largely ignore Matilda's expression of vacillation best exemplified by her complex relationship with IIR and Christianity, and its effect and dynamics.

The reviewed literature reveals that a number of studies have tentatively analysed *Arrow* and *Unburnable*'s concern with the interface between IIR and Christianity in the Igbo society of Nigeria and Dominica where the novels are respectively set. However, the ambivalence manifested in the religious performance of the characters epitomised by Ezeulu and Matilda is yet to receive the in-depth attention it deserves. This is more so with Matilda (*Unburnable*). Bearing in mind that religion can hardly be ignored because it is a prominent feature of human society and religious behaviour has an overwhelming impact on social relationships, this subject needs to be studied further. In addition, considering the role of religion and literature in understanding human behavior, and identifying cultural ties between different regions, the fictional expression of religious ambivalence deserves more attention. Here it is studied in terms of how it reflects the Igbo experience of religion at home and in the Diaspora.

This research employs Sigmund Freud's concept of Castration Complex/Anxiety as an analytical tool. Freud's most perceptive contribution to the Psychoanalytic domain is the "workings of the human psyche" (cited in Barry 1995: 96). The theorist postulates on the dominant role of the unconscious in determining characters' behaviours. The unconscious constitutes the hidden powers governing actions and inactions and one of such is Castration Complex. Castration complex claims that boys, at the oedipal stage (3 – 5 years), develop the fear of losing their penises on realizing that girls are without such. In patriarchal Victorian society, studied by Freud, the presence of penis confers social power, privileges, dominance and superiority on the male gender. Lois Tyson (1994: 28) defines Castration Anxiety as the "fear of domination to the powerless position occupied by the females". Eagleton (2006: 136) adds that anyone who comes out of the Oedipal process is "a *spilt* subject" precariously torn between the conscious and unconscious with the later having an overwhelming influence on such. In Eagleton's (2006) view, the contradiction engendered by the presence of two opposing forces in the human subject is articulated. This research is motivated by such contradiction as portrayed in *Arrow* and *Unburnable*.

Literarily, Castration Complex describes the fear of loss of sexual potency and supremacy. Metaphorically, it represents the fear of being demoted, dominated, or made irrelevant. As such, it implies fear emasculation. The fear can become so overpowering as to cause the human subject to interpret insignificant occurrences as humiliating, feel powerless, and take extreme measures to preserve his/her relevance. Thus, the feeling could be injurious to mental well-being. This study employs the metaphoric use of the term with all its noted connotations. Armed with Castration Complex, it examines the hardly noted portrayal of belief and doubt revealed in attempts to simultaneously belong to no god/God and every god/God. It analyses this tendency as an unconscious process of striving for power and relevance in a changing world and, therefore, a manifestation of fear of emasculation. This it does by looking at two characters, Ezeulu and Matilda, as they individually relate with IIR and Christianity, their devotees and informing cultures.

3. Methods of Data Collection and Analysis

This study adopts the first part of its title from Charles de Gaulle's statement: "I am a man who belongs to no-one and who belongs to everyone." It derives its primary data from two literary texts respectively set in the Igbo society of Nigeria and what could be classified as remnants of the same group in Dominica. Both countries host both Christianity and IIR. The texts are Achebe's *Arrow of God* (1964) and Marie-Elena John's *Unburnable* (2006). Analysis is further enhanced by relevant data obtained from secondary materials. Textual interpretations are guided by Freud's Psychoanalytic concept of Fear of Castration. It is based on four considerations. First is how characters' affiliation with the two religions in his/her environment, and with their adherents and supporting culture, manifests ambiguity as revealed in thoughts, words and actions. The second is the effect of such on social relationships, while the third is the underlying forces driving such conducts. The last is correspondences and departures between the regions covered by the novels. Consequently, the study engages in an in-depth character analysis that involves two religious leaders in both settings.

4. Data Analysis and Result

Guided by the concept of Anxiety Complex, this study engages in a close reading of *Arrow* and *Unburnable*, set in comparative societies of Nigeria (African) and Dominica (West Indies). It undertakes an exhaustive analysis of the religious behaviours of Ezeulu and Matilda to identify and discuss instances of religious ambivalence as well as their impact and dynamics.

Ezeulu's ambivalent religious conduct is mainly established through three incidents in *Arrow*. These are his relationship with IIR gods – Ulu, Eru and Idemili, donation of his son, Oduche, to Christianity and rejection of the warrant chief offer. The priest's vacillation is foreshadowed early in the text through his feelings towards the new moon. Even as an old Chief Priest of Ulu "the fear of the new moon which he felt as a little boy still hovered round him. ... The fear was often overpowered by the joy of his high office; but it was not killed. It lay on the ground in the grip of the joy" (Achebe 1964: 2). Ezeulu's dilemma is reminiscent of Okonkwo's bravery motivated by the fear of being called weak (*TFA*). In the excerpt above, the Chief Priest's contrastive emotions are portrayed as irretrievably bound. Consequently, he is "perplexed and uncertain" (Carroll 1980: 91) and this implies ambivalence. In addition, the fear is traced to his childhood in a manner that corresponds with Freud's idea that the fear of castration is developed at the early years. Again, Ezeulu's delight at his exalted position suggests his quest for power and relevance.

The adroit juxtaposition of the vacillation illustrates Achebe's (1964: 70, 192) creative discretion observed throughout the novel. Moreover, the character's refusal to belong totally to one side of the religious divide is given a concrete expression in the ceremonial painting of his body in black and white and his classification as half man and half spirit. Ezeulu's religious ambiguity tends to draw from Ulu, described by Ezeulu as the god that "kills and saves" (Achebe 1964: 72). In the character, one understands the complexity embedded in the human person.

Ezeulu's relationship with Ulu, his principal, exhibits ambivalence evident in his thoughts. This is displayed in his mental examination and interpretation of the nature and scope of his priestly authority and power. Using the analogy of the child goat-owner and the metaphor of a mere watchman, the narrator discloses Ezeulu's comprehension of his subordinate position in relation to Ulu and Umuaro. Thus, he realizes "the immensity of his power" but wonders "what kind of power was it if it would never be used" (Achebe 1964: 3). Ezeulu's frustration over his subsidiary position seems prompted by a desire for supremacy and control. It displays a tacit attempt at averting demotion by usurping Ulu's powers. Consequently, the chief priest practically accepts his 'servant' position as Ulu's messenger but, theoretically, rejects its second-rate status and as such refuses to belong totally to Ulu. Ambivalence is contained in the character's reverence and submission, as well as impudence and defiance towards the same god. In this episode, one sees many religious leaders in African countries, like Nigeria, who easily transform from taking instructions as 'men of God' to giving commands as 'gods of men'. Again, the employment of dramatic monologue in the scene further demonstrates Ezeulu's dilemma. The two debating voices in the monologue suggest a raging battle which illustrates the impact of vacillation on the subject. By foregrounding this episode, Achebe forecasts Ezeulu's dilemma.

Another testimony of Ezeulu's religious equivocation is found in his words which exhibit reverence for Eru, the god of wealth, and contempt for Idemili, a higher god and owner of the venerated sacred python. The Chief Priest eulogizes the god of wealth, as "Eru, the Magnificent", benevolent and a just god "the One that gives wealth to those who find favour with him" (Achebe 1964: 9). Through authorial interpolation, the text reveals that Ezeulu was "carried away by his praise of the god of wealth" and his passionate adoration makes him seem like the "proud priest of Eru rather than Ulu who stood above Eru and all the other deities" (Achebe 1964: 9). Adetugbo (2001: 10) explains that pre-colonial African societies "had a pantheon of deities above which most often a supremo presided". Ulu reigns supreme in *Arrow*'s Umuaro. Thus, the homage could be considered as another act of defiance to Ulu, who will not allow any other god "come to power" (Achebe 1964: 192) in Umuaro. As such the full implication of the character's effusive adoration of Eru is that Ulu's foremost votary momentarily shifts his loyalty to a lesser god. His religious behaviour displays vacillation between Ulu – the most prominent and Eru – the wealthiest. As such, Ezeulu belongs exclusively to neither Ulu nor Eru but to both gods. The wealth trope inserted into his praise of Eru unmasks a longing for Eru's favour which, in turn, exposes Ezeulu's fear of emasculation by poverty.

The Chief Priest symbolises African 'big men' who court several gods in their struggle for survival and pursuit of power. Atiku Abubakar, a prominent Nigerian politician and former vice president, exemplifies such 'big men'. According to El-Rufai (2013: 145), Abubakar "placed his faith in the prediction" of a Cameroonian marabout, even as Muslim. El-Rufai (2013: 146) submits that "one must never underestimate the influence of both Islamic and Christian spiritualists on African politicians".

Considering his veneration of Eru, it appears that Ezeulu holds the gods of Umuaro in high esteem. However, his later thoughts, utterances and behaviour suggest otherwise. They disparage Idemili and interrogate Ezeulu's faith in Umuaro deities. Ezeulu's disloyalty to the god is displayed in his reaction to his son, Oduche's unprovoked assault on Idemili's royal python which he imprisoned in his school box. In the Chief Priest's thinking, Oduche is "an arrow" and Chris-

tianity "an ally" recruited by Ulu to check Idemili's excesses and keep the treach-
erous and jealous god in his secondary position, after Ulu (Achebe 1964: 192). The
chief priest of Ulu as such patronizes not only his god but also Christianity in an
attempt to emasculate Idemmili in order to retain his position as the priest of the
most powerful god in his changing society. His behaviour is reminiscent of Bo-
lanle's mother who "used God at her own convenience" in Shoneyin's *The Secret
Lives of Baba Segi's Wives* (Achebe 1964: 147). Moreover, Ezeulu "hurl(s) defiance" at the priest of Idemili (Achebe 1964: 59) and by extension, Idemili, as he
tells the priest, through his messenger, to "go and fill his mouth with shit" (Achebe
1964: 54). He disregards the narrator's warning that "a man might have Ngwu and
still be killed by Ojukwu" (Achebe 1964: 39). Ezeulu's unconcealed discourtesy
towards Idemili's adherents, even in the face of their seeming impudence, implies
irreverence and contempt towards a major Umuaro god as well the culture that
establishes such god.

The origin of Ezeulu's attitude towards Idemili is identified in the narrator's
account that he understands the "religious implication" of his son's sacrilege but
"did not want anybody to think that he was troubled or make him appear like an
object of pity" (Achebe 1964: 60). This implies that his religious behaviour is
goaded by a desire to evade humiliation by appearing invulnerable. Ezeulu's refusal to belong exclusively to any god/God impacts negatively on Umuaro. By the
virtue of his office, Ezeulu is saddled with the responsibility of energising Umuaro
gods and culture but by his attitude, he enervates both. His tacit support and justification of Oduche's irreverence deepens the polarization in Umuaro. It widens the
social gap between him and Ezeidemili as well as his village and Ezeidemili's and
so dislodges the society from within. This is why Pearse (2008: 114) says that
Oduche's unwarranted attack on an Idemili snake is "an alarming threat to communal survival". The Chief Priest's vacillation also sets the wrong precedence for
Umaro to disrespect her gods and by extension enervate IIR. Achebe, through this
episode, holds religious leaders in Africa responsible for destroying the very institutions that accord them relevance. Therefore, the character of Ezeulu has "a lot of
lessons (for) leaders" in Nigeria and the entire world (Akinkurolere &
Ariyo 2015: 144).

The ambivalence reflected in Ezeulu's choices finds its most lucid portrayal in
his tenacious hold on Ulu and indirect alliance with Christianity. Ezeulu's decision
to belong to Ulu exclusively is manifested in his audacious rejection of the warrant
chief proposal tendered by the British colonial administration represented by Win-
terbottom in *Arrow* on account of his position as Ulu's votary. He declares thus:
"Ezeulu will not be anybody's chief except Ulu" (Achebe 1964: 175). His unwa-
vering loyalty to Ulu is emphasized by the account that all overt and covert lobby-
ing and coercion employed to get Ezeulu to "change his mind ... had failed" to the
chagrin of the colonial administration (Achebe 1964: 177). By introducing his deity into the conversation, Ezeulu shifts the argument from political to spiritual fix-
ing it within the ambit of religious plurality. Ezeulu's use of language tends to
apotheosize neither Ulu nor any other god, but himself. The Chief Priest's stance

seems heavily influenced by his fear of being demoted to the chief of a lesser god since Ulu is the most prominent god in Umuaro. In addition, by his action, the character turns on its head his logic that "those who do not befriend the white man today will be saying *had we known* tomorrow" (Achebe 1964: 45-46). According to Eruvbetine (2014: 13) it is "paradoxical" that when the British offers him the power he desires he rejects it in Ulu's name. This episode again conveys his religious ambivalence.

Ironically, the same Ezeulu who rebuffed the white man's offer for the sake of Ulu consorts, by proxy, with the new Christianity by sending Oduche, his son, to go and "learn the new ritual" and to "see and hear" (Achebe 1964: 42, 220) for him. Mgbemere's (2014: 19) notes that the Chief Priest is the "chief ambassador" of IIR and Christianity is totally "at variance" with IIR (Achebe 1964: 19). Thus, as the Chief Priest of Ulu and against strong domestic and communal disapproval, he sent a representative to an emerging Western institution he refuses to stand for in Umuaro. This makes it difficult to identify which god/God he belongs to. His position represents a reversal of Okonkwo's choice in *TFA*. Okonkwo disowns his son, Nwoye, for joining Christianity and is, therefore, hardly burdened by Ezeulu's dilemma.

Ezeulu's vacillation is engendered by Western-engendered "euphoria of ambivalence" (Mgbemere 2014: 19). The chief priest observes, from tales and prophecies, that Westernization arrives with "great power and conquest" to dominate and control and it "would be wise" to have a family member among those rulers (Achebe 1964: 42). Ezeulu's mission statement to Oduche reveals his motive, thus:

> "The world is changing … I want one of my sons to join these people and be my eye there. If there is nothing in it you will come back. But if there is something there you will bring home my share. The world is like a mask dancing. If you want to see it well you do not stand in one place (Achebe 1964: 45-46).

The mask trope is a major member of Achebe's rural novels. The dancing mask symbolises shifting existential circumstances and illustrates Ezulu's conscious refusal to belong completely to one god/God. Ezeulu's hidden fear of emasculation and move towards "making himself lord" over Umuaro (Achebe 1964: 28) tend to govern his religious conduct. They are unmasked by Achebe using Nwaka who observes that the Chief Priest is "a man of ambition" who desires to be both the political and spiritual head of Umuaro (Achebe 1964: 27). Nwaka's opinion seems flawed when placed before Ezeulu's rejection of the warrant chief offer which would have placed him above others (Achebe 1964: 177). However, his intension for sending Oduche to school proves Nwaka right. Both incidents indicate Ezeulu's faith in both Ulu and Christian God and his doubt in the capacity of each to meet the challenges of his early 20th century Igbo society. They are extreme measures which exhibit his fear of dethronement and an attempt at perpetuating his supremacy. In the Chief priest is found several African religious and political leaders who position their children to take over the mantle of leadership after them.

The consequences of Ezeulu's inability to belong to one god are overwhelming and cut across his person, family and Umuaro society. It facilitates confusion, costs him his integrity, claims his son and sanity, and engenders Ulu's demise. The effect on Umuaro is articulated through dialogue using Ogbuefi Ofoka, a respected elder statesman and Obierika, Ezeulu's closest friend. First, Ofoka tells Ezeulu that Umuaro, represented by the elders, "are confused (and) are like the puppy in the proverb which attempted to answer two calls at once and broke its jaw" (Achebe 1964: 188). The proverbial puppy's condition illustrates Ezeulu's in-between position and its consequences. Second, Obierika tells the Chief Priest that Umuaro will interpret Oduche's school business as Ezeulu's contribution to "desecrating the land" and an act of betrayal (Achebe 1964: 131). Moreover, the colonial government misunderstands him and considers the Chief Priest mad for his refusal to accept a plum job for the sake of Ulu. Thus, Ezeulu's reluctance to belong to one god/God causes confusion in his society and questions his intergrity and sanity. Ofoka's figurative discourse, works with scenes like Ezulu's rendition of Ulu's institution (Achebe 1964: 70-71) and Obika's *ayaka* chant (Achebe 1964: 226) to create sound and spectacle which vivifies the message of text. All these contribute to making *Arrow* a classic African novel in English.

Furthermore, the priest loses some of his authority in his family. His son and wife, Edogo and Matefi, pelt him with blame for Oduche's misdeeds and Umuaro's economic recession caused by his refusal to convene the New Yam Festival. Again, Obika's death is remotely caused by the New Yam crisis. His tragic outing in Ogbazuluobodo, in spite his infirmity is an "attempt to redeem the effect of his father's action" (Anyadike 2008: 286). Moreover, Ulu's demise is facilitated by Ezeulu's attempt "to test and demonstrate … the power" he wields by strictly adhering to pre-New Yam festival rituals against the counsel of elders (Eruvbetine 2014: 14). His rigidity, invalidates his dancing mask thesis, distorts the spirit of the festival, 'kills' Ulu and dislodges the basis of his socio-economic authority and relevance.

Perhaps, the most tragic consequence of Ezeulu's dilemma is the loss of his sanity preceded by his feeling of humiliation at the desertion of Ulu and death of Obika. The insanity tale is casually inserted as part of the concluding statements of the novel thus: Ezeulu lived his last days "in the haughty splendor of a demented high priest" (Achebe 1964: 229). This demonstrates Freud's delusions of grandeur. The revered chief priest as such ends up like his demented mother, just like the phenomenal Okonkwo ends up in the evil forest like his indolent father. Ulu's eventual castration and Ezeulu' madness are foreshadowed in the priest's dream at Okperi prison and disturbing laughter which leaves his friend Akuebue frightened and uncomfortable like one who meets a laughing mad man on a "solitary path" (Achebe 1964: 131). This technique functions to create suspense and, at the same time, cushions the effect of an on-coming tragic incident. Consequently, Ezeulu's extreme measures to preserve his relevance in an unstable culture prove injurious to his mental well-being. His tragedy appears self-made, arising from his refusal to belong to one god/God. At last, the protagonist of *Arrow* becomes Achebe's archetypal allegory of insecure and over-ambitious religious leaders in Africa and the West Indies.

Unburnable, set in the West Indies Dominica, display elements of religious ambivalence engendered by anxiety over possible emasculation in a changing world. Vacillation is observed in Matilda's relationship with IIR and Christianity. It is mostly exhibited in three incidents and two are connected to her only child, Iris. The three are her meeting with Sister Mary-Alice, choice of a Catholic school for Iris and concept of death. While the first and third events display loyalty to IIR and rejection of Christianity, the second demonstrates alliance with Christianity in a way that suggests infidelity to IIR.

Matilda's brief encounter with the white American Catholic religious, Sister Mary-Alice, over Iris' welfare exhibits total loyalty to IIR and contempt for Christianity. The text recounts that Matilda, unlike the typical black rural Dominican woman, attends the meeting with dirty fingers, sweaty body and uncovered hair (John 2006: 220). The narrator adds that:

> The unsmiling woman had come in everyday farming cloths to meet her - knowing that *a sister of God* was waiting to see her, had not extended her the respect of dressing appropriately ... Matilda had looked at her with indifference, without deference, with no regard for *her nun's habit* ... treated her worse than one would have treated a donkey (John 2006: 220-1) (Emphasis mine)

The 'God factor' fixes the entire incident within the context of religion. Matilda's stern face and contemptuous attitude represent her refusal to negotiate with the nun, who is the face of Christianity in the episode. It is a symbol of her devotion to IIR. Matilda's refusal to maintain the asymmetrical relationship between the slave-master/colonizer and slave/colonized reveals her rejection of the orient label as it refuses to endorse Mary-Alice's occidental position. It seems regulated by fear of emasculation and desire to dominate. By recounting what Matilda fails to do, the novel equally gives a concise picture of the power Christianity and colour wield over the ordinary Black in West Indies post-slavery and colonial society. The combination of race and religion demonstrates Crenshaw's (1989) concept of Intersectionality. John's depiction revises the White/Christian and Black/IIR relationship pattern in the colonial Dominica by placing both sides on the same pedestal. The episode displays John's post-colonial creative attitude and "refusal to accept the self-hatred" as an aspect of Westernization (David 2006: 1).

The novel traces Matilda's behaviour to her experience as "a Black person who had never lived in that subjugated place under the double authority of the colonizer and the colonizer's religion" (John 2006: 276). This implies that Matilda's Noir village is hardly influenced by the Christianity which dominates its Dominican larger society. It also explains her devotion to IIR. Matilda's rejection of Christianity and its informing culture is intensified in her non-English complex, yet rich and totally comprehensible, Creole (John 2006: 222). Moreover, her "you will never understand" (John 2006: 223) response to the nun's tearful pleas over Iris' welfare sets her cultural acuity against Mary-Alice's ignorance. Matilda's utterance reveals a desire to demote the white religious, sense of superiority and demonstration of power. It tends to express Matilda's belief that Christianity lacks the ability to understand her reality and so cannot fulfill her spiritual needs. Therefore, it becomes her justification for rejecting Christianity in Mary-Alice.

In addition, Matilda's disloyalty to Christianity is demonstrated by her use of her exposed black breasts to deal several "hard slaps" on Mary Alice's face (John 2006: 222). The action symbolises the trashing of Christianity by IIR. Matilda's breasts are in this episode symbolic in more than one way. They function as an instrument of repudiation, serve as a different expression of fertility and sexuality and a mockery of the modesty and celibacy ingrained in Mary-Alice's vocation. John intensifies the ridicule by the narrator's account that Mary Alice was only a nun in theory (John 2006: 221). The enervating impact of Matilda's religious behaviour on interpersonal relationships is reflected in the narrator's explanation that it "threatened her (Mary-Alice), had deeply stirred her to fear. She wanted to step away but could not" (John 2006: 222). The nun's fear and shock demonstrate the ability of ambiguity to unsettle one, create enmity and facilitate division.

Moreover, Matilda's unalloyed fidelity and seeming trust in IIR is conveyed through her final thoughts as she awaits death by hanging, after being wrongly condemned for murder by Western powers. According to the narrator, she does not fear death which the Noir citizens live to expect as they believe that it is "the beginning of their everlasting lives as ancestors". Matilda also hopes that her entrance into the revered ancestor class would enable her to acquire "the kind of power" people believe she has (John 2006: 272-273). The character's last thoughts exhibit her total assimilation of the IIR concept of life after death and her refusal to interpret reality through other means except her religion and its supporting culture. It also illustrates Matilda's thirst for more power borne out of fear of demotion. Margaret's assertion that Matilda is "more powerful dead than when she was alive" (John 2006: 173) validates IIR idea of after-life. The idea is extended in Matilda's appearance to Lillian, her granddaughter, in an Obeah man's mirror. Thus, the character is phenomenal in life and in death. However, despite her seeming loyalty to IIR, her religious attitude manifests equivocation.

One significant instance of Matilda's religious ambivalence is her decision to send her daughter Iris to a Catholic school. This choice interrogates her loyalty to IIR. In spite of all her contempt for colonialism and attendant Christianity, Matilda allows herself to be persuaded to send Iris to "have a Catholic education" in a convent in Roseau (John 2006: 56). This is because Iris is very special and due to the post-World-War II socio-political developments in Dominica (John 2006: 54). Doig (2006: 1) explains that "after World War II, old customs were disappearing and modernism was on the rise" and this is portrayed in the middle the novel. Thus, though Matilda lacks interest in the world outside Noir (John 2006: 32), she needs to register Iris into that bigger world where the admission requirement is Western education. Therefore, she is compelled to give out her only future to be nurtured by the same system she had debased and trashed. By her action, she belongs to neither IIR gods nor Christian God. This injects ambiguity into her character.

Matilda's equivocation is a tactical approach to social dynamics like Ezeulu's. It is motivated by her fear of emasculation in a society that is increasingly accepting modernism. However, unlike Ezeulu, Matilda's society is also burdened by slave experience, apart from colonialism. In addition, Matilda's dilemma appears more complex than Ezeulu's. Both, even as leaders in an IIR dominated societies, submit their children to Western civilization but While Matilda offers her only child, Ezeulu gives out one of his sons. This shows correspondence and discrepancy of experiences between Nigerian and Dominican Igbo societies. Based on her antecedents, Matilda's decision to send Iris to a Catholic convent school, even when that decision is orchestrated by forces beyond her control, heightens the surprise component of the novel. Perhaps the equivocation contributes to her reputation as a mysterious woman in Roseau. Matilda's reputation and death by hanging suggest that the ambiguous religious consciousness is injurious to contemporary Black society. Moreover, Iris' tragic end illustrates the consequences of Matilda's ambiguity on her family.

5. Conclusion and Recommendations

The study discovers that *Arrow* and *Unburnble* represent Ezeulu and Matilda as the most prominent IIR leaders in the Igbo societies of Nigeria and Dominica respectively. Thus, their religious conduct, observed through their relationship with IIR and Christianity, could be described as ambivalent because their thoughts, words and actions display equivocation. Moreover, the research reveals that the characters' vacillation creates doubt, fear, suspicion, and confusion which impact negatively on social relationships and human development. In addition, the study discovers that the religious behaviour derives from Ezeulu and Matilda's respective fear of emasculation and quest to gain strategic advantage over others in their changing societies. Lastly, it finds that the characters' individual religious expressions and experiences reveal cultural and historical correspondences and disparities between Igbo society of Nigeria and the remnants of the same society in Dominica. Based on the findings, one cannot but agree with Soyinka's argument that "the cloak of religion is a tattered alibi, the real issue – as always – being Power and Submission..." (Soyinka 2013: 60). Indeed, Ezeulu and Matilda's individual manipulation of IIR and Christianity is motivated by fear of emasculation and speaks thus: "I belong to no god/God and I belong to all gods/God."

There are other manifestations of religious behaviour in the texts which could form the subject of further research. The attitudes can also be studied in non-literary fields in order to determine how cultural interface engender or hamper healthy human relationships.

References

Abussamen, A. E. (2018). Chinua Achebe and the postcolonial ambivalence: Gratitude and revenge in *Things Fall Apart, No Longer at Ease* and *Arrow of God. American Journal of Creative Education* 1(1): 1-12. Retrieved April 2, 2018 from http://www.onlinesciencepublishing.com.

Achebe, C. (1964). *Arrow of god*. London: Heinemann.

Adetugbo, A. (2001). *African continuities in the diaspora*. Lagos: CBAAC.

Akanbi, Olarongbe A., Noor Hashima A. A., & Rohizaz H. (2018). The God and people's power in Chinua Achebe's *Arrow of God*. *Journal of Humanities and Social Sciences (IOSR- JHSS)* 23 (2): 11, 68-77. Retrieved June 6, 2018 from http://www.iosrjournals .org.

Akinkurolere, Olajoke S. & Ariyo K. S. (2015). Speech act: Features of select extracts in Chinua Achebe's *Arrow of God*: Leadership perspective. *British Journal of Education, Society and Behavioural Science* 9 (2): 139-145. Retrieved April 11, 2018 from http://www.science-domain.org.

Ali, T. (2010). (Re-)Visiting Dominica's pasts; (Ad-)Venturing into her future: Interrogating identity formation in Marie-Elena John's *Unburnable*. In Anyadike, N. C. (2008). *The cracks in the wall and the colonial incursion: Things fall*.

Bailey, C. (2013). Destabilizing Caribbean critical orthodoxies, interrogating orality. in Marie-Elena John's *Unburnable*. *Caribbean Quarterly* 59 (1): 31-49. Retrieved May 3, 2015 from http://www.questia.com.

Barry, P. (1995). *Beginning theory: An introduction to literary and cultural theory*. New York: Manchester University Press.

Bryce, J. (2006). Unforgettable fire. (Review of the book *Unburnable* by Marie-Elena John). *Caribbean review of books*. Retrieved Sept 28, 2012 from http://marie elenajohn.com.

Carroll, D. (1980). *Chinua Achebe*. London: Macmillan.

Chukwuma, I. (2016). An augury of the world's ruin and the making of the tragic hero in Chinua Achebe's *Arrow of God*. *Literator* 37 (1): 1- 10. Retrieved April 10, 2018 from http://litera-tor.zaorg.

Chuma-Ude, N. (2014). Ezeulu in the binary systems of Chinua Achebe's *Arrow of God*. *An African Journal of New Writing* 52: 216-233. Retrieved April 10, 2018 from www.unn.edu.ng.

Clark, R. (2010). What's the idea? Where the personal is political. Retrieved Oct. 3, 2012 from www. rootsandrightswordpress.com.

Crenshaw, K. (1989). Demarginalizing the Intersection of race and sex: A Black feminist critique of antidiscrimination doctrine, feminist theory and antiracist politics. *University of Chicago Legal Forum*, 139-167.

David, P. E. (2006). A new Caribbean classic. (Review of the book *Unburnable* by Marie-Elena John). *Amazon reader reviews*. Retrieved Oct. 3, 2012 from www.amazon.com.

Denison, S. (2009). Walking through the shadows: ruins, reflections, and resistance in the post-colonial gothic novel. Retrieved Feb. 4, 2012 from http://dspace.iup.edu.

Doig, D. M. (2006). *Unburnable*. (Review of the book *Unburnable* by Marie-Elena John) *Black issues book*. Retrieved Sept. 28, 2012 from www.findarticles.com.

Eagleton, T. (2006). *Literary theory: An introduction*. 2nd ed. USA: Blackwell.

El-Rufai, Nasir A. (2013). *The accidental public servant*. Ibadan: Safari Books.

Eruvbetine, E. A. (2014, April). Fractured societies and issues of good governance in Achebe's *Arrow of God*. Paper presented at *Chinua Achebe's* Arrow of God *at 50: International Collo-quium on Literature, Leadership and National Unity*. University of Lagos.

Harrison, S. (2017). Twenty-first-century west Indian fiction. *Oxford Research Encyclopedia of Literature*. Retrieved April 13, 2018 from www.literature.oxfordre.com.

Hillhouse, J. Author Unleashes Myriad Realities. (Review of the book *Unburnable* by Marie-Elena John). *The Daily Observer*, March 24, 2006. Retrieved from www.myspace.com/jho-hadli.

Irele, A. (2000). The crisis of cultural memory in Chinua Achebe's *Things Fall Apart*. *African Studies Quarterly* 4 (3): 1-40. Retrieved Nov. 24, 2011 from asq.africa.ufl.edu.

John, M. (2006). *Unburnable*. U.S.A.: Haper Collins.

Mgbemere, C. D. (2014). Cues in Igbo cultural matrix: Analysis of Achebe's *Arrow of God*. *Jour-nal of Culture, Society and Development* - An Open Access International Journal 4: 19-26. Retrieved Jan. 8, 2016 from http://www.iiste.org.

Mudimbe, V.Y. (2007). African literature: myth or reality. In T. Olaniyan and A. Quayson (Eds.) *African literature: An anthology of criticism and theory.* USA: Blackwell, 60-64.

Ngugi, W. (2007). Writers in politics: The power of words and the words of power. In T. Olaniyan & A. Quayson (Eds.) *African literature: An anthology of criticism and theory.* USA: Blackwell, 476-483.

Ojinmah, U. (1991). *Chinua Achebe: New perspectives.* Ibadan: Spectrum.

Ogwude, S. (2011). History and ideology in Chimamanda Adichie's fiction. *Tydskrif vir Letterkunde* 48 (1): 110-123. Retrieved April 15, 2013 from http://www.scielo.org.

Pearse, A. (2008). Challenges of leadership in Chinua Achebe's rural novels. (Special edition). *LARES: A Journal of Language and Literary Studies* 16 (3): 103-122.

Ruano, H. L. (2010). In search of new believers: How the Guatemalan religious panorama has changed in recent decades. *Brigham Young University Law Review* 895-920.

Shoneyin, L. (2010). *The secret lives of Baba Segi's wives.* Abuja: Cassava Republic.

Soyinka, W. (2007). A voice that will not be silenced. In T. Olaniyan & A. Quayson (Eds.) *African literature: An anthology of criticism and theory.* USA: Blackwell, 141-143.

Soyinka, W. (2013). Remembering Kofi Awoonor: Humanity and against. *The News* 41 (14): 60.

Tyson, L. (1994). *Critical theory today: A user-friendly guide.* New-York: Routledge.

Whose Boko Haram? A Critical Discourse Analysis of Print Media - News on Terrorism in Nigeria

Olarotimi Daniel Ogungbemi

Adekunle Ajasin University

Abstract

This study employs critical discourse analysis to analyse the representation of social actors in print media coverage of the Boko Haram insurgency between 2009 and 2014. Data for the study were texts of systematically chosen news stories from five private Nigerian newspapers: *The Nation, The Guardian, Daily Trust, Vanguard* and *Leadership*. Critical Discourse Analysis (CDA) (with bias for Wodak's (1999) framework and Halliday's (2004) ideational meta-function), containing predicational and referential strategies, and transitivity choices, mainly guided the analysis. Lexicalization, presupposition, and material and relational choices were used in representing social actors and constructing identity for them. The findings demonstrate considerable similarities in representation patterns among the five newspapers. However, the newspapers were divided in portraying politicians and the northern elders as playing politics with the Boko Haram insurgency. *Daily Trust* and *Leadership* were very critical of the Federal Government of Nigeria, arguing that the government has politicised the crisis. *Vanguard* indicted some northern elders, claiming that they were using the insurgency for political gains. Further, the study discovered that the stereotype that 'Boko Haram members are Muslims' prevailed in all the news reports that were analysed. In addition, the selected newspapers were consistent in recognizing both Muslims and Christians in the country as victims of Boko Haram insurgency. Two types of ideologies – radical Islamism and us/them dichotomy– manifested in the discourses on Boko Haram. Radical Islamism, represented through naming choices, evaluative adjectives, transitivity and presupposition created a polarisation at two levels: between moderate Islam and extremist Islam, and between Muslims and adherents of other faiths, such as Christianity. The differentiation strategy provided *Vanguard, The Guardian* and *The Nation* with great flexibility to denigrate the enemy, the Boko Haram members, and to praise moderate Muslims. A strong link exists between linguistic representations and ideologies in the newspaper reports on the Boko Haram insurgency, which project security issues and social concerns in the Nigerian print media.

Keywords: Boko Haram terrorism, critical discourse analysis, politics, Nigerian print media, religion

1. Introduction

1.1. Terrorism and Boko Haram

Terrorism came into existence during the French Revolution, the 'Reign of Terror' (Bizovi 2014). Despite the numerous studies (Gibbs 2012, Jackson 2007, Rapoport 2001) on the topic of terrorism covering the motivations, actors, and methods, there is yet to be a consensus in various communities as to what constitutes a terrorist organization. The age long adage, 'one man's terrorist is another man's freedom fighter' underlines the main discourse concerning who is classified as a terrorist. Terrorist motivations can be classified into categories, including religious, ethnic, state-sponsored, and politically motivated terrorist acts (Spindove and Simonsen 2013). The claim of Spindove and Simonsen (2013) does not agree with the observation of Hoffman (2006) that all forms of terrorism can be subsumed under the political category. Terrorism has also been interpreted as a social construct. Elaborating the above, Turk (2004: 271) maintains that terrorism as a social construct "is an interpretation of events and their presumed causes". In other words, terrorism is fuelled by certain ideological and political motivations, and the need to challenge and change the status quo. Until recently, terrorism seemed to have been restricted to a few isolated places in the world (Jenkins 1975). In the last several years, however, it has become a common experience in many places like Ireland, France, United States of America, including Nigeria.

Boko Haram became famous in 2009 for its incessant violent attacks in northern Nigeria. The group was effectively managed under the leadership of Mallam Mohammed Yusuf, a fiery Islamic scholar in Maiduguri. Boko Haram did not adopt open violence before 2009. After an open confrontation with the Nigerian government, it was violently suppressed in July 2009. After this time, nothing was heard of the group until 2010 when it resurfaced and appeared better prepared for guerrilla warfare.

According to Sani (2011: 26), Boko Haram sees "western influence on Islamic society as the basis of the religion's weakness". The group is in opposition to secular government, and Western education; it believes Western education is especially not predicated on sound ethical teachings. This is why the group is generally branded as Boko Haram (literally, "Western education is forbidden"). The expression *Boko Haram* is derived from a blend of the Hausa word *boko*, meaning *book*, and the Arabic word *haram*, meaning *forbidden*. The group's ideology is entrenched in Salafi Jihadism which is interested in purging Islam of external influences (European Commission's Expert Group on Violent Radicalisation 2008).

The Boko Haram insurgency is one crisis that has dominated print media all over the world for years now. Through the media, especially print media, volumes of information on the crisis is disseminated in Nigeria and all over the world on daily basis. A huge and significant concentration of news reports on the Boko Haram insurgency was observed between 2009 and 2014. The year 2009 marked the beginning of the violent clashes between the Boko Haram group and security forces. It was in 2009 that the group's leader, Muhammad Yusuf, and many members were reported in the media to have been unlawfully killed by the security forces. Those six years saw the newspapers give a blow by blow accounts of the Boko Haram insurgency which include, among other things, military operations in the affected areas, positions of different interest groups and organisations, the positions of the government both at the federal and state levels, the positions of the Christian organisation in Nigeria, the Islamic organisation(s), the international communities, such as the Amnesty International, etc. Though the Boko Haram insurgency is commonly reported in Nigerian newspapers, there are conflicting and divergent interests and ideological leanings projected by the different newspapers and the different actors in the crisis. These ideological leanings become manifest in their use of language in the news reports on the Boko Haram insurgency.

The motivation for this study derives from the observation of Curran and Seaton (1997) cited in Behnam and Zenouz (2008: 199) that the media are "the machinery of representation" in modern societies. The mass media as a very powerful institution can construct meanings about an event, a problem, culture, etc. according to dominant ideas and interpretations through choices that are made at various levels in the process of producing texts. The media can influence how we think about a subject, whether as a benevolent or a malevolent construction. The media are instrumental in the processes of gaining public consent and media texts never simply mirror or reflect 'reality', but instead, construct hegemonic definitions of what should be accepted as 'reality' (Carter and Steider 2004). In reporting on the activities of Boko Haram in the Nigerian newspapers, the media create constructions of the world through language. This paper seeks to particularly explain the textual and linguistic features that are accountable for depicting a specific representation of the actors in discourses on Boko Haram in the Nigerian print media.

2. Previous Studies and Problem Statement

Existing studies on terrorism and associated topics have turned its attention to media reporting of the issues and events involved in terrorism, principally whether their reports represent correct and impartial reporting (Azeez 2009, Abdullah 2014). These studies, especially Abdullah's (2014) opines that the Arabic news channels, Al-Jazeera, and Al-Arabiya, which were analysed were biased in their reportage on terrorism. In recent times, various studies have examined the responses to terrorism offered by media outlets such as TV, twitter, newspapers, and film (Banuri 2005, Martin 2006). They both agree that, while the news media perform its function of informing people, reporting extensively on terrorist attacks gives terrorists visibility all over the world.

Previous studies such as Chiluwa and Adegoke (2013), Odebunmi (2016) and Agbedo et al. (2013) on the Boko Haram crisis have carried out sociolinguistic and pragmatic analyses. Some have looked at terrorism discourse from historical anthropology (Ajayi 2012, Loimeier 2012). However, most of these studies do not deal with the relationship between linguistic representations, and religious and political cleavages in the representation of the conflict. However, comparatively, few researchers have paid attention to how political and religious cleavages are constructed through linguistic devices in discourses on Boko Haram (Osisanwo 2016, Roelofs 2014). While it is not their primary focus, the two scholars, Roelofs (2014) and Osisanwo (2016), reveal how discourses on Boko Haram in the Nigerian media establish a connection between Boko Haram insurgency and Islam by referring to Boko Haram members as fundamental Muslims. Therefore, the present study examines how, through linguistic devices, certain topics and themes are high-lighted and prioritized, while others are excluded and obscured with a view to es-tablishing the ideologies underlying the discourses on Boko Haram in the Nigerian print media, and revealing the kinds of power constructions behind the discourses. The findings of the study will allow us to see clearly and appreciate the ideological representations that are couched in the news reports.

3. Methodology

The data for the study were newspaper reports on the Boko Haram insurgency published between 2009 and 2014. The data were sourced from five private Nige-rian newspapers (*The Nation, The Guardian, Daily Trust, Vanguard* and *Leader-ship*). *The Nation* is owned by a politician, *Vanguard* by a business man, and *The Guardian* was established as a business entity (Nwammuo, Edegoh and Iwok 2015). *Daily Trust* and *Leadership* are owned by some northern businessmen in Nigeria. These five newspapers are published daily in English. These newspapers were selected because they are national newspapers and are among the largest me-dia outlets in terms of circulation. They also have the largest coverage on the Boko Haram insurgency and enjoy a measure of prestige among a cross section of Nige-rian readership. The period between 2009 and 2014 was the period that Boko Ha-ram became a serious national issue. Thus, 2009 to 2014 was chosen because the Boko Haram insurgency was a constant item in the coverage of news outlets in the country at this period.

My sources of data collection included the newspaper archive of NISER's li-brary, Federal College of Education Kontagora's main Library, and the internet sites of some of the newspapers. The data consisted of news reports, opinion col-umns, and feature articles that were purposively sampled between 2009 and 2014. The news reports included both institutional and individual perspectives on the Boko Haram insurgency. Necessary headlines and relevant stories were written out and details such as the name of the paper and date of the publication were marked out. The newspapers were scanned manually and relevant language features were classified and discussed.

4. Conceptual framework

The provision of information by the media is crucial to determining and influenc-ing public understanding of, and responses to, any mounting crisis. This study is interested in how language is used to highlight and prioritize certain topics, while others are obscured in discourses on Boko Haram. To accomplish this, Halliday's (2004) lexico-grammar and Wodak's (1999) CDA are deployed in the analysis. Critical Discourse Analysis is interested in analysing obscure, as well as translu-cent structural relationships of dominance, discrimination, power and control, manifested in language (Wodak 1995). Wodak's (1999) approach considers criti-cal discourse analysis as a homogenous school, consisting of various theoretical and methodological approaches. She believes that CDA should be thought of as "a theoretical synthesis of conceptual tools" (Wodak 2002: 15). For Wodak (2002), discourses are socially constitutive because they add to the creation of some social conditions, reproducing, justifying, and maintaining a certain condition. Further, discourses change or transform the status quo, dismantling or destroying the status quo in some cases. The Discourse Historical Approach advocates the contrasting of linguistic manifestations of inequality and prejudice with historical facts. Discourses, according to Wodak (1999:190), must also "integrate systematically all available background information in the analysis and foregrounds the historical contexts of discourse in the process of explanation and interpretation". Wodak's (1999) approach attempts to incorporate available knowledge about historical sources and the social and political contexts in which discursive events are entrenched.

The Discourse Historical Approach follows the principle of triangulation involving interdisciplinary, multi-methodological work on the basis of a variety of empirical data which include background information. This approach involves linguistic analysis, as well as systematic historical, political, sociological and/or psychological analyses. This approach is based on four contextual levels: (i) the immediate linguistic co-text; (ii) the intertextual and interdiscursive relations between texts, genres and discourses; (iii) the context of situation involving social variables and institutional frames; and (iv) the broader socio-political and historical contexts, e.g. the history of the event (Reisigl and Wodak 2001, Wodak and Meyer 2001).

For Wodak (1995, 2006), power and ideologies are integral part of discourse and background knowledge plays a role in the interpretation of a discourse. Derogation and euphemisation are two key tools for discussing ideological struggle between in-groups and out-groups under this framework. Wodak and Koller (2008: 302) identify five discursive strategies that are involved in "positive self-presentation" and "negative other-presentation". They are: reference/nomination, predication, argumentation, framing/discourse representation, and intensification and/or mitigation.

In providing a framework for identity construction, Wodak (2010), cited in Aboh (2013: 86), examines:

- the persons named and referred to linguistically;
- the traits, characteristics, qualities and features that are attributed to the negative other;
- the arguments and argumentations scheme which specific persons or social groups try to justify and legitimize the exclusion of others or inclusion of some;
- the perspectives or point of view that such labelling, attributions and arguments are expressed and
- whether the respective utterances are articulated overall, or they even intensified or mitigated.

Wodak's (1999) discourse historical model, which illuminates how language in context-specific ways aids identity construction, is appropriate for a critical discourse analysis of print media news on Boko Haram terrorism in Nigeria. Her identity framework investigates the phenomenon of the in-group and the out-group and subscribes to the view that identities are constituted through a process of difference.

Reisigl and Wodak's (2001) ideas of predicational and referential strategies which manifest in evaluative attributions of positive or negative traits are applied to identify power contexts and the dichotomy between the in-group and out-groups. These are realized through the following identity specific forms: lexicalization, forms of reference, predicative nouns and adjectives, and rhetorical figures. Analysing lexicalization involves studying the denotations and connotations of lexical items. Further, her concept of presupposition is appealed to in the present study. Wodak (2007: 214) claims that "presupposed content is, under ordinary circumstances, and unless there is a cautious interpretive attitude on the part of the hearer, accepted without (much) critical attention (whereas the asserted content and evident implicatures are normally subject to some level of evaluation)". Thus, an analysis of presuppositions discloses encoders' beliefs and what they want their recipients to take as a given (van Dijk 1998).

There is a meticulous deployment of several transitivity processes in the discourses on Boko Haram in the print media texts under study. Hence, Halliday's (2004) Systemic Functional Grammar, an appropriate theory in revealing concealed projections, becomes very useful for our purposes in the study. The systemic functional grammar emphasises the importance of language as a resource for making meaning; it also claims that meanings reside in systemic patterns of choice (Halliday 1991, 2004, Gotzsche 2009). What matters to systemic linguists when analysing texts is the linguistic choices made by interlocutors within the context of other potential choices available to the user. The present study benefits from this notion of choice since, as Simpson (2004) notes, language functions ideationally to produce preferred meanings. The present study vehemently believes that critical discourse analysis of terrorism news is often about what is foregrounded or backgrounded by the linguistic choices.

Within Halliday's Systemic Functional Grammar, the ideational component of meaning argues that speakers or writers deploy lexico-grammatical features to construct patterns of experience or form their opinion of the world (Litosseliti 2002). This meta-function is realized through transitivity patterns. Transitivity "construes the world of experience into a manageable set of process types" (Halliday 1967, Halliday and Matthiessen 2004: 170, cited in Sahragard and Davatgarzadeh 2010) and codifies the actors of those processes as Actor in Material Processes, Behaver in Behavioural Processes, or Senser in Mental Processes, Sayer in Verbal Processes, or Assigner in Relational Processes. The experiential centre of every clause is constituted by the main verb in the clause structure and the actor participant as it is inherent in the action denoted by the verb. In the present study, we focus attention on material and relational processes.

In the analysis of transitivity structures, attention is paid to how syntactic structures account for the representations of the different actors and their actions. This can have serious implications as it affects readers' understanding of the actors and their actions and responsibility for their actions. Here, the actions undertaken by the different actors are examined, in line with the choice of transitivity structures and affected participants.

5. Data Analysis/Discussion

Textual features that are examined in the study revealed that three textual strategies provided the most appealing results. The tools for textual analysis include: lexicalization and predication, presupposition, and material and relational processes.

5.1. Conflating Religion and Boko Haram

The following examples show instances of labels or naming strategies which conflate religion with Boko Haram in the selected Nigerian newspapers.

No.	domain	Newspaper
1	*Sharia fundamentalists of Boko Haram*	("Boko Haram, Buhari and northern elite", *Vanguard*, December 19, 2014, p.18)
2	*Militant preacher*	("Boko Haram: Former commissioner among sect members killed," *The Nation*, August 1, 2009, p. 5)
3	*Jihadist*	("Islam and Boko Haram: Sultan of Sokoto's voyage of discovery," *Vanguard*, June 3, 2014, p. 19)
4	*Religious bigots and extremists*	("Boko Haram, Muslims and Northerners", *Vanguard*, June 10, 2014, p. 18)
5	Religious fanatics	("Restrict Boko Haram to nest areas," *Vanguard*, May 9, 2014, p. 19)
6	*Extremist Islamic sect*	("Boko Haram Threatens to Attack Lagos, Claims Link to al-Qaeda," *The Guardian*, August 15, 2009, p. 16)
7	*Islamic militants*	("The Kano bomb blast," *The Guardian*, July 16, 2014, p. 14)
8	*Islamic fundamentalists*	("Boko Haram: Cleric seeks ICC probe," *The Nation*, Saturday, August 8, 2009, p. 5)
9	*Islamic fundamentalists*	("Boko Haram Crisis: CAN Blames Northern States, FG," *The Guardian*, August 8, 2009, p. 49)

Table 1:   Constructing Boko Haram Insurgency as Religiously Inspired through Labelling or Naming Strategy

In the data, the most frequently found labels include *Sharia fundamentalists* (domain 1), *militant preacher* (domain 2), *Boko Haram Jihadists* (domain 3), *religious fanatics* (domain 4), *religious bigots and extremists* (domain 5), *extremist Islamic sect* (domain 6), *Islamic militants* (domain 7) and *Islamic Fundamentalists* (domain 8). The excessive use of these labels reveals that the society, which the media represents, sees the Boko Haram crisis as a religiously motivated crisis.

To put these domains in context, I would present some of the texts from which the domains were taken below.

(1)   Domain 4 - there is no doubt that leaders from the North have failed to tame excesses and recklessness of *religious bigots and extremists*, which have led to insecurity in the region. ("Boko Haram, Muslims and Northerners", *Vanguard*, June 10, 2014, p. 18)

(2)   Domain 6 - two weeks after the crackdown on the *extremist Islamic sect*, Boko Haram, the group regained its voice yesterday, threatening to cause more violence with the southern part of the country as its major target. ("Boko Haram Threatens to Attack Lagos, Claims Link to al-Qaeda," *The Guardian*, August 15, 2009, p. 16)

(3)   Domain 9 - we are addressing this press conference with a heavy heart as a result of the mindless killing of Christians and destruction of their churches in Maiduguri, the Borno State capital, by members of the *Islamic fundamentalists* known as Boko Haram. ("Boko Haram: Cleric seeks ICC probe," *The Nation*, Saturday, August 8, 2009, p. 5)

(4)   Domain 3 - it means therefore that either the Sultan wants to admit or not, the Islamic religion organisation he heads in Nigeria cannot be separated from the Boko haram metamorphic display. He needs to accept one truth that *Boko Haram Jihadists*, to those of us who are uninitiated, is a full package of Islam. ("Islam and Boko Haram: Sultan of Sokoto's voyage of discovery," *Vanguard*, June 3, 2014, p. 19)

The noun phrase (*Sharia fundamentalists of Boko Haram*) in domain 1 contains two target words, *Sharia* and *fundamentalists*. Sharia refers to the Islamic law code dealing with the total religious, political, social, domestic, and private life of Muslims. A fundamentalist is strongly convinced that he is right, and others are wrong. The noun phrase *Sharia fundamentalists of Boko Haram* makes it possible to 'package up' (Jeffries, 2010: 19) the information that Boko Haram members are Sharia fundamentalists which the reader is unlikely to question and rather takes for granted. These Sharia fundamentalists of Boko Haram, according to *Vanguard*, hanker after the old certainties, and strive to bring Nigeria and Nigerians back to what they feel are proper moral and doctrinal foundations. They do all in their power to force others to live according to a "correct" moral code and system of doctrinal beliefs. To *Vanguard*, Boko Haram members are determined not only to preserve for themselves a traditional structure of doctrines or way of life but to impose these on others, to change social structures so that they conform to the fundamentalists' beliefs. Little wonder, the news report sees Boko Haram as Sharia fundamentalists who oppose even the president of Nigeria, Goodluck Jonathan, because of his different religious ideology.

The *Nation's* use of the adjective *militant* in domain 2 contributes to an initial construction of negative identity of Yusuf, the founder of Boko Haram and its members. In representing Yusuf as a militant preacher, *The Nation* highlights to its reader that he is determined and willing to use force on whoever does not subscribe to his religious ideology, a theology of rage and hatred to people who hold different beliefs. The use of the noun phrase *militant preacher* to refer to the founder and spiritual leader of the group speaks volume about how the group is perceived by *The Nation*. To support the ideology that the group is religiously inspired, *The Nation* uses the word *preacher* as the head of the noun phrase *militant preacher*. The relative clause in *the militant preacher, whose Boko Haram sect wants a wider adoption of Sharia* reveals that the goal of Boko Haram is to en-trench Sharia in Nigeria. This definitely has a religious ideology because Sharia, as a concept, is inherently Islamic. For *The Nation*, Boko Haram has an Islamic agenda: the Boko Haram movement is a way of advancing and propagating Islam in Nigeria.

In Example 4 (domain 3), there is the use of the noun *jihadists*. The Arabic word *jihad*, according to the Webster English dictionary, means *a religious war against infidels or Mohammedan heretics*. It is possible that the decision to use the term *jihadists* by *Vanguard* in domain 3 would invoke the reader's schematic knowledge of a discourse of 'Islam and Jihad', given that "Jihad" ("holy war" or "holy struggle") is viewed as a sixth pillar by some Muslims. Its purpose, accord-ing to *The New Encyclopædia Britannica* (2013: 8), "is not the conversion of indi-viduals to Islam but rather the gaining of political control over the collective affairs of societies to run them in accordance with the principles of Islam." The writer of the view point believes strongly that Boko Haram is inspired by Islam. The third person pronoun *he* refers to the Sultan of Sokoto, the President of the Nigerian Supreme Council for Islamic Affairs, who declared that terrorism has no place in Islam (cf. example 4). The writer is in effect saying that Boko Haram members are backed by Islam and are trying to force the religion on others through jihad.

One aspect that makes up the identity of Boko Haram members, according to *Vanguard*, is their devotion to their religion. In domains 4 and 5, the adjective *religious* is used to modify nouns such as *fanatics, bigots,* and *extremists*. These nouns clearly show how Boko Haram members are saliently complimented on their bad qualities. They are described not for their social fanaticism, bigotry and extremism but for their religious fanaticism, bigotry and extremism. Also, worth mentioning in these examples is the consistent inclusion of *religious* to modify those negative labels. The choice of the adjective *religious* as such explicitly per-petuates a view of Boko Haram members' attachment to their religion.

The Guardian in domain 6 deploys the noun phrase *extremist Islamic sect* in reference to the Boko Haram members. The label *extremist* is used to delineate the Boko Haram members. The label, *extremist* has the feature +irrationality, +abnor-mal, +violence and +illegal. In the data for the study, the Boko Haram members are largely represented as not just Islamists but as extremist Islamists. They are constructed as the Muslim 'enemy' within and outside Islam itself. The demoniza-tion of Boko Haram is found at play within the binary that divides Muslims into liberal Muslims and extremist Muslims. In the Nigerian print media, Boko Haram members are largely constructed as backwards, primitive, excessively religious, and oppressive. Therefore, they occupy the 'enemy' role both within and outside Islam.

Certainly, the pre-modifying adjective *Islamic* in domains 7, 8 and 9 (cf. Table 1) is instrumental in giving the Boko Haram crisis a religious face. In addition, the headwords in each of the underlined noun phrases are labels that connote a rejec-tion and exclusion of the Boko Haram members. They are seen in the Nigerian print media as a terrorist cell of religious zealots accused of wanting to create a fundamentalist Islamic state in Nigeria. Then, they are labelled as militants whose motives appear to rise no higher than the profit they reap from using force to cause social disorder and perpetrate crime. In (7), the antisocial activities of the Boko Haram members should give Nigerians serious concern. The journalist is at a loss as to what motivates them to do what they do. *The Nation* and *The Guardian* often give voice to the concerns of groups such as the Christian Association of Nigeria (CAN) to portray the conflict as a religious crisis. This is evident in domains 7-9. *The Nation* in (8) presents the Northern Christians as victims of some violent incidents like the destruction of their churches, and of other significant ones like losing their lives. The Boko Haram members are said to do this with the aim of implementing Sharia in Nigeria.

5.2. Constructing Boko Haram Insurgency as Religious through Presupposition

(5) Existential presupposition

   a) With few demands of the murderous gang called Boko Haram, enumerated above, it becomes an exercise in futility for anyone, the most reverent Sultan inclusive, to say that "Boko Haram should not be associated with Islam." Terrorists in religious matters; mostly of the Islamic dynasty, preach the Koran, say prayers in the Islamic manner, performs every other religious obligation in consonance with Koran injunction, "kills" for Allah, and do all these other atrocities in the name of the great prophet Mohammed. ("Islam and Boko Haram: Sultan of Sokoto's voyage of discovery," *Vanguard*, June 3, 2014, p. 19)

Example 5, which details how the Boko Haram members engage in religious activities, presupposes that they are highly religious. This existential presupposition in Text 5, relate to the following noun phrases, *terrorists in religious matters, the Koran, Islamic manner, Koran injunction* and *the name of the great Prophet Mohammed*. The implication is, certainly, that the Islamic religion cannot be separated from Boko Haram, rather Boko Haram is inspired by Islam.

(6) Logical presupposition

   a) It is therefore, ipso facto, a difficult one not associating Islam with Boko Haram, for it is a common saying that "by their fruit you will know them." By violence of jihad, core Muslims are known. ("Islam and Boko Haram: Sultan of Sokoto's voyage of discovery," *Vanguard*, June 3, 2014, p. 19)

   b) As Obasanjo approached the group they sent very strong signals of non-cooperation by killing those who tried to negotiate with Obasanjo, *stepped up the violent killing of non- Muslims* and non- northerners in the North with several murderous attacks in several northern cities, including an attack in Kano that killed over 200 people including scores of police officers and a journalist. ("Boko Haram, Buhari and northern elite, *Vanguard*, December 19, 2014, p.18)

c) *If Yorubas will not take this matter serious because they have Muslims among their kith and kin, Igbos should not emulate them.* If Northerners will not take the fight against terrorism serious, for their own reasons, Igbos should ignore them. All Southern governors, especially the Igbos, ought to wake up now and plan to stop Boko Haram, Fulani herdsmen and the jihadists before they creep into the South, especially the South East, because Christianity has become part of the Igbo culture. *There is hardly any gathering in the South East where opening and closing prayers are not offered in the name of Jesus. We are surely different and that makes us target of the religious fanatics and their blood thirsty political fathers.* ("Restrict Boko Haram to nest areas," *Vanguard*, May 9, 2014, p. 19)

d) "The president *had never visited* any of the theatres where Muslims were massacred. He was never in Jos to commiserate with the families of dozens of Muslims that were massacred. He was not in Kaduna or Kafanchan," Qaqa said. ("Boko Haram: State of emergency meant to attack Muslims," *Daily Trust*, January 2, 2012, p. 7)

e) Sheik Khalid further *questioned* why such action was not taken when Muslims were affected stressing: "I don't know why they take this kind of action when the incident now involves Christians." ("Mixed reactions trail emergency rule in Plateau," *Daily Trust*, January 2, 2012, p. 7)

The presupposition that Boko Haram is indeed motivated by religion arises from the adverb *ipso facto* in example 6a, which functions as a logical presupposition device. This extract also uses pragmatic presupposition to imply that Boko Haram is not only religiously inspired, but also that Boko Haram is inspired by Islam, by bringing in a comparative construction *by their fruit you will know them*, and connecting this with the existentially presupposed relationship between jihad and Islam. Therefore, the world knowledge of the reader(s) comes into play in understanding the different presuppositions in the extract.

In addition, in example 6b, the material process, *stepped up the violent killing of non- Muslims*, presupposes that the killing is selective and motivated by religious sentiment. *Vanguard* claims that non-Muslims, such as Christians and adherents of other religions, are being killed by Boko Haram members, the unnamed Actor of the material process *stepped up*. The Goal of the process, *the violent killing of non-Muslims* is strategically placed to convey the intention of *Vanguard*. The newspaper believes that the crisis is religiously motivated.

Further, there is presupposition in the dependent clause in example 6c, *if Yorubas will not take this matter serious because they have Muslims among their kith and kin, Igbos should not emulate them*. The dependent clause shows that the Boko Haram crisis is religious. The Yoruba can afford not to take the crisis serious, according to *Vanguard,* not because they do not feel the pain and the effect of the activities of the Boko Haram members but because they have kith and kin who are Muslims. The implication of this is clear. There is a clear polarisation between adherents of Islam and Christianity. Muslims in the South West in Nigeria, according to this news report, have a soft spot for Boko Haram because of the religious affiliation. The religion script is introduced through the Circumstantial Element of Purpose, *because they have Muslims among their kith and kin*. This implies that the crisis is religiously motivated. In the process, it projects that the ideology that the Boko Haram crisis has religious connotations.

In example 6d, the verb phrase *had never visited* presupposes that the president is being biased against the Muslims. The president is accused of not considering it important to visit grief-stricken Muslims in Jos, Kaduna and Kafanchan when Muslims were massacred. If it were to be the other way around, if Christians had been the victims, Qaqa, the spokesman of the Jama'atu Ahlis Sunnati Lidda'wati Wal Jihad, reported in the *Daily Trust* newspaper, claims that the president would have paid the Christians a visit, to at least sympathize with them. This indicates religious undertone. In example 6e, the presupposition that the Goodluck Jonathan led administration is playing politics with the Boko Haram crisis is further advanced. The verb *questioned* presupposes the clausal element *when Muslims were affected*, implying that the president does not give two hoots concerning the safety and security of Muslims in the North. The implication is, certainly, that the president hates Muslims and that they do not mean anything to him.

Transitivity	Linguistic cue	Newspaper
Text 11	**Since it is obvious that *there is a religious dimension to the crisis*	("The Kano bomb blast", *The Guardian*, July 16, 2014, p. 14)
Text 12	Boko Haram is an Islamic religious instrument	("Islam and Boko Haram: Sultan of Sokoto's voyage of discovery", *Vanguard*, June 3, 2014, p. 19)
Relational process	*"Boko Haram is the core Northern Muslim leadership's instrument of war* to fulfil the promised making of Nigeria ungovernable."	("Islam and Boko Haram: Sultan of Sokoto's voyage of discovery", *Vanguard*, June 3, 2014, p. 19)
	The principal demand of Boko Haram is religious supremacy and interfaith intolerance...	("Boko Haram, Buhari and northern elite", *Vanguard*, December 19, 2014, p. 18)

Table 2: Boko Haram Insurgency as Religiously Inspired through Relational Process

Text 11 consists of a complex sentence; in the subordinate clause, we have a Relational Process. This relational clause establishes a relation which is factual, that is, the Carrier and the Possessor are treated as real and indubitable. This indubitability appears in the process *is,* that constructs a relation marked by no modalisation. No *would, should* or *could* is used, revealing that there is no space for possibilities and probabilities or doubts in the relation. Text 11 shows the ideological view held by *The Guardian* regarding the Boko Haram insurgency. The newspaper is saying that the crisis has a religious dimension. Little wonder, it calls on people with deep knowledge of the faith (Islamic faith to dialogue with members of the group).

Another relational process (Text 12), intended to advance the ideology that the crisis is religious, is in *Vanguard*. The newspaper establishes this ideology by relating in a factual way the participant *Boko Haram* to the attributive clause *an Islamic religious instrument of prosecuting a political agenda of the core Northern Muslims to the leadership of Nigeria back to Northern control*. It tries to sell the idea that Boko Haram is just a tool in Islam in Nigeria to return political power to the Northern Nigeria.

Vanguard further depicts Boko Haram crisis as religious in Text 12. The newspaper's impression about the sect is represented by the Carrier *Boko Haram* and the attribute *the core Northern Muslim leadership's instrument of war to fulfil the promised making of Nigeria ungovernable.* From the attribute, it is implied that Northern Christians are not behind Boko Haram; it is only the core Northern Muslim leadership who are bent on making Nigeria ungovernable because the then president, Goodluck Jonathan, is a Christian from the South.

It is quite interesting to point out that the Identifiers of Text 12 are presented, in a factual way, in a relation of "this-is-equal-this", that is, *the principal demand of Boko Haram* is equal *religious supremacy and inter-faith supremacy. Vanguard* entertains no doubt about the affirmation. It is part of a persuasive positivism and finality by the newspaper to promote the ideology that Boko Haram is religiously motivated.

5.3. Boko Haram as Politically Inspired Insurgency

The Boko Haram crisis is believed to have political undertones in the Nigerian print media. The Northern Elders and the government are widely represented as playing politics with the crisis. One example is the constructing politics in discourses on Boko Haram through presupposition as shown below:

(7) "Unlike in Kano, BirninGwari and Rigasa areas of Kaduna state, all these obnoxious and sacrilegious acts elicited not a single passive or active resistance from the locals who in the absence of security agencies were there when the inhuman acts were committed." ("JTF: Borno people condoning Boko Haram," *Daily Trust*, January 2, 2013, p. 6)

(8) The people of Borno understood this. They have always known that their own feudalist leaders are behind the kidnapping of the girls. ("#Bring Back our Northern Domination," *Vanguard*, August 19, 2014, p. 17)

Example 7 reveals that the politicisation of the crisis could also come from the locals. In the news article "JTF: Borno people condoning Boko Haram", the inhabitants of Borno are accused of encouraging the terrorists by not doing anything while the terrorists are carrying out obnoxious and sacrilegious acts. The use of the negator, not before the noun phrase *a single passive and active resistance from the locals*, presupposes that the locals have not in any way done anything to discourage or repel the Boko Haram members. The negative-other representations do not end with the Borno locals.

In example 8, the adverb *always* creates the existential presupposition that the people of Borno know that the kidnapping of the Chibok girls is sheer politics and the adverb upholds the truthfulness of the noun clause *that their own feudalist leaders are behind the kidnapping of the girls.*

Transitivity	Linguistic cue	Newspaper
Text 15. Relational process	*The kidnapping of the Chibok girls is part and parcel of a cynical plan by some Northern elements...*	("#Bring Back our Northern Domination," *Vanguard*, August 19, 2014,p. 17)
Text 16. Material process	*The President Jonathan- PDP administration has* actively *sustained the crises,* profiteering from it!	(Politicization of Boko Haram Insurgency, Bane of Nigeria's Anti Terror Fight, *Leadership*, September 12, 2013, p. 12)
Text 17. Relational process	*President Jonathan's handling of the Boko Haram insurgency has been a spectacular failure,* and *This is deliberate* for political reasons.	(Politicization of Boko Haram Insurgency, Bane of Nigeria's Anti-Terror Fight, *Leadership*, September 12, 2013, p. 12)

Table 3: Boko Haram Insurgency as Politically Inspired through Transitivity Choices

What emerges from Text (15) is the allegation that there is a political mischief to the kidnapping of the Chibok girls. Femi Aribisala, whose view is reported by the *Vanguard* newspaper, accuses some Northerners as being the brain behind the said kidnap of the Chibok girls. Lexical items such as *cynical plan, Northern elements*, and *Goodluck Jonathan's re-election plans* help to establish the assumption that Femi Aribisala is discussing politics. The link between the Chibok girls' abduction and the 2015 General elections are signified by these explicit phrases. Aside from that, the sentence is a relational process which has the structure X serves to define Y, as in *The kidnapping of the Chibok girls is part and parcel of a cynical plan by some Northern elements to embarrass the government and militate against Goodluck Jonathan's re-election plans.* Here, the relational process is a formal accusation of some Northern elements who believe political power must return to the North. The author of the article, Femi Aribisala, constructs a discourse of negativity about those he refers to as Northern elements. This allows them to be categorised as the other. For the purposes of negative-other representation, the targets, the Northern elements, are discursively disconnected from the in-group, Nigerians who are genuinely seeking an end to the Boko Haram crisis.

Text 16 is taken from *Leadership. The President Jonathan- PDP Administration* is the Actor, the material process is realized by the verb group *has sustained* and *the crises*, the Goal. *Leadership* refers to its out-group in stating that *The President Jonathan- PDP administration has actively sustained the crises, profiteering from it*! The assertion is thought of as a negative other presentation of the political and military planning of the Jonathan Administration and an appeal of persuasive discourse to influence beliefs about the unserious ways the Jonathan Administration has been going about fighting the Boko Haram insurgency in northern Nigeria. The president is accused of benefiting from the crisis; that is why it is sustained and allowed to linger on indefinitely. The affected Northerners who suffer the effect of the elongation of the prolonged Boko Haram insurgency are the in-group, identified with *Leadership*.

Text 17 is taken from *Leadership*. The representation of irresponsibility and failure on the part of the president is actualized by the Relational Process with *a spectacular failure* as an attribute in the first clause, and *deliberate* as an attribute in the second clause, while the prepositional phrase *for political reasons* functions as a Reason Circumstance. *Leadership* accuses President Jonathan of politicizing the Boko Haram insurgency. The ideology in the Northern part of the country that the president is deliberately prolonging the Boko Haram crisis is advanced by *Leadership* here. In some quarters in the North, it is believed that since the Boko Haram crisis is more serious in states where opposition party to the president's PDP is ruling, the president is not willing to prosecute the war against Boko Haram wholeheartedly in the hope that elections would not hold in the opposition strongholds.

6. Conclusion

The critical discourse analysis of print media coverage of the Boko Haram insurgency between 2009 and 2014 reveals different patterns of representation of social actors in discourses on the insurgency. In denigrating the Boko Haram members, the five newspapers resemble each other. They were united in denigrating the enemy, the Boko Haram members, and praising moderate Muslims. Nevertheless, the newspapers were divided in portraying politicians and the northern elders as playing politics with the Boko Haram insurgency. *Daily Trust* and *Leadership* were very critical of the Federal Government of Nigeria, arguing that the government has politicised the crisis. *Vanguard* indicted some northern elders, claiming that they were using the insurgency for political gains. Radical Islamism and us/them dichotomy manifested in the discourses on Boko Haram. Radical Islamism was represented through naming choices, evaluative adjectives, transitivity and presupposition. This created a polarisation at two levels: between moderate Islam and extremist Islam, and between Muslims and adherents of other faiths, such as Christianity.

As demonstrated by the present study, the print media, like any other communicative event, can be used as influential instruments to construct identity, impose or legitimize, and emphasize certain ideologies that positively represent a specific group and negatively represent the other. When readers are exposed to this kind of discourse, their perceptions about reality can be shaped in line with the dominant ideology, and unless they contest, they further reproduce it in their discourses. The study, therefore, has implication for readers of the news reports on the crisis who may read the texts uncritically, disregarding that the news reports may be imbued with a particular ideology which the newspapers position it to adopt. If readers become fully aware of the subtleties involved, they may take appropriate precautions.

References

Abdullah, S.A.N. (2014). A study of reporting about terrorism on two Pan-Ara television news channels. Thesis. Mass Communication. University of Leicester.

Aboh, R.A. (2013). Lexical and discursive construction of identity in selected twenty-first century Nigerian novels. Thesis. English, Arts. The University of Ibadan.

Ajayi, A.I. (2012). Boko Haram and terrorism in Nigeria: Exploratory and explanatory notes. *Global Advanced Research Journal of History, Political Science and International Relations 1.5*: 103-107.

Agbedo, C.U. Ebere C. Krisagbedo, E.C. and Buluan, D. (2013). Socio-pragmatic analysis of Boko Haram's language of insurgency in Nigeria: Implications for global peace and security. *Developing Country Studies 3.8*: 45-63.

Azeez, A. L. (2009). The role of the media in reporting terrorism: A personal viewpoint. *Journal of Communication and Media Research, Volume 1,1*, 1-15.

Banuri, S. (2005). The nature and causes of international terrorism: A look at why terrorists believe measures are necessary. (Honors Thesis, Department of Economics). University of Texas: Dallas, TX.

Behnam, B., & R. M. Zenouz, (2008). A contrastive critical analysis of Iranian and British newspaper reports on the Iran nuclear power program. In N. Nørgaard (ed.) *Systemic functional Linguistics in use. Odense Working Papers in Language and Communication 29*: 199-218.

Bizovi, O.M. (2014). Deviant women: Female involvement in terrorist organisations. Thesis. Ridge School for Intelligence Studies and Information Science. Mercyhurst University, Erie, Pennsyivania.

Carter, C., Steinder, L. (2004). *Critical readings: Media and gender.* Berkshire: Open Press University.

Chiluwa, I. and Adegoke, A. (2013). Twittering the Boko Haram uprising in Nigeria: Investigating pragmatic acts in the social media. *Africa Today 59*, 3: 82-102.

Curran, J., Seaton, J. (1997). *Power without responsibility: The press and broadcasting in Britain.* London: Routledge.

Fowler, R. (1996). *Linguistic criticism.* 2nd Ed. Oxford: Oxford University Press.

Gibbs, J.P. (2012). Conceptualisation of Terrorism. In Horgan, J. and Braddock, K. (Eds.). *Terrorism studies, A reader.* New York: Routledge, 41-62.

Gotzsche, H. (2009). Key ideas in linguistics and the philosophy of language. In S. Chapman & C Routledge (Eds.). *Systemic Functional Grammar.* Edinburgh: Edinburgh University Press.

Halliday, M.A.K. 1967. Notes on transitivity and theme in English, Parts 1–3. *Journal of Linguistics 3.1*: 37–81, 3.2: 199-244 and 4.2: 179–215.

Halliday, M.A.K. (1991). Towards probabilistic interpretations. In E. Ventola. Ed. *Functional and systemic linguistics: approaches and uses.* Berlin/ New York: Mouton de Gruyter.

Halliday, M.A. K. (2004). *An introduction to functional grammar.* 3rd ed. Rev. Mathiessen C. London: Edward Arnold.

Hoffman, B. (2006). *Inside terrorism.* 2nd ed. New York, NY: Columbia University Press.

Jackson, R (2007). Constructing enemies: 'Islamic terrorism' in political and academic discourse. *Government and Opposition 42(3)*: 394–426.

Jeffries, L. (2010). *Critical stylistics. The power of English.* Basingstoke: Palgrave Macmillan.

Jenkins, B. M. (1975). *Will terrorists go nuclear?* Santa Monica, CA: The RAND Corporation; (P-5541 in the RAND Paper Series)

Litosseliti, L. (2002). "Head to head": Gendered repertoires in newspaper arguments. In Litosseliti, L. and Sunderland, J. *Gender Identity and Discourse Analysis.* Netherlands: John Benjamins, 129-148.

Loimeier, R. (2012). Boko Haram: the development of a militant religious movement in Nigeria. *Africa Spectrum 47.2-3*: 137-55.

Martin, G. (2006). *Understanding terrorism: Challenges, perspectives, and issues.* 2nd ed. Thousand Oaks, CA: Sage Publication.

Nwammuo, A.N., Ededegoh, L.O.N. and Iwok, U. (2015). Nigerian press coverage of the 2015 elections: What has ownership got to do with it? *International Journal of African and Asian Studies* 14, 81-88.

Odebunmi, A. (2016). Frames and pragmatic strategies in Nigerian newspaper reports on Boko-Haram insurgency. In Odebunmi, A. and Ayoola, K (eds). *Language, context and society.* Ile-Ife: Obafemi Awolowo University Press, 265-288.

Osisanwo, A. (2016). Discursive representation of Boko Haram terrorism in selected Nigerian newspapers. *Discourse and Communication 10* (4) 341-362.

Rapoport, D. C. (2001). The fourth wave: September 11 in the history of terrorism. *Current History*, 100(650), 419-424. Retrieved from http://search.proquest.com/openview/402567f2c2f64a77974c34fff586d309/1.pdf?pq-origsite=gscholar&cbl=41559

Reisigl, M., Wodak, R. (2001). *Discourse and discrimination.* London: Routledge.

Roelofs, P. (2014). Framing and blaming: Discourse analysis of the Boko Haram uprising, July 2009. In Pérouse de Montclos, Marc-Antoine, (ed.) *Boko Haram: Islamism, politics, security and the state in Nigeria.* French Institute for Research in Africa / Institut Français de Recherche en Afrique (IFRA-Nigeria), 110-131.

Sahragard, R., Davatgarzadeh, G. (2010). The representation of social actors in Interchange third edition series: a Critical Discourse Analysis. *The Journal of Teaching Language Skills* (JLTS) 4, 29, 67-89.

Sani, S. (2011). Boko Haram: History, ideas and revolt. *Vanguard*, Friday, July 8, pp. 26.

Simpson, P. (2004). *Stylistics: A resource book for students.* London & New York: Routledge.

Spindlove, J. R. & Simonsen, C. E. (2013). *Terrorism today: The past, the players, the future.* 5th ed.). Boston, MA: Pearson.

The New Encyclopædia Britannica (2013). Volume 22. Encyclopaedia Britannica Inc, 1-964.

Turk, A. T. (2004). Sociology of terrorism. *Annual Review of Sociology 30*, 271-286.

Van Dijk, T.A. (1998). *Ideology.* London: Sage.

Wodak, R. (1995). Critical linguistics and critical discourse analysis. In J. Verschueren, J.-O. Östman, J. Blommaert and C. Bulcaen (Eds.) *Handbook of pragmatics.* Amsterdam: John Benjamins, 204-201.

Wodak, R. (1999). Critical discourse analysis at the end of the 20th century. *Research on Language and Social Interaction 32.2*: 185-193.

Wodak, R. (2001). What CDA is about - a summary of its history, important concepts, and its developments. In R. Wodak & M. Meyer (Eds.) *Methods of Critical Discourse Analysis.* London: Sage, 1-33.

Wodak, R. (2002). Aspects of Critical Discourse Analysis. *Zeitschrift für Angewandte Linguistik 36*: 5-31.

Wodak, R. (2006). Images in/and news in a globalised world: Introductory thoughts. In I. Lassen et al. (Eds.) *Mediating ideology in text and image: Ten critical studies.* Amsterdam: John Benjamins.

Wodak, R. (2007). Doing Europe: The discursive construction of Europeans identities. In R.C.M. Mole (Ed.). *Discursive constructions of identity in European politics.* Basingstoke: Palgrave Macmillan, 70-94.

Wodak, R. (2010). The politics of exclusion: The haiderisation of Europe. In A. Landwehr (Ed.). *Diskursiver Wandel.* Frankfurt: VS Verlag, 355-376.

Wodak, R., Meyer, M. (2001). *Methods of Critical Discourse Analysis.* London: Sage.

Wodak, R., Koller, V. (2008). *Handbook of communication in the public sphere.* Berlin: Mouton de Gruyter.

A Multimodal Critical Discourse Analysis of Religious Discourse: The Study of Selected Church Programme Handbills[1]

Charisa Dada

Benson Idahosa University

Abstract

This paper examines religious discourse from a systemic functional multimodaldiscourse perspective by exploring the ideological messages and critically analysing the verbal and visual elements contained in church programme handbills in order to demonstrate that the meaning constructed in the handbills, reflects the power of ideological discourse to produce better citizens. Kress & Van Leeuwen's (2006) visual grammar approach, and Cheong's (2004) analytical tools of multisemiotic print advertisement were used in the analysis of data. The multimodal analysis image software 2013 was further used to empirically analyse and corroborate findings. The specific focus of this paper is on representation and interaction between the producer and viewer of imagery. Four purposively selected handbills were examined and analysed to give insight into their function as powerful ideological tools. The study reveals that meaning constructed in handbills, from a systemic functional multimodal discourse perspective, contributes to a better understanding of religious discourse.

Keywords: ideology, print advertisement, representation and interaction, systemic functional multimodal discourse analysis, image analysis software

1. Introduction

The present study is concerned with how multimodal resources have been effectively utilised in church programme handbills to communicate some levels of Christian ideology. Handbills can be categorised as outdoor advertising which, according to Oyebode & Unuabonah (2013: 812) "is a rich research area that captures and reflects the value system of any society as well as its ideological beliefs". Ideologies are concepts that drive the direction of our thoughts or work ultimately culminating in a mindset reflected in all we represent consciously or subconsciously. They can be enforced overtly or covertly in order to solve humanity's perceived problems. The ideology of Christianity is centred on the gospel of Jesus

---

[1] Many thanks to the director of CLAREP, Dr A. U. Esimaje, for the opportunity to be a part of the writing workshop, to my mentor, Dr Christine Ofulue, for her invaluable guidance, and to other anonymous reviewers.

Christ and its power to change lives. Christianity encompasses a wide range of de-nominations with their own set of doctrines that could exhibit slight variances or exceptions. Four handbills from the programmes of four Christian denominations the *Higher Life Conference* (HLC) of Christ Embassy, the *Holy Ghost Congress* (HGC) of the Redeemed Christian Church of God, *Annual Anointing Service (Power must Change Hands)* of the Mountain of Fire and Miracle Church (MFM), and Shiloh of the Living Faith church were analysed. The main tools of Kress and van Leeuwen's (2006) visual grammar were applied for the analysis of the images. Cheong's (2004) framework for the articulation of meaning in print advertisement was used to expand the analysis of both linguistic and non-linguistic features while the multimodal analysis image software was empirically applied to correlate find-ings. The study investigates the underlying ideologies of Christianity that inform the semiotic choices made in Christian programme handbills from a multimodal critical discourse perspective. In so doing, it sheds light on the power of ideological discourse to produce better citizens. It also contributes to a better understanding of religious discourse as it demonstrates the usefulness of the systemic functional ap-proach to critically account for multimodal phenomenon within this discourse do-main. The practical approach involves the use of multimodal analysis image soft-ware to enhance the systematic semantic and ideological interpretation of the imagery contained in the handbills. In what follows, a brief background of the use of handbills in Christian religious discourse is presented. This is followed by a review of some existing religious discourse studies and an overview of the theory underlying this study, the critical analysis of the handbills, and the presentation of findings and conclusion.

Handbills or fliers are simple, easy to read or view promotional materials dis-tributed by hand for an event, service or a product. Their main purpose is to dis-seminate quick information and their text often appear in large fonts accompanied with pictorial representations designed in attractive colours to draw viewers' atten-tion to the information contents. In the religious context, and within the context of this study, handbills are meant to be handed out to invite people for a church pro-gramme. In the bid to fulfill the great commission of "... Go ye into all the world and preach the gospel to every creature" (Bible, Mark 16:15, King James Version), churches often organise moderate to massive church programmes where members of the church serve as "mobile adverts on the go" disseminating these handbills, and thereby creating the much needed public awareness for these programmes. Such programmes are often geared towards filling the void in people, which only their interaction with a supreme being can make possible (Graham 2017). The quality of a handbill varies depending on the financial capacity of the church or-ganisation or on the value they place on a programme. The current trend is that there is the preponderant use of handbills for church programmes and it is this high prevalence and reliance of churches on these materials that necessitated this re-search interest.

The goal of the study is to use the analytical tools of systemic functional mul-timodal discourse analysis (SF-MDA) to project how ideologies of Christianity are constructed through the visual and verbal imagery in handbills. Discourse analysis approaches such as SF-MDA are designed to expose ideological underpinnings.

2. Review of Existing Studies

Scholarly works abound in religious discourse with specific reference to sermons, magazines and language. Eun Young (2016) examines the process of interpreting biblical texts of a religious scholar. The paper defends and justifies the Southern Baptist Convention's opposition to women's ordination using a sociocognitive approach as an underlying theoretical framework. It also demonstrates the usefulness of employing Critical Discourse Analysis in understanding how a religious text both assumes and tries to formulate unified mental models to control the beliefs of the audience and promulgate dominance by assigning sovereign values to certain interpretations so that readers will understand certain texts as they see them. Eldin Sharaf (2014) adopts an ideological approach within a critical discourse analysis (CDA) to investigate Islamic discourse by tracing the ideological devices in Amr Khalid's sermons. It shows how the language employed in Khalid's sermons reflects the common conceptual structures and interrelationships between him and his audience. It equally uncovers certain forms of ideological disguises in the sermons thereby exposing the tension between idealism and pragmatism, the conflict between 'us' and 'them'.

One interesting research that was of main significance to the present research is that of Olowu (2013) in which he carries out a critical analysis of some selected editions of *Christian Women Mirror* magazine of the Deeper Life Church, using the theoretical framework of Multimodal Discourse Analysis. His focus is on exposing Christians' perception of the two concepts of death and judgement. The reason this work is of particular significance is that there are not many works on religious discourse that adopt the multimodal approach as an analytical tool as adopted in this study. His article is divided in two parts. First, he examines the euphemistic expressions used, and second, the visual components focusing mainly on the analysis of the images and colours used in the magazine. This study will extend beyond Olowu's (2013) analysis because of its use of the multimodal analysis image software.

Esimaje (2012) identified the words most associated with Christian sermons in English, in Nigeria. She uses a corpus of present-day sermons in Nigeria and compares it to a reference corpus of sermons from other parts of the world in order to find out those lexical items which are characteristic of sermons in terms of types, frequency and usage. Milada Burianova's (2010) thesis discusses the ideological messages contained in Christian advertising in the magazine *The Church and Christian Business Guide in the United States* using the pragmatic analysis of the Relevance Theory (Sperber & Wilson 1986, 2004; Tanaka 1994 cited in Burianova 2010). The ideological messages are captured and interpreted via ostensive stimuli revealing product names, headlines and slogans as the most typical ostensive, overt strategies mainly adopted in Christian advertising. Taiwo (2005, 2006) conducts an investigation into the various ways pulpit preachers in Christian religion elicit responses from their congregation and the general style of interrogation in Charismatic Christian pulpit discourse, respectively. In both investigations the framework of sociolinguistics and discourse analysis are adopted. His (2005) study shows how preachers control the pulpit discourse, while the congregation share in the process of creation of the text as it unfolds. By contrast, his (2006) article that looks at the peculiar use of interrogatives by charismatic Christian preachers concludes that interrogation is not only used as a tool for getting feedback information and responses, but also used to regulate the linguistic behaviour of the congregation in the process of the discourse. Taiwo's (2005, 2006), and Esimaje's (2011) works differ from this study in the area of focus and framework adopted but they are similar only as religious discourse.

Sharaf Eldin's (2014) study shares some aspects of similarities with this present work because it is a critical discourse analysis of religious discourse; its emphasis is, however, on Islamic sermons. Burianova's (2010) work comes close as it deals with print advertisement of magazines only that we differ in our underlying theory and area of focus. The present study explores the ideology of Christianity projected in Handbills, that is, print advertisement and works in this area are scanty. The multimodal discourse approach is a relatively new trend in discourse analysis, not so popular in Nigeria, which focuses on the systematic deconstruction of the elements of a text in which semiotic resources of various kinds work in partnership to create the meanings that we attribute to such texts. Additionally, the use of the multimodal analysis image software enables intensive annotation and analysis which exposes meanings that an otherwise cursory descriptive study would not have captured. The need to contribute to scholarship in this regard became necessary.

3. Theoretical Framework

This study employs and extends the functionality of the SF-MDA approach to religious discourse. Multimodal analysis is a systematic approach to understanding how words, images, sounds, etc., make more meanings together than any one of them can make alone. Kress and Van Leeuwen (2001: 20) define multimodality as "the use of several semiotic modes in the design of a semiotic product or event" and this is seen in the design of handbills which is the focus of this study.

The systemic functional (SF) approach to multimodal discourse analysis (MDA) is concerned with the theory and practice of analysing meaning arising from the use of multiple semiotic resources in discourses (O' Halloran 2008).This approach has its base on SF theory initially fomulated by Halliday (1978) as a semiotic theory, and "a theory of meaning as choice, by which language, or any other semiotic system, is interpreted as networks of interlocking options" (Halliday 1994: xiv). The term *systemic* refers to the centrality of the system network framework to represent the meaning potential available in a semiotic resource (Lim Fei 2011: 72). In other words, it is composed of systems of choices that communicators select from to make desired meanings. It is functional "because the conceptual framework on which it is based is a functional one rather than a formal one" (Halliday 1994: xiii, cited in Lim Fei 2011: 76); basically, the approach is meaning focused. The focus in Systemic Functional Theory is to understand and evaluate meanings in context. Meaning is function in context, that is, functional meanings are made through the semiotic resources in a society.

This theory has been comprehensively applied to language and has been adapted by foremost writers like Jewitt (2009), Kress & Van Leeuwen (2006), Lemke (1998), O'Halloran (2008, 2016, 2017), O'Toole (2010), and a host of others in their analysis of how semiotic modes and resources interact to achieve specific objectives. SF-MDA is a social semiotic theory where meaning is seen to be context-dependent. Halliday (1978, cited in O'Halloran et al. 2017), states that

> One of the key tenets of social semiotic theory is the premise that language and other semiotic resources are structured according to the functions which the resources have evolved to serve in society: (a) experiential and logical meaning to structure our experience of the world; (b) interpersonal meaning to enact social relations and create a stance towards happenings and entities in the world; and (c) textual meaning to organise experiential, logical and interpersonal meanings into coherent messages (e.g. Halliday & Matthiessen, 2014).

Kress & Van Leeuwen (2006: 14) adapted this principle for images when they stated that "... visual design, like all semiotic modes, fulfils three major functions" which are as stated above. This study entails a combination of Critical Discourse Analysis with Multimodal Discourse Analysis known as Multimodal Critical Discourse Analysis. The linguistic principles found in SFL are also adapted and applied in Multimodal Critical Discourse Analysis (MCDA) to show how images, architecture, colour, dress, etc., along with language, work together to create meanings communicated by a text.

According to Machin and Mayr (2012: 10), the job of MCDA ... is to uncover "ideas, absences, and taken-for-granted assumptions" in both the images and linguistic elements in order to reveal the kinds of power interests buried in them. The approach to SF-MDA adopted in this study demonstrates how the combination of the linguistic and visual components in handbill fulfill a threefold function of ideationally construing reality interpersonally attracting attention and textually developing the central idea or theme, all in a way intended by the advertisers. Specifically, however, through the transitivity process of ideational meaning we will explore how visual structures in the form of images can convey ideological meanings, as well as do language. Kress & Van Leeuwen (2006: 14) "see images of whatever kind as entirely within the realm of the realizations and instantiations of ideology, as means – always – for the articulation of ideological positions", while Wernick (1991: 42, cited in Cheong 2004) states that "The meaning of the entire advertisement, [...] delivers back to the people the culture and values that are their own . . . [it is] a reinforcement of whatever ideological codes and conditions [that have] come to prevail".

In a similar vein, Ravelli (2010) expanded on this notion when he claimed that "in the case of ideational meaning it is the choice of process and participants and circumstances which construes a particular version of an event; that is, through the grammar, a picture is created of 'what is going on'". Exploring the ideational meaning through the transitivity process will therefore enable us capture whatever ideological meaning entrenched within the religious milieu of a particular society. The next session explains the materials and methods used in the study.

4. Materials and Methods

Twelve handbills of specific programmes held from 2015 - 2017 were collected, but four were purposively selected as data representation of the twelve because each denomination's handbills within this period were alike in form and representation. They often maintained a basic pattern according to the orientation of each ministry even in the midst of slight variations. The 2017 programme handbills were chosen as arepresentative sample because they are the most recent productions. In advertising, designs fluctuate with the tide of time according to societal values, personal/organisational innovations, creativity, and the dynamism of digital technology. The four purposively selected handbills are from four church denominations whose headquarters are based in Nigeria. These denominations are Christ Embassy, the Redeemed Christian Church of God, the Mountain of Fire and Miracle Church, and the Living Faith Church. These are international ministries with global focus and they have national and international branches. Their mission is to take the supernatural power of Jesus to the world and to make the kingdom of God the governing system of our social order, a social order operating biblical principles as unifying and meaningful responses to the challenges and opportunities of life, thus making better citizens of the peoples of the world.

The selected handbills sourced from the internet (google images) are aimed at specific programmes held annually by these ministries. These programmes are the Higher Life Conference, the Holy Ghost Congress, the Annual Anointing Service, and the Shiloh conference, respectively. These are convocation, home-coming programmes. They are organised as means of establishing believers through the spirit which is in line with the biblical injunction which states that "For I long to see you, that I may impart unto you some spiritual gift, to the end ye may be established" (Bible, Romans 1: 11).

The framework for the study is taken from Kress & van Leeuwen's (2006) visual grammar and Cheong's (2004) approach to the analysis of multi semiotic print advertisements and complemented with the multimodal analysis image software. The software and the two approaches of Kress & van Leeuwen (2006) and Cheong (2004) adapted the SFL principles for multimodal texts analysis. The software highlights the elements analysed under the catalog for advertisement which contains a predefined system of available choices utilised in print advertisement according to the ideational, interpersonal, and textual metafunctions. It is from these available choices that specific choices are made according to what pertains to the particular print advert being analysed. Under the experiential metafunction, two participant types involved in a text were identified by Kress & van Leeuwen (2006). These are the represented participants, and interactive participants (Kress & van Leeuwen 2006: 114).

Represented participants produce representational meaning under narrative images with identified four processes in the multimodal analysis image software. These are action process, reactional process, interaction process, and state process. These processes have corresponding participant roles which are actor, reactor, target, and concept. Interactive participants, essentially under the interpersonal metafunction, consist of represented participants interacting with each other inside the text, or represented participant(s) interacting with the viewer of the text. Interactive participants produce interactive meanings in three ways. Firstly, there is the system of contact classified as either *demand* (represented participant looking at the viewer, in other words demanding something from the viewer) or *offer* (represented participants looking away from the viewer, in other words, offering something to the viewer). In the Image analysis software, this is categorised under gaze-visual address (direct and indirect visual address). Secondly, there is the system of social distance classified in the image analysis software as *closeness* and *distance* (close shot = intimate, medium shot = social/friendly, long shot = neutral/impersonal). Thirdly, there is the system of attitude depicted as *visual power* in the image analysis software which is the angle of interaction between viewer and participant; high angle = superiority of viewer over represented participant, low angle = inferiority of viewer/superiority of represented participant and eye-level = equality of viewer and represented participant. When the angle of interaction combines with closeness and distance, a certain level of relationship is suggested between viewer and participants, such as intimacy, involvement, detachment, or friendliness.

At the textual level, there are elements of composition involving arrangement in space from left to right (before and after, given/new), top = important information/promise, bottom = less information value (ideal/real). Elements of visual attraction involve visual prominence, with emphasis on the salience of depicted objects, and can be achieved through colour contrast, sharpness of focus, size, lighting, background, foreground, etc. Other elements captured in the image analysis software focused on in this analysis are visual reality depicting realistic detail (photograph, digital graphics and digitally enhanced image, cartoon etc.), typography (typeface design and style such as fonts, case etc.), visual-verbal relations which involve similarity and difference in terms of whether the visual illustrates, elaborates, enhances, repeats, contrasts, or gives additional information to the text and vice-versa. Lastly, grammar at text level involves the type of cohesive devices, and word classes used, and their visual-verbal relationship.

Cheong (2004: 173) identified certain macro-structural elements in the Generic Structure Potential of print advertisements consisting of Lead^(Display)^Emblem^ (Announcement)^(Enhancer)^(Tag)^(Call-and-Visit-Information). According to Cheong (2004), Lead is an obligatory visual element in print advertisement defined by its size, position and colour. It consists of the Locus of Attention (LoA), and of the complement to the Locus of Attention (Comp.LoA). Display refers to the visual display of the product or service in the advertisement which may be explicit or implicit. The Emblem, another obligatory element, can be realised visually by the logo of the product/service, and linguistically by the brand name of the product/service. The Announcement (Primary and Secondary) is the most salient linguistic resource and has "relative prominence in scale, colour, font and size" (Cheong 2004: 173). The Enhancer comprises linguistic items which build on the meaning "emanating from the interaction between the Lead and the Announcement" (Cheong 2004: 173).

The Tag is a one-line statement that captures information not indicated in the Enhancer, while Call and-Visit Information is a non-salient item that comprises contact information about the product/service. These terms are applied in the analysis of the church programme handbills selected for this study because handbills fall under the category of print advertisement. Cheong (2004) further elaborates on four strategies for ideational meaning in print advertisement consisting of the *Bi-Directional Investment of Meaning* across visual and linguistic components; the resulting *Contextualization Propensity* (CP) of the linguistic and visual selections opens up an *Interpretative Space* (IS) in which the *Semantic Effervescence* (SE) can be assessed (O'Halloran 2008). These four strategies again have four functional stages within a triumvirate interaction between the Lead, Announcement, and Enhancer. In the first stage, the Lead is what gets the attention of the viewer. It is, therefore, the most salient but encumbered with diverse meaning potentials. This leads to the announcement stage where there is bi-directional investment of meaning between the Lead (a visual code), and Announcement (a linguistic code). For this juxtaposition, Cheong (2004) proposes setting up transitivity processes that invest meaning from the linguistic code to the visual code and vice versa. At this stage, the narrowing of meaning begins through certain contextualization elements and ideologies begin to emerge as well. This is further fine-tuned at the secondary announcement stage, and meanings built upon at the Enhancer stage, when the socio-cultural context is taken into consideration. With this, the particular meaning desired comes to fore. Since one of the objectives of this study is to unravel the ideologies behind the linguistic and visual imagery in handbills, the framework adopted becomes appropriate as handbills fall under the category of multisemiotic print advertisement, and the use of the image analysis software further systematises the analysis and lends credence to the findings. This study also deploys the analytical tools of SF-MDA to deconstruct the visual and verbal elements in order to expose the ideology of Christianity in the handbills of selected church programmes. The analysis that follows in the discussion and results section will clarify interpretations and understanding of the underlying ideologies projected in the handbills.

5. Discussion and Results

The multimodal analysis image software was used to generate a table of inventory of the elements depicted in the selected church programmes handbills. Below, there is the tabularised generic structure potential for Handbill (Table 1).

Atalog Advertisement	Combination of Choices Utilised			
	MFM	HGC	HLC	SHILOH
Design elements	Visual elements - main visual display, focus of attention, logo, icons and symbols, 'offer'	Visual elements - main visual display, focus of attention, logo, icons and symbols, 'offer'	Visual elements - main visual display, focus of attention, icons and symbols, 'offer'	Visual elements - main visual display, focus of attention, icons and symbols, 'demand'
	Verbal elements - Headline, brand name, slogan, call to action, call and visit invitation	Verbal elements - Headline, brand name, call and visit invitation	Verbal elements - Headline, brand name, call and visit invitation	Verbal elements - Headline, brand name, slogan, call to action, call and visit invitation
Elements of composition	Centre	Top, bottom, centre	Left-right, centre, top, bottom	Left-right
Elements of visual attraction	Foreground, background	Foreground, background, sharpness of focus	Foreground, background	Foreground, background
Visual reality	Digital graphics, stylised background	Digital graphics, stylised background	Photograph, Digitally enhanced images	Photograph, abstract background
Typography	Uppercase, big fonts	Uppercase, big fonts, bold	Uppercase, italic, small fonts	Uppercase, italic, small fonts, big fonts
Interpersonal relations	Indirect visual address high angle, medium shot	Indirect visual address high angle, medium shot	Indirect visual address eye level, medium shot	direct visual address, eye level, medium shot
Emotional involvement (Text and Image)	Positive emotion	Positive emotion	Positive emotion	Positive emotion
Agency and Action	Participants 1, 2, 3, 4 Concept	Participants 1,2,3. Concept	Participants 1,2,3.4,5,6,7, Actor, Concept, Target, interaction, reaction	Actor, Concept, interaction, reaction
Visual-Verbal Relations	Illustration, Addition	Illustration, Addition	Addition	Illustration, Addition
Grammar at text level	Mental verbs, commands, Present tense, relating	Mental verbs, commands, Present tense, relating	Statement, Adjectives, relating	Mental verbs, commands, Present tense, feeling

Table 1: The Generic structure potential for handbills

The handbills under focus have three main underlying themes running through them. These are, firstly, the theme of spiritual warfare, and assured victory. Secondly, there is the theme of a higher life in Christ - a life of all-round prosperity and general wellbeing (Bible, 3 John 1:2) where congregants are inspired to higher ideals. Thirdly, closely linked to this, is the theme of supernatural transformations, that is, there is always room for change in any circumstance, and such changes could be instantaneous depending on how strong one's desire is to allow for the

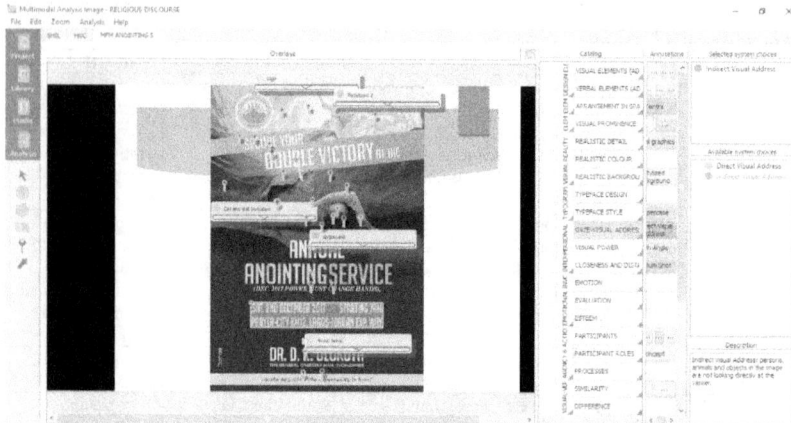

Figure 1:   Screenshot of MFM handbill on *Multimodal Analysis Image* software showing overlays, catalog, annotations, available system choices, selected system choices, and description of system choices.

flow of the anointing or auction of the Holy Spirit. These are the main selling points of these churches as reflected in the selected church programme handbills. Their themes are a reflection of societal values of Christianity depicted in the communication of the advertisers with their target audience - their immediate community of believers and the global Christian community.

The MFM handbill (Figure 1) and the HGC handbills share similar themes in their headlines, one of which is spiritual warfare. These headlines and tags presuppose that spiritual warfare is inevitable for a Christian, and such warfare is always from a standpoint of victory. They make use of different colourful fonts ranging from big (suggestive of the importance of the programme, as big fonts serve the purpose of emphasis) to small (suggesting modesty, and humility), to attract the attention of the viewer. They also make use of illustrative backgrounds to demonstrate the meaning intended in the headline as part of their advertising techniques.

The headlines which consist of the primary and secondary announcements (PA/SA) and tags are examples of covert communication where implication is conveyed through the use of imperatives, statements or phrases like *Secure Your Double Victory at the Annual Anointing Service* (P A)/ Dec 2017, *Power Must Change Hands* (PA)/ *Make hay while the opportunity is here!* (Tag)/ *The Redeemed Christian Church of God* 2017 *Holy Ghost Congress* (PA)/ *Songs of Victory* (PA). The first sentence in the MFM handbill is an imperative which emphasises the need to secure your double victory.

Our attention is drawn to the word *double* which is further illustrated with digital graphics and stylized through the visual background the Bible story of Elisha who asked for a double portion of his master anointing when he, Elijah, was about to be raptured (Bible, 2 Kings 2: 9). The red cloak of Elijah in the graphics represents the assurance that Elisha had received the double portion of the anointing upon Elijah. The word *double*, in this context, therefore, signifies the right of the first born, authority (Oyakhilome 2018, July 9), inheritance, and conquest. Thus, intertextually transposes into presupposing that anyone who attends this programme will have (or recover) their rights of first born, inheritance, and authority secure in the area of life intended. There is, therefore, a bi-directional investment of this meaning from the visual elements to the verbal elements as we see power metaphorically being handed over to Elisha by Elijah. In the same token, the brethren are to expect handover of power from those people, things, or elements, who supposedly stole them away from them. The change of ownership is the value exemplifying the token (power) and the double victory (phenomenon) is that which is wanted. Therefore, there must be an urgency and time constraint (contigency) about it; hence, the beneficiary has to make hay (attribute) while the opportunity lasts.

(9)

Secure	*your*	*double victory*	*at the annual anointing service*
process: mental	beneficiary/recipient	phenomenon	circ. location

(10)

Dec 2017 Power	*must*	*change hands*
identified token	process: circ. identifying	identifier value

(11)

Make hay	*while the opportunity*	*is*	*here*
attribute	circ. contingency	process: intensive	cir. time

Figure 2:   Screenshot of HGC handbill on *Multimodal Analysis Image* software showing overlays, catalog, annotations, available system choices, selected system choices, and description of system choices.

In the Holy Ghost Congress (HGC) handbill in Figure 2, we also see similar words and graphic illustrations used to depict the theme of the congress. The adjectival phrase *Songs of Victory* is aptly illustrated with the Bible story of David and Goliath in graphics where we see David squatting over the target, Goliath whom he slew with a sling shot, and then the people rejoicing in songs of victory.

It is interesting to note that, in the graphics, the people rejoicing are made more prominent. They are foregrounded with sharpness of focus, while David and Goliath are in the background because their prominence is dimmed or blurred. This, therefore, presupposes that the congress is about coming together to rejoice about victory(ies) that are accomplished over life battles. As the viewers attend the congress, every 'Goliath' in their lives will be slain, ultimately resulting into *Songs of Victory*. The headline, therefore, provides the context within which the meanings of the Locus of Attention (LoA) are negotiated and established. The viewers read the following experiential meaning:

(12)

The redeemed Christian Church of God 2017 Holy Ghost Congress	(presents)	*songs of victory*
carrier	process: intensive	attribute

Those who become victorious, (class membership - carrier) congress participants, are those who sing songs (attribute) of victory. There is also the assumption that the viewer already has a relationship with God which can be upgraded 'to higher levels' of experiences. However, this has to be inferred by the viewers, who will experience a higher level of relationship with God when they attend the Higher Life Conference with Pastor Chris, though implicitly expressed through the complement to the Locus of Attention (Comp. LoA) in the HLC handbill where we see captions of beautifully dressed people listening with rapt attention to the message of the gospel as exposed by Pastor Chris. There is a Relational Attributive, Intensive process, between the Primary Announcement (Headline), and the Lead (Main Visual Display). The Attribute *Higher Life* in the headline or Primary Announcement is invested into the Carrier (that is, the LoA in the Lead) by virtue of their proximity, thus causing viewers to see the LoA as a higher life personality. This headline provides the context for the viewers to adopt a preferred thread of meaning intended by the advertisers. The sophisticated looking LoA in Figure 2 is a visual exemplification of the statement *"Higher Life"* (in Christ). Again, a Relational Identifying: Intensive process occurs in the investment of meaning from Lead to Announcement. Through this Identifying, Intensive process, viewers read the following meaning in the advertisement: a higher life is the value exemplifying the token Pastor Chris.

(13)

The LoA	represents	'higher life (in Christ)'
token	identifying: intensive	value

The meaning which emanates from this juxtaposition between the verbal to the visual element portrays what higher life is all about, that of a beautiful life in Christ without sickness and disease, and that Pastor Chris represents this reality. The meaning is further exemplified in the Comp. LoA showing clips of healing miracles that characterize the ministry of the LoA. This can be deduced from the Relational processes that invest meaning bi-directionally from the headline/primary announcement to Lead, and vice-versa, resulting in semantic equivalence between Lead and Announcement, which Barthes (1977) refers to as anchorage. This is an advertising strategy used by advertisers to foreground the LoA as viewers' attention are directed to salient characteristics of the LoA which are contextually relevant for the purpose of the programme. The Comp. LoA captions depicting participants 2, 3, and 4 presuppose that anyone who comes needing a healing miracle will receive it, thus, interpersonally and ideationally, enhancing the salience of the LoA (Cheong 2004: 168). The word of God has the power to transform lives and move a person from one level of relationship to a higher level (Bible, John 7: 8, 10: 10). This is a life of all-round prosperity, general wellbeing (Bible, 3 John 1: 2), and aspirations to greater ideals that can produce better citizens with positive mindsets out of a nation; hence, such programmes are characterized by mass crowd as depicted in the background of the HLC handbill. The importance of the above is hinged on the fact that without Christ one cannot enjoy the benefits of a higher life.

Figure 3:   Screenshot of HLC handbill on *Multimodal Analysis Image* software showing catalog, annotations, available system choices, selected system choices, and description of system choices.

In the above Figure 3, the principal actor's reactions are non-transactive because Pastor Chris is looking out of the frame at something the viewer cannot see. These choices relate to his personality as 'a man of God', a prophet imputed with supernatural powers. However, the sub shots (Comp. LoA) in the bottom of the handbilll contain images of people in the real world, people with real problems who seek solutions from powers beyond the physical realm. This is alluded to in the Scriptures which state that Christians live in this world, but they are not of this world (Bible, John 17: 16). So, we see Pastor Chris inviting the unseen viewer to contemplation between the natural and spiritual world.

(14)

(You)	(attend)	*Higher life conference*	*United Kingdom*	*with Pastor Chris*
beneficiary: recipient (Goal)	process: material	*Actor*	circ. location	circ: prep phrase (accompaniment)
participant	process	participant	circ.	participant

From the point of view of interactive meaning, the viewer is positioned closer to Pastor Chris than to the other images in the Comp. LoA. This is expressed through camera angle known as eye level which represents the view point of the viewer because the viewer is looking straight at the image (LoA) captured in medium shot, while the Comp. LoA are long shots, with the crowd behind the LoA, and the miracles in front, below the image of the principal actor. His gaze, that is not so directly at the viewer, constitutes an image act known as *offer*, in tandem with the explanation above, which is that the viewer is the subject, while the represented participants are the object of the viewer's scrutiny because no direct contact is

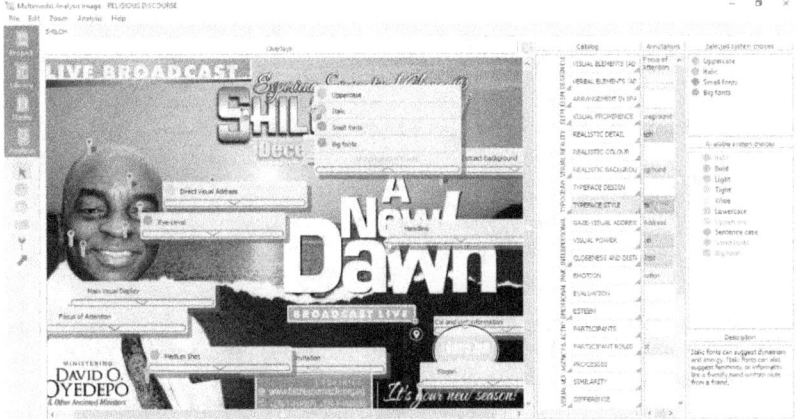

Figure 4:   Screenshot of Shiloh handbill on *Multimodal Analysis Image* software showing catalog, annotations, available system choices, selected system choices, and description of system choices.

made. The LoA is 'offered' to the viewer, as item of information, object of contemplation; hence, he is depicted as a concept. The higher life becomes the Actor who unfolds Pastor Chris (Accompaniment) to the viewer (Goal) who must attend the conference to experience an upgrade.

The Shiloh handbill has a similar orientation which correlates that of the HLC handbill (Figure 4). However, the reverse is the case, in terms of representational meaning, depicted by camera angle. While the gaze-visual address is *offer* in the HLC handbill, it is a *demand* act in the Shiloh handbill. The advertisers 'demand' that the viewers experience a life characterized with supernatural transformations. This is seen in the use of mainly imperatives and an adjectival phrase as analysed below. The meaning generated through the transitivity process is that Bishop Oyedepo, the Actor, addresses the Recipient to sign up for a life of supernatural transformation. This is realised through the bi-directional investment of meaning between the linguistic and visual components (LoA and Headline) where the Tag enhances the meaning projected by the headlines (PA). The investment of meaning from the headline to the LoA is that the supernatural change will be felt (phenomenon) as an experience in Shiloh; hence, the Actor directly addresses the Sensor, who is the Viewer. In the second most prominent headline which is the theme of the conference, it is expressed the fact that participant viewers (beneficiary) will be identified (identifier) with the new dawn acquired from the programme, while the tag further amplifies the meaning already generated as a result of the juxtaposition between Headline and Lead:

(15)

s/n	sensor	mental: affect	phenomenon	circumstance: location
1	(You)	*experience*	*supernatural change*	*at Shiloh 2017*
2	(It)	(is)	*a new dawn*	(for you)
	identified	rel. process: intensive	identifier	beneficiary

(16) Headlines Tag

(It)	(is)	*your*	*new season*
identified	Intensive	beneficiary	identifier
token			value

The positive emotion radiated by the actor (a smiling face) represents a direct address at the viewers as he is looking directly at the viewers. Thus, the subject is relating with the object transactively.

The typeface style used, and the abstract background, further reinforces the direct address to the viewer who is compelled to dwell more on the main visual display as there is no detailed background to serve as distraction, hence adopting the preferred reading path intended by the advertisers.

6. Conclusion

This study has attempted a critical multimodal discourse analysis of church programme handbills. The objective of the study was to reveal the ideological messages contained in these handbills and findings indicate that producers of church programme handbills effectively utilise multimodal resources to direct viewers into their intended meaning, thereby projecting certain ideological stance such as victory in spiritual warfare, aspirations to higher ideals, and supernatural tranformations. The analysis is based on Kress & van Leeuwen's (2006) visual grammar approach and Cheong's (2004) Generic structure potential for multisemiotic text. The multimodal image analysis software 2013 deployed in the analysis further correlates findings. The interpretative space (IS) in religious advertising is narrow and the semantic effervescence is further constricted because the context is strictly religious. There is, therefore, no rigmarole or confusion to arrive at the meaning of elements since there is already a context of situation, and culture, within which interpretations must occur. The interaction between visual components (the Lead, LoA, and the Compliment to the Locus of Attention), represented in the software as Main Visual Display, Focus of Attention, Visual prominence (foreground, background), Interpersonal relations (gaze- visual address), Visual power (camera angle), Closeness and Distance (camera shot), the linguistic components (Headline, primary and secondary announcement), and the tag (where available in religious print discourse) create the narrow interpretative space, and semantic effervescence under which interpretations occur. Therefore, this study succinctly accounts for the interactions between the purposive juxtaposition of verbal and visual elements of a text by the producers/advertisers in order to impart their ideologies to their viewers. The analytical frameworks for this study have been successfully applied to unravel the underpinning meanings communicated in church programme handbills and lend credence to the power of ideological discourse to produce better citizens.

References

Barthes, R. (1977). In S. Heath, (Ed.) *Image-music-text*. London: Fontana.
Burianova, M. (2010). A relevance-theoretic perspective on the ideology of Christian advertisement. Retrieved from http://www.iiste.org/Journals/index.php/RHSS/article/download/342779/35262.
Cheong, Y. (2004). The construal of ideational meaning in print advertisements. In K.L. O'Halloran (Ed.) *Multimodal discourse analysis*, London: Continuum, 163-195.
Eldin S. (2014). Critical discourse analysis of religious sermons in Egypt-case study of Amr Khalid's sermons. *International Education Studies* 7 (11): 68.
Esimaje, A. (2012). A corpus-based lexical study of sermons in Nigeria. Retrieved from http://dx.doi.org/10.5539/elt.v5n9p24.
Eun-Young, J. (2016). Persuasive strategies in a chauvinistic religious discourse: The case of women's ordination. *Critical approaches to discourse analysis across disciplines* 8 (1): 58-83.
Graham, B. (2017). *The Mystery of incarnation*. Retrieved from https://www.billygraham.org/decision-magazine/december-2017
Halliday, M. (1978). *Language as social semiotic*. London: Arnold.
Jewitt, C. (2009). (Ed.). *The Routledge handbook of multimodal analysis*. London & New York: Routledge.
Kress, G. and van Leeuwen, T. (2006). *Reading images: The grammar of visual design*. 2nd ed. London: Routledge.
Kress, G. and van Leeuwen, T. (2001). *Multimodal discourse: The modes and media of contemporary communication discourse*. London: Arnold.
Lemke, J.L. (1998). Multiplying meaning: Visual and verbal semiotics in scientific text. In J.R. Martin & R. Veel (Eds.), *Reading science* (87-113). London & New York: Routledge.
Lim Fei, V. (2011). *A systemic functional multimodal discourse analysis approach to pedagogic discourse*. Retrieved from http://www.multimodalstudies.wordpress.com/.
Machin, D. and Mayr, A. (2012). *How to do Critical Discourse Analysis: A multimodal introduction*. Los Angeles: SAGE.
O'Halloran, K. (2008). Systemic functional-multimodal discourse analysis (SF-MDA): Constructing ideational meaning using language and visual imagery. *Visual Communication*. Retrieved from http://vcj.sagepub.com/content/7/4/443.
O'Halloran, K. Tan. S, Wignell, P., & Lange, R. (2017). Multimodal recontextualisations of images in violent extremist discourse. In S. Zhao, E. Djonov, A. Björkvall & M. Boeriis (Eds.), *Advancing multimodal and critical discourse studies: Interdisciplinary research inspired by Theo Van Leeuwen's social semiotics*. London/NewYork: Routledge.
Olowu, A. (2013). Christians' perception of the concepts of death and judgment: A multimodal discourse analytical study of selected editions of *Christian Women Mirror* Magazine. *International Journal of English and Literature* 4 (10): 508-515.
O'Toole, M. (2010). *The language of displayed Art*. 2nd ed. London & New York: Routledge.
Oyakhilome, C. (2018). *Rhapsody of realities*. Lagos: Love World Publishing.
Oyebode, O., Unuabonah, F. (2013). Coping with HIV/AIDS: A multimodal discourse analysis of selected HIV/AIDS posters in south-western Nigeria. *Discourse and Society* 24 (6): 810-827.
Ravelli, L. (2010). Systemic-functional grammar. In K. Malmkjær (Ed.). *The Routledge Linguistics encyclopaedia* (3rd ed.). London/New York: Routledge, 524-537.
Sperber, D., & D. Wilson. (1986). *Relevance: Communication and cognition*. 2nd ed. Oxford: Blackwell.
Sperber, D., & D. Wilson. (2004). Relevance Theory: In L. R. Horn &G Ward (eds.) *The handbook of pragmatics*: 607-632.

Taiwo, R. (2005). Forms and functions of interrogation in christian pulpit discourse. *Nebula* 2 (4):117-131.

Taiwo, R. (2006). Response elicitation in English-medium christian discourse. *Linguistic Online*, 26 (1/06): 127-143.

Power in Institutional Discourse: An Analysis of Admission Letters of some Public Universities in Ghana[1]

Kodwo Adam-Moses & Charles Marfo

Kwame Nkrumah University of Science and Technology (both)

Abstract

The major concern of this paper was to explore the ways power is enacted, expressed, and concealed within the social context of University Admission Letters (UALs) in three public universities in Ghana. With the use of van Dijk's (1989) framework of social power and discourse control, it was observed that power manifests in UALs in the form of threats, command, regulation, and recommendation. It was also found that passives, declaratives, and abstract rhetors are rhetorical strategies employed to conceal power in this discourse type. The study makes a contribution to the literature on the relationship between discourse and institutional power and draws attention to the role of ideology in this discourse, especially in terms of the theory of social cognition.

Keywords: institutional discourse, Admission letters, Ideology, Power, Control

1. Introduction

The study of power as an ideology often enacted, concealed and/or legitimized in discourse is as old as language itself. At the macro level, whereas some studies have concentrated on the role that power or dominance plays in language variation and style (e.g. Scherer & Giles 1979), others have discussed the role of power in cultures (e.g. Saville-Troike 1982). Here, feminist studies on male dominance and power in language have also received considerable attention (e.g. Kramarae, Thome & Henley 1983). At the micro level, on the other hand, are studies which have approached the study of power/dominance as an ideology from the perspective of societal power (Kramarae, Shulz & O'Barr 1984, Mey 1985). Others on this level have looked at the phenomenon from the viewpoint of personal power, especially in the area of interpersonal communication (Berger 1985, Seibold, Cantrill & Meyers 1985).

Central to most of the studies we have examined is the issue of discourse control, where questions such as who can say or write what to whom and in what situations are often raised. Also, frequently asked is who has access to the various forms or genres of discourse or the means of its reproduction. In all of these, there appears to be only one answer – the less powerful people are, the less they have

[1] We would like thank an anonymous reviewer for comments and suggestions made to this paper, which helped to improve and properly shape it. Of course, all imperfections are solely ours.

access to various forms of text or talk and that, ultimately, the powerless such as children, prisoners, defendants, students, and in some cultures, women have nothing to say when the more powerful are speaking. According to van Dijk (1989: 229), the production mode of articulation is controlled by what he describes as "symbolic elites". These include journalists, writers, artists, directors, academics, and other groups that exercise power on the basis of symbolic capital (Bourdieu 1977, 1984). He describes the symbolic elites as very powerful in deciding the discourse genres and even determining the topics, styles, or presentation of discourse. Indeed, besides the political, military, and economic elites, the symbolic elites play an essential role in the ideological framework for the exercise or maintenance of power in the realms of information and communication in societies. This symbolic capital is not limited to articulation per se; it also extends to the mode of influence, it wields to set the agendas of public discussion, influences topical relevance, and manages the amount and type of information. This power, thus, becomes the manufacturer of public knowledge, beliefs, attitudes, norms, values, morals, and ideologies. Hence, symbolic power is also a form of ideological power.

As has been observed by scholars such as Ragan (1983), West (1984), Edelman (1974), Edu-Buandoh & Ahialey (2012) and Harris (1984), one of the domains of discourse where power is believed to be constantly at play is institutions of social bureaucracy; e.g. business corporations, the hospital, prison, court and, especially, the school. The popular notion observed by these scholars and others who share a similar opinion is that the less powerful almost always assume a more passive stance in the discourse in such institutions. They are, thus, expected to speak or give information only when they are requested or ordered to do so. Even though the literature (such as cited above) abounds on the suggestion that there is a great deal of scholarship on power dynamics in institutional discourse, there is one discourse type in higher institutions that seems to have received no attention; i.e. University Admission Letters (hereafter, UALs).

As in all other forms of institutional discourse, in UALs, the relation between discourse and power is dire. There is, however, a direct manifestation of the power of class, group, or institution of position or status (Bernstein 1975, Mueller 1973, Schatzman & Strauss 1972). Following van Dijk (1989), we observe that the production of power in UAL discourse type is made manifest in some resources that are exclusive to the representatives of the universities. That is also to say, in UALs, the more powerful group is that of administrators or representatives of the universities who tend have access to an increasingly wide and varied range of discourse roles, genres, occasions, and styles. They also control the discourse they engage the applicants with. In most cases, the applicant is obliged to completely heed to the content of the document and without any questions. This study, therefore, sets out to investigate the strategic role of the agents of the UAL discourse in the reproduction of the sociocultural hegemony we have identified or professed. It seeks to examine how power is signalled, expressed, or concealed in the UAL discourse. We also pay attention to the various strategies that are used to do so. The main aim of the study is to show that language use in this way should not be seen as a mere means of enacting or indicating power. Rather, power should be viewed as a relevant societal force behind discourse.

The rest of the paper is structured as follows: in the following section (2), we adopt and explore a conceptual framework within which our analysis will be captured. Section 3 is devoted to our methodology of analysis and data gathering. Results of the study are determined and discussed in section 4. Section 5 concludes the study.

2. Conceptual framework

2.1. The concept of ideology

In both classical and modern senses, ideology is a very complex concept whose definition usually generates controversies. However, it is generally described as a set of beliefs underlying the socioeconomic, political and cultural practices of group members in such a way that their interests are realized (Brown 1973, Kinloch 1981, Manning 1980). More often than not, the ideological practices derived from the ideology are acquired, enacted, or organized through various institutions such as the state, the media, the church or education, as well as informal institutions such as the family (van Dijk 1989). From the classical Marxist perspective, the dominant ideology in a given period is usually the ideology of those who control the ideological reproduction, namely the ruling class. Conversely, the dominant groups or classes tend to conceal their ideology (i.e. interests) and aim to get their ideology accepted as a general or natural system of values, norms, and goals. In that case, ideological reproduction assumes the nature of consensus building, and the power derived from it takes on a hegemonic form. We assume this understanding or sense of ideology as the traditional one.

In this study, our use of ideology deviates a little from the traditional sense of the word. Following van Dijk (2008: 34, 2012: 24), we assume that 'ideology is a form of social cognition shared by members of a group, class, or other social formation' and that 'their sociocognitive nature is more elemental'. An ideology, for us, therefore, is a complex cognitive framework that controls the formation, transformation, and application of other social cognitions such as knowledge, opinions, attitudes and social representations, including social prejudices (e.g. Fiske & Taylor 1984, van Dijk 2012). In this case, the relevant social norms, values, goals, and principles are selected, combined and applied in a way that favours perception, interpretation and action in social practices that are in the overall interest of the group. That is, an ideology assigns coherence among social attitudes, which in turn co-determines social practices. From the foregoing, therefore, we contend that our position is different from much of the classical works on ideology which focus on macro-analyses of society. Rather, we pay attention to the actual structures and processes at the micro level of the operation of ideology. This helps to establish a link between societal or group ideologies and the power structures they determine, conceal, or legitimize with concrete social practices of intra or intergroup interaction, including the precise role of discourse in ideological formations.

Discourse and communication remain central to institutions and groups. For that matter, they are connected to institutional and group ideology in their establishment, understanding and transmission. In fact, they can be described as central role players in the formation of ideology. In this regard, the examination of who controls the processes that control the means, or institutions of ideological (re)production such as the media or education, becomes relevant. Therefore, as Roloff & Berger (1982) explain it, it is important to note that discourse and, in particular, the discourse of powerful institutions and groups is the essential social practice that manages the beliefs that underscore an ideology.

2.2. The concept of power

In the broad field of language and discourse studies, what 'power' is, where it is located, and how it can be analysed are questions that continue to be vehemently debated. In this study, however, we attempt to give a scant discussion on the various positions on the phenomenon and see how it has informed sociolinguistic and critical discourse analytic research. We conclude by paying attention to its relevance to the analysis of institutional discourse.

From the behavioural perspective, power is conceptualized as a matter of individual agency, something which resides in individuals rather than in organizations (Dahl 1957). Power in this sense, therefore, can be compared to the notion of power in physics where the action of one force can be measured in terms of the effect it has on another. In contrast to this position is the structural model in which power is conceptualized as ideological and hegemonic (Lukes 1974). Hegemonic power is capable of shaping people's perceptions, cognitions and preferences and, on this, Hall (1982: 65) contends as follows:

> in such a way that [social agents] accept their role in the existing order of things, either because they can see or imagine no alternative to it, or because they see it as natural and unchangeable, or because they see it as divinely ordained or beneficial.

This view of power has been pervasive in many accounts of the relationship between power, ideology and social discourses. A more recent view of power within the poststructuralists' theories is that it is a community of practice. Eckert & McConnell-Ginet (1992: 492) particularly explain a community of practice as '[where] social meaning, social identity, community membership, forms of participation, the full range of community practices, and the symbolic relationship of linguistic form are being constantly and mutually constructed'.

The understanding of power in this way makes the symbolic function of language key, lending credence to Bourdieu and Wacquant's (1992) account of power as 'symbolic capital', which has been found by many sociolinguists to be an effective framework for understanding the relationship between language and power. In this framework, Bourdieu reiterates that some social practices are more valuable than others. Thus, knowledge and/or exhibition of those practices put some people in potentially more powerful positions than others. This is the conceptualization of power this paper uses; i.e. power from the angle of society, hence social power, where one group (or its members) could be said to have power over another group (or its members) and where the potential actions of the more powerful group is an exercise of social control over the less powerful one.

3. Methodology

We apply discourse analysis in its broad sense as methodological basis in the current study, on the grounds that it provides a fruitful method for research in communication, culture and society. As an interdisciplinary approach, discourse analysis is helpful in analysing the role of language in many different social domains, including organizations and institutions (Jorgensen & Phillips 2002). It particularly deals with how entities such as 'language' and 'the subject' are to be understood. Thus, it suggests that our ways of talking do not neutrally reflect our world, identities and social relations but, rather, play an active role in creating and changing them.

3.1. Data description

The study focuses on three public universities in Ghana – University of Ghana (UG), Kwame Nkrumah University of Science and Technology (KNUST), and University of Cape Coast (UCC). These are public institutions with the autonomy to run all manner of programmes and degrees. These three universities were selected because they seem to represent the traditional institutions of higher learning in the country, probably due to the length of time they have been in operation as compared to the other ones. Also, considering the fact that these public universities in Ghana are the mother institutions from which the other public universities gained their autonomy, drawing data from them to represent all the public universities in Ghana is appropriate.

For the purposes of providing common grounds for comparison, letters from the same year and level were chosen from these universities and that is undergraduate admission letters for the 2013/2014 academic year. Since the contents of the undergraduate admission letters from each of the universities are the same, only three admission letters, one from each of the universities, were used for the extraction of data.

3.2. Data analysis procedure

In an attempt to understand the types, characteristics and organisational aspects of the UALs as social products, we employed content analysis as a methodological means of analysing written texts. The actual analysis of the data was done at two levels. First, each clause was numbered, and the clause type assigned against it. Based on the perspectives of Downing & Locke (2006) and Quirk et al. (1985), the pragmatic function (i.e. illocutionary force communicated) of each of the clauses was determined. An inter-rater reliability test was conducted to authenticate the correlation between each of the structural types of the clause and its function. The result of the respondents' ratings yielded 89% reliability. The clauses whose illo-cutionary force suggested enactment or concealment of power were then coded, using the number of the clause and an abbreviated form of the institution.

4. Results and discussion

Following the provision of a theoretical framework on the notion of power through succinct analysis and the observation of our methodology, in this section, we con-tinue by looking into how power is actually expressed, signalled, concealed, re-produced, or legitimized in our defined domain of institutional discourse; i.e. UALs of public universities in Ghana. We set out to analyse the strategic role of discourse and its agents (i.e., university administrators) in the reproduction of the suggested form of sociocultural hegemony. As noted earlier, we argue especially that, rather than merely looking at language as a means of enacting power, power should be viewed as a relevant societal force behind discourse within our observed framework of social power and discourse control.

4.1. Manifestation of power in UALs

Based on the framework of social power and discourse control, we suggest four main signals as means through which power is enacted or indicated in UALs. These are threat, command, regulation and recommendation. As speech acts, they demonstrate that power in UALs may be enacted to exhibit certain illocutionary force that are all geared towards controlling the minds of the less powerful ones. It will become evident that whereas some of these signals of power could be overt, in other cases they are covert, bringing to the fore the possibility of concealing the acts of power. Table 1 presents a distribution of how the four main signals of power are expressed in their respective numbers in admission letters from the three se-lected universities.

Signals of Power	UCC		UG		KNUST	
	No.	%	No.	%	No.	%
Threat	13	46.4	5	16.1	6	35.3
Command	12	42.9	13	41.9	7	41.2
Regulation	3	10.7	10	32.3	3	17.6
Recommendation	0	0.0	3	9.7	1	5.9
Total	28	100	31	100	17	100

Table 1:   Distribution of signals of power in UALs

4.1.1. *Threats*

In line with our assumed typology, which postulates that discourses have the abil-ity of directive pragmatic function to control actions, we observe from Table 1 that the discursive enactment of power in UALs comes amply in the form of overt threats to the poor applicant, particularly in those of UCC (46%) and KNUST (35%). Examples of extracts given in (1) below illustrate how the universities issue direct threats.

(1)

    a) UCC 8: If you do not indicate your acceptance by the date indicated above, your place will be offered to another candidate on the waiting list.

    b) UCC 12: You will be withdrawn from the University if you fail to do the medical examination.

    c) UG 8: You will also be personally held liable for any false statement or omission made on your application form

    d) UG 21: This admission is, however, conditional.

    e) KNUST 3: Should the information you have provided be found at any instance to be false, … you will be dismissed from the University.

It can be seen from the above that each extract contains some element of threat. In UCC 8, UCC 12, UG 8 and KNUST 3 extracts, the threat can be understood as sanctions that will be applied to the applicants or students if they fail to meet certain conditions spelt out by the institutions. These sanctions, depending on what the applicant or the student is expected to do, range from complete expulsion or forfeit of admission. In UG 21 extract, the threat is even more serious as it suggests that the student's entire stay in the institution is probationary. We observe that the threats contained in the extracts in (1) are not far-fetched. That is, there are instances where one needs to dig deep to uncover the concealed threat. The data in (2) exemplify the concealed instances of threats.

(2)

    a) UCC 4: You will be on probation for the full duration of your program.

    b) UCC 5: Satisfactory academic work and good conduct are required for your continuous stay on the program.

    c) UG 2: The University requires that you be declared medically fit by the Director of University Health Services.

    d) KNUST 10: Applicants are advised, in their own interest, to communicate with the University by correspondence.

On a critical look, one realizes that extracts in (2) suggest that the University reserves the right to apply any sanctions it deems appropriate to the student until and unless they conform. More importantly, in all of these there is the demonstration of hegemonic power, as the agents of this discourse are able to influence people's perceptions into believing that issuing threats is a natural way of communicating in such institutions and cannot be changed (Hall 1982). The ideological implication of this analysis is that the enormity of power these symbolic elites wield does not only shape public knowledge, but also transforms public beliefs and opinions as well as attitudes (Petty & Cacioppo 1981, Roloff & Miller 1980). Thus, no matter how pervasive and entrenched this hegemonic display of power may seem, it is considered by the students and, by extension, the general public as legitimate.

4.1.2. Command/Instruction

As also found in the study, power is also signalled by the use of command/instruc-
tion in the UALs of all the universities to an appreciable extent (40%+). As noted
earlier, by virtue of their symbolic capital, the agents of this discourse wield social
power that enables them to control the actions of the students through command.
The command is indicated in the letter by some specific expressions of direction.
Some of the commands are exemplified in (3) below.

(3)
  a) UCC 17: Your admission number and programme should be quoted on the back of
     the pay-in slip.
  b) UG 11: Ensure that your ID number is quoted on the pay-in slip.
  c) KNUST 13: You should indicate in writing whether or not you accept this offer of
     admission …

While the statements given in (3) profess a sense of command, we observe that the
expressions should be, ensure, and should indicate in particular, underscore the
command to control the less powerful (i.e. the students). This, by no small measure, helps to maintain the power base of the more powerful, in this case the agents
of the institutions.

4.1.3. Regulation/Law

Although minimally, it was again found in the data that the use of regulation/law
is yet another means of expressing power in UALs. As observed by van Dijk
(1989), the power of the university administrators is an institutional power which
finds its source in some laws that support. In the extracts below, we get the impression that the decisions being communicated by the administrators in the letters
are policies that the students are obliged to abide by. The data in (4) exemplify
instances of this case.

(4)
  a) UCC 2: It should therefore be noted that the University does not award scholarship
     to students.
  b) UCC 8: A change in programme is NOT ALLOWED.
  c) UG 2: You will be required to take and pass all prescribed courses during the first
     year.
  d) UG 12: The University itself does not offer financial assistance to students.
  e) KNUST 4: In line with current University policy, you have been affiliated to
     QUEENS Hall.

Observing the data in (4), admittedly, the signal is not immediately evident except
in KNUST 4. It is evident only in KNUST 4 where the expression university policy
is used to explicitly inform us of a source to a regulation/law. Thus, it could be
overlooked. However, as could be discerned from all the examples, some individual pieces of information provided are policy inclined; i.e. 'the University does
not' in UCC 2, 'NOT ALLOWED' in UCC 8, 'take and pass all prescribed courses

during the first year' in UG 2, and the 'The University itself does not offer' in UG 12. These suggest that, ideologically, the policies are laws in themselves, and that one cannot contest them even in the court of law and be successful. It, then, becomes binding on all so long as the services of the university are still required.

4.1.4. *Recommendation/Advice*

Last but not least, recommendation was identified as another way by which universities in Ghana signal power in their admission letters. As could be observed from Table 1, however, it is interesting to note that the use of this signal was hardly prevalent. As compared to the others, it hardly featured on the UALs of the selected universities. We exemplify it in (5) below.

(5)
    a) UG 12-13: The University itself does not offer financial assistance to students. There is, however, an optional Students' Trust Fund (SLTF) under which registered Ghanaian students, who are not on study-leave, may obtain a loan.
    b) UG 22: For your information, however, there are graduate hostels for which you may apply separately for accommodation.
    c) UG 23: You may, if interested in graduate hostels, make enquiries from the Manager of the hostels: P. O. Box LG571, Legon.
    d) KNUST 12: To apply for accommodation, please check for availability of bed space at your Affiliated Hall.

As the symbolic elites, the administrators of this institution entrench the base of their power, capitalizing on the knowledge they have on how things operate within their setup. Thus, by providing assistance such as those given in (5) to the student, they assume the position of the knowledgeable who should always be relied upon whenever information is needed. It is undisputable that providing such guidance falls within their mandate as administrators. However, the ideological role beneath this gesture far outweighs the notion that they are doing their work as administrators. It may be disputable to claim that power play is more at work than the call of duty. However, from the perspective that it is commonplace among symbolic elites to be blinded by the institutional power they are entrusted with, our claim here is in reality not far-fetched. In fact, we also determined this from an 'extra data'. Through a quick check with some students at UCC and KNUST, it became evident that the university administrators are definitely indispensable, and they do well in presenting themselves as such. However, these students, also generally and forcefully, made the point that the administrators have often portrayed the student as a novice whose survival depends on their (administrators') guidance. For us, this suggests nothing less than exhibition of power and cannot be explained to exclude power play.

From the foregoing, we postulate that discourses have the ability of directive pragmatic function (i.e. elocutionary force) to control actions following van Dijk (2008; 2012). According to this typology, and as we have variously observed, speakers (in the present case, administrators) often have an institutional role and their discourses are often backed by institutional power. Thus, compliance in this case is often obtained by legal or other institutional sanctions.

4.2. Concealment of power is in UALs

Following van Dijk (1989), it has been noted that dominant groups attempt to conceal their interest, but with the aim of getting their ideology generally accepted as a general or natural system of values, norms, and goals. This section strives to examine the linguistic strategies that are used to mitigate or conceal the illocutionary force the observed signals/speech acts suggest. From our data across the universities, three strategies were identified: the use of passive structures, declaratives, and the university as an agent. The distribution of these strategies is summarily captured in Table 2 below:

Rhetorical Strategies	UCC		UG		KNUST	
	No.	%	No.	%	No.	%
Passives	16	76.2	10	62.5	4	44.4
Declaratives	2	9.5	4	25	4	44.4
Univ. as Agent	3	14.3	2	12.5	1	11.2
Total	21	100	16	100	9	100

Table 2:   Distribution of strategies used to conceal power in UALs

4.2.1. *Passive constructions*

As suggested in Table 2, one of the linguistic strategies employed by the administrators of the institutions to conceal power is the passive construction. Even though the use of passives in an official institutional discourse like UALs certainly marks a form of formality, its preponderance in the current data denotes concealment of ideological power (of distance). In this manner, the social agents of the discourse consciously attempt to make use of passives to give directives in order to mitigate the threat the directive might be to the face of the recipients. The data in (6) elucidates this.

(6)
    a)   UCC 19: A change of programme is NOT ALLOWED [by ...].
    b)   UG 3: The conditions spelt out in paragraph 2 below [by ...] will have to be met for you to assume the full status of a student.
    c)   UG 8: You will also be personally held liable [by ...] for any false statement or omission made on your application form.
    d)   UG 24: You are required [by ...] to indicate acceptance of this offer as soon as possible.
    e)   KNUST 9: Fees must be paid [by ...] through any branch of the listed banks and major post offices as specified in the attached schedule fees.
    f)   KNUST 15: Any acceptance letter delivered by hand SHALL NOT be processed under any circumstances.

It is interesting to note here that, although all the extracts in (6) can be described as passive constructions as indicated, per their communicative functions, they can further be grouped into two. That is, on the one hand, UCC 19, UG 3, UG 8, and KNUST 15 as one group only give information. On the other hand, UG 24 and KNUST 9 constitute the other group that gives direct order for an action to be carried out with the use of the expression required, and must, respectively. Generally, however, through the use of passive voice as an ideological tool, the agents cleverly hide their involvement, or make themselves unknown or unimportant, so that the unpleasant nature of the message would not be felt by the student and blamed on them.

4.2.2. *Declaratives*

Another linguistic strategy this study found in the data as concealment of power was the use of declaratives to issue commands. Indeed, there are a few instances in the data where instructions are given in direct imperatives as exemplified in (7) with the use of the expression note that and ensure that in UCC 11 and UG 9 respectively. That is to say, the bulk of similar instructions are given in declaratives. This choice can be said to be ideological in nature since declarative structures, rather than imperatives, help mitigate the illocutionary force meted out in direct imperative structures. Thus, instead of giving the instruction in an imperative structure as in (7), they are issued in a declarative in the structure/pattern '[subject + be + to infinitive]' as the data in (8) below exemplifies and indicates in bold. In a few instances, as in (9), the pattern is that of '[subject + aux verb + main verb]'.

(7)
    a)   UCC 11: Note that attendance at matriculation is compulsory for all fresh students.
    b)   UG 9: Ensure that your ID number is quoted on the pay-in-slip.

(8)
    a)   UCC 6: You are to note that if the University discovers later that you do not in fact possess the qualifications by virtue of which you have been offered admission to this programme, you will be withdrawn immediately.
    b)   You are also to note that your admission is subject to your being declared medically fit to pursue the programme of study in this University.
    c)   KNUST 17: You are to quote your reference number (xxxxxxx) and programme (xxxxxx) in all correspondences and payments to the university.

(9)
    a)   KNUST 13: You should indicate in writing whether or not you accept this offer of admission ...

The import of the illocutionary force (i.e. command/instruction) given in each of the extracts above could have equally been achieved by simply asking the recipient/student in a more direct imperative form. However, as a negative politeness strategy (Brown & Levinson 1987), the writer chooses the declarative structure to reduce the force of the command which may be face threatening to the student.

Even better, there is the use of the auxiliary will for the sole purpose of making the instruction the verb denotes more futuristic. In this manner, as found in the examples given in (10) below, it is believed that the illocutionary force in the utterance is made distant and somewhat delayed in its threat to the face of the student.

(10)

a) UG 15: You will need your student number and PIN stated above to gain access to the University's online registration.

b) UG 20: You will be required to bring with you a chest X-ray for … examination.

4.2.3. *Use of the University as social agent*

The final rhetorical strategy we observed as having been employed in the data to conceal power is the absence of writer agentivity. Here, unlike the use of passive constructions to reduce the author's responsibility as seen above, the institution itself (i.e. the University) is depicted as a social agent who directly gives the information. The data in (11) below show this situation.

(11)

a) UC 16: The University reserves the right to revise the fees anytime without notice.

b) UC 21: The University re-opens on Saturday, August 11 … and all fresh students should report to their assigned halls of residence.

c) UG 12: The University itself does not offer financial assistance to students.

d) UG 18: The University requires that you be declared medically fit by the Director of University Health Services.

e) KNUST 6: The University re-opens for the 2014/2015 Academic Year of Friday, August 15, 2014.

From (11), the University is presented as a human being and is made to assume full responsibility of whatever is being given to the student. According to Hyland (1995: 34), the use of this strategy he calls "abstract rhetors" suggests that the situation described is independent of human agency. The motivation of its use is that the writer does not wish to be associated with, committed to, or personally held responsible for the information given. By so doing, the administrators of the institutions hide behind the faceless institution to show their power. In this way, they attempt to conceal their demonstration of power, which in itself is ideological.

5. Conclusion

We have examined the relationship between social power and discourse throughout this paper. Appealing to the framework of social power and discourse control toward the achievement of sociocultural hegemony, which has substantially been explained as usually in the interest of the powerful, we focused on social power in terms of institutional control over actions and cognitions of other people. Exploiting data from admission letters of three public universities in Ghana, dubbed discourse of UALs, it has become evident that power manifests through directive speech acts such as threats, commands, regulations, and recommendations.

In furtherance of our analysis, it has also been exhaustively observed that the illocutionary force of these directives is often concealed in some rhetorical strategies including passive constructions and declaratives, rather than imperative structures and agentless clauses in the form of abstract rhetors where the university is presented as a social agent.

References

Berger, C. R. (1985). Social power and interpersonal communication. In M. L. Knapp & G. R. Miller (Eds.) *Handbook of interpersonal communication*. Beverly Hills, CA: Sage, 439-496.

Bernstein, B. (1975). *Class, codes, control* (Vols. 1-3.). London: Routledge & Kegan Paul.

Bourdieu, P. (1977). *Outline of a theory of practice*. Cambridge: Cambridge University Press.

Bourdieu, P. (1984). *Home academicus*. Paris: Minuit.

Bourdieu, P. and Wacquant, Loïc J. D. (1992). *An invitation to reflexive sociology*. Chicago: The University of Chicago Press.

Brown, L. B. (1973). *Ideology*. Harmondsworth: Penguin.

Brown L. B., Levinson S. C. (1987). *Politeness: Some universals in language usage*. Cambridge: Cambridge University Press.

Downing, A. and Locke, P. (2006). *English grammar: A university course* (2nd Ed). London and New York: Routledge.

Edu-Buandoh, D. F. and Ahialey, H. O. (2012). Exploring the ideological implications of questions in elicitation in courtroom cross-examination discourse in Ghana. *Language, Discourse and Society* 2(1): 11-30.

Edelman, M. (1974). The political language of the helping professions. *Politics and Society* 4: 295-310.

Fiske, S. T. and Taylor, S. E. (1984). *Social cognition*. Reading, MA: Addison-Wesley.

Hall, S. (1982). The rediscovery of "ideology": Return of the repressed in media studies. In M. Gurevitch, T. Bennett, J. Curran and J. Woollacott (Eds.), *Culture, society and the media*. London: Methuen.

Harris, S. (1984). Questions as a mode of control in magistrates' court. *International Journal of the Sociology of Language* 49: 5-27.

Kinloch, G. C. (1981). *Ideology and contemporary sociological theory*. Englewood Cliffs, NJ: Prentice-Hall.

Kramarae, C., Schulz, M. and O'Barr, W. M. (1984). Towards an understanding of language and power. In C. Kramarae, M. Schulz, & W. M. O'Barr (Eds.) *Language and power*. Beverly Hills, CA: Sage, 9-22.

Kramarae, C., Thorne, B. and Henley, N. (1983). Sex similarities and differences in language, speech, and nonverbal communication: An annotated bibliography. In B. Thorne, C. Kramarae, and N. Henley (Eds.) *Language, gender and society*. Rowley, MA: Newbury House, 151-331.

Lukes, S. (1974). *Power: A radical view*. London: Macmillan.

Manning, D. J. (Ed.). (1980). *The form of ideology*. London: George, Allen & Unwin.

Mey, J. (1985). *Whose language: A study in linguistic pragmatics*. Amsterdam: Benjamins.

Mueller, C. (1973). *The politics of communication: A study of the political sociology of language, socialization, and legitimation*. New York: Oxford University Press.

Petty, R. E. and Cacioppo, J. T. (1981). *Attitudes and persuasion: Classic and contemporary approaches*. Dubuque, IA: Wm. C. Brown.

Quirk et. al. (1982). *A comprehensive grammar of the English language*. London: Pearson Longman.

Ragan, S. L. (1983). Alignment and conversational coherence. In R. T. Craig and K. Tracy (Eds.) *Conversational coherence*. Beverly Hills, CA: Sage, 157-171.

Roloff, M. E. and Berger, C. R. (Eds.). (1982). *Social cognition and communication*. Beverly Hills, CA: Sage.

Roloff, M. E., & Miller, G. R. (Eds.). (1980). *Persuasion: New directions in theory and research*. Beverly Hills, CA: Sage.

Saville-Troike, M. (1982). *The Ethnography of communication*. Oxford: Basil Blackwell.

Schatzman, L. and Strauss, A. (1972). Social class and modes of communication. In S. Moscovici (Ed.) *The psychosociology of language*. Chicago: Markham, 206-221.

Scherer, K. R. and Giles, H. (1979). *Social markers in speech*. Cambridge: Cambridge University Press.

Seibold, D. R., Cantrill, J. G., & Meyers, R. A. (1985). Communication and interpersonal influence. In M. L. Knapp and G. R. Miller (Eds.) *Handbook of interpersonal communication*. Beverly Hills, CA: Sage, 551-611.

van Dijk, T. A. (2012). Structures of discourse and structures of power. In J. A. Anderson (Ed.) *Communication yearbook 12*. London, UK: Routledge, 18-59.

van Dijk, T. A. (2008). *Discourse and power*. New York: Palgrave MacMillan.

van Dijk, T. A. (1989). How "they" hit the headlines: Ethnic minorities in the press. In G. Smitherman-Donaldson and T. A. van Dijk (Eds.) *Discourse and discrimination*. Detroit: Wayne State University Press, 18-59.

West, C. (1984). *Routine complications: Troubles with talk between doctors and patients*. Bloomington: Indiana University Press.

Stance-Taking in Online Political Discourse: A Study of News Report and Opinion Articles

Helen Ufuoma Ugah

Abstract

There are daily evaluations by Nigerians on the progress or otherwise of All Progressives Congress (APC) in heralding change in Nigeria. Nigerians take their stances on, and also evaluate President Muhammadu Buhari's and APC's general performance since the party took over the rein of leadership from President Goodluck Jonathan, the PDP candidate, in 2015. This study examines the grammatical markers of stance-taking in news reports and opinion articles on the APC's "Change" agenda posted on *Nairaland,* and *Sahara Reporters.* It sets out to test Biber's (2006) theory of grammatically marked stance, which has hitherto been applied to only academic context, and on online political discourse. Ultimately, stance-taking in this study can be firmly grounded in the way news and opinion article writers portray their opinions of the politicians through their use of grammatical stance markers.

Keywords: political discourse, stance, news writing, grammar

1. Literature Review

Interactions in writing include positioning one's self or adopting a point of view in relation to the topic of discussion, as well as the contrary opinion of other participants that might partake in the interaction. Stance, which is one of the ways of managing interactions, according to Hyland (2005: 176), expresses a textual voice and can be seen as "an attitudinal dimension which includes features that refer to writers' representation of themselves and how they stamp their personal authority into their arguments, or step back and hide their involvement".

Stance, as a linguistic phenomenon, can be investigated and classified from different angles. Several researchers have characterised stance in different dimension: stance is socially constructive and dynamic (Dubois 2007: 163, Maroko 2013: 49), stance is relational and psychological (Scherer 2005: 706), stance is socially and culturally bound (Precht 2003: 243), stance is epistemic and interactional, stance is investigative and is expressed through intensifiers (Martin & Rose 2003: 38), and stance is used to show opinion and authority (Sayah et al. 2014: 594).

Biber's (2006) model has been previously applied to academic genre and this is seen in the works of Adams and Quintana-Toledo (2013). A number of the earlier studies on stance-taking have focused on academic contexts, political interview, legal genre, offline job portals, etc. (Haddington 2004; Moini & Salami 2015). For instance, Biber (2004) examined the entire system of stance devices in order to explore historical change in the preferred devices used to mark stance. This shows that stance devices change over time, across genres, and registers. This is proved to be true in Biber (2006), where the use of a range of lexico-grammatical features for the expression of stance, and the major pattern of register variation in the marking of stance in academic and student management registers were compared. Findings revealed that the expression of stance is important in all university registers and that there are important register differences in the particular kinds of stance meanings that are expressed. Hyland's (1998) study on the pragmatics of academic discourse across twenty-eight research articles portrays that metadiscourse reflects a way in which context and linguistic meaning are integrated. This, in his opinion, is to allow readers to derive intended interpretations. However, current studies on stance-taking are situated within the context of online communication.

Several linguists have examined language as a tool for communication, as well as its use in different contexts, especially on the Internet (Noci 2012: 86). Moreover, research efforts have focused on people's opinion on several phenomena and situations in different online forums. For instance, Chiluwa (2011a) analysed participants' interactional norms and pragmatic strategies used to express political opinion in *Nolitics,* a Nigerian online political forum. He concludes that Nigerians are willing to participate in political matters that affect them, and that the internet is a viable tool for political mobilization and participation. In Chiluwa (2011b), he analysed participants' expressions in giving out unsolicited advice in the life-style blogs of *NaijaPals,* an online community website, and arrives at the conclusion that participants give unsolicited advice through the use of narrativity, and directive and indirective speech acts. David et al. (2006) examined features of identity, language use, and gender in teenage blogs. Ifukor (2010b) evaluated readers' comments on the Nigerian 2007 general elections and discovered that Nigerian bloggers and tweeters, during elections, use the tool of mobilisation to educate, enlighten, and encourage eligible voters to avail themselves of the opportunity to perform their civic duties. Taiwo (2009) analysed the use of interrogations in online forums and concluded that *wh-* and *yes/no* questions are the predominant questions types used by the participants in the forums. Silva (2013) has investigated audience participation, and modes of political discussion in Brazilian presidential election. All these studies noted above do not have a clear portrayal of the opinionated use of language in political online news, neither do they make clarifications on how language is used by online news, and opinion article writers, to give opinion about election processes, political leaders and their political parties, and the actualization or otherwise of political party manifesto. They also do not evince how Nigerian citizen journalists use language to construct their perception of Nigerian political leaders in power before and after elections.

Several scholars have also carried out research on the use of stance features in different online forums. Meyer (2010) looked at the way writers of blogs mark their stance as a way of presenting their own contribution as distinctive, showing their entitlement to a position. Putman et al. (2012) examined the use of stance in student participants' responses and postings on online discussion forums. Taiwo (2016) investigated the use of cognitive verbs and stance taking in Nigerian jobs, and career portals online, and discovered that the expression of cognition through the use of the verb *think* in the corpus is similar to its use in English as a mother tongue speech context. Chiluwa (2015b) examined the features of stance in tweets of *Boko Haram,* and *Al Shabaab,* and discovered that self-mention and attitude markers are the most prevalent features of stance in radicalist discourse.

From the foregoing, some gaps emerge. One, it appears that there is an impasse on news report and opinion articles: are reporters being objective, or do they take a stance in their reporting? Two, can Biber's (2006) model be applied to other genres aside from academic genre, for example, political discourse? Thus, this study set out to fill these two gaps: examine online political discourse whether it is objective, or reporters use stance taking, and test out the applicability of Biber's (2006) model on political discourse.

2. Materials and Methods

The data for this study was downloaded from *Sahara Reporters,* and *Nairaland* between November 2016 and May 2017. *Sahara Reporters,* and *Nairaland* were selected because they have more content than other online forums such as *Premium Times, Nigerian Village Square, Pulse,* etc. In addition, both forums cover a lot of political discourse of the APC's 'change agenda' and the forums are popular among Nigerians who publish stories, comment on and assess politicians and political events in Nigeria. *Sahara Reporters* is a website created to provide up-to-date news, especially political news, while *Nairaland* is a general interest site that also features news and opinion articles. The data comprises forty news and opinion articles on the All Progressives' Congress' 'change agenda (henceforth APC) before (2013-2015) and after (2015-2017) Nigeria's 2015 general election. The news items are those received from citizen journalists and reported by *Sahara Reporters,* and *Nairaland,* while the opinion articles are written by Nigerians that have something to say about Nigerian politics and the activities of Nigerian politicians. Though the data cuts across pre and post 2015 general election, the study does not compare the data between the two periods, 2013-2015, and 2015-2017. Twenty news and opinion articles were selected for each forum and further categorized into two: Pre-election data (PRE-A1-20), and Post-election data (POST-A1-20).

The analysis is purely descriptive. We used both qualitative and quantitative methods for the analysis. The news reports and opinion articles were read and instances of grammatical markers of stance were identified and categorised using Biber's (2006) framework of grammatically marked stance. Biber's (2006) framework encompasses the description of the lexico-grammatical features used for the expression of stance. It describes how many lexico-grammatical features in English can be used to indicate the personal stance of the speaker's or writer's personal feelings, attitude, value judgments or assessments. In other words, it approaches the study of grammatical expression of stance from the first-person subject since this contains the most overt expressions of speaker/author stance (Biber 2006: 98). The description of the lexico-grammatical features used for the expression of stance focuses on three major structural categories: Modal and Semi-modal verbs,

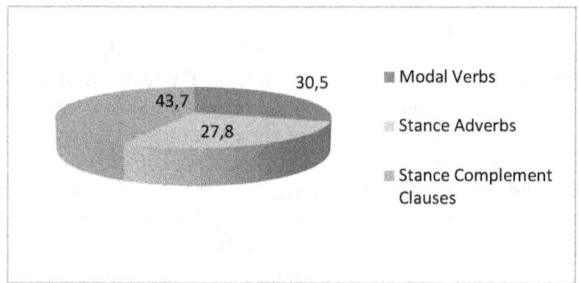

Figure 1: Grammatical stance markers in news reports and opinion articles on the APC's 'Change Agenda'.

Stance adverbs, and Stance complement clauses. The frequency of occurrence of the features are presented in tables and illustrated using figures. The main objectives are to identify stance features, and their functions in the data. This is to enable us test out the applicability of Biber's (2006) framework to the data.

3. Results and Discussion

In this section, we analyzed the data using Biber's framework that identifies three semantic categories of stance, namely: Modal Verbs, Stance adverbs, and Stance Complement clauses. Their frequency of occurrence is captured in the figure below.

From the chart in Figure 1, it can be noted that stance complement clauses (the *-to* and the *-that* clause) are more frequently used when compared to modal verbs and stance adverbs. The interpretation of the use of grammatical stance markers is further explicated in the sub-sections below.

3.1. Modal Verbs

3.1.1. *Frequency distribution*

In this sub section, we identify the frequency of modal verbs in the data. Biber (2006) grouped modal verbs into three categories, according to their main meanings: possibility/permission/ability, necessity/obligation, and prediction/volition.

Modals	Frequency	%
Prediction/Volition	152	50
Possibility	70	23
Ability/Necessity	81	27
Total	**303**	**100**

Table 1: Frequency of modal stance markers

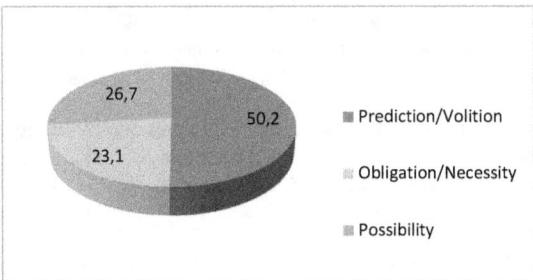

Figure 2:   Frequency of modal stance markers.

Table 1 shows preponderance use of modal verbs as stance markers with Prediction/Volition modals occupying the highest frequency (50%), followed by ability/necessity modals (27%), and possibility modals (23%). This result shows that modal stance markers are not evenly distributed in the data, although ability/necessity, and possibility modals are almost evenly distributed in the data. The frequency pattern is illustrated in Figure 2.

3.1.2. *Functions of Modal Verbs*

The prediction/volition *will* is the most common of all the modals used in the news reports. In the pre-election news report, it is used to make predictions on the politicians who will run under the umbrella of a party, the party that would likely herald positive development in Nigeria, the party that would most likely win the election, and general predictions about the elections. Consider below an extract from the data:

(1)   **PRE-A14** "If the Federal Government allows a level playing field for all contestants, if the security agencies stop acting as the armed wing of the ruling PDP, if the electoral umpire **will** carry out its duties without fear, favor or bias and if citizens are allowed to exercise their franchise unmolested, the stage **will** be set for non-violent, free, fair and credible polls"

The use of *will* in the extract above, though consistent with the general meaning of prediction/volition modal, appears conditional as parties involved need to play their parts in ensuring violent free election. The parties involved need do their part and play their appropriate role for the election to be violence free.

The modal *would*, on the one hand, is used to disseminate information that can be regarded as a rumour, while *can*, on the other hand, is used to show epistemic likelihood. Consider the examples below.

(2)   **PRE-A2** "Our investigations have confirmed that ... Lagos, and the entire South West, being a stronghold of the All Progressives Congress (APC), has been marked for massive disheveling commotion that **would** involve killings, maiming and kidnapping".

(3) **PRE-A9** "APC has no moral right to pioneer the affairs of this nation. **Can** a good leader talk about Nigerian seeing the THUG in them if they loose come 2015. To me this is the voice of cowards who knows quite well he or she **will** be defeated in an open context".

Can, in example (3), is used to question the leadership quality of the APC. The use of *will* and *should* in the latter part of the extract above is an admonishment to the APC to desist from the violent acts they have been known for. *Will* is also used to show certainty in the data:

(4) **PRE-A8** "Former Nigeria's president Olusegun Obasanjo has spoken about General Muhammadu Buhari (retd). Obasanjo said that incumbent President Goodluck Jonathan ... do not want him to contest because they believed that he **will** win and come for them. ... "Buhari **cannot** listen to anyone about his certificates because as a General of Nigeria Army, he will speak when he chooses".

Will, in example (4), is not just used for prediction/volition, as indicated by Biber (2006) in his work, but it is also used as a marker of certainty.

Obligation/necessity modals, which are the least used modals in the data, are used to take a stance on what has to, or should not be done, by political participants before and after they win the election. One of the most popular modal in this category is *must,* though there are others like *ought to, need to,* etc. Instances of their use can be seen in the extracts below.

(5) **PRE-A1** "To do that, the APC **must** demonstrate the capacity, not just the rhetoric, for democracy... **must** set clear standards, and demonstrate that those standards are higher than partisan politics and the APC itself".

(6) **POST-A17** "The parlous state of the Nigerian economy by the 29th of May, 2015 **should have** instructed an incisive and urgent macroeconomic stabilisation programme to realign the price levels in the economy The incoming administration **should not** have been told that we were weak and vulnerable. ...So, it is accurate to conclude that both the preceding and successor governments conspired by their actions and inactions to throw the Nigerian economy into the deep throes of economic recession of which it **must** be rescued in order to avoid social implosion."... "The citizens **must** place a demand on the government to implement right economic policies".

(7) **PRE-A8** "APC **should** prepare to bomb police stations like they did in the last election. Tinubu **should** bring out money to sponsor juju men that **will** use oruka ano sare (hit and run amlet) and oruka warapa (amlet for epilepsy)... they **should** prepare themselves to take over power by force. ....obasanjo and his friends **should** be ready to count the cadavas on the street of nigeria since they want to see Nigeria plung into the Former state of Rwanda".

In PRE-A1 *must* is used to show a passionate expression of stance that strongly emphasises what the APC is obliged to do, while, in PRE A8, *should* is used to demonstrate a weak obligation, as well as sarcastically insinuate that members of the APC are thugs. But in POST A17, *should* is used to express disappointment in Nigerian leadership.

According to Biber (2006), Possibility modals express several meanings ranging from likelihood to in/ability and permission. Although they are the least used modals in the news report, they are used by the news and opinion article writers to express their opinion of what might have been done to forestall or prevent a negative occurrence, and sometimes used as hypothetical statements. The most common of these modals in the news reports and opinion articles are *can/could*, with and without the negator *not*.

(8) **POST-A17.** "Had the government made quick and necessary adjustment ..., our story **could** have been different today. .... We needed a policy response that **could** have enabled that adjustment to happen ... That response **could** have helped the economy to absorb the shock. It **could** have reassured the investors. It could have reassured the consumers. It **could** have helped us...."

(9) **POST-A10.** "According to the party's statement, no serious governance could go on if the billions of naira in a few hands were not recovered... In addition, the APC disclosed that $2.1 billion from the Excess Crude Account **could not** be accounted for".

(10) **POST-A19**"....our problem is self centredness. ... "Tell me, how many of our leaders can make sacrifices for our country?"

In POST-A17, the writer uses *could* hypothetically to insinuate that Nigerian current and past leaders are incompetent. The writer in POST-A19 above uses the modal *cannot* to express disappointment in the APC and dissatisfaction with Nigerian politicians' method of leadership, while, in POST-A18, *could not* is used to indicate that the statement is a fact.

3.1.3. *Stance Adverbs*

Biber (2006) grouped stance adverbs into four categories, according to their main meanings: epistemic certainty, epistemic likelihood, attitude and style/perspective.

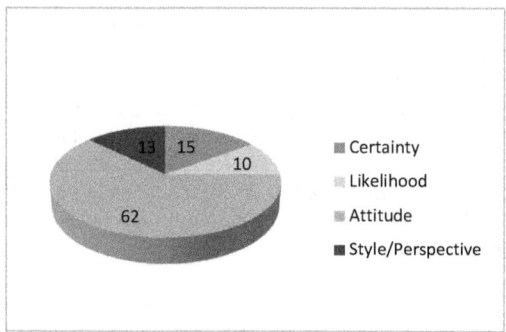

Figure 2:   Frequency of stance adverb markers.

Figure 2 above shows a cornucopia of the use of adverbs that express attitude in the data. Adverbs in this category occupy the highest frequency (62%), followed by the adverbs that express certainty which have a frequency of 15%, style/perspective adverbs of 13%, and adverbs that express likelihood of 10%. It appears that the last three adverbs are rarely used in the data.

3.1.4. *Functions*

In this section, the functions of stance adverbs are described. This section analyses the data describing the functions of the stance adverbs. Epistemic adverbs, according to Biber (2006), are known to express the speaker's judgement about the certainty, likelihood or reliability of the proposition or the source or information. Consider the examples below:

(11) **POST-A11** "The Governor of the Central Bank of Nigeria, Mr. Godwin Emefiele, has predicted that the nation's economy will **likely** come out of recession by the fourth quarter of this year when the result of the various measures put in place by the Federal Government. ... While reacting to the governor's optimism that the recession would start easing off in the fourth quarter, economic and financial experts said on Sunday that it would be **nearly** impossible for the nation to come out of recession this year".

(12) **PRE-A1** "The new party has outlined its priorities to include agricultural development, jobs, free education, ... Does the APC have the political and patriotic capital to pay for it? I **certainly** hope so, but the new party may be looking at the microscope from the wrong end. **Regrettably**, that is the same exhaust pipe from which the PDP has always looked at the country ... How is the APC to be seen to be programmed to serve, and not **simply** to serve its members?"

(13) **PRE-NR12** "Nigeria and Nigerians are not **truly** ready for change, they prefer the status quo, because many of them are benefitting **immensely** from the many loopholes of the system".

(14) **POST-NR8** "One might as well add unpaid salaries to millions of workers in the public and private sectors. These are the realities of our lives these days. Were these part of the change agenda? Were these the promises made to Nigerians during the campaigns? **Probably** not, at least, I never heard anybody in the APC campaign trail saying things were going to get so bad for us. So the Vice President of Nigeria was right; CHANGE was a slogan devoid of content during the last elections".

The five examples above engage the four different types of adverbs treated in this theory: epistemic, likelihood, attitude and style/perspective. In the example PRE-A1, the opinion article writer uses the epistemic adverb *certainly* emphatically to express absolute confidence in the APC's ability to fulfill the promises in their manifesto. However, registers have doubts about the APC being different from the PDP by using the advert *regrettably,* which is an adverb of attitude, to presume that the APC might make the same mistake made by the PDP which caused them to fail in governance. The use of *simply*, which is also a marker of attitude, is used by the writer to strengthen the truth value of his/her position on the reliability of the APC. In the example POST-A11, Emefiele's choice of the hedging expression *likely* indicates the state of his understanding and, at the same time, reduces the strength of his claims simply because a stronger statement would not be justified. In the same report, other financial experts are reported to negate his opinion with the use of the epistemic adverbs *nearly impossible*. The writer in PRE-NR12 uses *truly* as an assertion of certainty to clarify his/her attestation that Nigerians are not ready for 'change' despite their claims that they are.

The examples below encompass the use of attitude adverbs.

(15) **PRE-A17** "It is **largely** around this question that a choice will probably be made. It is **pointlessly**, and **dangerously** provocative to present General Buhari as something that he probably was not. It is however just as purblind to insist that he has not **demonstrably** striven to become what he most **glaringly** was not, to insist that he has not been chastened by intervening experience and most **critically** - by a **vastly** transformed environment both the localized and the global".

(16) **POST-A19** "As far as I am concerned, a lot of what we heard from Buhari, from the leading members of the party was sloganeering and that **unfortunately** hasn't helped him. This cannot be reversed it is **absolutely** absurd for people who haven't won election, who cannot organise a ward election, to be making the pronouncement they are making on behalf of Buhari ... **Frankly** speaking, I find that disgusting and disgraceful and I want to assure you that whether Buhari is well enough to talk or not well enough to talk, ...those spokespersons cannot claim to speak on behalf of Buhari, because **occasionally** they don't have the true picture. ... Nigeria's president must be a man who is **nationally** and **internationally** exposed ... That's not the case with Buhari, we need somebody who is **sufficiently** confident of himself, so that the country can move forward".

(17) **POST-A18** "The APC noted with satisfaction that the vast majority of Nigerians "are **vehemently** opposed to the few who would rather have the government of the day turn a blind eye to the looted funds and ... According to the APC, 3.8 trillion naira out of the 8.1 trillion naira ... was **illicitly** withheld by the Nigerian National Petroleum Corporation (NNPC)".

(18) **PRE-A20** "We believe Nigerians shall speak **eloquently** on 28th March, 2015 and this brutality on the psyche of the Nigerian people shall cease."

The writer in PRE-A17 uses the attitude adverb *pointlessly and dangerously provocative* to register his opposition to the presentation of Buhari as a saint or a repented dictator. The use of the adverbial phrase shows the passion of the writer towards his stance, as well as his resolve to strengthen the truth-value of his claim. The writer's use of *demonstrably*, *glaringly* and *critically* increases the force of his statement, and also shows that his opinion is not just a bare assertion but a fact. The use of *vastly* by the writer intensifies this.

In example POST-A19 above, the opinion article writer expresses his disdain for Buhari's and the APC's inability to fulfil their 'change' mantra by using several attitudinal adverbs (*unfortunately, absolutely, sufficiently*) and few perspective adverbs (*frankly, nationally*, and *internationally*). By deploying the attitudinal adverb *unfortunately*, the writer insinuates that the 'change' mantra has been to Buhari's disadvantage and has had bad effects on him and his style of governance. Through the use of the attitudinal adverbial phrase *absolutely*, which is both a booster as well as a marker of intensification, the writer registers his/her disappointment in Buhari's sick leave. There are several instances of the use of style/perspective adverbs in the data. For instance, the writer's use of *frankly*, which is a style/perspective adverb in POST A19 above, evinces that his/her opinion of President Buhari's actions is honest and not in any way biased. The use of *nationally* and *internationally* by the same writer shows the magnitude of Buhari's lack of exposure as a leader.

Stance adverbs are not only used by news reporters and opinion article writers. They are also used by the members of the APC at the pre- and post-election news reports. Members of the APC use stance adverb in the pre-election news reports to register their confidence in the vote of Nigerians at the election. This is usually done through the use of attitude adverbs. For instance, in PRE-A20, the APC expresses their belief that the results of the general elections will show who Nigerians are in support of: APC or PDP. The use of the word *eloquently* indicates that the APC is confident that the APC is sure that the result of the election will show who Nigerians are in support of and that they are not afraid of the outcome. Stance adverbs are also used by the APC leaders in the post-election news reports to promote themselves, defend their actions, and demonstrate to Nigerians that they are working very hard to bring their manifesto to reality. For instance, the extract from POST-A18 above, the reporter uses *vehemently* as an attitudinal adverb that projects intensification to point out that they agree with most Nigerians that the APC

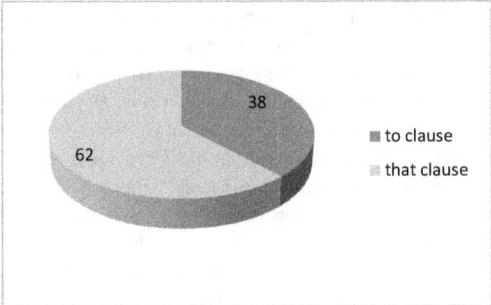

Figure 4: Frequency of stance complement clauses.

should recover all the public fund looted by the PDP. Through the use of the attitudinal adverb *illicitly* in the same article, the writer strengthens the force of his stance about the PDP being financially motivated.

3.2. Stance Complement Clause

Biber (2006) categorized stance complement clauses into *-that* clauses, and *-to* clauses. This is captured in Figure 4.

The chart above portrays that there is a much more frequent use of *-that* clauses than *-to* clauses in the data. This section will analyse the use of the *to*-clause and the *that*-clause by the reporters or reported voices, and opinion article writers, to indicate their stance on the proposition or topic of discussion.

3.2.1. Functions of Stance Complement Clauses

The *-that* complement clause can be preceded by nouns, verbs, or adjectives. They usually express the writer's attitude or assessment of likelihood. The *-that* clause is used by the reporters or opinion article writers to state a writer's opinions or report someone's opinion. They are also used to state what members of the APC said before and after the election, what people said about the APC, as well as to show the attitude of the writers. These types of clauses abound in the pre-and post-election news reports and opinion articles. The extracts below are examples of some *-that* complement clauses found in the pre-election data.

(19) **PRE-A1** "This will **demonstrate that the party understands the quality of the challenge that is before our nation**, and that it intends to subordinate itself to it. The APC must **understand** that it will be held to a higher standard than the PDP because, by its nature, it has proclaimed itself to be the superior of the two".

(20) **PRE-A5** "We have **heard** from Nigerians who are so afraid about possible violence during the forthcoming election **that they are even willing to relocate to other countries
until after the elections.** But, as the biggest opposition party in Nigeria and a major
stakeholder in our nation's democracy, we are **assuring**, on our part, **that there will be
no violence.** The party **added** that it demonstrated, during its recent rancor-free and
festive national convention in Lagos, that elections should be a celebration of democracy,
rather than a moment of fear, violence, and threat to lives. The **APC stated that it had
taken practical steps, as far back as May 2014, to work with the PDP to ensure vio-
lence-free polls in 2015**".

(21) **PRE-A18** "However, the APC does not intend to ride into power on a mere rhetoric of
'change'. **The change that we   propose is fundamental in many ways as it is critical
to the very survival of our country.** .... . How can a party or a government even begin to
solve a **problem** that it does not believe exist? Like in all things, PDP is stuck in denial.
The **promises** that we make reflect our innermost **belief that the people must be at the
centre of development**. Especially, we believe that any economic growth that leaves the
majority of the people behind, and does not protect the weakest and the vulnerable among
us, is merely delusionary".

The extracts from PRE-A1 and PRE-A5 above contain instances of verb
headed -*that* clauses. The verb headed -*that* clause in the second sentence from
PRE-A1 above acts as the object of the certainty verb *understand*, which is preceded by a high modality verb of obligation *must*. Certainty verbs are used to show
that a case is true to the extent that it is almost regarded as a fact. The use of this
verb by the writer purports that the statement embedded in the -*that* clause is a fact
and not just the writer's opinion. The -*that* clause of first sentence in the same
extract, which is preceded by the attitudinal verb *demonstrate*, connotes expecta-
tion. This is an indication that the writer is not indifferent about the outcome of
APC winning the election.

In PRE-A5, the writer uses the -*that* clause that is preceded by the epistemic
verb *heard* to epistemically show the APC is sympathetic towards Nigerians and
their concern about safety during the election. The -*that* clause preceded by the
verb *assuring* evinces a stance of commitment. The writer uses it to show that the
APC is committed to protecting the lives and properties of Nigerians. The latter
part of this extract contains communication verbs-headed -*that* clauses. This type
of -*that* clause marks the information in the complement clause as non-factive;
hence, it can be concluded that the information in the last two sentences of PRE-
A5 as used by the writer cannot be totally relied upon. The use of the communication verbs *added* and *stated* in the extract can also be interpreted as a strategy used
by the reporter to avoid responsibility for the truth value in the news report.

In PRE-A18, all the complement clauses identified are noun headed -*that*
clauses. These clauses usually comprise of the head noun (which is usually a pre-
sumption or an idea), plus the -*that* clause as a post modifier in the form of a subordinate clause. Noun headed complement clauses are sometimes used to enable
writers to demonstrate their position towards the proposition objectively by not
referring to anyone but to entities (Charles 2007). This makes the opinion or stance

in the sentence less open to dispute. The first three identified noun headed *-that* clauses in the extract contain nouns that perform epistemic functions and identify the information embedded in the sentences they are found as claims. Hence, the noun phrases *The change*, *A problem* and *The promises* that head the *-that* clauses identified indicate that the stances expressed in the clauses are all claims made by the APC. The use of this type of complement clause indicates a stance that is an expression of confidence in the APC. The noun headed *-that* clause in the last sentence of the extract contains a fact. The writer uses the *-that* complement clause headed by the noun phrase *our innermost belief* to portray that the APC has the interest of Nigerians at heart. The extracts below are some instances of the use of *-that* clauses after the election.

(22) **POST-A11** "I am not **sure that** *we can come out of recession this year. Already, we are at the end of the third quarter.* If the policymakers allow liquidity into the system and adopt appropriate measures, we may be lucky to come out of the recession early next year," a professor of Economics at the Olabisi Onabanjo University, Sherriffdeen Tella, said,"

(23) **POST-A17** "It was a major **mistake that the economy did not get timely and right type of** *policies that could have helped us avoid the calamitous collapse into negative growth in the* last three quarters of 2016. ... She stated, "The attendant fiscal pressure and the delayed right policy responses *were* **severe enough that by 2015, economic growth had sharply declined from 3.8 to 2.7 per cent**".

(24) **POST-A18** "The APC listed some of the instances of massive looting by former public officials, *declaring that it was important to arm Nigerians with the information to enable them to be aware of the gravity of the situation"*.

In the post-election data, *-that* clause preceded by verbs, nouns, or adjectives is used by opinion article writers to express disdain, dissatisfaction, and contempt at the APC and their actions, or to advocate on their behalf. Hence, *-that* clauses are used by the writers in the post-election articles to antagonise the APC or defend them.

In POST-A11, the adjective headed stance complement clause expresses negative epistemic likelihood. Through the use of the adjective *sure* as the head of the *–that* clause in extract 25 above, the writer expresses his/her doubt about the claims of the Central Bank Governor. In POST-A17 above, the writer expresses his/her dissatisfaction with the economic policies of former President Jonathan and current President Buhari through the use of the *–that* complement clauses headed by the adjectival phrase *severe enough*. This is both attitudinal, as well as evaluative.

To clauses are similarly preceded by nouns, verbs and adjectives. They are used by the reporters or the reporting voices to share other people's opinion regarding the topic of discussion. They are also sometimes used as indirect directives to the set of people being discussed or to defend an action. Consider the extracts below:

(25) **PRE-A5**. "All Progressives Congress (APC) presidential candidate Gen. Muhammadu Buhari yesterday asked Nigerians not to lose hope because change is imminent in the country. ... He **pledged** *to change the nation's debilitating dependence on crude oil to earn revenue*. Gen. Buhari, ..., **pledged** *to provide mass employment, adequate security, fight corruption, improve infrascptructure and good health care*".

(26) **PRE-A9** "To Nigerians, ApC has no moral **right** *to pioneer the affairs of this nation.* Can a good leader talk about Nigerian seeing the THUG in them if they lose come 2015. To me this is the voice of cowards who knows quite well he or she will be defeated in an open context...."

(27) **PRE-A18** "And if this government was more **sensitive** *to the enormity of the challenge that this presents*, it would be *reluctant to jump all over the place in self celebration while so many of our youths are wasting away*".

Just like what obtains in the use of *-that* clauses, *-to* clauses are also used by the writers in the pre-election articles to endorse the APC, state clearly their manifesto and how ready they are to make things better in Nigeria, and to make disparaging remarks about them. For instance, the verb *pledge* in verb headed *-to* clause of PRE-A5 above is used to portray Buhari as someone that can be trusted to improve the Nigerian economy.

The stance complement clause headed by a noun in PRE-A9 is used to indicate that the writer is disappointed at the APC. In PRE-A18 above, the adjective headed *-to* clause is accusative; it is used to portray the PDP as insensitive to the plight of Nigerian youth, while the APC is not. The stance embedded in this clause is an evaluative emotional assessment aimed at presenting the APC as competent, considerate, and sensitive. The extracts below contain *-to* complement clauses found in the post-election data.

(28) **POST-A16** "Many Nigerians are unhappy with the current state of the nation under the administration of President Muhammadu Buhari. Many **took** *to social media to lament the hardship the people are passing through, especially the persistent fuel scarcity in parts of the country* ... However, some other Nigerians called for patience, noting that the president has only spent 10 months in office and it still too **early** *to judge his administration*"

(29) **POST-A15** "President Muhammadu Buhari has said that before Nigerians **demand to see** *the changes he promised them during the 2015 election, they must first change their own attitude by shunning corruption and other social vices*. He adds that change is not about economic or social progress, but it is in terms of citizens' personal behavior".

(30) **POST-A1** "Since his inauguration, the President has been chasing after corrupt politicians and businessmen. But now, it has become **necessary *to remind President Buhari and his APC government that recovery of stolen money cannot be categorised as change by any stretch of the imagination*.** Recovery of stolen money was not exactly what Nigerians had at the back of their minds, or what they bargained for when they voted for change. ... From the look of things, Nigerian leaders will eventually not implement the change Nigerians desired and voted for because they have a mission. While, I do not **wish *to stoke any fire of discontent among Nigerian citizens,*** *is it not necessary to observe for instance that ever since the case was made to investigate the Senate President on certain charges, nothing seems to be happening?*"

Most of the articles in the post-election data contain opinions, attitudes, and reports that show Nigerians' disappointment with the APC's 'change agenda'. The extract above portrays the use of *-to* clauses to express these opinions. The verb headed *-to* clause in POST-A16 which contains the verb of intention/decision *took*, connotes the desperation of Nigerians and their persistence at insisting that something should be done about it. However, the adjective headed *-to* clause in the latter part of the extract is used evaluatively to insinuate that Nigerians are insatiable.

POST-A15 also contains a verb headed *-to* clause used as a communication or non-factual verb. The use of this type of verb also indicates that the information in the report may not be totally relied upon and the reporter cannot be held liable for the information since it is only a news report. POST-A1 above contains an adjective headed *-to* clause used for evaluative purpose. Through the use of this stance complement clause, the opinion article writer expresses his dissatisfaction with the APC government.

This section has portrayed that all the sub-categorisation of Biber's (2006) theory of grammatically marked stance are identifiable in political online news and opinion articles. The functions of the sub-categories in the data used for this study align with what obtains in Biber's (2006).

4. Discussion of Findings

Every news report contains the news writer's stance towards the text and also indicates how to understand their perspective or opinion towards the text (Haarman & Lombardo 2009). This is as a result of the fact that during the process of interaction, a range of linguistic features, according to Hyland (2005a: 173), contribute to writers' projection of a stance. This study uses online political discourse to validate the claim. In doing this, Biber's (2006) framework, which has been widely tested out on academic writing, is used on a different kind of data – online political discourse to ascertain its applicability on unfamiliar data. This study has so far identified in the data the frequency of occurrence of the grammatical stance markers categorized by Biber (2006). The application of the theory to the data revealed that the features of grammatical stance markers categorized by Biber (2006) are found in the data. Subsequent paragraphs below will interpret and discuss the findings.

There are copious uses of stance features in the data and they serve different functions to convey the positions of the writers/reporters. Through the use of modals, for instance, the writers make reference to salient issues in the Nigerian socio-political context like corruption, secession, endorsement of political aspirants, party manifesto, election malpractice, revolution, etc. These issues were quite pertinent to the successful conduction of the elections and subsequent development of Nigeria. More so, the repletion of prediction/volition modal in the data demonstrates that, at both election periods in the history of Nigeria, Nigerians were greatly interested in what the future holds for them in the light of the change of power. The occurrence of possibility modals in the data connotes that the writers are interested in how the actions or inactions of political leaders affect the country negatively or positively. The different manifestations of modals of obligation/permission connote the idealized perception of how the writers think elections should be conducted, politicians should behave before and after the election, and political leaders should perform their duties of ruling the country.

Stance adverbs in the data connote the different perception of the APC by the writers. Through these adverbs, the writers evince their feelings and attitude towards members of the party and their performance at different times. The use of epistemic adverbs indicates the level of certainty, or otherwise, of the writers. They are used to qualify their commitment, or otherwise, to the truth value in the proposition. Attitude adverbs, which are the most common of all the adverbs in the data for this study (about 61.7%), are the most significant for meaning. Through them, the writers express their feelings and attitude towards the proposition and the general topic of discussion, which is usually the APC, their 'change agenda' or their general performance. Stance adverbs indicate the portrayal of value judgments and assessments by the writers. Style/perspective adverbs indicate that the writers are always interested in how their readers take what they have written. The writers, through the use of these adverbs, evince that they want to be understood, believed, and classified as knowledgeable.

The choice of the use of stance complement clauses by the writers implies different degrees of support for the truth value of their opinion communicated through the use of verbs and other lexical items. They are used to show attitudinal or epistemic meanings directly or indirectly.

Biber's (2006) analysis of the use of stance in academic context was restricted to first-person pronoun expression of stance. However, in this research, it has been demonstrated that third-person pronouns are also core markers of stance. It has been also demonstrated that the theory is self-sufficient to account for the use of stance in political online forum; hence, it is highly applicable to online political discourse.

The findings from this study corroborate with the findings of previous studies which show that news report and opinion articles are difficult to be taken as objective, rather they contain the stance of the writers. Thus, this study lends to support to the report that news report and opinion articles (political discourses) are "…ideologically disseminated due to reporters' stance taking" (Martin &

White 2005: 300). This suggests that political discourse should not be taken and analyzed as neutral discourse without considering the ideological underpinnings.

The use of Biber's (2006) model for this study has confirmed its appropriateness in analysing political discourse. This underscores the point that, aside from academic genre, Biber's (2006) model can be applied to other genres, e.g. political discourse, as this study has shown. However, this latter claim is subject to further research in other genre because any generalization can be made.

5. Conclusion

According to the idealized view of new discourse, news article is objective. Thus, there would be no need for stance expressions. This study underscores, among other things, that online political discourse has a high degree of subjectivity as writers/reporters have been shown to be engaged in stance taking. In addition, the applicability of Biber's (2006) model to other genres other than academic discourse, which has dominated the literature or studies that have applied his model so far, the model can be applied to other genres although more studies must be carried to show the validity of the claim that there is a measure of subjectivity in online discourse. This study has so far proven that there is a degree of subjectivity in online news reports, especially political news. The expression of stance cuts across all facet of human communication, and the frequency of occurrence of grammatical stance markers found in the data has shown that online political forums are not left out. This study has so far proven that Biber's (2006) theory of grammatically marked stance, which has hitherto been used to analyse stance in academic context, can also be used to analyse stance in online political context. Though the interpretation of the use of stance in both contexts is not the same, the theory can adequately account for the use of stance in political contexts. Moreover, online forums have proven to be forums where people can express their views and opinions without fear or reservation; hence, the use of language in them is highly subjective and evaluative.

This study contributes to recent literature on political discourse in New Media Studies, and to empirical studies on the implication of 'free discourse' featured on the internet since the internet serves as a virtual window to understand the nature and reasoning of its users. The theory can also be applied to other contexts of human communication in order to ascertain its applicability to them.

References

Adams, H., Quintana- Toledo, E. (2013). Adverbial stance marking in the introduction and conclusion sections of legal research articles. *Revista de Linguistica y Lenguas Aplicados* 8, 13-22.

Biber, D., Johasson, S., Leech, G., Conrad, S. & Finegan, E. (1999). *Longman grammar of spoken and written English*. Harlow: Pearson Education Limited.

Biber, D. (2004). Historical patterns for the grammatical marking of stance: Across-register comparison. *Journal of Historical Pragmatics* 5(1), 7-136.

Biber, D. (2006). Stance in spoken and written university registers. *Journal for English for Academic Purpose* 5, 97-116.

Biber, D., Finnegan, E. (1988). Adverbial stance type in English. *Discourse Processes* 11,1-34.

Chandrasegaran, A., Kong, C. K. (2006). Stance taking and stance support in students' online forum discussion. *Linguistics and Education: An International Research Journal* 17(4) 374-390.

Charles, L. C. (2008). The processing foundation of head-final relative clauses. *Language and Linguistics* 9 (4) 813-838.

Chiluwa. I. (2011a). On political participation: Discursive pragmatics and social interaction in politics. *Studies in Literature and Language* 2(2)80-92.

Chiluwa, I. (2011b). Discursive pragmatics of unsolicited advice in the life-style blogs of *Naija-Pals* online community website. *Papers in English and Linguistics*, 12, 148-179.

Chiluwa, I. (2011c). *Labelling and ideology in the press: A corpus-based study critical study of the Niger Delta crises.* Frankfurt: Peter Lang

Chiluwa, I. (2014). Online negotiation of ethnic identity. *Current Issues in Linguistic and Literary Issues* 81-110.

Chiluwa, I. (2015a). Radical discourse: A study of the stances of Nigeria's Boko Haram and So-malia's Al Shabaab on *Twitter. Journal of Multicultural Discourses.* Retrieved from: http://dx.doi.org/10.1080/17447143.2015.1041964.

Chiluwa, I. (2015b). Occupy Nigeria 2012: A critical analysis of *Facebook* posts in the fuel sub-sidy removal protest. I CLINA 1 (1), 47-69.

Chiluwa, I., Ifukor, P. (2015). War against our children: Stance and evaluation in *#BringBackOurGirls#* campaign discourse on *Twitter* and *Facebook. Discourse and Society,* 1-30.

Chiluwa, I., Odebunmi, A. (2016). On terrorist attacks in Nigeria: Stance and engagement in con-versations on *Nairaland. Communication and the Public* (2016), 1(1), 91-109.

Crismore, A. (1983). *Metadiscourse: What is it and how is it used in school and non-school social science texts.* Urbana-Champaign: University of Illinois.

David A. H., Calvert, S. L. (2006). Gender, identity and language use in teenage blogs. *Journal of Computer Mediated Communication.* Vol.10, (2), 324-331.

Davis, A. (2010). New media and fat democracy: The paradox of online participation. *New Media and Society.* Sage Publications 12(5), 745-761.

Dubois, J. W. (2007). The stance triangle. In Englebretson, R. (Ed.). *Stance taking in discourse: subjectivity, evaluation, interaction.* Philadelphia: John Benjamins, 39-82.

Haarman, L., Lombardo, L. (2009). (Eds.). *Evaluation and dtance in war news: A linguistic anal-ysis of American, British and Italian television news reporting of the 2003 Iraqi war.* Contin-uum: New York.

Haddington, P. (2004). Stance taking in news interviews. *SKY Journal of Linguistics* 17, 101-142.

Hyland, K. (2005a). Stance and engagement: A model for interaction in academic discourse. *Dis-course Studies* 2005 (7), 173-192.

Hyland, K. (1998). Persuasion and context: The pragmatics of academic metadiscourse. *Journal of Pragmatics* 30, 437-455.

Hyland, K. (2005b). *Metadiscourse.* London: Continuum.

Ifukor, P. (2010a). Spelling and simulated Sibboleths in Nigeria computer-mediated communica-tion. In *English Today* 27, 35-42. doi:10.1017/S0266078411000368.

Ifukor, P. (2010b). "Elections" or "selections"? Blogging and twittering the Nigerian 2007 Gen-eral Elections. In *SAGE Bulletin of Science, Technology & Society* 30(6), 398-414.

Ifukor, P. (2011). Linguistic marketing in "... *A marketplace of ideas":* Language choice and intertextuality in a Nigerian virtual community. *Pragmatics and Society* 2(1), 109-147. doi 10.1075/ps.2.1.06ifu.

Maroko, G. M. (2013). Learning about author positioning in written academic discourse. *Argen-tinian Journal of Applied Linguistics* 1(2), 47-60.

Martin, J. R., Rose, D. (2003). *Working with discourse: Meaning beyond the clause.* London: Continuum.

Martin, J. R., White, P. R. R. (2005). *The language of evaluation: Appraisal in English.* Great Britain: Antony Rowe Ltd, Chippenham and Eastbourn.

Meyer, H. K., Carey, M. C. (2013). In moderation: Examining how journalists' attitudes towards online comments affect the creation of community. *Journalism Practice* 8 (2), 213-228.

Moini, R., Salami, M. (2015). Stance and engagement discourse markers in journals' author guidelines. *The Journal of Teaching Language Skills (JTLS)* 7(30), 109-140.

Noci, J. D. (2012). Mubarak resigns: Assessing the quality of readers' comments in online quality media. *Trípodos* 30, 2012, 83-106.

Precht, K. (2003). Stance moods in spoken English: Evidentiality and affect in British and American conversations. *Text* 23, 239-257.

Putman, M., Ford, K. & Tancock, S. (2012). Redefining online discussions: Using participant stances to promote collaboration and cognitive engagement. *International Journal of Teaching and Learning in Higher Education* 24(2), 151-167.

Sayah, L., Hashemi, M. R. (2014). Exploring stance and engagement features in discourse analysis papers. *Theory and Practice in Language Studies* 4(3), 593-601.

Scherer, K. R. (2005). What are emotions and how can they be measured? *Social Science Information* 44 (4), 695-729.

Silva, M. T. (2013). Online forums, audience participation and modes of political discussion: Readers' comments on the Brazilian Presidential Election as a case study. *Comunicación y Sociedad* 26(4), 2013, 175-193.

Silva, M. T. (2014). Portuguese news organisations and online audience participation: policies and self-perceptions. Paper presented at *JSS-ECREA: Journalism Studies Section Conference – Journalism in Transition: Crisis or Opportunity*, Greece, 2014.

Taiwo, O. O. (2007). Language, ideology and power relations in Nigerian newspaper headlines. *NEBULA: A Journal of Multidisciplinary Scholarship* 4(1), 218-245.

Taiwo, O. O. (2009) Interrogation in online forums. In Adika, G. S. K., Fabunmi F. A. & Salawu, A. S. *current perspectives in Phono-Syntax and Dialectology,* 342-368.

Taiwo, O. O. (2010). Social identity and discursive practices in Nigeria online forums. In Ekeanyanwu, N., Okeke, C. (Eds.). *Indigenous societies and cultural globalization in the 21st century: Is the global village truly real?*, 70-91.

Taiwo, O. O. (2016). Cognitive verbs and stance taking in Nigerian jobs and career portals online. *Marang Journal of Language and Literature*, 2016.

Zamith, R., Lewis, S. C. (2014). From public spaces to public sphere. *Digital Journalism* 2 (4), 558-574.

Hedging in Academic Discourse in Nigeria

Alexandra Esimaje

Benson Idahosa University

Abstract

The aim of this paper is to examine how hedging is marked in the scholarly articles of Nigerian academics. It identifies the linguistic forms frequently employed to hedge propositions in academic discourse in the context and compares that with established practice in other academic communities and cultures. Data for this study is a corpus of approximately 257,000 words representing 54 journal articles published in peer reviewed journals between the years 2010 and 2016. The work adopts the corpus method and is premised on the systemic functional view which sees language as social semiotic (Halliday 1978). The study showed that Nigerian academics are deliberate in the application of hedging in their writings and that the choice and frequency of use of such hedges as the modals - may, would, could, might and the evidential verbs – seem, appear, attempt, report and then judgment verbs – suggest, indicate, believe, which are among in the writing of senior academics in Nigeria. However, the quotative form notes, the judgement verb argue, and the adverbial form according to, seem to be peculiarly frequent in the Nigerian context.

Keywords: Academic researcher, academic discourse, hedging, journal articles.

1. Introduction

In academic communities, discourse is the mainstay of all activity; whether it is the creation, transfer, negotiation or the dissemination of knowledge. Therefore, the study of academic writing has, in the past three decades, attracted substantial attention. One of the areas of interest is stance, which is a desiderative practice in academic literacy because it establishes the status of the researcher in relation to other discursive participants and positions them to contribute to knowledge. Epistemic stance, hedging, which is the immediate focus of this paper, enables a writer to convey the level of his commitment to claims and is marked by the use of epistemic verbs, epistemic modals, epistemic adverbs, epistemic adjectives, and epistemic nouns.

Hyland (1997: 50, 2005: 178-181) defines hedges as "devices that indicate the writer's decision to withhold complete commitment to a proposition, allowing information to be presented as an opinion rather than accredited fact", and boosters as allowing "writers to express their certainty in what they say and to mark involvement with the topic and solidarity with the audience". Therefore, writers use hedges when in doubt of the veracity of a proposition, and boosters when certain of the claim of a proposition.

Furthermore, Hyland (1998: 349) argues that hedging and boosting enable "academics gain acceptance for their research claims by balancing conviction with caution, either investing statements with the confidence of reliable knowledge, or with tentativeness to reflect uncertainty or appropriate social interactions". As he says, and as is supported by Nkemleke (2011: 21), hedging prevents a face-threatening reaction from the reader which may result from a firm assertion and enables the building of a harmonious relationship. Hyland (1998: 352) summarises the importance of hedging, thus:

> minimises the potential threat new claims make on other researchers by soliciting acceptance and challenging their own work; [makes it] easier to satisfy disciplinary gatekeepers when negotiating peer review procedures by observing community expectations concerning collegial deference and limits on self-assurance; [and softens] interpersonal imposition. Moreover, hedges have also been seen as a way of anticipating the possible negative consequences of overstatement and the eventual overthrow of a claim. [Finally], by limiting their commitment with hedges, writers offer an assessment of the status of a claim, attesting to the degree of precision or reliability that it carries. Hedges imply then, that a statement is based on plausible reasoning rather than certain knowledge and allow readers the freedom to dispute it.

Nkemleke (2011: 22) corroborates these views when he says that academic language is a world of indirectness and non-finality. Citing Crismore and Fransworth (Nkemleke 2011: 22), he notes that "hedging is the mark of a professional scientist; one who acknowledges the caution with which he/she does science and writes science". In other words, a researcher needs to recognize that knowledge is in a state of constant flux, hence the need for caution, distance, politeness, respect, deference, seeking acceptance, for establishing tentativeness rather than absoluteness in presenting claims, making propositions, and for reporting findings. Hedging enables the negotiation of knowledge between writer/speaker and reader/listener to confirm that academic writing is a social act. The overall aims of hedging are, therefore, to create a harmonious relationship between the writer and his audience, whether immediate or extended, and to confirm membership of the academic community by conforming to agreed principles. Hedging, then, is a practice of the global academic community, a convention without which a scholarly work would attract resistance rather than acceptance, and the writer considered unprofessional or immature rather than credible. After all, knowledge is what people can be persuaded to accept (Rorty 1979 in Hyland 2009).

1.1. Hedging: state-of-the-art

A great deal of research has been reported on hedging in academic writing. For instance, Hyland & Milton (1997: 184) undertook a comparison of UK and Hong Kong students' use of doubt and certainty in their writings and finds that although both groups of students depended on a narrow range of hedging items, the Hong Kong students exhibited greater difficulty in manipulating the items, employing more syntactically simpler sentences and even a more limited range of items while making stronger commitments. Also, in a study of hedges and boosters in the argumentative essays of Japanese first-year university students, Macintyre (2013) reveals that students use them in their writing, even though they are confused about exactly how to use them, and this is because hedges and boosters have not received adequate pedagogical attention. He reports a study by Vassileva (1997: 3) in which the occurrences of hedging in a corpus of English research articles by native speakers, Bulgarian research articles, and articles written in English by Bulgarians were compared. This study shows notable differences in both the overall number of hedges and their distribution throughout the articles, which Vassileva (1997: 3) believes is due to "native-language transfer of academic writing standards where the Bulgarian language shows a higher degree of commitment and, therefore, a lower degree of hedging".

Ignacio Vázquez & Diana Giner (2009) examined the extent of conviction in the research articles in the academic disciplines of marketing, biology and mechanical engineering in order to investigate the effect of disciplinary conventions and epistemologies on the choice of interpersonal rhetorical strategies. The study portrays differences in the occurrence of boosters and hedges in the RAs selected and the researchers attribute this to "the nature of the data used for the research in each discipline, [as] each discipline tries to fulfill social needs in different areas [and] this appears reflected in the presence of these interactional elements" (Vasquez & Giner 2009: 235). The study points to "different rhetorical patterns in the construction of information as regards disciplinary variation, [and thus] different social needs constructing different disciplines. [Hence] whereas softer sciences seem to present a stronger need for enhancing the propositional content in the containing statements, harder sciences rely on the exactness of the data used in their research as sufficiently evidential to show the truth of their statements" (Vasquez & Giner 2009: 235).

In another study, Serholt (2012) investigated the use of epistemic modality by Swedish advanced learners of English to express doubt (hedges) and certainty (boosters) in their academic writings, and to interrogate whether there were gender-related differences. The study shows that females more than males demonstrated a slightly higher propensity for stronger commitments to propositions, but both displayed a substantially higher use of hedges than boosters. In his discussion of research articles from eight academic disciplines, Hyland (1998) noted that the use of hedges exceeds boosters by nearly 3 to 1 and remarks the need for claims to be presented provisionally rather than assertively. The study also showed disciplinary differences in terms of frequency of occurrence.

Other recent works on hedging in non-native Englishes are those of Beyer (2015) who examined hedging by German students and how they apply epistemic adjectives and adverbs in their BA and MA theses. The study indicates a preference for epistemic adverbs and a higher frequency in MA theses, which shows that advanced writers are more aware of hedging devices and their importance in academic writing. Similarly, Trajkova (2015) compared the application of hedging in the writings of Macedonian and German undergraduate students and discovered that although both categories of students hedge their writings, there were variations in both their distribution and pragmatic functions due to cultural differences. However, the German students were more productive in their use of hedges and boosters.

There are also a few studies of hedging in the African contexts. For instance, Nkemleke (2011) examined hedging in Cameroon English and found that modal verbs are in the highest frequency, followed by epistemic adjectives and evidential verbs. Likewise, Atechi (2016) studied the use of hedges and boosters by advanced learners in Cameroon and also determined whether gender plays a significant role in the use/choice. He reported that hedges were used more frequently than boosters, and females are more likely to use hedges than their male counterparts. Edusei (2016) examined hedging in Ghanaian English and compared the use by novice writers and expert Ghanaian writers on the one hand, and expert Ghanaian writers' and native speakers' writers on the other hand. The results show significant differences in the choice of hedges by academic writers in Ghana which point to the roles of language proficiency and experience. However, no notable differences were found in the use of hedges by expert writers in Ghana and native speakers' expert writers. Despite the importance of this phenomenon in academic writing and the rising interest in it, research into hedges and boosters in the academic contexts of Nigeria is very scanty. This study, therefore, attempts to draw attention to how hedging is deployed by expert writers in Nigeria to encourage its conscious use and draw pedagogic attention to it.

2. The Journal Article

Among the genres of academic writing, the research article has received the most academic attention. As Hyland (2009: 67, 78) says, "the research article (RA) remains the pre-eminent genre of the academy; it is not only the principle site of disciplinary knowledge–making but… 'the master narrative of our time'; it is the jewel in the crown of academic communication". Hyland (2009) explains that the pre-eminence of the research article derives from the systematicity of its production and structure. It goes through the dual processes of review and revision, which are control mechanisms for transforming beliefs into knowledge, the process of restructuring of knowledge to establish a discourse for creating scientific facts, and language is the technology tool for achieving this, for presenting interpretations and positioning participants in particular ways to establish knowledge.

The process of producing an RA involves the chain activities of producing an original draft, passing it through reviews and undertaking painstaking revisions, navigating the terrain of existing knowledge to argue for justification and relevance for the work, seeking credibility for findings by arguing for the validity of the method employed, discussing findings and seeking support for, or invigorating new claims, in order to 'sell' the research, taking a stance to present the researcher as credible by forming solidarity with others, and engaging the readers by including them as participants in the discourse while guiding them to interpretations. No doubt, the RA is a complex rhetorical activity which requires initiation, apprenticeship or mentoring. The relevance of the RA requires no effort to defend because, as Hyland (2009: 2) argues, "no new discovery, insight, invention or understanding has any significance until it is made available to others and no university or individual will receive credit for it until it has seen the light of day through publication".

The journal article serves the primary purpose of reporting scholarly work. As a genre, the article has peculiar characteristics of structure, content, and language. For international publications especially, a journal article must follow established guidelines and meet international standards to qualify for publication. Often, becoming a member of the community of academic writers is generally challenging for young academics, but much more for the non-native speakers of English. For them, it requires extensive learning and practice. In many cases, young academics have to be 'introduced' or 'initiated' into this community by experienced writers who are senior academics. This is simply because, as Bhatia (1997) affirms, academic English has its own generic conventions and membership of the community requires a mastery of those conventions. Academic writing is characterized by clarity, focus, conciseness, abstraction, technicality, indirectness, and appropriateness of style. It is the aim of this paper to examine the characteristic of indirectness in the language of the journal article, technically called hedging.

3. Data and method

A total of 54 research articles (RAs) published in high ranking local and foreign journals constitute data for the study. The reason for combining local and foreign publications is to see if writers exercise more caution in writing for the global community. All selected articles were written between 2010 and 2016 to capture the current state of article writing. In terms of discipline, the articles were chosen from the three language fields of English studies, English literature and English linguistics. These are communities that should be most aware of the demands of academic writing. Of the 54 RAs, 19 were taken from high profile foreign journals such as English Today, World Englishes and Journal of Pragmatics while 35 were sourced from high ranking local journals such as JNESA and Okike. Of these 35, 15 were taken from literature domain, while 20 were sourced from English language and linguistics domains. For all the articles, only the online, transcribed versions were used to prevent the introduction of errors that retyping would have occasioned. Permissions to use these articles were obtained from the individual authors in some cases, and from the publishers of the journals in other cases.

After collating the 54 articles, the data were sorted and cleaned up, and sections not required for the study, like direct quotations, tables, figures, references, and appendices were removed. This left the main IMRD sections as the texts for examination. The next step was the division of the data into the 2 main groups of local and foreign, and then into disciplines. The main and sub groups of the data were saved as separate word files. All the word files were later converted to text files to enable their use in Antconc, which is the chosen software for the analysis. Therefore, there are four sets of data saved in two formats. These are articles in local journals irrespective of disciplinary differences, articles in foreign journals, articles in literary journals, and articles in linguistics and English language journals.

A quantitative analysis was done using Antconc 3.2.4. (2014). This entailed word searches of specified hedges to determine their occurrences, frequencies and contexts. This was done using the concordance program to identify both the occurrences and contextual uses of the predetermined hedges. Following the quantitative analysis, a qualitative analysis was carried out to reveal the implications of the results. The discussions were guided by the objectives of the study, namely to determine what hedging devices are frequently used in the scholarly articles of Nigerian academics, and to see how this compares with the practice of academics in other communities and cultures as evidenced in the literature of academic writing.

To search for frequent hedges in the data, a list of hedges which have been shown to be highly productive both in ESL contexts and the native contexts of English was compiled from previous studies. In addition, those hedges, which a preliminary look at the data revealed to be commonly used, were isolated and examined as they may reveal some peculiar uses in the Nigerian context. The following 26 hedges were, therefore, isolated for analysis and a recourse was made to lists of hedges compiled in such studies as Biber et al. (1999), Hyland (1998), and Nkemleke (2011). The results are shown in Tables 1, 2, 3, and 4 below and then discussed.

4. Results

We can see in the table above the categorization of epistemic hedges into five classes: modals, adverbs/adverbials, adjectives, verbs and nouns, following established traditions (see Biber et al. 1999; Hyland 1998). The data shown represent those hedges identified in past studies to be frequent. These are marked using the plus sign for those that are found to characterize native English writings and marked with asterisks for features that characterize non-native English writings in the African contexts (see Atechi 2011; Edusei 2016; Nkemleke 2011), excluding Nigeria, while those features marked in square brackets represent features found in the present study, for Nigerian writers. Where there is a double sign, whether of the asterisk, plus or square bracket, it means that such a linguistic form occurs very frequently. Then, the numbers represent the frequencies of the forms found in the present study. Whereas low frequencies are marked in black, high frequencies are marked in red. High frequency means an occurrence of up to 50, and very high frequency means occurrence up to 80.

Modals	Adverbs/ adverbial	Adjectives	Verbs-Evidential	Verbs-Judgement	Nouns
++**[[May]] 362	++**Probably 26	++**[possible] 74	++**[[seem]] 108	++*[suggest] 87	*possibility 16
++[[might]] 99	++perhaps 41	**likely 27	**Tend to 39	++*[indicate] 81	*assumption 11
++**[[could]] 160	+*possibly 07	*relatively 13	*[appear] 86	*think 36	
++[[would]] 221	+[[according to + NP]] 149	*+clear 46	+[[note]] 109	*[believe] 52	
			+[report] 54	++assume 14	
			+[attempt] 61	[argue] 64	

Table 1:   Epistemic hedges examined in the study in comparison with earlier studies.
Legend:
+ Hyland (1998), Biber (1999): high frequency hedges in native contexts
*Nkemleke (2011), Atechi (2016), Edusei (2016): high frequency hedges in African contexts
[ ] Items with frequency > 50 in Nigerian context [[ ]] Items with frequency > 100 in Nigerian context.

As can be seen in the Table 1, the modals are generally used most frequently whether in the native or non-native contexts of English, while the use of the other classes of hedges differs both in the type and extent of usage. The data shows, for instance, that academic writers in Nigeria use mostly modals and verbs as hedging devices more than adjectives, nouns and adverbs. Where adverbs are used, it is the adverbial form 'according to…' that predominates. This factor of variation will be discussed in more detail later. As the quantitative result shows, the modals have the highest total raw frequency of 842, that is, an average occurrence of 15 per paper. In the case of verbs, which manifested the second highest raw frequency with a total occurrence of 791, this represents 14 occurrences per paper, although forms may cluster in individual papers. However, when we calculate the relative frequencies, it becomes obvious that modals have much higher frequency than verbs because, while only 4 modal forms accounted for the frequency of 842, there are 12 verb forms which accounted for the frequency of 791. Therefore, the ratio is 3:1; modals are three times as frequent as verbs. From Table 2, which shows actual examples of hedging, we gain more insight into this language act and this will enable a fuller discussion of its use in the academic context of Nigeria.

(1) Political actors functioning in a political setting can only be effective when they understand that the level of action of discourse will **possibly** provide crucial conditions for restructuring part of the conventions that make (political) utterances acceptable.

(2) It **appears** that the language practice among many educated Nigerians **tends to** shift towards English-only.

(3) These enabled the establishment of associative, pragmatic word meanings, which **according to** Lewis (1997) **may** differ radically from literal meanings.

(4) **Perhaps** the differences between the studies **may be** accounted for in the differences in their data, methods of data collection, analysis and focus, while the common grounds **suggest** areas where Holmes (1986) **might** have adapted from Pomerantz (1978), in a manner that future studies **may** emulate.

(5) In fact, our data reveal a striking consistency (in the use of *as in*), that rules out **the possibility** of it being a mistake or a mere hesitational device, and **suggests** that a well-structured, rule-governed linguistic phenomenon is in operation.

(6) Specifically, this paper **argues** that *as in* in various ways and in diverse contexts signals the speaker's desire to get the hearer to recognize that a crucial aspect of his meaning is being communicated....

(7) In the context of this present study of the speech act theory therefore, the basic **assumptions** as **proposed** by Austin and Searle serve to highlight the importance of speech act to discourse analysis.

(8) The study **attempts** to flesh out claims regarding the indigenization of English in Nigeria and **asserts** that ....

(9) Students' recurrent disappointing performance in university semester examinations **seems** to **suggest** that there **could** be a number of problems that teachers and educationists need to attend to.

(10) *As in,* just like Anderson **notes** of the use of *like*, usually precedes lexical material with high information value.

(11) I **assume** that compliments are speech acts or performative utterances that perform certain social actions and that these actions leave conventional effects when issued in the appropriate circumstances.

(12) While the typology presented in the paper may not yet be evidence of a national problem, it **indicates**, at least, that many of our students are yet to get the hang of the essential requirements of academic writing.

(13) That Wazobia remains king despite the anger of high-ranking male members of the community **clearly argues** for the participation of women in politics and societal governance.

(14) What's more, the paper **stoutly asserts** that students' poor scores in examinations **may be** a reflection of certain neurologically-based processing problems which have their exponents in the students' poor basic writing as well as expressive writing skills.

(15) **According to** Pomerantz (1978:82), accepting compliments **arguably** confirms the assumed friendship, familiarity or solidarity. In other words, acceptance engenders good feelings between participants, which Pomerantz (1978) **believes** is the preferred next action. Thus the preference for acceptance in NE compliment responses **might** be indicating interest in fostering good relationships/feelings with conversational partners, a preference which **tends to** override any other consideration among participants.

The above list shows actual examples of hedging in the study data. In each example, there is at least one proposition and one writer's reaction to the proposition. In many cases, the reaction precedes the proposition as clearly shown in examples 2, 6, 7, 8, 11. The examples also demonstrate the two types of claims found in academic writing, either the claim made by the writer as in examples 6, 11, 12 or those claims made by other writers or discursive participants in the literature as in examples 3, 4, 7. In either case, a writer's reaction is required to show support or hesitation to existing claims or to his own claim. Of course, all the data types manifested this act of hedging whether in response to the claims of others or in the report of research findings, their own claims. Therefore, academic writers in this context are well aware of the dangers of overt claims, the need for caution, as well as inclusiveness in negotiating knowledge. Moreover, the results show that writers were conscious of hedging irrespective of whether they were writing for international or local audiences. This was confirmed, for instance, in the spread of *may* the most frequent hedger which occurred 362 times in the data. The analysis showed that 182 cases were found in international papers, while 180 cases where found in local papers. Therefore, no variation in terms of publication context was found. Some of the examples called attention to themselves, and some raised interesting questions. Example (9), for instance, reveals a case of triple hedging of a single proposition. What this portends is probably that the degree of uncertainty is quite high, but then, too much hedging stifles the idea of a sentence as it saps it of its power. On the other hand, examples 13 and 14 are interesting for another reason, the fact that a single proposition is hedged and boosted at the same time as shown below.

(16) "Students' recurrent disappointing performance in university semester examinations **seems** to **suggest** that there **could** be a number of problems that teachers and educationists need to attend to for standards to be redeemed".

(17) That Wazobia remains king despite the anger of high-ranking male members of the community **clearly argues** for the participation of women in politics and societal governance.

(18) What's more, the paper **stoutly asserts** that students' poor scores in examinations **may be** a reflection of certain neurologically-based processing problems which have their exponents in the students' poor basic writing as well as expressive writing skills.

Examples (16) and (17) raise a question of whether the writer's stance is confused or contradictory. Whichever is the case, the expression of stance in the two examples is not clear even though it appears that the writers intended the exact opposite by the pre-modification of the verbs argue and asserts. It seems to me, however, that the both forms clearly and stoutly introduce certainty rather than emphasise uncertainty as expected. This feature raises an interesting question for research – to determine the collocates of reporting verbs, as well as to examine their pragmatics. Of equal interest was the need to investigate how the hedging practice of Nigerian academics compare to those in other academic and cultural contexts as reported in the literature. The result of this investigation is reported in Table 2 below.

HEDGE Hyland 1998(56 RAs)	FQ	HEDGE Nkemleke 2011(156 diss.)	FQ	HEDGE Esimaje (present study (54 RAs))	FQ
may	646	seem	300	may	362
would	385	may	296	would	221
possible (ly)	306	possible (ly)	287	could	160
could	269	likely	121	according to ...	149
might	265	tend	102	notes	109
suggest	258	could	76	seem	108
indicate	141	would	70	might	99
seem	138	might	48	suggest	87
assume	128	probably	96	indicate	81
				possible(ly)	81

Table 2:   Comparing hedge frequencies across studies and contexts

This table presents, in the first column, a list of hedgers considered to be the most commonly used in academic writing. Their uses are compared in three contexts: native English context (Hyland 1998, in columns 1 and 2), and the non-native contexts of Cameroon (Nkemleke 2011, in columns 3 and 4) both as reported in previous research, and then with the Nigerian context in columns 5 and 6 as found in the present study. One can see clearly from this table that the priority usage is not the same in the contexts. Whereas in Hyland (1998) and Esimaje may is the most frequent hedger, in Nkemleke (2011) seem was found to be most frequent. It is also obvious that some forms which are frequently used in one context are not so frequent in other contexts, while some forms found to be in constant usage in one context are completely missing in other contexts. This indicates both preferential uses and even peculiar uses. These points will be discussed further later.

5. Discussion

In relation to the objectives of the study, the study reveals that academic communities in Nigeria, like others, are conscious of hedging and apply them in large numbers in their works although at a relatively lower rate than their English native-speaker counterpart writers. For instance, whereas Hyland (1998) shows an average occurrence rate of 120 hedges per paper, this study showed an average occurrence of 38 hedges per paper. In terms of frequency of use, although the study showed general high frequencies for modals in all the studies, both in the native and non-native contexts of English, it revealed preferential uses of certain modals verbs. For example, whereas may was found to be the most frequent modal hedge in Hyland (1998), with 646 occurences, and the present study, 362 occurences, it was found to be the second most frequent in Nkemleke (2011), 296 occurences. Might showed interesting variation in its use. It had a very high occurrence rate in native-speaker writing, a comparatively high occurrence rate in the Nigerian context, and a very low occurrence rate in such other non-native contexts as Cameroon (see Atechi 2016; Nkemleke 1998). Contrarily, in Nkemleke (1998), a very high occurrence rate was recorded for seem and an equally high frequency was found for tend to. Although seem was also found to be in frequent use in Hyland (2011) and Esimaje (present study), its position as the most frequent hedge in Nkemleke (1998) is interesting but tend does not have significance occurrence in both Hyland (1998) and Esimaje (present study). There is, therefore, the likelihood that Cameroon writers have preference for these forms and this might account for the low frequency of might in the context.

Another surprising finding is that of the use of would which in most studies, including the present one (also see Biber et al. 1999; Hyland 1998), is often among the top three most frequent hedges, but it recorded a low frequency in Nkemleke (2011) and Atechi (2016). Both studies focus on academic writing in Cameroon and, thus, confirm preferential uses of hedges across social, linguistic, and cultural contexts reported in the literature. Yet another fascinating result is the use of possible(ly) in Hyland (1998) and Nkemleke (2011) where very high frequencies were found, but the Nigerian academic context showed low frequency for the form (present study). However, academic writers in Nigeria seem to like the adverbial form according to and the quotative verb form notes which are not preferred forms in the other two contexts. Generally, therefore, it appears that expert academic writers in Nigeria compare reasonably to native speaker academic writers in their choice of hedgers. Edusei (2016) made a similar conclusion for Ghana expert academic writers. It is likely though that some writers utilize hedging devices merely as linguistic forms of academic writing without the alertness of involvement in interaction, the presence of other discursive participants, nor the negotiation of knowledge (this was clearly revealed in the oral interviews with my colleagues). Beyond being a social act, hedging has been proved to be a cultural act (Trajkova 2015) and could, therefore, account for its prevalence in some cultures.

6. Conclusion

Although the academic practice of hedging claims to be a cultural act and, thus, negotiating knowledge cuts across academic communities, its use is less profuse among non-native English writers such as in Nigeria. This is probably due to the low awareness of the feature as demonstrated also in Nkemleke (2011). Perhaps, generally, writers in such contexts are primarily at a disadvantage as they struggle not only to think and create knowledge in a foreign language, but also to communicate through it. The internationalisation of English, the globalization of the academic world, and the fact that English is the language of communication have been identified as possible causes of the poor competence in academic writing and the reason for the low participation of non-native writers in international scholarship and knowledge creation. Nonetheless, the ability to communicate knowledge in a particular and globally acceptable way remains an index of academic maturity and visibility. Thus, this competence is critical for academics irrespective of their social, linguistic and cultural backgrounds. Therefore, the points remain, and which constitute our interest here, that journal article writing is a practice of the academic community, it is a genre that has its own rhetoric and other structural conventions. Therefore, to be counted in this community, one needs to master the art of writing scientifically by employing appropriate linguistic resources to balance conviction with caution in negotiating and constructing knowledge.

References

Atechi, S. (2016). Exploring gender differences in the use of hedges and boosters among advanced ESL learners in Cameroon. In Schmied J. & Nkemleke D. (Eds). *Academic writing across disciplines in Africa: From students to experts.* Göttingen: Cuvillier: 81-88.

Bhatia, V. (1997). The power and politics of genres. *World Englishes* 16 (3), 359-371.

Beyer, D. (2015). "It is probably the reason why..." Hedging in BA and MA theses by German ESL students. In Schmied J. (Ed.). *Graduate academic writing in South Eastern Europe: Practical and theoretical perspectives.* Göttingen: Cuvillier, 81- 98.

Biber, D. et al. (1999). *Longman grammar of spoken and written English.* Pearson Education Limited.

Edusei, J. (2016). Academic writing in Ghana: Hedging among advanced L2 users of English. In Schmied J. & Nkemleke D. (Eds). *Academic writing across disciplines in Africa: From students to experts.* Göttingen: Cuvillier, 103-116.

Halliday, M.A.K. (1978). *Language as social semiotic.* London: Arnold.

Hyland, K. and Milton, J. (1997). Qualification and certainty in L1 and L2 students' writing. *Journal of Second Language Writing* 6(2): 183-205.

Hyland, K. (1997). Is EAP necessary? A survey of Hong Kong undergraduates. *Asian Journal of English Language Teaching* 7, 77-99.

Hyland, K. (1998). Boosting, hedging and the negotiation of academic knowledge. *Text* 18(3): 349-382.

Hyland, K. (2005). Stance and engagement: A model of interaction in academic discourse. *Discourse Studies,* 7 (2): 173-192.

Hyland, K. (2006). *English for specific purposes: An advanced resource book.* London: Routledge.

Hyland, K. (2009). *Research discourses - academic discourse.* London: Continuum.

Macintyre, R. (2013). Lost in a forest all alone: The use of hedges and boosters in the argumentative essays of Japanese university students. *Sophia International Review,* 1-24.

Nkemleke, D. (2011). Hedging in Cameroon English. In Nkemleke D. (Ed.) *Exploring academic writing in Cameroon English: A corpus-based Perspective.* Göttingen: Cuvillier, 19-33.

Serholt, S. (2012). Hedges and boosters in academic writing: A study of gender differences in essays written by Swedish advanced learners of English. PhD Thesis. Department of Languages and Literatures, Goteborgs Universitet, ENGELSKA.

Trajkova, Z. (2015). Expressing commitment and detachment in non-native English. BA Graduate papers. In Schmied J. (Ed.). *Graduate academic writing in South Eastern Europe: Practical and theoretical perspectives.* Göttingen: Cuvillier, 143-162.

Vassileva, I. (1997). Hedging in English and Bulgarian academic writing. In Duszak, A. (ed). *Culture and styles of academic discourse.* Berlin: Mouton de Gruyter, 203-221.

Vázquez, I., Giner, D. (2009). Writing with conviction: The use of boosters in modelling persuasion in academic discourses. *Revista Alicantina de Estudios Ingleses,* 219-237.

A Rhetorical Move Analysis of Research Article Introductions in Selected Academic Arts Journals in Nigeria

Faith Amuzie

Benson Idahosa University

Abstract

This paper explores research article (RA) introductions written by advanced academics in Nigeria with a view to describing their rhetorical structures (moves) and investigating the extent to which they converge and/or diverge with CARS Model, a widely-used model for writing research introductions. The study involves 31 RA introductions from four academic arts journals in Nigeria, namely *Journal of Nigeria English Studies Association, English Language Teaching Today, Okike, an African Journal of New Writing,* and *Journal of the Literary Society of Nigeria.* Findings reveal that most introductions written by Nigerian academics do not conform to CARS. Whereas CARS is linear in sequence, most introductions in the Nigerian academic contexts investigated are predominantly cyclic. The study has implications for academic writing, teaching, and publication.

Keywords: Rhetorical structure, CARS Model, research article introductions, Nigerian academics

1. Introduction and Background

1.1. Academic Genre, Discourse and Writing

Academic genre is an overarching term for academic discourse text types that exist in the academia. Within the ecology of academic writing, the research article (RA) is a fundamental academic genre and it is one of the four basic categories of academic discourse types (the Research article, Instructional discourse, Students discourse, and Popular discourse) identified by Hyland (2009). The RA is not only the main channel for presenting new knowledge claims (Hewings 2001) and presenting evidence for such with the intention of persuading other members of the community of the validity of a particular claim, it is also a fact that university researchers and lecturers are assessed more on their publications in refereed journals than on any other scholarly activity within the academic community (Corbett 2007). Therefore, academics are constantly under pressure to publish in scholarly journals. It is agreed that peer recognition, ethical as well as professional compulsion to communicate one's research, the desire to contribute and transfer knowledge (Soule 2007) and promotional purposes may account for motivations to publish.

The scholarly RA is the common currency of the academic community (Corbett 2007) and a very authoritative source of information for past or older research work. The RA comprises segments (the abstract section, introduction section, methods section, discussion section, and the results section) that have been the object of serious academic research among academic scholars (Neff van 2011, Salager-Meyer (1990), Nkemleke 2016, Santos 1996, Swales 1990, Taylor and Chen 1991, Yang and Allison 2003) in recent times. Such scholars have engaged in genre analysis of these sections and have placed specific focus on the organizational arrangement of the RA sections in terms of their constituent moves with a view to understanding their underlying structures and language choices utilized in their realizations. Each of these components is highly structured and tends to play a vital role in contributing to the overall rhetorical purpose of the RA.

The introduction section, for instance, is acclaimed to be a vital component of the research article (Corbett 2007, Nkemleke 2016). This is because it acts as a mental road map that leads an academic audience (reader, editor, other gatekeepers) into what a research area is all about. It allows a writer to show the relevance of his work by stating the importance of his research area, situating his research in relation to previous literature and announcing the current research in order to sell the general research area to the academic community. It has been observed that the writing of introductions to research papers is an extremely important academic exercise that scholars regularly engage in with acuity because RA introductions are highly structured genres written with the intention of convincing an academic audience by arguing for relevance (Nkemleke 2016). Corbett (2007) equally commented that the suitability of any research article for publication and to individual interest is first determined from the introduction. Swales' (1990) Create-a-Research-Space (CARS) model has been devised to enable scholars effectively organise and write the introduction text of a research article.

This study explores research article introductions written by advanced academics in Nigeria with a view to describing the rhetorical moves found in them, and investigating the extent to which the moves converge and/or diverge with the CARS model. Two objectives guided this research: (1) identifying the rhetorical structures in language arts introduction texts, and (2) comparing the rhetorical structures of Nigerian academics to the CARS model.

1.2. The CARS Model

Swales' (1990) CARS is the model of analysis for this study. It is a well-known ESP genre-based model, first suggested by Swales in 1981, then further refined in 1984, 1990, and 2004 for writing and organizing the rhetorical structure of a research article introduction. The model aids to explicitly reveal the underlying rhetorical structure of an RA introduction, as well as the pattern that academics may follow to advance their arguments. As observed, the RA introduction presents information, and such information is presented to readers in a structured format, and predictable patterns of organization that enable readers to follow the line of argument in the write-up (Swales and Feak 2004: 10). Corbett (2007: 25) equally stated that the value of Swale's model is that "it expresses the purpose that any introduction should serve [… that of] communicating to the reader the research area and the author's stance with respect to it". Nkemleke (2016: 40) noted that the model has "a strong explanatory power and has been very useful in research article writing instruction and pedagogy". CARS is a three-staged model, namely: establishing a territory (move 1), establishing a niche (move 2), and occupying a niche (move 3).

1.3. Previous Studies

The CARS model has been applied in analysing RA introductions in varied academic genres across disciplinary fields because of its importance in RA writing instruction and pedagogy. Samraj (2002), for instance, applied CARS in analyzing RA introduction sections in Conservation Biology and Wildlife. Her study revealed that there are disciplinary variations on how both fields structure RA introductions. The study indicated that, while Conservation Biology carried out the justification of research through real or phenomenal world matter, Wildlife made use of the epistemic world of research (i.e. reference to research activities in the field) to justify research. The study also revealed that one element "the discussion of previous research" was not only found in move 1 (Establishing a territory, as it is the case with CARS), but was equally found in the other two moves (Establishing a niche, and Occupying the niche) where they played very important roles. A similar study conducted by Neff-Van (2011) on RAs in Applied Linguistics and Literature indicated that there was the need for an additional step in move 1 to make provisions for introductions in English Literature. This step entails inserting a literary example that is followed by an intense discussion of the argument. The author also discovered that, while Literature academics made less use of step 3 of move 1, Applied Linguistics RA introductions realized move 1 through the use of step 3 (the review of previous literature). Within the field of medicine, Kevin Ngozi Nwogu (1997) conducted a comprehensive study on the different components of the medical RA and the results obtained showed that a typical medical research paper may comprise eleven schematic moves of three moves each from the introduction and methods sections, while two from the results section and four from the discussion section.

In addition, Lakic's study (2010) on RA introductions in Economics showed that, despite similarities with Swales' (1990) model, differences exist in Economics RA introductions. A vital aspect of the result highlighted the division into four moves, rather than the three canonical moves of Swales. Therefore, there was the need to introduce a separate move known as 'Summarising previous research', which appears to be an indispensable move in Economics introduction texts. In addition, 'Summary Review' is seen as another possibility in referring to previous research, while other moves appear to contain more steps than those found in Swales' model. Equally, Nkemleke's study (2016) on 51 RAs in the language arts shows that introductions of RAs in Cameroon do not have uniformity in rhetorical pattern; about four categories of rhetorical structures were identified. While only nine texts (18%) of the corpus conformed to the linear sequence of the CARS model, the remaining 42 articles in the corpus made up the other three patterns of organizations identified in the introductions.

A significant finding from these researches is that 'moves' and 'steps', as rhetorical strategies in RA introductions, reflect disciplinary variations. In investigating introductions found in language arts RAs in Nigeria, the current study contributes to the existing literature on academic writing by identifying the rhetorical structures of language arts RA introduction within the Nigerian academic space to further an understanding of the exiting and predominant pattern.

2. Data and Methodology

This study was done harmonizing the qualitative method of textual analysis and the quantitative method of frequency count of moves and steps variation. The research covered 31 introductions gathered from 31 articles published in selected academic journals from Nigeria: *The Journal of Nigeria English Studies Association, English Language Teaching Today, Okike, an African Journal of New Writing*, and *Journal of the Literary Society of Nigeria*. The period considered spanned the years from 2010 to 2015. The CARS model is the framework employed for analysis (cf. section 1.2 above).

The initial procedure embarked on in the course of analysis was to convert the soft copies of the introduction texts into hard copies by printing them out from the computer to do a manual analysis. Following the manual print-outs, the next step was to do a move coding through textual analysis to identify the different moves contained in each of the introduction texts. A follow-up to this action was the grouping of similar introductions into one set, and a subsequent classification of the different sets into four categories mentioned in Nkemleke's format (2016). The format classified introductions, based on the moves (M) identified in them, into four categories, as follows: linear structure, semi-linear structure used for introductions that have been written in just two out of the three conventional moves, a cyclic structure, and a single move structure. The sequence may be chronological as M1 - M2 or non-chronological as in M3 - M2. The linear structure is used for introductions that follow the linear sequence of the canonical moves in the CARS model which follows a sequence of M1 - M2 - M3. The cyclic structure refers to introduction structures that have a sequence of repeated moves. In other words, it presents a situation whereby an initial move x is followed by move y and then another backward movement to x, so that we can have a case of a M1 - M2 - M1. In this structure, moves are recursive. The Single Move structure refers to introductions that present only one move.

2.1. Samples of Data/Analysis: Rhetorical Move Identification

2.1.1. *Sample 1: Move 1 - Step 2 - topic generalization*

(1)

    a) Title of paper: The Nexus of Idioms, Tropes, Themes and Characterization in Tanure Ojaide's *Matters of the Moment*

    b) Tanure Ojaide is renowned for his collections of lyrical poetry which have won him many prizes. His prose works include *The Activist, Sovereign Body, Great Boys: An African Childhood,* an autobiographical work, and *Matters of the Moment (MOM).* The author's use of idioms and tropes and their effects are treated from lexico-semantic and literary perspectives. *MOM* is set in Nigeria of the 1980s and 1990s which is characterized by military coups and tyranny. Dede, the hero of the novel, is a Nigerian journalist trained in the United States of America. Brimming with enthusiasm and a revolutionary spirit, he returns to Nigeria after his study abroad and meets Franka in Warri. They became husband and wife later. But their marriage is beset with challenges which culminate in a scandalous divorce and child-custody debacle. Franka, his divorced wife, suffers disappointment in subsequent relationships and thereafter resolves to change her lifestyle by using her sexuality, otherwise known as 'bottom power' in Nigerian English, to influence highly placed men, climb to the upper class, attain and wield economic and political powers. Meanwhile, Dede is also facing serious socio-economic challenges. At a point, fortunes reverse for him when General Ogiso, the Military Head of State and Franka's biggest fancy man, dies in questionable circumstances. The trend of events brings Dede and Frank together again at a crisis point and together they unseat military tyranny.

The writers of example (1) above attempt to identify or establish their research area by making generalizations about a writer, the writer's works, and the book their research is about. In doing this, they have utilized a move 1 (M1), which is Establishing a research territory. This move comprises three steps: step 1 (Centrality claim), step 2 (Topic generalizations) and step 3 (Review of previous literature). A close attention to this introduction text reveals the use of step 1 (Topic generalizations) of M1. Establishing a territory, as the first move, requires an author to set the context for the research by providing a background for the topic under consideration.

2.1.2. Sample: Move 2- Step 1b - indicating a gap

(2)

    a) Title of paper: The Grammaticality and Acceptability of Nigerianisms: Implications for the Codification of Nigerian English

    b) Controversies still surround the linguistic status of certain features in terms of their grammaticality and acceptability. Systematic studies aimed at assessing whether these features are errors, deviations or deviances, let alone their codification, are still few (Grieve 1966, Bamgbose 1982, Jibril 1986, Adegbija 2004). To our mind, real progress in the codification of Nigerian English can only be made when results of systematic and close analysis of a large body of data on Nigerian English, coupled with the evaluation of their status in terms of grammaticality and acceptability are brought together (cf Bamgbose 1998).

The introduction text extract in example (2) highlights the author's attempt to establish a niche in the first three lines, and this he achieves through indicating an existing gap in previous studies. The niche means an open "space" or "gap" in the existing research. This move involves a process whereby a writer tries to show how and where prior research has failed, is inadequate or incomplete in addressing the issues raised in the research, and, therefore, presenting that there are areas of the work that need further research. An author can establish a niche by counterclaiming, indicating a gap, raising a question or continuing a tradition. The use of contrast or negative evaluation lexical items is often used to signal this stage. Some words include *however, nevertheless unfortunately, few, less, ignore, question, challenge, unclear, unsatisfactory, hence*, etc.

2.1.3. Sample 3: Move 3 - Step 1b - announcing present research

(3)

    a) Title of paper: Indigenous Oral Poetry in Nigeria as a Tool for National Unity

    b) The paper explores and illuminates indigenous oral poetry in Nigeria as a tool for national unity. It comprises six sections, section one being this introduction. Section two focuses on a review of literature germane to the study, three on the critical approach used for the study and four on ten (10) selected ethnic poetic forms in Nigeria.

In example (3), the writer announces the focus of the current study: "The paper explores and illuminates indigenous oral poetry..." By this, the writer has deployed the rhetorical strategy of move 3 (Occupying the niche) through the use of step 1b known as Announcing the present research. Under this move, writers unveil their solution to assist in filling the gap that was created in Move 2. This is often done by stating and describing the aim of the paper, arguing for a position, and evaluating findings.

Following the analysis, the different rhetorical moves identified were grouped into different categories based on areas of convergence. Table 1 below presents the different rhetorical patterns of the 31 research article introductions in the corpus. It captures the type of introduction structure (e.g. semi-linear), the percentage and number of times such structure occurred in the corpus (9.7% and 3). The table also presents the individual description of the particular moves and the trajectory that (establish territory → occupy territory) the rhetorical patterns have followed.

Type of Structure	Frequency		Rhetorical Move Patterns
Semi-linear Structure	**3**	**9.7 %**	
M1→M3	3		establish territory → occupy niche
Linear Structure	**3**	**9.7 %**	
M1→M2→M3	3		establish territory → establish niche → occupy niche
Cyclic Structure	**21**	**67.7%**	
M1→M3→M1→M3→M1→M2→M1 →M3→M1	1		establish territory → occupy niche → establish territory → occupy niche → establish territory → establish niche → establish territory → occupy niche → establish territory
M1→M3→M1	2		establish territory → occupy niche → establish territory
M1→M2→M1→M2→M1→M2→M1	2		establish territory → establish niche → establish territory → establish niche → establish territory → establish niche → establish territory
M1→M3→M1→M2→M1→M2→M1 →M2→M1→M3→ M1	1		establish territory → occupy territory → establish territory → establish niche → establish territory → establish niche → establish territory → establish niche → establish territory → occupy niche → establish territory
M1→M2→M1→M3	1		establish territory → establish niche → establish territory →occupy niche
M1→M2→M3→M1→M3→M1	1		establish territory → establish niche → occupy niche → establish territory → occupy niche → establish territory
M1→M2→M1	4		establish territory → establish niche → establish territory
M1→M2→M1→M2→M1→M3	1		establish territory → establish niche → establish territory → establish niche → establish territory → occupy niche
M1→M2→M3→M1→M3	2		establish territory → establish niche → occupy niche → establish territory → occupy niche
M1→M2→M1→M3→M1→M2	1		establish territory → establish niche → establish territory → occupy niche → establish territory → establish niche
M3→M1→M3→M1	1		occupy niche → establish territory → occupy niche → establish territory
M1→M2→M1→M3→M1	1		establish territory → establish niche → establish territory → occupy niche → establish territory
M1→M3→M1→M2	2		establish territory → occupy niche → establish territory → establish niche
M1→M3→M1→M3→M1→M2	1		establish territory → occupy niche → establish territory → occupy niche → establish territory → establish niche
Single Move Structure	**3**	**9.7%**	
M3	3		occupy niche
Dissimilar Pattern	**1**	**3.2%**	
M1-M3-M2	1		establish territory → occupy niche → establish niche

Table 1:   Summary of the different rhetorical patterns.

3. Results and Discussion

Following objective 1 (cf. section 1.1) of the current study, four types of RA introduction structures, along with an introduction text that had a dissimilar structure, were identified (cf. Table 1 above). With respect to objective two, the result showed that the RA introductions written by Nigerian academics indicate some form of divergence from the rhetorical pattern of the CARS model. For instance, the CARS model follows a linear ordering of three schematic structures, where the moves proceed from 1 to 2, and then to 3 in a sequential manner. However, the RA introductions in Nigeria predominantly exhibit an element of non-linearity (cf. Table 1 above), so that the moves do not progress in a linear sequence, but in a recursive order as reflected in the following pattern: M1→M2→M1→M3→M1→M2. There were also cases of move embedding/merger and step repetitions.

The rhetorical structures or patterns have been identified using the move sequence structures utilized by different academics in the disciplinary fields under study. Considering the three-move pattern M1-M2-M3 as the logical sequence or steps in introduction writing, the results of this research indicate that only 9.7% (i.e. 3/31) introductions conform to the CARS Model, 67.7% (21/31) consist of cyclic structure, 9.7% (3/31) are semi-linear in structure, 9.7% (3/31) contain a single move structure, and one introduction, which constitutes 3.2% (1/31), does not fit into any of the patterns. An overview of the results shows that introductions in Nigeria have diversified rhetorical structures, the cyclic structure being the most diversified with about fourteen (14) different move sequence types. In addition, one introduction reflects a move sequence that was not catered for by Nkemleke (2016) in his framework. In order to account for this introduction, a new category was added as the dissimilar category. Thus, instead of M1-M2-M3, the introduction has a M1-M3-M2 sequence.

The outcome of these findings is that the results reflect a mixed perspective on how Nigerian academics in the disciplinary fields of English, Linguistics, and Literature structure RA introductions. The implication of this may be a seeming absence of a uniformed structure for RA introduction in Nigeria that would be or indicate a standard model to follow. This may pose a major challenge to young academics that may not have any standard to follow, or know how to structure an effective RA introduction, especially as the writing of the RA introduction has been considered a major challenge for the young ESL writer (Gupta 1995, Nkemleke 2016, Shaw 1991). Nkemleke notes that "for junior scientists who aim at quality publications, knowledge of how academic papers are structured and written is required..." (2016: 50). He further adds that "one of the handicaps that junior scientists face in ESL contexts ... is the limited availability of journals in their area of discipline, where they can read about how research papers are structured and written" (2016: 50). Furthermore, the diverse nature of the data means that the writing of RA introduction by Nigerian academics is idiosyncratically determined. According to Nkemleke, this "illustrates what happens when conventional ways of text organization in academic writing is overlooked" (2016: 49).

In addition, the results further show a high level of disparity in the rhetorical patterns of introductions written by Nigerians and the CARS model. The first thing observed is that the CARS model is a linear straight forward sequenced three-move structured format (i.e. a move that proceeds from M1 to M2 to M3). However, as earlier noted, a large portion (67.7%) of the introduction texts in the corpus present a cyclic structure with a high level of recursive moves so that there is a back and forth movement of rhetorical moves made (i.e. from M1-M2-M1-M3-M1 or from M1-M2-M1-M2-M1-M2-M1-M2-M1). Furthermore, the results also show that some academics skip certain moves. This is particularly common with the semi-linear and single move structures. And even though some cyclic structured introductions appear to have move 2, they are often not clearly stated. Thus, such moves are quasi-moves, unlike the CARS model where move 2 is expected to be clearly stated to identify the research problem.

It is important to note that the omission of a move 2 (Establishing a niche), where writers often establish their own credentials and nature of their contribution to the field, (as seen in the semi-linear, single move, and some cyclic structured introductions) may indicate the inability of a writer to clearly identify the research problem he may want to resolve and "consequently it becomes difficult to situate the study in the context of others, since no gap has been identified and logically, no contribution can be argued for" (Nkemleke 2016: 43). In addition to this is that the use of M2 as a rhetorical strategy is a very important component of scientific writing which is characterized by a problem/solution approach. The issue here is if academic studies done in the language arts are scientifically driven? Do these studies clearly identify any problem that require solutions that would help solve language problems? These questions are presented here to engender further studies in these areas.

The data also indicated that Nigerian academics have a preference for step 2 (Topic generalizations) and step 3 (Review of previous literature) of move 1 more than the use of centrality claim (step 1), where a writer needs to show the importance of the research area. This explains the repeated use of M1, which, along with other repeated steps account for the long introductions in the corpus. For example, the longest introduction has over 3,000 words, while the introduction with the highest number of moves has eleven moves with the M1-M3-M1-M2-M1-M2-M1-M2-M1-M3-M1 sequence where M1 comprises six of the entire moves. The high propensity for the use of this move, on the one hand, may be the desire on the part of the writer to provide explanations, definitions, discussions, or remarks on concepts or research topic in order to provide extensive background information that would enable readers to understand his thrust. The use of the review of previous literature, on the other hand, is an indication of the need to enrich the study, as well as situate the current research in a wider academic context. Although M2 (Establishing a niche) and M3 (Occupying the niche) were not as recursive as it is the case with M1. The writers' repetitive use of these two moves showed that they indicated gaps (M2) in different instalments, as well as stating the intention (with M3) of the study in more than one location.

Another marked distinction observed in the current study between the CARS model and RA introductions in Nigeria has to do with move embedding/merger and step repetitions. This is a situation where particular moves are embedded under other moves or two different moves are merged in a single proposition or one move is achieved through a sequence of step repetitions. This is often not the case with the CARS model where each of the moves is separate to be able to account for their functions. The introduction texts used in this study frequently highlighted this phenomenon of move embedding/merger and step repetitions. Whereas the CARS Model is linear in its arrangement of steps for realizing the moves, so that a move 1 is realized by step 1(Centrality claim), and/or step 2 (Making topic generalizations) and/or step 3 (Review of previous literature), Nigerian academics may utilize a sequence of repeated steps to realize one move, for example, where the writer employs several steps to realize move 1. This was a unique feature mostly found in the long introduction texts (cf. Table 1)

4. Conclusion

This study aimed at examining the rhetorical structure of research article introductions written by Nigerian academics in the fields of English, Linguistics, and Literature with the purpose of identifying their rhetorical structure and determining the extent of compliance with the CARS model. With regard to objective one, four types of RA introduction structures were identified: the semi-linear structure constituted 9.7% (3/31) of the introductions examined, the linear structure was 9.7% (3/31), the cyclic structure was 67.7% (21/31), and the single move structure was 9.7% (3/31). A dissimilar structure, which indicated a clear disparity from any of the four patterns of introduction texts already categorized, was also identified and it represented 3.2% (1/31) of the introduction data. The findings from objective 2 showed that introductions in Nigeria indicate some form of departure from the CARS Model.

This study has provided insights into the rhetorical structural moves that introductions within the language arts in Nigeria have. RA introductions in the language arts exhibit a variety of rhetorical move patterns with the cyclic structured introduction being the most diverse among the four categories of introductions identified. This is a pointer to the fact that writers display idiosyncratic inclinations in the writing of RA introductions in Nigeria, thereby indicating that there is no specific or uniform standard for writing RA introduction. This lack of uniformity portends a lack of standard for writing RA introduction. By implication, there is no specific reference point for budding academics to acquire essential knowledge on crafting the RA introduction. The findings prove that Nigerian academics do not conform to the CARS model, rather introductions in Nigerian academic contexts are predominantly cyclic in rhetorical pattern, where writers seem to deploy more of the recursive moves instead of the linear sequence of the CARS model.

References

Corbett, J. (2007). Writing the introduction and conclusion of a scholarly article. In Soule D. P. J., Whiteley, L., McIntosh, S. (eds.), *Writing for Scholarly Journals, Publishing in the Arts, Humanities and Social Sciences*, 24-33.

Gupta, R. (1995). Managing general and specific information in introductions. *English for Specific Purposes*, 14 (1): 59-74

Hewings, M. (2001). Introduction. In Hewings, M. (ed.) Academic writing in context: Implications and applications. *Papers in Honour of Tony Dudley-Evans*. Birmingham: University of Birmingham Press, 9-16.

Hyland, K. (2009). Academic discourse. London: Continuum.

Lakic, I. (2010). Analysing genre: Research article introductions in Economics. JoLIE 383-399.

Neff van, A. (2011 July). Avenue towards Master: Teaching (Applied) Linguistics and Literary Studies as ESP. *Paper Presented at the 18th International Systemic Functional Congress*, Lisborn, Portugal.

Nkemleke, D. A. (2016). Analyzing research article introductions in the Humanities using the CARS model: How genre knowledge can help enhance academic writing skills of junior scientists. In J. Schmied & D. Nkemleke. *Academic discourse across disciplines in Africa: From students to experts*. Research in English and Applied Linguistics (REAL 10), 35-57.

Nwogu, K. N. (1997). The medical research paper: Structure and functions. *English for Specific Purposes*, 16 (2):119-138.

Salager-Meyer, F. (1990). Discourse flaws in Medical English abstracts: A genre analysis per research and text type. *Text* 10(4): 365-384

Samraj, B. (2002) Introductions in research articles: Variations across disciplines. *English for Specific Purposes*, 21:1-17.

Santos, M. B. D. (1996). The textual organization of research paper abstracts in Applied Linguistics. *Text*, 16 (4): 481-499.

Shaw, P. (1991). Science research students' composing processes. *English for Specific Purposes* 10:189-206.

Soule, D. (2007). Introducing 'writing for scholarly journals'. In Soule, D., Whiteley L., McIntosh, S. (eds.). *Writing for scholarly journals, publishing in the Arts, Humanities and Social Sciences*, 6-11.

Swales, John M. (1981). Aspects of article introductions. Aston ESP Research Report No. 1. Language Studies Unit. University of Aston in Birmingham.

Swales, John M. (1984). Research into the structure of introductions to journal articles and its application to the teaching of academic writing. In Williams, R., Swales, J., Kirkman, J. (eds.). *Common ground: Shared interests in ESP and communication studies*, 77-86. Oxford, UK: Pergamon

Swales, John M. (1990). *Genre analysis: English in academic and research settings*. Cambridge: Cambridge University Press.

Swales John M. (2004). *Research genres: Explorations and applications*. Cambridge: Cambridge University Press.

Swales, J. and C. B. Feak. (2004). *Academic writing for graduate students: Essential Skills and Tasks*. 2nd ed. Ann Arbor, MI: University Press Michigan.

Taylor, G. and T. Chen. (1991). Linguistic, cultural, and subcultural Issues in Contrastive Discourse Analysis: Anglo-American and Chinese scientific texts. *Applied Linguistics* 12(3): 319-336.

Yang, R. Y, and Allison, D. (2003). Research articles in Applied Linguistics: Moving from results to conclusions. *English for Specific Purposes*, 22(4): 365-385.

Investigating the Effects of L1 on L2 (English) Pronunciation among Tertiary Students in Southern Nigeria

Franca Okumo

Federal University Otuoke

Abstract

Mother tongue interference is a situation whereby the linguistic system of L1 is transferred into that of L2 in the process of producing the latter. The features of L1 are transferred to L2 at the phonological and morphological/syntactic levels. This paper, however, is focused on the former structure and analyses samples of spoken language of some Igbo, Ijo, and Urhobo tertiary students at the Federal University Otuoke, in Bayelsa State. Using a descriptive approach designed to show the complexity of language use by these speakers, I analyze their competence and rate of interference of L1 observable features on L2, and its effect on the phonological structure of their spoken form. The study identifies significant features of sound substitution, insertion, stress and intonation in the speech production of the learners in question. It is observed that when these learners encounter a gap in L2 phonological structures, they adjust the form of the L2 to sounds which are part of their L1. Further, when there is close similarity between the segments of L1 and L2, learners tend to mix-up both and, often, they apply the sound in L1 to L2. This leads to inappropriate L2 performance indicating interference. The study suggests that language instruction should involve both direct and indirect intervention which helps to teach learners specific linguistic properties and facilitate the process of SLA. Teachers can also identify the types of interference and proffer a stage-by-stage strategy to reinforce and facilitate learning.

Keywords: L1-L2 interference, substitution, insertion, stress and intonation, Southern Nigerian English.

1. Introduction

Communication is an essential element of language. It forms the core of our day to day activities since we share or transmit information, ideas, thoughts, feelings and messages from one person to another through it (Osikomaiya 2005). One major aspect of such communication is mastery of the sounds of the language. Since speech sounds are used to signal meaning, the sound system cannot be fully understood except they are carefully studied. To communicate effectively in any language, the language learner must be proficient in the pronunciation of words in the language. In line with this, Hyman (1975) and Osisanwo (2012) note that a language learner must master the production and perception of the sounds of a given language and know when to use the sounds. They argue that speakers must study the properties of the sound system which they must internalize in order to use their language for the purpose of communication.

Every language is unique in its own way. This is because, out of the entire sound inventory that the vocal organ is capable of producing, different languages select and combine these sounds depending on the phonological pattern of the language. Based on this unique selection, a non-native speaker of English, for instance, may find it difficult to pronounce English words because the sounds employed, and how they are structured to produce words, may not be in line with the pronunciation pattern of the speaker's L1.

Due to the international status and prestige of English, many ESL learners want to attain native-like proficiency (see Omachonu 2010). However, this requires some effort to achieve this objective, as the English manifests features that are not in the sound inventory of most L1. In English, for instance, there is no one-to-one correspondence between sounds and letters, neither is there consistency between spelling and pronunciation. One letter may represent more than five sounds as exemplified below:

(1) **Letter "A" as in:** /ɪ/ in *image* /ɪmɪdʒ/, /æ/ in *fan* /fæn/, /ɑ:/ in *father* /fɑ:ðə/, /ə/ in *above* /əbʌv/, /eɪ/ in *able* /eɪbl/, /e/ in *many* /meni/, /ɒ/ in *want* /wɒnt/, /ɔ:/ in *talk* /tɔ:k/

(2) **Letter "E" as in:** /e/ in *set* /set/, /i:/ in *secret* /sɪ:krət/, /ɪ/ in *explain* /ɪksplem/, /ə/ in *success* /seksəs/

These challenges make the teaching of pronunciation very important in any ESL context. In whichever environment learning a second language takes place, there is always a major target of every second language learner, which is to achieve significant target language proficiency at the level of pronunciation and writing, including knowledge of coherent structures, which leads to effective communication in the second language (Dulay, Burt & Krashen 1982; Ellis 1984; Rutherford 1987). Practical classroom experience has shown, however, that the accumulation of structural entities of the second language does not imply a perfect mastery of the second language. In reality, L2 learners still demonstrate difficulty in organizing this knowledge into appropriate coherent patterns. There is a major gap between accumulation and the organization of the knowledge. Second language learners tend to rely more on their L1 structures to produce the L2. The major concern of this paper, therefore, is to observe such noticeable features of interference among tertiary students of Igbo, Ijo, and Urhobo origin in Southern Nigeria. They obtained their L1 input from their individual learning process. These habits interfere with their acquisition of English.

2. Conceptual Studies on Interference in SLA

This section comprises two components: conceptual discussion of the key concepts of sound substitution, insertion, stress and intonation (2.1), and an extended review of empirical studies on SLA at the global level (2.2).

2.1. Some SLA-Related Concepts

In the study of SLA, some concepts are very fundamental for an effective analysis and understanding of the patterns that operate in languages. This includes sound substitution, insertion, stress, intonation, and interference. Every language has its sound system which is patterned differently from that of other languages. Clark, Yallop & Fetcher (2007) describe a phoneme as a contrastive or distinctive sound of a language. In order to determine which sounds belong to the same class, it is necessary to examine the distribution of the sounds in question. When sounds are placed adjacent to other segments, they undergo certain changes caused by the environment in which they occur. These changes lead to different realizations of the sounds. According to Oyebade (2008), Osisanwo (2012), and Yul-Ifode (2007), phonological processes are those changes which segments undergo that result in the various phonetic realizations of the underlying phonological segments. They emphasize that these processes are the reasons why the systematic phonemic representation (underlying representation) of a segment is often different from its systematic phonetic representation (surface phonetic representation). A sound in L1 is substituted for that in L2 when there is a gap in the phonological structure of the L1. The sounds are completely changed to that in the learners' L1 for ease of communication.

Further to sound substitution is the process of insertion and stress. Most African languages operate an open syllable structure that does not permit a final consonant; hence, high vowels are inserted into loan words that end with consonants and also to break consonant clusters. Insertion is a phonological process that adds a vowel segment to a certain environment in other to conform to the syllable structure patterns of the L1 (Yul-Ifode 2007). Stress is a very important property of pronunciation. This is because words are made up of syllables and each syllable is pronounced differently from the other. While some syllables may be pronounced with some degree of exaction, others are pronounced without such pressure. Stress is the extra breath-force or pressure given to a syllable when pronouncing a word to make it more prominent.

The concepts of sound substitution, insertion, and stress and intonation so far discussed are the major features that interfere in the speech of the Igbo, Ijo, and Urhobo students investigated. Interference occurs when the patterns of the learner's mother tongue (L1) get in the way of learning the patterns of the L2. In the next sub-section, we look at some empirical research on interference in SLA.

2.2. Empirical Studies

The area of mother tongue interference on the teaching of L2 is not a virgin one in language study. Extensive research has been done in this area. Interference is the automatic transfer of L1 to L2 due to the habits of the surface structure of the first language into the surface of the target language. To Ellis (1997: 51), interference is the transfer that influences the learners L1 acquisition of the L2. He maintains that transfer is governed by learners' perceptions about what is transferable, and by their stage of development in L2 learning. In learning a target language, learners construct their own interim rules with the use of their L1 knowledge but only when they believe it will help them in the learning task, or when they have become sufficiently proficient in the L2 for transfer to be possible (Seligar 1988; Selinker 1971). It seems that there is a strong tendency on the part of anyone learning a second language to use the sounds, syllable structure, and rhythm of mother tongue in place of the sounds, syllable structure, and rhythm of the language he is learning.

Lott (1983) says that interference is the deviation in the learners' use of the foreign language that can be traced to the mother tongue. Scholars such as Albert & Obler (1978), Beebe (1988), Carroll (1964), Larson–Freeman & Long (1991) suggest that in learning a second language, L1 responses are grafted on to L2 responses and both are made to a common set of meaning response. The learner is less fluent in L2 and the kind of expression he uses in L2 bears traces of the structure of L1.

Essien (1996: 75) notes that we carry on the characteristics of our first language into English and can, therefore, be easily identified. If, therefore, you wanted to hide your ethnic identity by speaking English, you would unwittingly be betraying that very identity. This is because people are normally more relaxed and comfortable with their mother tongue since it gives them the leverage to express certain thoughts using nuances that depict their feelings and emotions, while, quite often, they lack adequate English vocabulary to express such thoughts (Ekah 2010: 71). These facts are evident in the speech of the Igbo, Ijo, and Urhobo learners of L2. The studies so far discussed the scope and relevance of interference in SLA research. This present investigation is a modest attempt to contribute to the discussion by highlighting interference features among the Igbo, Ijo, and Urhobo speakers of English in Southern Nigeria. It is hoped that such provision of original data would be a useful complementary material for English curriculum designers and classroom teachers in this part of Nigeria.

3. Methodology

This section gives a detailed explanation of the methodology used in this study. It is segmented into two sections: section 3.1 describes the population and sample size, and section 3.2 explains the method of analysis, showing, specifically, the procedures and instruments, and how the data was analyzed.

3.1. Population and Sample

The population for this study comprises the students of ENG 102, and 203 (Introduction to Phonetics and Phonology) in a language classroom at the Federal University Otuoke, in Bayelsa State, Nigeria. The total population of students was 300 from which a sample of 60 was drawn. The sample includes 30 students from ENG 102, and another 30 from ENG 203, comprising 10 from each of the following L1 groups: Igbo, Ijo, and Urhobo.

3.2. Method of Analysis

Using a descriptive approach designed to show the complexity of language use by the L2 speakers, I analyse the learners' competence and rate of interference, observable features of interference of L1 on L2 and its effect on the phonological structure of the spoken form of the second language learner using a qualitative approach· I am a competent native speaker of Igbo, a linguist and an L2 teacher. The data for the analysis were gathered through participant observation and interaction with the students of ENG 102, and 203 (Introduction to Phonetics and Phonology) in a language classroom at the Federal University Otuoke, in Bayelsa State, Nigeria. The study is limited to the analysis of speaking samples of some Igbo, Ijo, and Urhobo language learners. The Ibadan 400 wordlist was the research instrument used to elicit data from the respondents. The informants are competent native speakers of the languages under study. The list is presented with the use of phonemic symbols. This will help to show at a glance the features or patterns of interference of their L1 on L2.

4. Result

This section presents the results of the study. The findings show interference features of sound substitution, insertion, and tone and intonation. At the phonemic level, interference is predominant. This is because of the difference between the sound patterns of the Igbo, Ijo, and Urhobo languages and English. Section 4.1 presents the result for sound substitution, 4.2 gives those of insertion, and 4.3 shows that of stress and intonation.

4.1. Sound Substitution

As mentioned earlier, substitution is a process whereby a sound that has a similar feature is substituted for the other. This is like the assimilation process whereby sounds become more like their neighbouring sounds. But unlike assimilation, sound substitution occurs when a speaker or an L1 speaker of L2 does not have a certain phoneme in the phonemic inventory of the language. The resultant effect is the replacement of such sound with another close in approximation to those in the speaker's L1. Most sounds in English are not found in most African languages, thus, wherever they are used, there are mispronunciations by English language learners. In Igbo, for example, there are no dental fricatives /θ/and /ð/ and the approximants /l/ and /r/ are also absent in some Igbo dialects; hence, these sounds pose problems to Igbo learners of English.

Furthermore, Igbo has eight vowels while English has 20. There are no long vowels in Igbo. Thus, Igbo learners of L2 may find it difficult to articulate the long vowels, and also the diphthongs. Specifically, the pure vowels in English can be approximated to some of the vowels in English. Thus, for such similarities, there is the tendency to use the L2 structure with ease, but where there are differences, the learners will have difficulties. Such difficulty is observed in the pronunciation of the English vowel /e/. This vowel is approximated to the vowel /e/ in Igbo which is not produced with a retracted pharynx. It is an open-mid unexpanded vowel. Because of the difference in quality in this sound, there is a great deal of interference noticeable in most speakers of Igbo with regard to this vowel.

The quality of the Igbo /e/ is in close approximation with /eɪ/, thus the following words were realized in the following manner in the examples below:

(1)

a)	/bed/	→	[beid]	'bed'
b)	/jes/	→	[jeis]	'yes'
c)	/jet/	→	[jeit]	'yet'
d)	/sed/	→	[seid]	'said
e)	/leg/	→	[leig]	'leg'
f)	/bred/	→	[bleid]	'bread'
g)	/breɪn/	→	[blein]	'brain'
h)	/ðen/	→	[dein]	'then'
i)	/Θɔ:t/	→	[tɔt]	'thought'
j)	/raɪs/	→	[leis]	'rice'

Similarly, in Ijo, there are no dental fricative sounds /Θ/ and / ð/, the voiced and voiceless alveolar stops /s/ and /z/ replace the /ʃ/ and /ʒ/, and /ʧ/ and /ʤ/. In some other instance, the consonant /z/ is rendered as/ʒ/. As it is the case with Igbo, there are no long vowels or diphthongs in Ijo; hence, such sounds are naturally challenging to produce when an Ijo speaker speaks English. The close front vowel /ɪ/ and the central vowel /ə/ are not found in the language, either. Where the retracted /ɪ/ occurs, the Ijoid speaker replaces it with the unretracted form /i/. For the /ə/, which is found in unaccentuated syllables in English, the tendency is to substitute it with the accentuated form. This leads to a deviant pattern of production. Consider the following in example (2):

(2)

a)	/fɪʃ/	→	[fis]	'fish'
b)	/ʃɪp/	→	[sip]	'ship'
c)	/ʃu:/	→	[su:]	'shoe'
d)	/ʃaɪn/	→	[sain]	'shine'
e)	/meʒə/	→	[meze]	'measure'
f)	/dʒɒn/	→	[zɔn]	'John'
g)	/dʒʌmp/	→	[zɔmp]	'jump'
h)	/dʒi:p/	→	[zip]	'jeep'
i)	/ʧɜ:ʧ/	→	[sɔs]	'church'
j)	/zɪp/	→	[ʒip]	'zip'

Similarly, Urhobo speakers do not have the dental fricatives as in the case with Igbo, and Ijo. The voiced and voiceless palatal affricates /ʧ/ and /dʒ/ are replaced with the post-alveolar fricatives /ʃ/ and /ʒ/. In some of the dialects of Urhobo, the /r/ sound is rendered as /l/. These also affect their English pronunciation as shown below.

(3)

a)	/tʃɜ:tʃ/	→	[ʃɔʃ]	'church'
b)	/tʃeə/	→	[ʃe]	'chair'
c)	/tʃu:/	→	[ʃu]	'chew'
d)	/tʃeɪn/	→	[ʃen]	'chain'
e)	/dʒʌg/	→	[ʒɔg]	'jug'
f)	/dʒi:p/	→	[ʒip]	'jeep'
g)	/bred/	→	[buledi]	'bread'
h)	/raɪs/	→	[lais]	'rice'
i)	/bru:m/	→	[bulum]	'broom'

We can observe from the examples above that these English sounds which are not found in the languages under study are substituted. The learner, thus, transfers the knowledge of the close sound in the English into the pronunciation of English words. The implication is that there are errors in the performance of the L1 learner of L2 due to the interference of the L1 on L2. The speakers may recognize phonetic symbols and their environment of occurrence but yet find it difficult to verbalize the physical sounds accurately.

In the same vein, the presence of some sounds in the mother tongue that are found in the target language help to facilitate the acquisition of such similar sounds of the English language. Another common pronunciation error encountered by L2 speakers is insertion.

4.2. Insertion

Recall that insertion is a phonological process that adds a segment to break off clusters or, at word final position, to fit into the syllable structure pattern, which neither permit consonant clusters nor word final consonants. This is in line with Oyebade (2008: 74) who says that it is a process whereby an extraneous element, which is not originally present, is introduced into the utterance to break up an unwanted sequence. The insertion of vowel is a very common feature in the African languages. This is because the structure of these languages does not allow consonant clusters or word final consonant; so, when words of these patterns are borrowed into the language, an epenthetic vowel is inserted as exemplified below in example (4):

(4)

a)	/sku:l/	→	[sukulu]	'school'
b)	/bred/	→	[buredi]	'bread'
c)	/fæn/	→	[fani]	'fan'

4.3. Stress and Intonation

Stress, tone and intonation are features of spoken languages which are not easily identified as discrete segments. English words are pronounced with extra breath force, called stress, while intonation is the variation in pitch of a speaker used to convey meaning. This variation takes place in connected speech; hence, intonation deals with stress at the sentential level. English words and sentences are pronounced by the L2 speakers without the appropriate placement of stress and intonation. The following words are wrongly pronounced based on stress placement:

(5)   Example 5:

a)	/ɪmˈbærəs/	→	[èmbàráz]	'embarrass'
b)	/paːˈtɪsɪpeɪt/	→	[pàtìsìpét]	'participate'
c)	/ˈselɪbreɪt/	→	[sèlìbrét]	'celebrate'
d)	/ˈɪmɪteɪt/	→	[ìmìtét]	' imitate'
e)	/ˈtraɪbəlɪzm/	→	[traibálízìm]	'tribalism'
f)	/ˈbjuːtɪfaɪ/	→	[bjutifai]	'beautify'
g)	/ˈkwɔːlɪfaɪ/	→	[kwɔ'lìfái]	'qualify'
h)	/ˈedʒʊkeɪʃn/	→	[èdùkéʃɔn]	'education'

Observe that the Nigerian speakers of English reflect the suprasegmental feature of the MT which has either a high tone or a low tone in their speech. For stressed syllable, high tones are associated, while for unstressed syllables, low tones are applied. From the examples above, we can see that words are pronounced showing tonal variations. This is so because African languages are tonal languages, while English is an intonational language. The stress is wrongly placed as seen in a-b with stress on the second syllable, and c-h with stress on the first syllable.

4.4. Discussion

From the results presented in section 4.1, this study shows that the Igbo, Ijo, and the Urhobo L2 speakers of English exhibit some noticeable features in the production of the phonological structure of English. This is due to the effect of their L1 which interferes with the structure of their L2. The learners use the pattern of sound substitution, insertion, stress and intonation to achieve communicative competence. This is to buttress the point made by Ellis (1975) that learning a target language, learners construct their own interim rules with the use of their L1 knowledge, but only when they believe it will help them in the learning task or when they have become sufficiently proficient in the L2 for transfer to be possible. This is in line with Ekah (2010) who agrees that this kind of transfer is necessary since learners are more familiar with their mother tongue, and feel better expressing themselves in their language, since the language gives them leverage to make better expressions that show certain thoughts.

5. Conclusion

This paper has attempted to identify features of interference of L1 on L2, and its effects on the phonological structure of the English second language learner in Southern Nigeria. These features, which have been analyzed at the level of sound substitution, insertion, and stress and intonation have revealed that there is a significant influence of L1 over L2 in this context. These findings appear to be consistent with similar studies carried on in ESL context (Seligar 1988; Ellis 1997; Ekah 2010, and others) who said that there is a strong tendency on the part of anyone learning a second language to use the sounds, syllable structure, and rhythm of mother tongue in place of the sounds, syllable structure, and rhythm of the language they are learning.

This further enriches our understanding of the dynamic processes of language when it comes in contact with another one, and in this specific context adds to the existing body of literature on English varieties in Southern Nigeria. Findings of this nature are useful in that they inform the language teacher about existential and potential areas where L1 features diverged with L2 (English) features and thereby enables him to integrate them into the course design in teaching strategies. In addition, the findings may as well prove relevant for the English second language learners in Southern Nigeria, who could draw from the findings the necessary knowledge which will enable them to overcome the challenges of substitution, insertion, stress and intonation as they strive to learn English.

References

Albert, M., Obler, L. (1978). *The billingual brain: Neuropsychological aspects of bilingualism.* New York: Academic Press.

Ayodele, S. et al. (2006). *Manual for the re-teaching of primary school teachers (English Language).* Kaduna: NTI Press.

Beebe, L. (1988). *Issues in second language acquisition: Multiple perspectives.* (Ed). London: Newbury.

Carroll, J. (1964). *Language and thought.* Prentice-Hall: Englewood Cliffs.

Clark, J., Yallop, C. (2007). *An introduction to phonetics and phonology.* U.K: Blackwell Publishers.

Dulay, H., Burt, M. & Krashen, S. (1982). *Language two.* New York: Oxford University Press.

Ekah, M. (2010). The cultural impact in Nigeria. In Ndimele, O. (Ed.). *English Studies and National Development in Nigeria.* Port Harcourt: ELTAN Publication, 71-92.

Ellis, R. (1984). *Classroom second language development: A study classroom interaction and language acquisition.* Oxford: Pergamon Press.

Ellis, R. (1997). *Second language acquisition.* Oxford: Oxford University Press.

Essien, O. (1996). The case against English. *Calabar Studies in Languages* 11(4).

Hoffman, C. (1991). *An introduction to bilingualism.* London: Longman.

Hyman, L. (1975). *Phonology: Theory and analysis.* New York: Halt, Rinehart and Winston.

Larson–Freeman, D., Long, M. (1991). *An introduction to second language acquisition.* New York: Research Longman.

Lott, D. (1983). Analyzing and counteracting interference errors. *ELT Journal* 3 (37): 256-261.

Osisanwo, A. (2012). *Fundamentals of English phonetics and phonology.* (2nd Edition). Lagos: Femolus-Fetop Publishers.

Omachonu, G. (2010). Teaching English in Nigerian schools: the case of the blind leading the blind. In Ndimele, O. (Ed.). *English Studies and National Development in Nigeria.* Port Harcourt: ELTAN, 613-625.

Osikomaiya, M. (2005). Effective teaching of oral English. In Jitowo, A. (Ed.). *Schools in Language Teaching: A Book of reading.* Ibadan: Bounty Press.

Oyebade, F. (2008). *A course in phonology.* Ijebu: Shebiotimo Publication.

Rutherford, W. (1987). *Second language grammar: Learning and teaching.* London: Longman.

Seligar, H. (1988). Psycholinguistic issues in second language acquisition. In Beebe, L. (Ed). *Issues in second language acquisition: Multiple perspectives*. London: Newbury.

Selinker, L. (1971). The psychologically relevant data of second language learning. In Yul-Ifode, S. (Ed.). *A Course in Phonology.* Port Harcourt: Sunray Books Ltd.

Yul-Ifode, S. (Eds.) (2010). Word Power in Taboo Expressions as Instrument of Change in Nigeria. *The International Journal of the Humanities: Annual Review.*

A Descriptive Analysis of Compound Stress Patterns of Undergraduates Speakers of English as a Second Language (SESL)[1]

Julianah Akindele

Osun State University

Abstract

Nigerian English prosodies, especially stress, have raised interesting debates among linguists. Some of these features, particularly in relation to Nigerian English compound stress, have been observed repeatedly, hence the need for this study. The study sets to find out the stress patterns of speakers of English as a Second language (SESL) on English compounds and the implication for Nigerian English stress description. Two hundred university undergraduates (100 males and 100 females) were purposively sampled. Each of the participants was made to produce 15 English compound items into a digital language laboratory - *Speech Filing System* (*SFS*) installed on HP 250 laptop. Data gathered was statistically analysed and converted into simple percentages. For instance, out of the expected overall result of 3,000, appropriate articulations of participants, compounds whose stress is supposed to be on the first syllable as affirmed in Standard English (SE) forms was 99 (3.3%), while compounds with expected stress on the second syllable had 2,557 (85.2%) appropriate articulations. Component members of three syllable structure, where stress is expected to fall on the initial or penultimate syllable, SESL had a delayed primary stress, by articulating the primary stress on the final syllable at 344 (11.4%) instances of use. Through metrical stress rule, it is revealed that participants produced S/S articulation for majority of the compounds instead of the W/S or S/W of SE forms. Findings, therefore, revealed that SESL undergraduates place stress predominantly on the ultimate syllables of compounds with two syllables and penultimate syllables of component members, thus, manifesting expanding circle English, a variation of Standard English.

Keywords: Nigerian English, compound word, stress, speakers of English as a second language, Metrical Stress Theory

---

[1] This work would not have been possible, if not for the efforts of the Centre for Language Research and English Proficiency (CLAREP). The centre is sincerely appreciated for converging international scholars to a training workshop on academic writing for Africans. Loads of knowledge gathered from this training has further helped to improve this work. The painstaking efforts of the reviewers are also sincerely appreciated.

1. Introduction and Background

Empirical investigations have established the peculiarity of Nigerian English forms, in the spoken English of Nigerians, at all levels of linguistic analysis (Awonusi 2004; Jowitt 1991). Linguists have also commented that of all levels of linguistic analysis, differences in dialectal use of a language are more noticeable at the phonological level (Akinjobi 2004; Banjo 2012). Several linguists (Atoye 1989; Sunday 2010; Akinjobi 2002; Akindele 2008; Adepoju 2017; Muhammed 2017) who have worked on English stress claim Nigerian English word stress pattern differs remarkably from Standard English. Studies on NigE word stress seem enormous but studies on NigEng compound stress are not exhaustive, hence, the need for this investigation. The study sets to find out the stress patterns of speakers of English as a Second language (SESL) on English compounds and the implication for Nigerian English stress description. The following serves as objectives of the study:

- to examine the compound articulation patterns of Speakers of English as a Second Language;
- to find out if there is any significant difference between males and females' patterns in the compound articulation patterns of Speakers of English as a Second Language;
- to examine the extent of conformity in the compound articulation patterns of Speakers of English as a Second Language to Standard English forms;

Ogu (1992) remarked that trade contact between European merchants and the natives in the 15th century is one of the earliest factors responsible for the implantation of the English language in Nigeria. There was the need for communication between the Portuguese traders who arrived first in the West Coast of Africa and dominated the West African trade for about a century (1475-1575). Also, native traders were said to have necessitated the emergence of a kind of 'Pidgin Portuguese', which was used as a language of trade between the parties (Awonusi 2004; Christopherson 1953). Linguists (Awonusi 2004; Banjo 2012) have observed that English has been a language that links several ethnic groups in Nigeria such as the Hausa, Igbo, Yoruba, and other groups. Many authors and writers have stressed the important roles played by the English language in Nigeria. Among them are Adegbija (1989) and Akindele & Adegbite (1999). Adedimeji (2005) discusses the unifying role of English in Nigeria. He remarks that among the competing languages that scramble for national recognition or official status, whether indigenous or foreign, one must emerge as the official language, the language of relevance, for the purpose of unifying the nation. Fakeye (2012) observes that English is taught in almost all levels of the educational system in Nigeria. It is introduced to students from pre-primary to tertiary level of education. The present form and status of English in Nigeria is a result of the contact between English and Nigerian languages in the socio-cultural and political situation (Bamgbose 1995). Evidence of this world-wide phenomenon of language contact, variation and change is seen through such designation as: Nigerian English, Australian English, and Cameroon English, etc. The various varieties of "World Englishes" differ from Standard English (SE) at different levels of language organization. It has been claimed (Adegbija 2004) that Nigerian English differs systematically from SE at the levels of phonology, vocabulary, syntax, and semantics. Thus, some marked differences have been observed as they relate to suprasegmentals of stress, tone, rhythm, and intonation in the prosody of SE and NE (Akindele 2011, 2012; Akinjobi 2004; Oladipupo 2008).

2. The Stressing of Compound Words

In linguistics, compounds relate to words made up of two or more words. In other words, a compound is a lexeme (less precisely a word) that consists of more than one base. The component stems of a compound may be of the same part of speech as in the case of the English word *footpath*, which is composed of the two nouns *foot* and *path*. They may also belong to different parts of speech, as in the case of the English word *blackbird* i.e. the adjective *black* and the noun *bird*. With very few exceptions, English compounds have been remarked to be often stressed on their first component stem in SBE (Jowitt 2006, Akindele 2011), e.g. *WHITE-board, WHITEhouse, CRISScross, DOWNtrodden, WINDfall*, etc. Akindele (2008: 32) highlights the various types of English compounds as follows:

- True compounds: the two words are combined, without any space separating them. Examples are *sunshine, bookcase, chairman*, and *handshake*
- Hyphenated compounds: here, the two words are separated by a hyphen as in *drawing-pin, tape-recorder, good-looking, well-behaved*, etc.
- Phrasal compounds: the two words are separated by a space and they are compounds only in a loose sense. Examples are *motor cycle, gas cooker, free enterprise* etc.

Akindele (2008) further highlights in that study some rules guiding stress placement of English compounds. The main rules are as follows:

- In most compounds, the primary stress comes on the first syllable of the first compound member.
  - Examples: *DRAWingpin, SITingroom, MOtorcycle, WHEELbarrow, WHOOPing cough*, etc.
- Some compounds have the primary stress on the syllable of the second word. They include:
  - Adjectival compounds: *self-emPLOYed, goodLOOKing, farFETCHED, wellbeHAVED, fullGROWN and firstCLASS*, etc.
  - Numbers: *twentyONE, forty-FIVE*, etc.
  - Food/menu items: *roast CHICKen, baked BEANS*, etc.
  - Points of compass: *north WEST, south EAST*

3. Nigerian English Stress Assignment

The term *Nigerian English* (NE) is no more a myth to Nigerian linguists. This is because, at various level of linguistic analysis, differentiating linguistic features have been noticed at the lexical, phonological, morphological, and syntactic levels (Adegbija 2004). The position of English as a second language in Nigeria makes its subjection to Nigerians inevitable. Also, it has been observed, that Educated Nigerian English stress assignment has its base derived from SE forms, although with notable variations that differentiate it from SE forms (Akindele 2011). Akindele (2012) notes that conformity to the accepted norms of English usage has been the concern of linguists and other language teachers in English language teaching in Nigeria. For instance, the peculiar patterns of English as a Second Language stress patterns noticed in that study are (cf. Akindele 2008, 2012; Bolarinwa 2016):

- A shift of the main stress from the first syllable of a disyllabic word (SE) to the second syllable (NigE) as exemplified below:

(6) SE   NigE
   a) Urban   urBAN
   b) TRANSfer TransFER
   c) PERfume PerFUMe
   d) CHAos   ChaOS

- A shift of the main stress from the first syllable of a trisyllabic word in SE to the medial syllables in NigE as illustrated below:

(7) SE   NigE
   a) CHAracter character
   b) HOSpital   HospiTAl
   c) Interesting interesting

- A shift of the main stress from the first syllable of a tri-syllabic word in SE to the final syllable in NE. Thus:

(8) SE   NigE
   a) TELephone TelePHONE
   b) Educate   EduCATE
   c) Urinate   UriNATE
   d) IntERview   InterVIEW

Scholars (Kujore 1995; Jowitt 1991; Akinjobi 2004) have also remarked that some of the problems of mis-stress assignment of L2 speakers are that majority of Nigerians use delayed primary stress in the pronunciation of English words; which is due to the influence of indigenous languages with the rising rhythm as opposed to the falling rhythm of Standard English. Atoye (2005) also identified some English words in which the principal stress falls on the last syllable of verbs ending with -*ate*, -*bit*, -*sel*, -*ise*, and so on. It has been also observed that most second language learners of English came in contact with the language either in the classroom setting or learned English when they are of age or have had mastery of their native languages. Other reasons observed to be connected with the variation in use of stress of NigE speakers have also be linked to child learning error. This refers to NigE speakers who have been exposed to incompetent teachers, who themselves had deficiency in the use of stress as L2 speakers. The fact that English stress has a complex rule system has also been remarked to make the phenomenon complex to L2 speakers. Other linguists (Atoye 1991; Akinjobi 2002; Bolarinwa 2016) have also affirmed that NigE stress assignment differs significantly from SE forms. The characteristic stress patterns in NigE are such that almost every syllable is stressed. Nigerian English is considered as a variety of "World Englishes" which reflects the sociocultural sensibility of the Nigerian society. It co-exists with Nigerian languages in a diglossic relationship (Atoye 1991; Adepoju 2017).

Sunday (2010) investigated the compound stress pattern of 50 *Educated Yoruba English* (EYE) postgraduates from the University of Ibadan. He reported in that study that EYE stress pattern on compound nouns/adjectives/adverbs had a stable pattern of rise-fall pitch contour, except for compound verbs which had rise-fall or fall-rise pitch contour. This study differs from that of Sunday (2010) in the sense that more participants (i.e. 200) were purposively sampled, which helps to give a more concrete and scientific result for describing NigE stress articulation on compounds. Moreover, Sunday's (2010) interpretation of the results predominantly tilts towards a phonetic interpretation of pitch rise and fall, which is more of an intonation analysis. This study, however, encompasses phonetics and phonological description in the analysis of stress prominence through a simple statistical method on English compounds of SESL leaners.

4. Methodology and Theoretical Framework

In order to ascertain the phonological patterns of compound stress of speakers of English as a Second Language, two hundred informants (made up of 100 males and 100 females), who are university undergraduates from South-West, Nigeria, and L2 speakers of English as confirmed through interview, were purposively sampled for the investigation. University undergraduates were sampled because they meet Banjo's (1971, 2012) and Akindele's (2015) criteria of variety 3 as educated variety in NigE. As university undergraduates also, a level of proficiency is expected in their spoken and written English, having passed through the careful procedures of university screening examination before gaining admission into the university. Each of them was made to produce fifteen items of fused, separated, and hyphenated English compound words into a *Speech Filing System* (SFS), version 1.41 installed on HP 250 digital laptop. This was played back and transcribed, with the articulation of each of the participants adequately tracked and cropped for analysis. This was counted and converted to simple percentages, with the highest production taken as the norm for speakers of English as a Second language.

Metrical phonology (e.g. Liberman and Prince 1977; Kager 1995; Akinjobi 2004; Sunday 2010) is an offshoot of generative phonology. It is concerned with stress phenomena or linguistic prominence in natural languages. The innovative feature of this theory is that the prominence of a unit is defined relative to other units in the same phrase. It is distinguished from previous approaches in the sense that it posits a hierarchical structure reminiscent of the structures used in traditional discussions of poetic meter, hence the name metrical theory. Metrical phonology holds that stress is separate from pitch accent and has phonetic effects on the realization of syllables beyond their intonation, including effects on their duration and amplitude (Cruttenden 2008). It is an alternative approach to stress description due to the dissatisfaction with the *Sound Pattern of English* (SPE) system. The SPE considers stress as a feature of sound (such as nasality) such that a sound could be described as [+stress] or [–stress] using the binary approach.

Cruttenden (1986) defines stress on a tree structure in which nodes divide (only binarily) into S (strong) and W (weak) branches. Proponents of many branching trees point out that only multiple branches allow a limited number of tree levels, which correspond to predetermine levels of prosodic constituents, whereas binary branching trees require immediate levels that do not correspond to any prosodic constituent. Linguistic prominence in metrical phonology is partially determined by the strong and weak relation between nodes in a branching tree. The labels strong and weak have no inherent phonetic realization, and only have meaning relative to the rest of the labels in the tree. A strong node is stronger than a weak one. For instance, to say a syllable is stressed is to make judgement about its strength relative to an adjacent syllable as remarked by Clark and Yallop (1995) and Akindele (2008). In order to make some scientific statements on NigE stress assignment, which has been remarked to be problematic to L2 learners, and of which studies on the English compounds, also an aspect of stress, have been noticed to be inexhaustive in the literature of NE phonology. This study, therefore, make a concrete linguistic submission by engaging 200 (100 males and 100 females) SESL to produce fifteen English compounds items as represented below.

5. Analysis

From Table 1 below, it is observed that out of the expected result of 3, 000, appropriate articulation of participants for compound items whose stress is supposed to be on the first syllable of the stem was 99 (3.3%), while compounds with expected stress on the second syllable had 2,557 (85.2%) appropriate articulation. For component members of three syllable structure. where stress is expected to fall on the initial or penultimate syllable, SESL had a delayed primary stress, by articulating the primary stress on the final syllable at 344 (11.4%) instances of use.

Figure 1: Participants overall stress placement on English compounds

Items	Participants Stress Placement			
		1st Syllable	2nd Syllable	3rd Syllable
Sunshine /'sʌnʃain/	200	10	190	-
Headache/'hedeik/	200	10	190	-
Suitcase/'sju:tkeis/	200	10	190	-
Chairman /'ʧeəmən/	200	10	190	-
Checkmate /'ʧekmeit/	200	9	191	-
First name /'fɜ:st neim/	200	10	190	-
Sitting room /'sitiŋru:m/	200	30	10	160
Free kick / fri: 'kik/	200	0	200	-
Drawing pin /'drɔ:iŋ pin/	200	10	6	184
Team player /'ti:m pleiə/	200	0	200	-
Man-made /mæn-'meid/	200	0	200	-
Good-looking /gʊd'lʊkiŋ/	200	0	200	0
Well-behaved /weʎbi'heivd/	200	0	200	0
Well-dressed /wel- 'drest/	200	0	200	
High-handed /hai-'hændid/	200	0	200	0
Total	**3000**	**99 (3.3%)**	**2, 557 (85.2%)**	**344 (11.4%)**

Table 1: Participants' Overall Stress Placement on English Compounds

Figure 1 further gives a vivid and concrete description of the articulation of SESL on the compound items tested. Appropriate articulation of participants for compound items whose stress is supposed to be on the first syllable was 99 (3.3%) instances of use while instances of appropriate use for compound items whose stress naturally falls on the final syllable had 2,557 (85.2%). For compound members, whose stress are expected to fall on the initial or penultimate syllable, SESL placed stress inappropriately on the final syllable of the items at 344 (11.4%) instances of use. This means that SESL members have challenge in the placement of stress on compound items or component members, whose stress naturally falls on the initial syllable in SE.

Items	Participants Stress Placement							
	M	1st Syll	2nd Syll	3rd Syll	F	1st Syll	2nd Syll	3rd Syll
Sunshine /'sʌnʃain/	100	4	96	-	100	6	94	-
Headache /'hedeik/	100	4	96	-	100	6	94	-
Suitcase /'sjuːtkeis/	100	4	96	-	100	6	94	
Chairman /'ʧeəmən/	100	4	96	-	100	6	94	--
Checkmate /'ʧekmeit/	100	3	97	-	100	6	94	-
First name /'fɜːst neim/	100	4	96	-	100	6	94	-
Sitting room /'sitiŋruːm/	100	18	5	80	100	12	5	80
Free kick /friː 'kik/	100	0	100	-	100	0	100	-
Drawing pin /'drɔːiŋ pin/	100	7	3	92	100	3	3	92
Team player /'tiːm pleiə/	100	0	100	-	100	0	100	-
Man-made /mæn-'meid/	100	0	100	-	100	0	100	-
Good-loooking /gʊd'lʊkiŋ/	100	0	100	-	100	0	100	0
Well-behaved /weʌbi'heivd/	100	0	100	-	100	0	100	0
Well-dressed/wel- 'drest/	100	0	100	-	100	0	100	-
High-handed /hai-'hændid/	100	0	100	-	100	0	100	0
Total	150	48	1285	172	150	51	1272	172
Total %		**3.2%**	**85.7%**	**11.5%**		**3.4%**	**84. 8%**	**11.5%**

Table 2: Participants' sex placement on English compounds

Table 2 shows the sex performance of SESL. Out of the expected outcome of 1,500, only 48 (3.5%) males placed stress appropriately on English compounds as expected in SBE. For English compounds whose stress fall on the final syllable in SBE, male participants had appropriate use of 1, 285 (85.7%), while 172 (11.5%) instances of appropriate use was observed for English compound members, whose stress falls on the initial or penultimate syllables in SBE. The female participants had 51 (3.4%) instances of appropriate use for compounds with stress on the first syllable as confirmed in SBE while 1, 272 (84.8%) instances of appropriate use was observed on the final syllable of English compounds as expected in SBE, while 172 (11.5%) placed stress on the final syllable on compound members whose stress falls on the initial syllable or penultimate syllables in SE.

6. Results and Data Interpretation

Overall, SESL appropriate articulation of English compound words show that out of the expected result of 3, 000, appropriate articulation of respondents for compound items whose stress is supposed to be on the first syllable of the stem had a minimal use of 3.3%. English compounds whose primary stresses falls naturally on the final syllable of the stems had the highest instances of appropriate use, namely 85.2%. For component members whose stress naturally falls on the initial or penultimate syllable in SBE, also had minimal use of 11.4%. This noticed patterns, therefore, conform to Akinjobi's (2004) and Atoye's (2005) claims for English polysyllabic words stress pattern in educated Yoruba English, a sub-variety of NigE.

However, it should be noted that though phonologically, SESL placed stress on the second syllable of the English compound whose stress are expected to be placed on the second syllable appropriately. This does not invalidate the fact that, phonetically, participants could modulate pitch prominence between strong and weak syllables of the English compounds and compound members. Results from this study also show that SESL observed the affixation rule of Standard English which does not allow stress on an affix. The majority of the participants observed this rule even though they were L2 speakers. For instance, *good looking* /gʊdˈlʊkiŋ/, *drawing pin* /ˈdrɔːiŋ pin/, with affixes on the final and penultimate syllables, did not get any stress articulation from SESL.

Speakers of English as a Second Language stress articulation on the syllables of English compounds and compound members do not show any significant difference for sex performance. Overall, males' instances of use on the tested items was 23.2%, and females' 23.3%, with a difference of 0.1%. This insignificant difference, however, negates the claims of scholars such as Krammer (1975), Thorne and Henley (1975), Brend (1975), Trudgill (1975), and Ojareche (2009), who have conducted research on language and sex and have come up with claims that women are observed to use linguistic forms close to the standard and pronounce generally better than men.

Furthermore, to bring scientific justification for what was discovered from the production of the participants on the tested items, and specifically in relation to tables 1 and 2, participants' production was subjected to Prince and Liberman's (1977), Akindele's (2015) and Adepoju's (2017) Metrical Stress Rule, an aspect of metrical theory. This rule is exemplified below.

6.1. Metrical

6.1.1. *Stress Rule Analysis of Speakers of English as a Second Language (SESL)*

For the compound word *SUNshine* /ˈsʌnʃain/, SESL produced the first and second syllable of the item with the same pitch modulation as perceived. None of the participants could alternate between the strong and the weak syllables of the compound items, while in Standard English pitch modulation was confirmed. For *SUITcase* /ˈsjuːtkeis/, it was perceived that SESL produced the first and second syllable of the item with the same pitch modulation. None of the participants could alternate stress between the strong and weak syllables compared to what is obtained in SBE. Speakers of English as Second Language produced the first and second syllable of *TEAMplayer* /ˈtiːmpleiə/ at the same pitch level modulation, unlike SE, in which primary stress applies to the initial syllable of the stem. For *manMADE* /mæn'meid/, even though SESL articulated the second syllable of the stem phonologically, it was perceived that pitch modulation was not observed between the strong and weak syllable. Meanwhile, in SBE, two syllables cannot be adjacent to each other. The compound member, /'drɔ:iŋ pin/ *'DRAWing-pin* /'drɔ:iŋ pin/ will naturally take the primary stress on the initial syllable in SBE. Speakers of English as a Second Language produced the syllables on the same modulation. Pitch modulation was not observed, even though the final syllable was perceived to be more articulated.

Generally, the metrical tree patterns of participants show that speakers of English as a Second Language (SESL) compound stress pattern varies from Standard English (SE) form. This is because all the syllables were perceived to be given the same pitch prominence. Speakers of English as a Second Language did not apply pitch modulation between the weak and the strong syllables of the compound items and compound members. In SE however, two strong syllables cannot co-occur in a word. Hence, in NigE, a dual strong syllable articulation was obtained, but a shift of primary stress is often predominantly observed on the ultimate syllables of English compound words and component members.

7. Conclusion

Results from the data analysis of SESL revealed that stress on compound words for L2 varies from Standard English (SE) form. Even though the articulation of SESL shows that they could make the second syllable of the tested English compounds prominent as expected, participants did not show any modulation between the strong and weak syllables. The metrical tree of the participants clearly revealed Strong-Strong (S/S) articulation, instead of the Weak-Strong (W/S) or Strong-Weak (S/W) of SBE.

However, it should be noted that the SESL participants are from tone language background as affirmed through interview. As L2 speakers, tone characterises the majority of the indigenous languages spoken in Nigeria. As a second language speaker of English, therefore, it is likely to find out variation in the form of articulation of the participants from SE from. This is the reason for the phonological transfer observed by the participants. Hence, SESL stress pattern on compound words or compound members predominantly tilts toward the ultimate syllable. Thus, SESL stress should be accessed as a variety of one of the 'new Englishes', provided it is intelligible to other world users of English. Arising from the findings, therefore, speakers of English as a Second Language, and educated Nigerians generally, should strive at using spoken English forms with communicative features (i.e. expanding circle) in as much as it does not compromise with national and international intelligibility standard.

References

Adedimeji, M. (2005). The unifying role of English in a multilingual nation: The case of Nigeria. *A Festschrift for Okon Essien Aba.* National Institute for Nigerian Languages 67-75.

Adegbija, E. (1989). Lexico-semantic variation in Nigerian English. *World Englishes* 8 (2): 165-177.

Adegbija, E. (2004). The domestication of English in Nigeria. Lagos: University of Lagos Press.

Adepoju, O. (2017). *Phrasal stress in English as a second language.* Unpublished BA Project, Department of Languages and Linguistics. Osun State University, Osogobo, Nigeria, x-110.

Akindele, J. (2008). *Stress in Edo English.* M.A thesis. Nigeria: Department of English. University of Ibadan, xiii – 90.

Akindele, J. (2011). Variable word stress in spoken educated Edo English. MPhil Dissertation. Nigeria: Department of English, University of Ibadan, xv -169.

Akindele, J. (2012) The challenges of teaching and learning the English stress in ESL classroom: The case of Nigeria. *6ᵗʰ International Technology, Education and Development Conference.* Valencia, Spain, 1679-1685.

Akindele, J. (2015). *Duration as a determining factor in educated Edo English rhythm description.* Unpublished PhD thesis. Nigeria: Department of English, University of Ibadan. xv-175.

Akindele, F., Adegbite, W. (1999). *The sociology and politics of English in Nigeria: An introduction.* Ile-Ife: Obafemi Awolowo University Press.

Akinjobi A. (2002). Nigerian English or standard English suprasegmentals: The question of variety to teach. In Babatunde, S., Adeyanju, D. (Eds.) *Language, meaning and society.* Ilorin: Haytee Press and Publishing Co. Nigeria Limited.

Akinjobi A. (2004). *A phonological investigation of vowel weakening and unstressed syllable obscuration in educated Yoruba English.* PhD thesis. Nigeria: Department of Linguistics, University of Ibadan, xxiv-300.

Atoye, R. (1989). Progressive stress shift in Nigerian spoken English ODU. *A Journal of West African Studies* 35: 39-51.

Atoye R. (1991). Word-stress in Nigerian English. *World Englishes* 10 (1): 1- 6.

Atoye, R. (2005). Deviant word stress in Nigerian English: its implications for Nigerian's English oral literacy. Paper presented at the *22nd Annual Conference of Nigeria English Studies Association* (NESA). Ile- Ife: Obafemi Awolowo University.

Awonusi, V. (2004). Cycles of linguistic history: the development of English in Nigeria. In Awonusi, A., Dadzie, A. (Eds.) *Nigerian English influences and characteristics.* Lagos: Concepts Publications.

Babalola, E. (Eds.) *The domestication of English in Nigeria.* Lagos: University of Lagos Press.

Bamgbose, A. (1995). English in the Nigerian environment. In Bamgbose, A., Banjo, A. & Thomas, A. (Eds.) *New Englishes: A West African perspective.* Ibadan: Mosuro Publishers, 9-26.

Banjo, A. (1971). Towards a definition of standard Nigerian spoken English. *Annales de L'Universite d'Abijan Serie* H. (Linguistique) Fascicule hor Serie.

Banjo, A. (2012). The deteriorating use of English in Nigeria. Lectured delivered at the maiden edition of *English Language Clinic Forum*, Department of English. Ibadan: University of Ibadan.

Bolarinwa, P. (2016). *Stress patterns of selected Nigerian newscasters as model for Standard British English.* BA Project. Nigeria: Department of Languages and Linguistics, Osun State University, Osogobo, xiii-131.

Brend, R. (1975). Male-female intonation patterns in American English. In Thorne, B., Henley, N. (Eds.) *Language and sex: Difference and dominance.* Mass: Newbury House, 84 – 87.

Christophersen, P. (1953). Some special West African English words. *English Studies*, 34.

Clark, J. & Yallop, C. (1995). *An introduction to phonetics and phonology.* (2ⁿᵈ edition). London: Blackwell Publishing.

Cruttenden, A. (1986). *Intonation.* Cambridge: Cambridge University Press.

Cruttenden, A. (2008). *Gimson's pronunciation of English.* (7ᵗʰ edition). London: Roudlegde.

Fakeye, D. (2012). Teachers' qualification and subject mastery as predictors of achievement in English language. *Global Journal of Human social science* (12): 3.

Jowitt, D. (1991). *Nigerian English usage: An introduction.* Ibadan: Longman.

Jowitt, D. (2006). *Oral English for senior secondary schools*. Ibadan: Spectrum Books Ltd.

Kager, R. (1995). The metrical theory of word stress. *The Handbook of Phonological Theory*. In J. A. Goldsmith. (Ed.). Oxford and Cambridge: Basil Blackwell, 367-402.

Krammer, C. (1975). Women's speech: separate but unequal. In Thorne, B., Henley, N. (Eds.) *Language and sex: Difference and dominance*. Mass: Newbury House, 43-56.

Kujore, O. (1985). *English Usage: Some Notable Nigerian Variations*. Ibadan: Evans Ltd.

Kujore O. (1995). Whose English? In A. Bamgbose, A, Banjo, & A. Thomas. (Eds.). *New Englishes: A West African Perspective*. Ibadan: Musoro, 367-380.

Liberman, M., Prince, A. (1977). On stress and linguistic rhythm. *Linguistic Inquiry* (8): 249-336.

Muhammed, N. (2017). *Sentence stress in the English of second language learners' (ESL) conversion*. BA Project. Nigeria: Department of Languages and Linguistics, Osun State University, Osogobo, xiii-131.

Ogu, J. (1992). *A historical survey of English and the Nigerian situation*. Lagos: Kraft Books Ltd.

Ojareche, R. (2009). *A sociophonological analysis of Nigeria male and female television Newscasters' speech analysis*. MA Project. Nigeria: Department of English, University of Ibadan, xi -116.

Oladipupo, R. (2008). *English intonation patterns of television reporters in Lagos State*. MA. Project. Nigeria: Department of English, University of Ibadan, xi -118.

Sunday, A. (2008). Compound stress in educated Yoruba English. In Atoye, R. (Ed.). *Papers in English and Linguistics*. Ibadan: Linguistic Association, Obafemi Awolowo University, 9:40-58.

Thorne, B., Henley, C. (1975). *Language and sex: Difference and dominance*. Newbury: Rowley Mass.

Trudgill, P. (1975). Sex covert prestige and linguistic change in the urban British English of Norwich. In Thorne, B., Henley, N. (Eds.). *Language and sex: Difference and dominance*. Mass: Newbury House.

The Effects of Cooperative Language Learning on Students' Achievement in Composition Writing in a Selected Secondary School in Nigeria.

Uche Betty Gbenedio & Omawumi Osa-Omoregie

University of Benin (both)

Abstract

This study investigated the effects of cooperative language learning on students' achievement in English composition writing. The research design is based on a quasi-experimental non-randomized pre-test, and post-test control group design. The population of the study comprised all 243 students in Junior Secondary 3 (2017/2018 academic session) in a demonstration secondary school in Edo State, from which a sample of 80 students in two intact classes were selected, one class into the experimental group composed of 40 students taught using Cooperative Language Learning (CLL) which is a Process Approach, and the other class the control group composed of 40 students taught using the Product (traditional) Approach. Data were collected using English Essay Writing Achievement Test (EEWAT), a standardized instrument developed by the National Examination Council (NECO). The descriptive statistics of mean and standard deviation were used to analyse the research questions, while the t-test for independent samples and paired samples were used to test the hypotheses at alpha level of 0.05. Results showed that the subjects in the experimental group taught with Cooperative Language Learning (CLL) outperformed the subjects in the control group taught using the conventional teaching method which is the method commonly used by teachers for teaching composition writing. It was recommended that teachers should use student-centred methods that will make the students more involved in composition writing classes for enhanced students' performance.

Keywords: Composition writing, cooperative language learning (CLL), product approach, process approach, achievement, composition-writing.

1. Introduction and Background to the Study

1.1. Introduction

Writing is often considered the most complex and the most difficult of the four language skills, perhaps because it is not a natural activity as all learners have to be taught how to write. It involves many sub-skills some of which learners may master partially or may not be able to master until effectively taught and extensively practised. Some of the sub-skills are: knowledge of grammar; varied sentence structures, spelling, argument construction, effective organization of ideas and analytical skills, and even reading comprehension among others. When learners lack these sub-skills, their composition writing cannot but be deficient, especially in English as a second Language situations where learning to write the language is mainly dependent on classroom activities. Students need to master these writing sub-skills as mastery of these sub-skills will not only help them in their secondary school education in all school subjects, communication and self-expression, but also in the world of work.

1.2. Background

The importance of composition writing in the life of a Nigerian school child cannot be overemphasised. For learners to continue to the tertiary level after the secondary school education in the Nigerian system, they must pass the English Language at the Credit level; a simple pass in the subject, is not accepted and many prospective students have had to repeat the subject several times in order to obtain that credit pass at the end of their secondary education. Up till today, there is a persistent decline in Senior Secondary School students' performance in English language in Nigeria. A critical analysis of West African Senior Certificate Examination (WASSCE) results from 2006 – 2016 attests to this. In 2006, candidates who obtained the grades required for entry into tertiary institutions were 15.56%; in 2007, 25.54%; in 2008, 13.76%; in 2009, 25.54%; in 2010, 24.93%; in 2011, 30.70%; in 2012, 38.81%; in 2013, 36.57%; in 2014, 31.28%; and in 2015, 38.68%. This means that to the majority of the students will be denied access to tertiary education on the grounds of their unsatisfactory performance in English Language in the WASSCE examinations. Unfortunately, this has been attributed largely to gross deficiency in composition writing (Kolawole 1998, West African Examination Council (WAEC) Chief Examiners Report 2006-2015).

The Chief Examiner's Reports show that students cannot write good compositions. They have consistently and categorically stated that students' compositions were marred by wrong grammar, weak vocabulary, and poor content. This is a serious source of worry to stakeholders in the education sector. Observation by the researchers in some secondary schools in the country revealed that students are apprehensive whenever they are asked to write composition in class and that most teachers use the Product Approach to teach composition in their classes. It is possible that among other issues, the teacher-centred method used in teaching them composition writing is one of the factors responsible for students' poor attitude and performance in composition writing.

The art of composing is expected to motivate. But probably, it is indisputable that not all methods are able to motivate students' critical thinking, creativity, critical analysis, and organisation of ideas, problem solving skills, and the development of their ability to write efficiently. Methods which are process-driven, with peer review and feedback, are expected to enable students to learn from each other, thus training them in the art of constructive criticism, knowledge of extensive vocabulary and good writing skills.

The Process Approach is embedded in L. S. Vygotsky's (1978) Socio-Cultural Theory (SCT) which holds that socio-cultural interactions are critical to learning, and human behaviour, and that cognitive development occurs both in and through activity with other people. Two main principles of this theory which supports the above assertions are: the existence of a More Knowledgeable Other (MKO), and the Zone of Proximal Development (ZPD) to enable the learner to learn successfully. The MKO possesses more knowledge about a particular subject than the learner and can be a teacher, peer, text book, manual or even a computer. In other words, through the interaction with a more knowledgeable other, the composition writer can acquire skills and knowledge that he may not be able to acquire on his own, while the ZPD is the state of knowledge of the learner in which he would need a little push from without to learn a new idea or acquire a new skill.

Cooperative writing assignments and projects, such as creating a class newspaper, class bulletin, and group essays, among other group writing activities, make students to achieve group writing goals, as well as form deep and lasting social relationships as canvassed in Vygotsky's (1978) theory.

Halliday (2003), Kushner (2003), Juzwik, Curcic, Wolbers, Moxley, Dimling & Shankland (2006), all emphasise that writing proficiency is an essential need for students in the ESL environment in order to be able to communicate with people all over the world in English, the most widely used language not only for education and books, but also for sending different documents to one another and chatting, as well as sending e-mails across the globe.

Since this is the case, the methods of teaching it for effectiveness need close attention. So far, teachers in the Nigerian secondary school system seem to pay attention to teacher-centred methods, chief of which is the "product approach" to composition teaching and learning which is embedded in Behaviourism, a theory which believes that learning is best achieved through authority, through stimulus-response pattern of learning, Student–centred methods, among which is the CLL approach are often not utilised. Methods, if not the most important factor in learning, is definitely a very important factor. A teacher who utilises an effective method is likely to produce higher-achieving students. How would CLL, a process approach, compare with the Product to teaching and learning composition in a selected Nigerian secondary school?

1.3. Review of Related Literature

Previous literature on the effects of these two methods is available. However, in the Nigerian system, these are very few and include Oluikpe (2007) who conducted a study on enhancing student's achievement in expository writing using collaborative learning among university undergraduate students. The result showed that collaborative learning in essay writing is more effective than other methods. Ogbu (2009), in a study titled *Effects of cooperative and product teaching on senior secondary school students' achievement in Essay writing in Afikpo North Education Zone of Ebonyi State, Nigeria*, revealed that the students in the experimental group outperformed those in the control group, perhaps because they were made to work in groups. They interacted and gained better understanding of the essay topics, brainstormed, formed topic sentences and developed them together into paragraphs using varied and appropriate words and sentences. Okonkwo (2014), in a study using Senior Secondary 2 students titled *Effects of Collaborative Instructional Strategy on students' Achievement in Essay Writing in English in Abakaliki Urban Education Zone of Ebonyi State*, Nigeria, found that students taught Essay Writing with the collaborative instructional strategy outperformed those taught with the conventional, product method.

However, these studies were carried out either with University students or Senior Secondary students who can be considered as being fairly advanced in their knowledge and use of the English Language. This study, by contrast, applied the methods at the Junior Secondary level with the aim of finding out whether there will be a difference in the results obtained. In addition, the previous studies reviewed were carried out in public schools, while this study was carried out in a University secondary school which is considered a private, elitist school, and in a different State, Edo State, Nigeria. Perhaps these demographic differences would make a difference in the results?

1.4. Objectives of the Study and Hypotheses

The researchers therefore set out to investigate the relative effectiveness of the Cooperative Language Learning and the Traditional methods of teaching and learning Composition writing in a Junior Secondary School located in the University of Benin, Benin City, Edo State, Nigeria. The specific objectives of the study were explored through the hypotheses presented below, which guide this study:

> H1: There is no significant difference in composition writing achievement between students taught using cooperative language learning and those taught using the conventional method in junior secondary schools in Edo State.
>
> H2: There is no significant difference between the pre- and post-test mean scores in composition writing of students taught with cooperative language learning method.
>
> H3: There is no significant difference between the pre- and post-test mean scores in composition writing of students taught with the product approach learning.

2. Methodology

2.1. Language Learning Approach (LLA)

Cooperative learning (CL), which is a process approach, is a student-centred, instructor-facilitated instructional strategy in which a small team of four (4) heterogeneous ability students, is responsible for its own learning *and* the learning of all team members. The number four is not sacrosanct, except that you can have pairs working together at times, and four members working together at other times, without having an unwieldy group. This is said to promote peer interaction and cooperation for studying academic subjects (Slavin 1980).

CL holds each of the team members accountable for his/her own and the team's outcomes. Several essential characteristics must be present for a team to be called cooperative. Even though the teacher structures most of the activities, it is the team and each of its members that are responsible for learning. A team must exhibit interdependence, support one another's learning, hold each other accountable for the team's process and outcomes, exhibit acceptable interpersonal skills, and possess team dynamics (Brent 2001; Hamilton 1997; Johnson 2003; Felder, Johnson & Johnson 1994; D. W. Stahl 1994).

CLL tackles composition writing from three perspectives: idea generation during the pre-writing stage, meaning construction in the drafting stage, and peer review at the editing stage. This approach to teaching writing is informed by the Social Constructivist Theory in the sense that writing under this approach make the learners active in the classroom. They generate ideas, make multiple drafts, and engage in peer reviews through discussions, after which the composition is corrected. Social constructivists assert that guidance from MKO's, who might be the teacher or a more capable peer(s), should help learners to complete assigned tasks. Teacher-group and peer-peer conferences are held to discuss the written compositions, and corrective feedback offered to learners.

Usually, each student in the group has a specific role to play. The potential roles include: Facilitator (the student who ensures that the group stays on task), Recorder (the student who writes down group answers and decisions), Summarizer (the student who summarizes the groups answers), Reporter (the student who conveys the group's ideas/answers/decisions to another group or the entire class), and Time-keeper (the student responsible for making sure that the group keeps to the time assigned to accomplish the task).

These roles are not permanent but are rotated among the students as the groups desire and deem fit. Teachers are expected to help ensure that the same student does not serve in the same role every time a writing assignment is given, so that every student has an opportunity to serve in every capacity as the process approach CLL focuses on the stages that the students go through before the final draft of the composition (Hyland 2003). The above characteristics of the CLL which have been applied to this study are different from that of the Product approaches.

2.2. The Product Approach to Teaching Composition Writing

The product approach, often referred to as the conventional or "traditional rhetoric" (Matsuda 2003; Pullman 1999), emphasizes the final draft submitted by students to the teachers. In this approach, the students are told to write an essay by imitating a given model, going through four stages: familiarization, controlled writing, guided writing, and free writing. Writing is viewed as "mainly concerned with the knowledge about the structure of language; and writing development is mainly the result of the imitation of input, in the form of texts provided by the teacher" (Badger & White 2000: 154). It is, therefore, teacher-centred, as the teacher becomes the arbiter of the models used (Brakus 2003).

This method is based on Behaviourism, a theory of learning which sees learning in terms of the stimulus-response pattern. How the learner should approach the process of writing is ignored in this approach. What is important is the product or the finished work. This is the traditional approach currently in use by teachers in most schools in Nigeria (Aladeyomi & Adetunde 2007). The teachers seem to feel more comfortable with this approach either because they are not familiar with the other approaches or because of the often-large class-sizes that they handle. So far, the use of the product approach is said not to have yielded the expected positive results in terms of students' performance and achievement in writing tasks, and writing examinations, respectively. Instead, there has been steady decline in students' ability to write efficiently (WAEC Chief Examiner's Report 2015). Will this be found to be true in this study? Of the CLL and the Product Approach, which will lead to higher writing achievement for the students? In effect, which of the two methods would facilitate better students' performance in composition writing?

2.3. Study Design

To carry out the study the pre-test, post-test, a control group quasi-experimental design as diagrammatically represented below was adopted:

$0_1 \ X_1 \ 0_2$

$0_1 \ X_2 \ 0_2$

In this, 0_1 represents the pre-tests and 0_2 represents the post-tests. X_1 is the usual treatment (control group), i.e. the product approach, and X_2 is the unusual treatment (experimental group), i.e. Cooperative Language Learning (CLL).

2.4. The Population and Sample

The population comprised all 243 students in six (6) classes which made up the Junior Secondary School three (JSS3) in the Demonstration Secondary School at the University of Benin, Benin City, Nigeria in 2015/2016 academic session. Using the simple random sampling procedure, 80 students from two intact classes were selected from among the six classes. One class was termed the experimental group composed of 40 students taught using Cooperative Language Learning (CLL), while the other class, the control group also composed of 40 students, was taught using the Product Approach.

2.5. Instruments for Data Collection

One instrument was used to collect data for this study, namely the English Essay Writing Achievement Test (EEWAT), adopted from past questions administered by the National Examination Council (NECO) Junior Secondary Certificate Examination (JSCE) on Essay writing. NECO is the examining body charged with the final examination for this level of Education in Nigeria. The test was designed to cover those topics on which the pre-test and post-test observations were based. The same test was used for both the pre- and the post-tests.

Although the test was adopted from already standardized test items, it was still subjected to face and content validity test, by giving it to experts in the field of Educational Measurement and Evaluation and Language Testing for critical appraisal before administration. The instrument was adjudged to be valid. The reliability check of the instruments was conducted via pilot testing using thirty students who were randomly selected from a school outside the sampled school but within the population. The internal consistency reliability of the English Essay Writing Achievement Test (EEWAT) was estimated using the test-retest method. After two weeks of administering the instrument to the pilot subjects, the same test was re-administered on the same respondents. Using the Pearson product moment correlation statistic, the Reliability Coefficient of 0.82 was obtained showing that the instrument is reliable.

2.6. Experimental Procedure

The study lasted for twelve weeks and was carried out by the researchers. The first week was for administering the pre-test, ten weeks for treatment, and the 12th and last week for administering the post-test. The procedure for each treatment is summarized below.

2.6.1. *Experimental Group: Cooperative Language Learning (CLL)*

The researchers stated the learning objectives and explained the concept of the study. The researchers assigned the students into heterogeneous groups of four students each, with at least one good reader and one good writer in each group, rearranged the classroom to create face-to-face sitting arrangement so as to facilitate easy interaction among members of each group, assigned roles to the students in the different groups, and explained to them that the roles will be changed during every lesson.

The students worked together to write the first paragraph of each composition to ensure that they all have establish the keynote of their topics for the compositions, brainstormed on the topic collectively until a consensus was reached on every accepted point for the outline, wrote-up the outlines into full essays, proofread their work. They agreed on corrections in grammar, capitalization, punctuation, spelling, language use, and other aspects of writing specified by the teacher. Then, they signed their names to indicate that they have all read their submission and agreed with its contents as being what they all produced together. During the period of cooperative work, the teacher monitored the groups, intervening when appropriate, to help students master the required writing skills. At the end, the different groups' summarizers submitted their work for marking.

2.6.2. *Control Group: Conventional Strategy*

For this group, the usual conventional, traditional approach was utilised: the researcher wrote the topic on the board and explained it to the students, asked the students questions based on the topic and used their responses to develop an outline which she wrote on the board, and then directed the students to write a composition based on the outline given. Words that the teacher thought were essential to the composition were also, along with the outline, written on the board for the students to use should they require them. Students were then required to write the essay individually and, thereafter, submit their composition products to the teacher.

2.7. Procedure for Data Collection

The researchers first observed the two groups by administering a pre-test to them. The aim of administering the pre-test was two-fold: to establish the homogeneity of the two groups, and to ascertain the entry point of the subjects. The result, as shown in Table 1 reveals that the two groups were homogenous in essay writing achievement prior to the experiment.

Test	Groups	N	Mean	SD	t	df	$p_{\text{two-tailed}}$
Pre-test	Experi-mental	40	51.8000	10.80883	-1.395	78	.167
	Control	40	54.9500	9.33960			

Table 1:   Test of homogeneity of the groups using the pre-test.

After, the pre-test established that both groups were homogenous in their level of achievement in composition writing. The subjects in the experimental and control groups were exposed to treatment for ten weeks by the researchers, at the end of which they administered the post-test during the twelfth and final week of the study. The students' essays for the post-test were scored and the result subjected to statistical analysis.

2.8. Data Analyses

The data collected were analysed using descriptive statistics: mean and standard deviation, paired samples t-test, and t-test for independent samples. The hypotheses were tested for significance at the 0.05 alpha level.

3. Results and Discussion of Findings

3.1. Findings

3.1.1. *Differences in Writing Composition Achievement*

There is no significant difference in composition writing achievement between students taught using Cooperative Language Learning and those taught using the Conventional Method in Junior secondary schools in Edo State.

x	Groups	N	Mean	SD	t	df	$p_{two-tailed}$	Mean Difference
Post-test	Experi-mental	40	71.0000	10.56846	4.397	78	.000*	9.70000
	Control	40	61.3000	9.10677				

Table 2: T-test analysis of the difference in the post test scores of the students in the control and experimental groups (*Statistically significant at .05 level of significance).

Table 2 shows that the mean score of the students in the experimental group was 71.00, while the mean score of the students in the control group was 61.30. This shows that the students in the experimental group outperformed the students in the control group. To explore whether this was significant, an independent samples' test was conducted, revealing a t-value of 4.40, significant at .000 level. This indicated that there is a significant difference in the post-test mean scores between the students in the experimental and the control groups. Therefore, the null hypothesis is rejected.

3.1.2. *Differences between the Pre- and Post-Test Mean Scores in Composition Writing (CLL)*

There is no significant difference between the pre- and post-test mean scores in composition writing of students taught with the Cooperative Language Learning method.

	N	Mean	SD	t	df	$p_{two-tailed}$	Remark
Pre-test	40	51.80	10.81	8.655	39	.000*	Signifi-cant
Post-test	40	71.00	10.57				

Table 3: Paired samples t-test of differences between pre and post test scores of students in the experimental group (*significant at the 0.05 level of significance).

Table 3 shows that there was a statistically significant difference between the mean scores of the experimental group on the pre-test and post–test achievement in composition writing in favour of the post–test scores. The table shows a t- value of 8.66, significant at .000 level. This indicates that there is a significant difference in the pre and post-test mean scores of the students in the experimental group. Therefore, the null hypothesis is rejected.

3.1.3. *Difference between the Pre- and Post-Test Mean Scores in Composition Writing (Product Approach Learning)*

There is no significant difference between the pre- and post-test mean scores in composition writing of students taught with the Product Approach to composition writing.

	N	Mean	SD	t	df	$p_{\text{two-tailed}}$	Remark
Pre-test	40	54.9500	9.33960	-3.788	39	.001*	Signifi-
Post-test	40	61.3000	9.10677				cant

Table 4: Paired samples test of pre and post test scores of students in the control group (*significant at the 0.05 level of significance)

Table 4 shows that the difference in the pre- and post-test mean scores of the control group in composition writing was also statistically significant at the 0.05 level in favour of the post–test scores, with a t-value of -3.79, significant at .001 level. The null hypothesis is, therefore, rejected.

4. Discussion of Findings and Conclusions

4.1. Discussion of Findings

This study, which investigated the effects of Cooperative Language Learning (CLL) and the Product Approach on Junior secondary school students' composition writing ability, revealed that CLL is more effective than the traditional approach. At the onset of the study, there was no significant difference between the pre-test scores of the students in the Experimental and Control groups as evident in Table 1. This showed the homogeneity of the two groups.

After the experiment, however, the students who were taught with the Cooperative Language Learning (CLL) Approach performed significantly better than those in the Control group. The implication of this is that the Cooperative Language Learning (CLL), which is a Process Approach, empowered students to develop better composition writing skills and its attendant sub-skills in the course of learning to write. There is also a significant difference between the pre- and post-test achievements mean scores in composition writing of the students in the experimental group, as well as those in the control group. This shows that both approaches yielded some improvement. However, Cooperative Language Learning (CLL) was more effective, and the difference in the results of the two groups was significant. The students in the control group taught with the traditional method also improved on their performance, significantly, perhaps as a result of the passage of time, and perhaps also because the school is located in a university environment. The proximity to the university may have influenced the students to be self-directed in such a way that they did a lot of studying on their own. With educated parents, they may have been assisted in their homework, whether in composition writing or other language skills, which may have worked together to improve their pre-experimental performance.

The findings of this study are in agreement with the findings of Ogbu (2006), Okonkwo (2014), and Oluikpe (2007) that carried out similar studies in different States of Nigeria using either University students or students in the Senior Secondary schools respectively. Despite the class level and the State involved, the result turned out to be the same. From this result some conclusions were drawn.

5. Conclusion

The Cooperative approach is superior to the traditional approach to teaching composition in Nigerian schools irrespective of level or State. Difficulties encountered by students in composition writing which negatively affect their performance in English language examination stems, at least, in part, from the product to teaching composition writing. The researchers believe that the cooperative language learning approach, if adopted by teachers in teaching composition writing, will improve students' performance in composition writing in schools no matter the level.

6. Recommendations

Based on the findings of the study, and the conclusion drawn there from, the following recommendations are made: teachers should pay attention to the teaching of composition writing using the Cooperative Language Learning approach, which is a process approach and student-centred, to enable students participate actively in the lessons. This study can also be replicated in other States and perhaps for longer periods to see if the effect will be long lasting. Furthermore, the government should give English language teachers opportunities for in-service training, seminars and workshops to enhance their knowledge and use of methods other than the traditional product approach that they are currently familiar with and use. Other student-centred methods should also be tried out to ascertain if all student-centred methods will produce the same results.

References

Adegbile, J., Alabi, O. (2007). Effects of verbal ability on second language writers' achievement in essay writing in English language. *International Journal of African & African American Studies*, 6 (1), 61-67.

Akinwamide, T. (2012). The influence of process approach on English as second language students' performances in essay writing. *Journal of English Language Teaching* 5 (3): 16-29.

Aladeyomi, S., Adetunde, A. (2007). A balanced activity approach to the teaching of essay writing in English in Nigerian secondary schools. *MedwelJournals* 2 (3): 298-301.

Badger, R., White, G. (2000). Product, process and genre: Approaches to writing in EAP [Electronic version]. *ELT Journal*, 54 (2): 153-160.

Brakus, P. (2003). *A product/process/genre approach to teaching writing: A synthesis of approaches in a letter writing course for non-native English-speaking administrative personnel.* Unpublished MA dissertation, University of Surrey, Cambridge.

188 *Uche Betty Gbenedio & Omawumi Osa-Omoregie*

Chief Examiner's Report May/ June (2004-2006). *The West African examination council*. Lagos: Nigeria.
Chief Examiner's Report, May/June (2007-2015). *The West African examination council*. Lagos: Nigeria.
Halliday, M. (2003). Written language, standard language, global language. *World Englishes* 22 (4): 405-418.
Hyland, K. (2003). Genre-based pedagogies: A social response to process. *Journal of Second Language Writing* 12: 17-29.
Johnson, D. (2003). Social interdependence: The interrelationships among theory, research, and practice. *American Psychologist*, 58 (11): 931-945.
Johnson, D., Johnson, R. (1994). *Learning together and alone: Cooperative, competitive and individualistic learning*. (4th ed). Boston: Allyn & Bacon.
Johnson, D., Johnson, R. & Holubec, E. (1991). *Cooperation in the classroom*. Minnesota: Interaction Book Company.
Juzwik, M. et al. (2006). Writing into the 21st century: An overview of research on writing, 1999 to 2004. *Written Communication* 23, 451-476.
Kolawole, C. (1998). *Linguistic inputs and three methods of presentation as determinants of students' achievement in senior secondary students essay writing*. An Unpublished PhD thesis, University of Ibadan.
Kushner, E. (2003). English as global language: Problems, dangers, opportunities. *Diogenes* 50 (2): 17-23.
Matsuda, P. (2003). Process and post-process: A discursive history. *Journal of Second Language,* 12: 5-83.
Ogbu, C. (2009). *Effects of cooperative and product teaching on senior secondary school students' achievement in essay writing in Afikpo North Education Zone of Ebonyi State, Nigeria*. Unpublished PhD thesis, EBSU PG Abstract.
Okonkwo, A. (2014). Effects of collaborative instructional strategy on students' achievement in essay writing in English in Abakaliki urban education zone of Ebonyi State. *Research Journal of Education* 2 (3): 1-7.
Oluikpe, B. (2007). Enhancing students' achievement in expository writing using collaborative learning. *Journal of Applied Literacy and Reading* 1 (3).
Pullman, G. (1999). Stepping yet again into the same current. In Kent, T. (Ed.) *Post process theory: Beyond the writing process Paradigm*. Carbondale: Southern Illinois University Press, 16-29.
Sharan, S. (1980). Cooperative learning in small groups: Recent methods and effects on achievement, attitudes, ethnics, relations. *Review of Educational Research* 50:241-271.
Slavin, R. (1980). Cooperative learning. *Review of Educational Research* 50 (2): 315-342.
Vygotsky, L. (1978). *Mind in society: The development of higher psychological processes*. Harvard: Harvard University Press.

Providing Reading Choices in an English Language Classroom at ESUT: A Survey

Obiageli Nnamani

Enugu State University of Science & Technology

Abstract

Reading is an important language skill which fresh university students must acquire in order to succeed in school, yet research and experience show that many students do not read, and even when they do, they are not efficient. Several reasons have been adduced for this: learners do not read because the recommended books are difficult, the learners prefer other titles, or the learners just do not want to read. Consequently, this study investigated whether offering learners reading choices would make them read more and learn grammar better. The study used a qualitative survey design in which two instruments–the interview and the questionnaire- were used to elicit responses relevant to the study. Twenty- seven students who enrolled in the 2013/2014 ESUT/Gire American University, Cyprus programme, constituted the sample of the study. The research was carried out while the first semester classes were in progress. Simple percentage was used to analyse the data collected. Even though the population of this study was small, the result indicated that under the supervision of a teacher, reading choices and independent reading in the classroom will help learners not only read more and enjoy reading, but also excel in mechanical accuracy.

Keywords: Choice reading, book selection, independent reading

1. Introduction

One of the greatest ironies of the information age is that, while the 21st century has witnessed an avalanche of written information, students' interest in print reading has declined. The reading phobia which appears to have affected learners in both developed and under- developed nations has assumed such a huge significance that it has attracted the attention of world leaders around the globe. Consequently, in 2002, President Bush signed the *No Child Left Behind Act* into law. Along with this Act, came *Reading First* which, according to Johnson & Blair (2003: 182) "became a national initiative aimed at helping every child in every state become a successful reader by third grade". In Nigeria, a similar poor reading culture spurred Nigeria's immediate past president, Goodluck Jonathan, to launch the *Bring the Book Back* campaign in 2010. Although, that initiative did not have far-reaching effects on the educational sector as that of Bush's (Igwe & Uzuegbe 2013), the campaign itself was evidence that reading malaise had assumed huge proportions among Nigerians.

Whether books are recommended or not, learners read when they are determined to excel. But a majority of them read more when they are allowed to read what they want to read (Post 2017). Consequently, young people can become avid readers when they read book titles such as *Hannah Montana, The Diary of a Wimpy Kid,* as well as their cell phones. However, sometimes these same learners who read avidly for pleasure at home develop cold feet when it comes to reading school books recommended by their teachers.

In Nigeria, the state government and teachers recommend books used in Primary and Secondary Schools. Sometimes, these books do not fit the reading levels of the learners but are recommended to feather the nests of the publishers, who are often the sacred cows in the country (Nnamani 2015). In addition to the book imposition by government, the book-selection process by some secondary school teachers is equally arbitrary as is evident in Yankson's (1989: 140) claim that:

> This educated graduate was unaware that the choice of students ' books depended on her own pupils' mental age, interest, socio-cultural needs and not on feelings and that books appropriate to say University of Nigeria Secondary school class one pupils may be quite inappropriate for, say Ibagua or Ovogoro Community Secondary School.

In the university, the responsibility of recommending books rests with the teachers. These academics, who should be conversant with the guidelines for book selection, often recommend books for their financial benefits; hence, they select their own texts, those written by their relations, friends, allies, or in order to curry the favour of the author who is an influential member of the society. To ensure that these texts are bought, teachers not only give quizzes based on exercises in their chosen texts but insist that students present evidence that the books were bought. In Nigeria, many students are unsuccessful in examinations merely because they failed to buy a recommended text. When students are threatened in this way, they become biased about reading the text and may, in fact, not read at all. Other reasons why learners fail to enjoy reading recommended texts include the complicated language and the length of some texts (Ayebola 2011).

Apart from selecting books based on the whims and caprices of government and teachers, books are also sometimes selected because they are literary canons. For this reason, some teachers believe that since Chinua Achebe, William Shakespeare, and Wole Soyinka are literally giants, students should be made to read *Things Falls Apart, Macbeth,* and *The Interpreters*, for instance. Such teachers argue that when learners read classics, they learn the art of writing from the masters. However, learners who are uninterested in Soyinka's, Shakespeare's, or Achebe's subject matter may not read the text. In any case, many learners often get away with not reading the recommended school texts by asking fellow learners to write the book summaries for them or by cheating during the examination. It is for this reason that considering the learners' interest during the book selection process becomes imperative. Giving support to the recommendation of texts that align with the interests of readers, Emenyonu (1991: 16) states:

> We like to do frequently those things which give us most enjoyment and personal satisfaction at our first encounter so it is with reading. We must therefore not believe that a child must read anything thrust upon him which is the basis on which we prescribe reading lists.

What is true about children is also true about adolescents. Morgan & Wagner's (2013) study, from where the present study drew inspiration, provides empirical evidence for this claim. Their study reports how a high school teacher offered reading choice to fifty- seven students in a literature class. The students read books of their choice during the lesson and at home. Thereafter, the teacher discussed the selected books individually with each student and, then, used the books to teach concepts in literature such as point of view, conflict, plot, direct and indirect characterization, mood/tone, flashback, foreshadow, and irony. At the end of the course, the students read more books than when the teacher used the traditional method of using assignments and quizzes to ensure that the learners read the recommended texts. This approach to teaching literature is becoming rampant in Middle Schools in American and is referred to as *Reading Workshop* (Rich 2009). This paper seeks to discover whether using this choice approach to teach grammar at Enugu State University of Science & Technology, Agbani, Nigeria will make learners read more books and learn grammar better.

2. Theoretical framework

This study aligns with Krashen's (1988) Filter Hypothesis which supports the view that interest plays a vital role in second language learning. He argues that people acquire second languages when their affective filters are low enough to allow the flow of input. In his view, the variables that affect the comprehensive input include motivation, attitude and self-confidence. Indeed, students are more likely to be motivated to read a book they selected themselves. As they accomplish the feat of reading several chapters of the book, their self-confidence is likely to soar and their attitude towards the reading process is likely to improve. According to Swart & Peterson (2015), factors that influence learners' choice of a novel include: level of difficulty, length, format, author, series, interests, availability, setting, genre, popularity, gender appeal, cover, and recommendation. Arguelles (2012) adds that, while both students and teachers consider the level indicated on the back page and number of pages of a book, the teachers admitted that their choice was based on the book's representativeness of certain cultural movements and its relationship with a current affair.

Many researchers support the view that learners should be given a choice of what to read (Johnson & Blair 2003; Ihejirika 2017; Post 2017). Supporting the use of choice reading in the classroom, experts argue that, because effective reading involves the engagement of the reader, motivation is vital to make students read, and that choice is a major type of motivation. Engagement during reading requires effort and focus. It is highly unlikely that students will be engaged in a book they are uninterested in.

In Nigeria, from the Primary School to the university, learners are rarely given the power to choose the books they read. In addition to the texts they are forced to read at school, children do not get a respite from their parents who often ignore their preferences at bookstores, sincerely believing that being older and more learned, they are in a better position to determine the right books for their children and thereby save cost.

Giving learners a choice of reading texts should be taken more seriously by teachers of English when they realize that there is sharp contrast between the books the learners enjoy, and the books recommended by their teachers or school authorities. Ihejirika (2017), for instance, discovered that the 2015/2016 fresh learners admitted into the Federal University of Technology, Owerri, Nigeria (FUTO) preferred reading short stories on science technology, romance, adventure, crime, and sports, while Osakwe (1999) had earlier found out that students of Nnamdi Azikiwe University, Awka preferred reading for pleasure to reading academic texts.

This contrast in reading tastes is not peculiar to Nigeria. Morgan's and Wagner' (2013) study provides empirical evidence that even native speakers read more in school when they choose their texts by themselves. In that study, Chris, a high school teacher, sought to encourage learners to enjoy the process of reading by allowing them to select the books they would read during their lesson, rather than using assignments and quizzes to make them read more books. Chris made students discuss their favorite movies, television shows, videos, video games and, from there, the students recommended to each other book titles that fitted their interests. Chris used these books to teach concepts in literature such as *point of view*, *flashback*, *foreshadow*, and *irony*, to mention four. For example, the teacher asked learners to identify and write down in their journals three words on their current page. Beside each word, learners were to write another word with the same denotation or connotation. Learners were further required to guess why the author selected that particular word and to consider whether that word was important to the plot or revealed something about the character who uttered the word.

Chris taught for 10-15 minutes. Thereafter, he helped students connect the lesson to the book they were reading. In the process, he discovered fake readers. He also discovered that some readers were reluctant to read due to wrong book selection and that some students choose longer and more complex books because there were no book reports or quizzes at the end of the course. During the three weeks period, the teacher used a coding system to record students' performance. He assigned two points to students who brought their books to school and two points for reading the book at home. Points were deducted when students failed to bring their books to class, when they failed to bring their journals to class, and when they failed to read after school. At the end of the course, 81 books were read in three weeks, far more than the number they would have read had the teacher imposed a reading list on his students.

The benefits of choice reading notwithstanding, Perks (2010) contends that not all choices motivate students positively and lists four factors that make choices effective. They include: choices that promote feeling of control, choices that give readers a sense of purpose, choices that involve books that are meaningful to the readers, and choices that make students feel competent. In order to meet Perk's (2010) criteria, teachers need to strike a balance between positive censuring of students' choice (in order to avoid pornography, for instance) and negative censoring which impinges on students' freedom. Broz (2003) is worried about students' proficiency in the self- selection process and insists that teaching students how to select books they read is an important part of the reading curriculum.

Rich (2009: 1), however, cautions that making an entire class read one literary text has several benefits. It "builds a shared literacy culture among students, exposes all readers to works of quality and is the best way to prepare students for standardized tests" (Rich 2009: 1). He also wonders how only one teacher can cope with a class full of learners using different books. This fear may be justified in a literature class where theme, subject matter, and technique vary from one book to another, and where the teacher is inexperienced. Text variety is, however, more manageable in a class where mechanics is taught because here the teachers are dealing with conventions. Commas and colons are used in the same way irrespective of texts or authors.

The view canvassed in this study to allow learners choose some of their reading texts in order to lure them to read is even more compelling in Nigeria against the backdrop of the negative consequences of poor reading proficiency among learners. These consequences have been sufficiently documented. For instance, Akande and Oyedapo (2018) contend that the lack of enthusiasm of secondary school students for reading has contributed to their poor writing and limited understanding about the lessons taught in class. Anyaegbu, Aghauche & Nnamani (2016) note that because students fail to understand what they read, they are not keen on studying outside the classroom, a practice which makes it difficult for them to read up books required of them. These learners would certainly struggle to compete in foreign examinations, thereby confirming Igwe's (2011: 1) claim that the "absence of widespread reading culture is a barrier to Nigeria's development and international competitiveness".

Ihejirika (2014) paints a most sorry picture of the dire consequences of reading failure in Nigeria. First, he points out that primary and junior secondary school learners can hardly write their names correctly. Then, he recalls the encounter between the ex-governor of Edo State, Adams Oshiomole, and a primary school teacher, who, in spite of her many years of teaching experience, could not read the contents of an affidavit. These findings may indeed validate Udo's (2018: 1) report that the World Bank believes that only "20 % of young Nigerian youths who have completed primary education can read''.

With the current economic recession in Nigeria and the fierce competition from the television and social media – Youtube, Facebook, Instagram, and Twitter – Nigerian learners may continue to dislike print reading unless teachers of English and Literature in English change the way they teach reading. One change that the teachers can introduce to motivate students to read is to offer them choice instead of insisting that the whole class read one canonical text. The objective of this paper was to investigate if offering students reading choice in an English Language learning classroom would support students' reading multiple books and improve their knowledge of mechanical accuracy especially as Rich (2009) has noted that research on the effects of choice on academic reading is limited.

3. Method

This paper replicated the method used in Morgan & Wagner's (2013) study. The data for the present study was collected from 27 learners who were admitted into the 2013/2014 special academic collaborative programme between Enugu State University of Science & Technology (ESUT), Agbani, Nigeria and Girne American University, Cyprus. During this special programme, students spend one year at ESUT and complete their education in Cyprus. Because of the high cost associated with the programme, the learners are few and the criterion for admission is the ability to pay fees, and not necessarily academic performance. As a result, the class is made up of both brilliant and below average students. The course was a *Use of English* course offered under the General Studies programme. This group was selected for the study because the researcher's university has no English department, and this was the only programme where the researcher could exercise the liberty to ask the learners to select books of their choices. Under the regular programme, the university operates a team-teaching system where colleagues insist on selecting three recommended literature texts that would be used by all first-year students in the university. The lesson held for two hours once a week. The course lasted for twelve weeks, but the experiment lasted for six weeks. Thereafter, the researcher used other traditional methods to teach other topics such as the rules of grammatical concord, and tense.

At the beginning of the term, a total of 27 students, 11 female and 16 male students who registered for the course were asked to select two books of their choice from a list of books pre-selected by the teacher and brought to the class on the first day of school. The readability levels of these texts were not measured. The books were selected on the basis of the general interests typical of Nigerian youths: success, leadership, and marriage. African Writers series were included as some of these authors or titles may have been familiar to the learners. The book titles included Chinua Achebe's *Arrow of God*, Joyce Meyer's *The Confident Woman*, Ifeoma Okoye's *The Fourth World*, Ben Carson's *Think Big*, John Maxwell's *Make Today Count*, Malcolm Gladwell's *Outliers*, Joshua Harris' *Boy Meets Girl*, Chukwuemeka Ike's *Conspiracy of Silence*, Mason's *An Enemy Called Average*, Okey Adibe's *Arrow of Rain*, etc. While literary texts such as Chimamanda Adiche's *Purple Hibiscus*, and Ngugi's *A Grain of Wheat* are popularly described as prose texts, motivational books such as Joyce Meyer's *The Confident Woman*, and John Maxwell's *Make Today Count* are often not. Yet, Boulton (1954: 5-7), in identifying five types of prose writing, classifies books on instruction under informative prose. Motivational books are also books about instruction. Meyer's *The Confident Woman* instructs females about how to be confident, while Maxwell's *Make Today Count* teaches readers to make hay while the sun shines. Such books are informative. Students were asked to borrow any book of their choice from the teachers' mobile library. The variety of books provided by the teacher gave students an idea of the kind of books that they could bring along to the next class. The students showed preference for motivational books, rather for the African literature. On the first day, none of the students selected an African fiction. Thereafter, none bought an African series to class. When the learners brought their choice books to the next class, the teacher ensured that the contents of such books were acceptable before the students started reading.

The learners were given one-hour class reading time to ensure that they found time to read the books they selected themselves. Making students read during the class period may appear a waste of time, yet it was an important aspect of reading improvement because the more people read, the more they learn how to read, the more they enjoy reading and the more they learn. Morgan & Wagner (2013: 664) rightly point out another advantage of making students read during a lesson: "students have busy lives outside the classroom. Teachers can hope students read at home, but that simply is not always the case".

To ensure that students' reading was connected to the purpose of the course, the teacher wrote the course outline on the board. The topics included: Capitalisation, Punctuation, The Rules of Grammatical Concord, Tense, Types of Sentences.

During the mini-lessons, the teacher taught the uses of capital letters or punctuation for about 15 minutes on each day. The researcher decided to teach before the independent reading in order to present the principles to the learners. Then, during independent reading, learners would see the principles in use. Seeing the use of capital letters and commas in their proper places should reinforce their learning experience. Learners were encouraged to make notes inside their exercise books during the lesson. Thereafter, they were given one out of the two hours lecture period to read. During silent reading, they were made to write down in their journals sentences containing capital letters found in the books they were reading and the purpose for the author's use of each capital letter. The students were also to indicate instances where the examples they found in the books were contrary to what was taught during the lesson. They were also to write down their attitude towards the books they were reading and towards the self-selection experience. Learners were also told to indicate the page where they had stopped reading in class and to continue reading outside the classroom. Indicating the page where they stopped for the day helped the teacher to evaluate how much reading the student did outside the classroom. At the end of each class, while the learners went home with their exercise books, the teacher went home with their journals. This way, the teacher was certain that the learners wrote the journal entries by themselves.

During the independent reading, the teacher went around to ensure that reading was going on. In the process, the teacher interacted with the students, asking questions such as:

(1) Why did you choose this book?
(2) What is the book about?
(3) Why has the author used capital letters in this sentence?
(4) Why are the initial letters in the following words capitalised?
(5) Why did the writer use a comma in this sentence?

A learner who pretended to be reading was exposed when she was unable to give a correct recap of the pages she claimed to have read. Incidentally, the teacher had read the book, so it was easy to know that the student had not been reading. Some readers found it challenging to read and at the same time make connections between the book and the lesson. Others gave wrong reasons for the use of the capital letters in some of the sentences they selected. During the discussion with the teacher, the learners were relaxed because they were engaged in a discussion rather than in an assessment. Again, because they were involved in a one-on-one discussion with the teacher, they were shielded from mockery from their classmates. To enable the teacher keep track of students' progress, the teacher made notes. Examples of the notes included:

(6) Not very sure that initial letters of religions are capitalized.
(7) Able to identify proper nouns.
(8) Unable to recognize that capitalletters are used to begin proper nouns.

The notes enabled the teacher to prepare follow-up questions during the next class. To spend less time taking notes and give more time to discussing with students, the teacher opted to use Morgan & Wagner's (2013: 663) coding system where the numbers represented the following:

- 5 - complete answer that reveal thorough reading and connection of the concept.
- 3 - Surface level comprehension of the text and attempted connection of the concept
- 1 - Poorly supported answers and lack of connection of the concept
- 0 - Demonstrates lack of reading and connectionof the concept.

At the end of one hour of independent reading, learners asked questions, completed their notes, and commented in their journals. Those who no longer liked their choice of books and wanted to change their books were allowed to do so. While the slow readers were limited to only making connections between the lesson and the books they were reading, faster readers were assigned additional tasks. For example, a learner who was reading Carson's *Think Big* was asked to write about an experience where he was the worst in a class or in a team. Another learner reading Meyer's *The Confident Woman* was asked to write about an experience where she lost confidence in herself because of a mistake she had made. Those who read more than one book did not discourage the struggling readers because of the private conversations between the teacher and such students. Conceding the difficulty inherent in offering differentiated reading instruction in the classroom, Reutzel & Cooter (2009: 12) assert:

> Excellent teachers provide instruction that is responsive to the specific needs of every child based on on-going assessment findings.How one goes about differentiating reading instruction to meet each child's needs is of critical importance for all teachers.

This choice reading technique was used for teaching only capital letters and punctuation and lasted for six weeks. The teacher used other traditional teaching methods to teach the other topics in the syllabus. Finally, at the end of the semester, a three- item questionnaire was used to elicit students' responses to this practice. The first item asked students whether they preferred to select books by themselves. The second item required students to discuss how choosing the reading texts by themselves helped their study of English. The third question asked students to list the problems associated with the self -selection process.

The second and third questions were open- ended to enable students respond as objectively as possible. Responses to the first item required a *yes* or *no* answer, so it was converted into simple percentage. Even though the third item was open – ended, it was possible to count the number of respondents who said that they found book selection a challenge. Again, that figure was converted to percentage.

4. Results

The focus of this study was to investigate if offering students reading choice would enable them to read more books and understand better mechanical accuracy. The results of the study are presented in Table 1 below:

ITEMS	NUMBER	PERCENTAGE
Learners who completed the reading of two books	2	7.4%
Learners who completed the reading of one book	5	18.5%
Learners who did not finish reading the books they chose	22	81%
Learners who did not comprehend the books they chose	2	7.4%
Learners who changed their books	3	11%
Learners who had problem with the book- selection process	4	14.8%
Learners who preferred self- selection of school text to teacher –recommendation	27	100%
Learners who preferred instructional texts to African fiction	27	100%

Table 1: Learners' performance

The analysis of the questionnaire showed that 100% of the sample population preferred choosing their own reading texts and preferred motivational texts to African Literature. Seven percent of the population did not demonstrate knowledge of the contents of the pages of the book they had read. Seven percent of the sample population completed the reading of the two selected books during the six weeks the experiment lasted. 18% of the population completed the reading of one book while 81% of the population stopped at various points of their books. Whereas 14% of the learners faced difficulty choosing appropriate texts, and eleven percent changed their books after a few days, the rest knew exactly what they wanted and kept reading the same book until the end of the semester. Below are some of the learners' responses to the questionnaire:

(1) Research Question 1: Do you prefer to choose the text for this course or for the teacher to do so?
   a) Typical response of learners: "I prefer to choose by myself"

(2) Research Question 2: How did reading a book of your choice help your knowledge of English this semester?
   a) L1: Reading has become an important technique   of my day to day life activities. I have come to live with this reality after reading the book *Become a better you* by Joel Osteen in this semester [sic]. I not only learnt how to be patient and longsuffering towards others, but this singular act has helped me identify punctuation and the role they play in sentence, as well as helped to improve my vocabulary.
   b) L2: Reading a book of my choice has helped my knowledge of English this semester by knowing the use of punctuation marks and it has developed my reading skills. I can now read for enjoyment because people only thinks [sic] you read for examination but there is actually fun in reading for pleasure.
   c) L3: The benefit of reading another textbook helps me to understand that it is good to read as many books as you can, because what you will not know in a particular novel you read, another one will tell you about it. And you will still come across   the words which you were having problems with in the other book you read.
   d) L4: Reading the book of my choice has enlightened me on the use of punctuation marks and other reading skills I was ignorant of. I had to put all my concentration to draw out point [sic] which helped me understand that for me to write well, I   need to read well.

(3) Research Question 3: List the challenges you faced as you selected the book of your choice.
   a) L5: At the bookshop I am always confused. Getting into the bookshop each time I want to buy books, I end up being indecisive of the book to select.
   b) L6: The task of choosing has always been a burden, a burden that gets heavier each time I have to choose from a shelf of books.
   c) L7: Some books looks [sic] interesting but when you will start reading it, it will no longer be nice.
   d) L8: Choosing my own book is like when you want to buy clothes. The plenty clothes will be confusing you. That is how many books in the market will be confusing me.
   e) L9: wrote: I not only read the text for class work, but for the teaching in the text because I chose the text myself. If I was given the text to react, maybe I would have just read it for class work only but by choice, it gave me more [Sic]
   f) L10: one of those who finished reading two books wrote: Although I had read *The Big Picture* before, reading it again was like opening a big room with many hidden doors in it. I got to learn things and see things I hadn't seen before.
   g) L11: the second learner, who completed two books, commented in his journal: "My experience in the self- selection was quite interesting. I started with *Gifted Hands* by Ben Carson. After I had finished Ben Carson's book, I started with another one written by Zig   Ziglag   titled *Something to Smile About.* The book gave a lot of encouragement on how to go about our daily activities as well as how we can achieve success in any given opportunity.

In summary, the result of the study showed that 100% of the students preferred reading self-selected books to books selected by their teachers. Likewise, all the 27 learners preferred motivational books to African Fiction. Only two students completed the reading of two books at the end of six weeks, five finished reading a single book, two did not comprehend what they read, while the remaining 18 learners stopped at various parts of their books. Four learners indicated facing challenges with the self-selection process.

During the examination, the learners performed far better in questions based on the use of capital letters and punctuation than they did in questions related to the Rules of Grammatical Concord and tense which this Reading Workshop was not used to teach. 21 learners scored 15 marks and above out of 20 marks in the questions connected to capital letters and punctuation marks, while ten learners scored 15 marks and above in questions related to the rules of Grammatical Concord where the Reading Workshop technique was not applied.

5. Discussion

The finding from this study that learners preferred instructional literature to African Fiction confirms Osakwe's (1999) and Ihejirika's (2017) earlier finding that Nigerian learners prefer reading leisure books to academic texts. Ihejirika (2017: 104) noted that "some students would request the researcher to summarize the materials for them, the reason being that they could not make out time to read. But surprisingly, the same students who could not make out time to read the prescribed materials would be found occasionally reading non- prescribed reading materials individually on their own".

In this study, students' choice of instructional texts may be connected to the very harsh economic situation in Nigeria. Living in Nigeria is very difficult for a majority of the people. Consequently, young people appear to prefer books that give them direct instructions on how to cope with their various circumstances than the indirect counsel interwoven within the fabrics of a classic or an African fiction. The learners' preference for self-selection of school texts is also a great departure from teachers' conventional method of recommending a single text for the whole class. Though 100% of the population indicated a preference for self-selection of their school texts, only 14% admitted that they had challenges identifying books they liked. These learners may have expressed a desire for choice just for the sake of variety and a departure from the norm. Since some students expressed difficulty in identifying books of their choices, teachers should consider including self-selection of books in their curriculum. In addition, the fact that three students changed their minds about the books that they had earlier chosen is not necessarily a sign that they lacked self- selection skills. Firstly, even confident readers sometimes change their minds about their book choices. Secondly, the change may have been necessitated by the fact that the learners' initial expectations were not satisfied by the contents of the book, thereby validating the popular warning in reading parlance that books should not be judged by their covers. Indeed, the sheer fact that learners were free to change their minds about their book choices improved the teacher- learner relationship and increased the team spirit that pervaded the learning space.

Furthermore, although only a mere seven percent of the population finished reading two books during the six weeks and demonstrated knowledge of the books' contents through the book summaries they wrote, this can be considered an achievement in Nigeria considering the fact that the same learners may not have read an entire book had students not been given a choice to select their own titles. This claim is supported by Ayebola's (2011: 106) finding that science students from the University of Agriculture Abeokuta were so poor in reading recommended fiction texts "that 45 % of her respondents mixed up the genres listing novels as plays, plays as poems...".

The two students who were unable to read the books they chose belong to the category of learners who were admitted into the program merely because they were able to pay the fees. Those who did not finish reading the single books they chose still exhibited enthusiasm during classroom discussions of sections of the books they had read. They may not have completed the reading of one book because they were slow readers and because of the competing demands made on them from other courses.

The students' better performance in questions connected to the use of capital letters and punctuation marks compared to their performance in the rules of grammatical concord and tense where the choice reading technique was not applied appears to validate Benjamin Franklin's popular saying:

Tell me and I forget.

Teach me and I understand.

Involve me and I learn.

Allowing students to select their texts and insisting that the learners themselves explain the uses of capital letters and punctuation marks found in their choice texts were the teacher's ways of involving the learners in the learning process. One limitation of this study was the small size of the population of the study. Even though the study's population is too small to make generalisations about reading choice, the findings nonetheless suggest that choice reading can improve the reading competencies and mechanical accuracy of Nigerian learners.

This paper is similar and, at the same time, different from Morgan & Wagner's (2013) study in several ways. Both studies were carried out the same year and adopted the choice reading approach in the classroom. In both studies, the teachers taught for a while and allowed learners to use the remaining class time for independent reading and for one- on- one discussion with the teachers. However, while Chris's experiment was carried out in the United States of America, this study was carried out in Nigeria. Chris's population was 57, while the population in this study was 27. While high school learners constituted Chris' population, the population for this study was first year university students. While Chris taught literature, grammar was taught in this study. Chris's experiment lasted for three weeks, while this study lasted for six weeks. The population in Chris' study read far more books in three weeks than the population in this study read in weeks. While 22 of Chris's 57 students completed reading two books in three weeks, in this study, only two students finished reading two books in six weeks.

6. Conclusion

As the results of this study show, learners preferred their own choice of school texts to teachers' selection. Selecting books of their choice contributed to learners' enthusiasm in the reading and discussion of the texts. They also preferred motivational texts to African Literature. Independent reading during classroom period helped learners read more. It also provided the opportunity for the reinforcement of learning as the learners saw the rules of capitalization and punctuation in action, confirming that instructional texts can be used in teaching mechanics of English. Sadly, the study showed that very few Nigerian learners of English are confident readers, a good number are reluctant readers, some read without comprehension, while others struggle with book self- selection processes.

Based on the findings of this study, teachers of English and Literature in English should consider allowing learners choose by themselves one out of several books they are expected to read during a semester, as students were generally more engaged in reading than when books were imposed on them. If Nigerian learners must be helped to overcome reading inertia, teachers should include book self-selection processes in the curriculum and make independent reading an important aspect of language instruction because outside the classroom, students do not read as much as they should. Furthermore, instructional texts should be used to teach mechanics of English since Nigerian learners prefer them to classics or African fiction. Further research should involve a larger population and compare a group of learners who study English using teacher – recommended texts and another group who use their own choice of texts.

References

Akande, S. O, Oyedapo, R. O. (2018). Developing the reading habits of secondary school students in Nigeria: The way forward. Abstract. *International Journal of Library Science* 7 (10): 15-20, doi:10.5923/j.library.20180701.03.

Anyaegbu, M. I., Aghauche, E. E., Nnamani, E. (2016). Poor reading habit and the academic performance of Junior Secondary School students in Enugu South Local Government. Area of Enugu State. *Education Research Journal* 6 (8):112-121. Retrieved from http://resjournals.com/journals/educational-research-journal.html.

Arguelles, I. (2012). Student choice and reading in the EFL classroom. *Encuentro* 21, 104-114.

Ayebola, P. A. (2011). Challenges in the reading of fiction among ESL science students. *English Language Teaching Today.* 8, 106 – 107.

Boulton, M. (1954). *The anatomy of prose.* Boston: Routledge & Kegan Paul.

Broz, B. (2003). Supporting and teaching student choice: Offering students self-selected reading. *The Alan Review Professional Resource Connection,* 23-28.

Emenyonu, E. (1991). *Studies on the nigerian novel.* Ibadan: Heinemann Educational Books.

Ihejirika, R. C. (2017). Extensive reading in English: A study of the reading preferences of the freshmen at the Federal University of Technology, Owerri, Nigeria. *FUTO Journal Series,* 3(1): 64-76.

Ihejirika, R. C. (2014). Integrating extensive reading in the school curriculum: An effective strategy for enhancing and sustaining literacy in Nigeria. *Interdisciplinary Journal of Contemporary Research in Business* 5 (9): 590- 602.

Johnson, D., Blair, A. (2003). The importance and use of student self-selected literature to reading engagement in an elementary reading curriculum. *Reading Horizon* 43 (3): 181-202.

Krashen, S. D. (1988). S*econd language acquisition and second language learning.* New Jersey: Prentice Hall International.

Morgan, D. N., Wagner, C. W. (2013). What's the catch? Providing reading choice in a high school classroom. *Journal of Adolescent & Adult Literacy.* International Reading Association, 56 (8): 659-667.

Nnamani, O.C. (2015). *The language of selected prose texts for secondary schools in South Eastern Nigeria: A readability study.* (Unpublished Doctoral Dissertation) Ebonyi State University, Abakaliki.

Osakwe, N. (1999). The nature of students'reading problem at the tertiary level. *Literacy and Reading in Nigeria* 8, 138-148.

Perks, K. (2010). Crafting effective choices to motivate students. *Adolescent Literacy in Perspective* March/ April, 2-5.

Post, M. C. (2017). Children's choices 2017 List. *International Literacy Association.*

Reutzel, D., Cooter, R. B. (2009). *The essentials of teaching children to read: The teacher makes the difference.* New York: Pearson.

Swart, L., Peterson, S. S. (2015). *This is a great book.* Ontario: Pembroke Publishers.

Igwe, K. N. (2011). Reading culture and Nigeria's quest for sustainable development. *Library Philosophy and Practice.* Retrieved from http://digitalcommons.unl.edu/libphilprac/482.

Igwe, K. N, Uzuegbu, C. P. (2013). An evaluation of bring the book initiative of the Nigerian government. *Higher Education of Social Science.* 4 (2): 8-12.

Rich, M. (2009). Students get a new assignment: Pick books you like. *The New York Times,* August 30. Retrieved from https://wwwnytimes.com/2009/of/30reading.html.

Udo, B. (2018, March 31). 20% of young Nigerian adults who have completed primary education can read. *Premium Times.* Retrieved from https://www.premiumtimesng.com/news/headline/261106-p.1.

Yankson, K. (1989). *The language of literature.* Obosi: Pacific Publishers.

Exploiting Reviewers' Feedback to Develop Academic Writing Skills: An Empirical Report on a Research Seminar

Alexandra Esimaje & Uche Betty Gbenedio

Benson Idahosa University & University of Benin

Abstract

This paper reports on an academic writing workshop which modeled the process method of teaching writing. Using a corpus of reviews of 20 draft journal articles, and the questionnaire as an instrument of evaluation, the paper argues for the vital role of feedback in the writing process and how the scholarly reviews of papers can serve as resources for teaching writing. The study found learning from samples of existing reviews (indirect feedback) and reviews of authors' writings (direct feedback) to be quite useful. The feedback enabled writers to engage with the reviews of papers of others, model their writing through them, appropriate learning and even self-correct their writings. At the same time, the study proved that writers could utilize and internalize the direct reviews of their papers, thereby advancing their overall writing ability.

Keywords: academic writing, journal article, review, feedback, corpus-driven learning, writing process

1. Introduction

Academic writing has become a prominent issue which needs attention in many academies of higher learning all over the world. The low-level competence in the academic writing skills of our academy members - students and staff - is all too apparent in the products of our academies, the incidence of plagiarism and academic frauds which plague our institutions of higher learning, and also the denial of our society of the gains of research and education, in this case the Nigerian society.

This need for productive education underlines the significance of writing the journal article, the focus of this study, and the pre-eminent genre of academic writing. Writing successful journal articles is a skill that is acquired through practice and one that distinguishes the mature academic from the novice. No doubt, the journal article is a complex rhetorical activity which requires initiation, apprenticeship or mentoring. Its value is incalculable to the academic for, as Hyland (2009: 2, 67, 78) underscores, "no discovery, insight, invention or understanding has any significance until it is made available to others and no university or individual will receive credit for it until it has seen the light of day through publication".

This paper reports on a six-day academic writing workshop initiative of the Centre for Language Research and English Proficiency (Clarep). This workshop featured a writing retreat in which 30 young academics, from different universities in Nigeria, were taught the art of scientific writing through a series of writing interventions from seasoned academic mentors who provided feedback on the draft articles written by the participants. This paper examines this initiative to illustrate how reviewer's feedback can serve as a teaching resource in academic writing. To fulfill this aim, the paper set the following objectives:

RQ 1)   Did participants benefit from the indirect feedback on their papers?

RQ 2)   How much did participants gain from direct feedback on their papers?

RQ 3)   Which specific areas of writing targeted in the feedback/reviews?

RQ 4)   Is there a significant difference among the respondents in their views on the workshop obtained through their responses on the Likert-type questionnaire?

In the next sections, conceptual backgrounds to the study are given to enable a good understanding of the study as well as position it to make its contribution to existing literature. We, therefore, present studies on corpora in academic writing (subsection 1.1), and in subsection 1.2 studies on feedback in academic writing. Then in section 2, we discuss the method of the study, the discussion of results/findings follows in section 3, and then the conclusion of the study is presented in section 4.

1.1. Feedback in academic writing

There are different kinds of feedback. Poverjuc (2011), for example, identified oral, written, electronic, and peer feedback. His study revealed that students' major sources of difficulty in utilizing feedback arise from a host of attitudinal factors including the lack of willingness to critically examine one's point of view, a feeling that the teacher's feedback is incorrect, and a lack of sufficient knowledge to do the revision, amongst others. Beyond the attitude of the student to feedback, the type of feedback is also significant, as McGrath, Taylor & Pychyl (2011) found in their study of developed and undeveloped feedback and students' perceptions of the feedback. However, although the study showed students' preference for the developed feedback, it did not positively affect the quality of student writing in a significant manner.

Other modes of feedback advocated in the literature are the use of Facebook Notes (Yusof, Ab Manan & Alias 2012), as well as the use of online resources (Northcott, Gillies & Caulton 2016). Moreover, Huisman, Saab, Driel & den Broek (2018) explored the relationship between the nature of peer feedback, students' perceptions of the feedback, and their subsequent writing performance, and found that students' perception of the adequacy of the peer feedback and their willingness to improve based on the recommendations were unrelated to their trajectory increase in their writing performance. These perceptions do not mediate between the nature of the peer feedback and subsequent writing performance. Therefore, attitude may not be a significant index of feedback outcome.

Some studies have put their searchlight on the attitude of the teacher or reviewer rather than the student. For instance, Court and Johnson (2016) explored subject tutors' practices and beliefs about the provision of feedback and found that subject tutor markers seem to believe that there is more of a 'habitus' than reality. The paper claims that the practice helps to explain at least some of the individual variation that exists across the tutors regarding their marking/feedback practices, due to different experiences. This conclusion confirms Hyland's (2017) findings from a study of the motive behind the reviewers' feedback as well as the relationship that should exist between the tutors and the students. The paper showed that the yardstick used by reviewers is self-made and, thus, reflect personal attitudes and experiences. In another study, Hyland (2013) remarked that a possible reason for ineffective feedback is a relative lack of attention given to accuracy by faculty teachers in their feedback.

Although a host of factors, ranging from attitude of the student, attitude of the teacher, inadequate teacher attention to the practice, to sheer misconception of the practice as a uni-dimensional process rather than an interaction, influence the outcome of feedback, it is not in doubt the role that feedback can play in teaching writing. Hyland (2003: 17) corroborates this view in noting that "Few teachers now see writing as an exercise in formal accuracy, and most set pre-writing activities, require multiple drafts, give extensive feedback, encourage peer review, and delay surface correction". This conclusion is well supported in the literature and confirmed in the context of this study by recent works such as Sola & Olayinka (2015), Okurame & Ajayi (2017), Anani, Badaki & Kamai (2016), and Onuka & Junaid (2016), who agree that feedback has the potential to not only enhance student writing but also measure the quality of teaching. The salient question to answer remains how to deploy this tool in teaching. It is this question that this study tackles in its bid to make a methodological contribution to this body of knowledge.

2. Method of the study

2.1. Models of academic writing

There are many different approaches to academic writing in higher education. There is the trio of the older models, the skills, the socialization, and the academic literacy models, on the one hand. On the other hand, there are the newer approaches: process, genre, situated social practice, and text-in-context approaches. Each new model takes into account the older ones, and so there is an interweaving of approaches in any writing context. In this study then, these approaches interplayed to complement each other.

2.1.1. *Writing as skills, as socialization, as academic literacy*

As Curry & Hewings (2005) surmise, the skills model involves the teaching of study skills to students who are deficient in academic writing skills, the socialization model assumes that students will acquire academic writing skills through "implicit induction" and the academic literacy model "identifies writing as a social and disciplinary practice" (Lillis 1999: 26). However, none of these models is self-sufficient and they "are not mutually exclusive and do not follow a simple linear pattern" (Ganobscik-Williams 2004: 36). Therefore, all these aspects need to be taken into account in teaching writing and rather than focus on the written product, the focus should be on the process, namely what writers do as they write while also taking into account textual features (genre; Curry & Hewings 2003).

2.1.2. *Writing as a process*

The process approach relies on the assumption that writing is iterative and involves many stages which do not necessarily take a linear order (Murray 1987). The first stage is pre-writing - where a writer generates ideas and collects information for the writing task. The next stage is planning – where a writer organizes his ideas to produce a sort of mind map or outline, and then drafting – where a writer begins to structure and develop his ideas. The next stage is reflection – when a writer lets the work lay fallow to come back to it at a later time, followed by review – where a writer seeks external support through reviews by peers for insight and input to the writing. Subsequent stages are revision – where the reviewer's comments are implemented to develop the writing further, and, finally, editing/proofreading – wherein focus shifts ideas to surface-level features such as the general mechanics of writing, issues of structure, and language accuracy. The drafting stage is revisited many times after reflection, after peer review, and during revision, such that the final draft eventually shows little resemblance to the initial draft having undergone series of interventions. The review process, which involves seeking and receiving feedback, is a crucial stage in the writing process because it prepares the writer for the all-important stage of revision. As Murray (1978: 56) opines " few, if any, writers ever get it right the first time; they write to catch a glimpse of what they may see and then revise - and revise, and revise, and revise - to make it come clear".

2.1.3. *Writing as a genre*

A genre is merely the term for a set of language practices that identify a language community. As Hyland (2007: 4) says, it "is a term for grouping texts together, representing how writers typically use language to respond to recurring situations". Earlier, Hyland (2003: 20, 21) explicates the assumptions that underpin genre as the belief that "the features of a similar group of texts depend on the social context of their creation and use, and that those features can be described in a way that

relates a text to others like it and the choices and constraints acting on text producers". Therefore, language constructs social realities and creates relationships
through the use of conventional recurrent patterns. He identifies three schools of
genre theory. First, there is the new rhetoric approach, which emphasizes the rhetorical contexts in which genre is employed. Second, there is the ESP approach,
which emphasizes the linguistic structure of communicative events in specific discourse communities. The third school is the systemic functional linguistics which
emphasizes "the purposeful, interactive, and sequential character of different genres and the ways language is systematically linked to context" (Hyland 2003: 20,
21). In the application of genre theory to teaching writing, what is crucial is the
understanding of the language practices that typify particular discourse events and
communities and how to utilize this knowledge in the classroom. Thus, the focus
is on text types (awareness of what the target discourse looks like), and their contexts (the social situation that creates the discourse). The pedagogy necessarily entails the use and discussion of model texts (as visible pedagogies), the deconstruction of the text (joint negotiating/analysis), and then the construction (through
drafts, reviews and revisions). But like the models before it, the genre approach
has its limitations, and so a complementary use with other models remains the
suggestion.

2.1.4. *Writing as a situated social practice*

Green (2016) explicates the notion of academic writing as a "situated social practice", which is influenced by works on Rhetorical Genre Studies (Bawarshi & Reiff
2010) and Academic Literacies theory (Lea & Street 1998; Lillis 2001, in Green
2016). Green (2016) notes the implications for academic writing to be that: 1) the
notion of *situation* implies specific disciplinary or institutional community; hence
writing is shaped by the values of the community; 2). social practice implies com-
munity-based activities/interactions that are system-based, and as a result, students
must know the practices of their community; 3). there is also the understanding
that different strands of knowledge characterize the practice, as well as the existence of the practices of representation, construction or communication of this
knowledge. Therefore, the teaching of academic writing will need to take this complexity into account.

2.1.5. *Writing as a text-in-context (genre-based model)*

The text-in-context model is a genre-based pedagogy that seeks primarily to uncover the defining stages, moves and informational structures of key genres and to
relate these to the contexts of culture and situation in which these texts are produced and consumed (Green 2016: 100). As Green (2016: 99) earlier remarks, this
is a slightly different model of academic literacies which has emerged in the UK
and is influenced by genre studies in Systemic-Functional Linguistics (SFL)
(Swales 1990) and the English for Specific Purposes (ESP), a *text-in-context* model

of genre-based pedagogy. This model, the text-in-context, is akin to the one advocated in this study and is fully described by Green (2016: 100), thus:

> This text-in-context design is typified by the four-stage sequence developed within SFL
> which begins with an exploration of writing context, defined concerning audience and
> communicative purpose, followed by the introduction and analysis of sample genre texts
> concerning rhetorical structure, function and linguistic realization. 'Construction' stages
> follow this 'deconstruction' stage, first scaffolded and collaborative, then independent, and
> may include an element of process instruction.

Although this approach has its criticisms (see Green 2016; Wingate & Tribble
2012), it is important to note the important observation of Tardy (2006, 2009 in
Green 2016: 100), about "the necessity for writers to engage in actual, disciplinary
genred writing, to structure and proceduralize nascent genre knowledge ... in order
to fully understand how to use genres". Our study fully illustrates this idea. Therefore, our approach adds an element, that is, exposure to genred writing, to the three
key elements of the text-in-context approach: an extensive exploration of the writing context, analysis and guided noticing of genre features, and scaffolded construction of texts.

3. Research design

3.1. Population

According to the universities regulation body, National Universities Commission
(NUC), as at 2017, there were a total of 158 universities in Nigeria, 40 Federal, 44
State, and 74 private universities. 158 universities constitute the population of this
study. To reduce the population to a manageable size, we classified it following
the zonal grouping of the country into North, South, East, and West. Therefore, we
adopted the stratified random sampling procedure to select 30 universities, which
translates to approximately 20% of the total number of Universities and from these
universities, 30 participants were further selected through the random sampling
technique, one from every institution. This way, some level of representativeness
was achieved since all zones, as well as the three types of universities, were represented although equal representation could not be achieved for the various categories. Consequently, whereas the target population for the study is 158 universities,
the accessible sample from the population stands at 30.

3.2. Sample

From a sample of 30 universities, and 30 participants, one was randomly selected
from each university to participate in the academic writing workshop. All 30 un-
derwent the writing retreat for six days, during which period there were extensive
reading and writing activities. Of this number, 20 were purposively selected using
the criterion of heterogeneous selection to ensure variability in the sample. Such
factors as sex, type of university (private/public) and level of qualification (Pre
PhD, PhD) were some of the considerations applied in the selection. Based on the
fact of the smallness of the primary data, the researchers consider their judgment
reliable, hence the choice of the purposive sampling method. The selection of 20
or 67% out of 30 also makes for a very representative sample.

A Comparative Analysis of the Paralinguistic Features of the Igbo and Yoruba Ethnicities of Nigeria

Odochi S. Akujobi

Nnamdi Azikiwe University

Abstract

Paralinguistic communication in recent times has continued to gain more acceptance in linguistic and communication studies. Increasingly, scholars have realised the need for its application in various spheres of human endeavour to ease dialogue, especially among people of diverse cultural, social and linguistic backgrounds. The study compared the paralinguistic features of the Igbo and Yoruba peoples of Nigeria using Ferdinand de Saussure's semiotic theory to discover the degree of similarities or differences between them. A high degree of similarities of the two languages should encourage conviviality and so enhance communication, while a high degree of differences could contribute to inter-ethnic conflicts. The study was carried out using the Survey Research Design. A sample population (n=63) was drawn through a random sampling technique and partici-pant interview data were collected using systematic observation and interviews. The find-ings show more similarities than differences in the paralinguistic features of both ethnic groups. Since the ethnic groups share more similarities than differences in paralinguistic features, it is expected that these features should enhance communication.

Keywords: paralanguage, Igbo, Yoruba, Nigeria, semiotics

1. Introduction

Paralanguage plays a pivotal role in comprehending the actual meaning of words in every speech environment and can be conscious or unconscious. Information can be communicated verbally or nonverbally, but paralanguage falls under non-verbal communication and it is used to interpret the intention of the speaker in a speech environment. Comprehending paralinguistic signs of other ethnic groups or call systems of people could lead to peaceful co-existence among them. Both the speaker and receiver must understand the nonverbal stimuli in their communi-cation settings, and their implications. Nigeria is a linguistically diverse country with several ethnolinguistic groups. It also houses a lot of emigrants and tourists, who do not understand the indigenous languages. These people rely heavily on nonverbal communication to communicate. So, there is need for them to learn the paralinguistic cues of the major ethnic groups in Nigeria, which at present are not adequately documented. The paralinguistic cues in one's culture can depict some-thing different in another and could lead to problems that arise from miscommu-nication. No discourse can be successfully completed in the absence of paralan-guage and the non-comprehension of such unspoken rules may lead to social, religious (insurgency), and political rivalry. Therefore, a good perception of paralinguistic cues of others that relay danger, warnings or emotions, can enhance communication.

This study examines the paralanguage of two major ethnic groups in Nigeria, namely: the Igbo, and the Yoruba ethnic groups. This is because previously more comparative work has been done for the Igbo and the Hausa ethnic groups, so this serves as a continuation of that comparative work.

The theoretical framework of this work was based on the theory of semiotics by Ferdinand de Saussure (1916). Semiotics is the study of signs and sign processes. It studies the structure and meaning of language. It is divided into three branches: Semantics, Syntax and Pragmatics (Morris 1938). According to Saussure (1916), language can be categorized as signs. He divided these signs into two: the Signifier, and the Signified. The Signifier is the sound/gesture, while the Signified is the meaning or the image associated with such a sound/gesture.

2. Review of Related Literature

Kalin et al. (2018) classifies Paralinguistics as the process of communicating through sending and receiving wordless (mostly visual, but also auditory) signals between people. Paralanguage can also be seen as: (1) narrowly, non-segmental vocal features in speech, such as tone of voice, tempo, tut-tutting, sighing, grunts, and exclamations like w*hew!*, and (2) broadly, all of the above plus non-vocal signals such as gestures, postures and expressions – that is, all non-linguistic behaviour which is sufficiently coded to contribute to the overall communicative effect (Trask 1996).

There are no spoken words that are devoid of paralanguage due to voice dynamics. According to Karpinski & Klessa (2018: 29),

> [d]ialogue participants adjust mutually to each other in a range of complex and often unconscious processes. Their results can be observed in the behavior of communicating humans: in language use, including facial, syntactic and stylistic or pragmatic choices in speech prosody, gestural behavior (hand gesture, body posture, head movements etc.

As a form of discourse, paralanguage extends beyond words. The vocal paralanguage is made up of all the clues except the words used. The Nigerian environment cannot do without the help of paralanguage due to the security threat and insurgency in the country. There is need for intercultural familiarity and awareness among ethnic groups in the country.

Section 2 discusses the literature review and the theoretical framework, leading to Section 3 which focuses on Methodology and the research tools used in this work. The analysis is presented in section 4 as Analysis of Data and, finally, section 5 is the conclusion.

Paralinguistic devices are the major tools for the determination of the direction and purpose of every discourse, especially ambiguous ones. It amply empowers conversationalists to observe the sincerity among one another. Paralinguistic voice qualifiers feature as discourse markers for effective communication. Brown (2017) views paralinguistic features of speech as those which contribute to the expression of attitude by the speaker. Gestures, facial expressions, voice quality, shrugs, eye gaze, winks, whispering, giggling, and laughing are some of the paralinguistic devices mentioned by Brown.

Some researchers in this field have also done some related works. Khalifa & Faddal (2017) conducted a research on *the Impacts of Using Paralanguage on Teaching and Learning English Language to Convey effective Meaning*. Their target participants were three hundred level students of the English Department, Albaha University, Saudi Arabia. Their sample was selected randomly to include a total of 33 students and 16 teachers to answer 12 and 16 questions respectively. The tool of data collection was a structured questionnaire. Their results showed that:

- Smiling teachers teach more effectively than serious ones.
- It is easy to communicate with the teachers who usually encourage students by nodding their heads.
- Teachers who vary their tone, pitch, volume and rhythm of their lectures, are more successful.

Zi & Lausberg (2018) also conducted a research project titled *Koreans and Germans: Cultural Differences in Hand Movement Behaviour and Gestural Repertoire*. The study compared hand movement behavior and gestural repertoire between the Korean and German participants. Video clips of the hand movement behaviour of participants during description of their appreciation of dance stimuli were analyzed with NEUROGES system. The result showed that the German participants in general exhibited significantly more gestures than the Koreans. Concerning gesture repertoire, the Germans showed more emotional and emphasizing gesture, and gesture presenting motion quality, while the Koreans displayed more pointing and pantomiming gestures. Their differences were discussed in line with cultural differences.

Akujobi (2005) investigated the paralinguistic features between the Hausa and Igbo extractions of Nigeria using Ferdinand de Saussure's (1916) semiotic theory. Forty-five respondents were presented with five interview questions and the data generated were analyzed with the Semiotic Theory. The result shows that there is a higher percentage similarity between them than difference. There are nonverbal vocal communications that communicate meaning and two types of paralanguages examined were vocal and non-vocal paralanguage. Some gestures from the study fall under the non-vocal paralanguage. These are movements made with any part of the body in order to express meaning or emotion, or to communicate an instruction/feeling or action, like shrugging, making a fist, making a thumb up sign, or spreading the hand to say 'waka', etc. The gestures from the data were classified into two: vocal paralanguage and non-vocal paralanguage. These gestures are culture specific and can be misunderstood unintentionally, or misinterpreted, which can lead to offence and, so, hinder communication. Gestures hold specific meanings for members of varied cultures and are likely to be misunderstood by people unfamiliar with them. For example, the American OK sign depicts obscenity in Russia or Turkey. Also, the Yoruba gesture, where a woman removes her head gear and ties it on her waist, holding her waist and shaking one leg, means that she is ready to fight but it doesn't mean the same in the Igbo paralanguage.

Cooperrider et al. (2018) investigated the nonverbal reactions of speakers and how speakers commonly rotate their forearms so that their palms turn upwards. Some of these gestures are made in an incoherent manner during discourse, like touching someone incoherently during discourse. Gestures are different from the vocal paralanguage, like the sigh, gasp, *mm!*, *shii*, cry, *sigh*. Bronckart (2018) uses Saussure's (1916) semiotic theory to analyse the way semiotic units and linguistic signs were conceptualised, and the implications of this conceptualization for the human significant process.

Two states from each of the geographical zones were selected to represent the two ethnic groups, namely Anambra state and Imo state for the Igbo ethnic groups, while Lagos state and Ogun state were selected for the Yoruba ethnic groups. A sample of 63 participants from the study area were randomly selected for this study.

3. Methodology

An unstructured five interview questions were designed, validated and administered to 63 respondents. The purpose of the interview was to discover:

- The awareness of paralinguistic devices in the study areas.
- Whether these paralinguistic devices are culture bound.
- The awareness of voiced paralanguage.
- Which gestures indicate what?

The sample (n=63) comprised indigenous members of the study areas resident in Awka and students of Prescience Programme of Nnamdi Azikiwe University, Awka. The data were collected through systematic observation and interview. Data obtained were categorized and illustrated with tables (see Appendix 1). The data were categorized into two: the vocal paralanguage, and the gestures. Using the semiotic theory, the data were analyzed by identifying the sign, the signifier, and the signified. Examples of vocal paralanguage and gestures are presented showing the similarities and differences between Igbo and Yoruba. The Table below summarizes the theoretical framework to analyze data in this study.

Textual data (Sign): Signifier	Signified
The sound or gesture.	The meaning or the image associated with such a sound or gesture.

Table 1: Selected textual data and method of analysis: semiotic theory.

4. Data Analysis and Results

The Semiotic theory's framework of signs and signifiers was used to analyse the data and examples of similarities between the two languages are presented below in Table 2, and analyses for differences are presented in Table 3.

Sign	Language	Signified	Context
Shii!	Yoruba Igbo	Sound made with clenching the teeth, rounding the lip and exhaling air to draw attention someone's attention to stop doing something.	Used to hush children to keep quiet.
Ah!	Yoruba Igbo	To indicate surprise	Used to express surprise at an unexpected ugly occurrence.
M..m..m..m!	Igbo	Sound made in the glottis when one notices something dangerous around.	Used to indicate danger.
Ahhh!	Yoruba	Sound made when one notices something dangerous around.	Used to indicate danger.

Table 2: Voiced Paralanguage

The presence of the signifiers displays the fact that there are vocal paralinguistic signs in the two ethnic groups. The first two (Table 2) show cross-cultural similarities in the ethnic groups, and the last two (Table 2) show cross-cultural differences in their paralanguage.

The semiotic theory's framework of signs and signifiers was used to analyse the data and examples of similarities between the two languages are presented below in (3), and analyses for differences are presented in (4).

Sign	Language	Signifier	Context
Calling someone with the forefingers	Yoruba/Igbo	Derogatory, for animals	Used when to degrade someone.
Opening one's lower eyelids with one's hands.	Yoruba/Igbo	Used to Indicate 'Serves you right'	Used when someone deserves a bad thing that he/she experienced during an encounter with the other person.
When a Queen intertwines her fingers, turning them upwards while kneeling before her king.	Yoruba	Asking for forgiveness.	Used when a queen offends her king and is asking for forgiveness.
When a queen kneels before her King with bowed head.	Igbo	Asking for forgiveness.	Used when a queen offends her king and is asking for forgiveness.

Table 4: Gestures

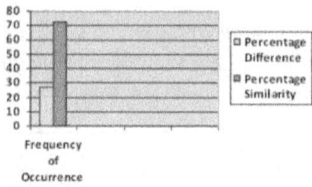

Figure 1:   Paralinguistic bar chart of similarities and differences

The presence of the signifiers highlights the fact that there are non-vocal paralinguistic signs (gestures) in the two ethnic groups. The first two (Table 4) show cross-cultural similarities in the ethnic groups and the last two (4) show that there are cross-cultural differences in their gestures.

The similarities and differences in terms of sign and the meaning in the two languages were calculated in percentages to find out the percentage difference and similarity as shown below.

Figure 1 further explicates the percentage similarity and difference of the two languages in terms of sign and meaning. Percentage similarity is 73%, and represented in the figure with the red bar, while the percentage difference which is 27% is clearly represented in the figure with the blue bar. This goes to show that there are more intercultural similarities than differences between the paralinguistic features of the two languages.

The results of the data were discussed hereunder in relation to the questions presented for this study. The different questions were specific to the textual data used for the study. Generally, the findings unravelled some forms of paralinguistic devices in the two major ethnic groups in Nigeria, highlighting their similarities and differences. Moreover, it discovered that developing a paralinguistic template for intending emigrants and tourists to Nigeria is crucial and possible. The tables were classified into two sections, namely: vocal paralanguage, and gestures. The different forms of paralinguistic devices among the studied ethnic groups are highlighted in the above stated tables.

There is great need for people to understand one another's language to make for effective communication. Gaps in communication can lead to great misunderstandings among people living together; which, when not properly handled, can lead to inter-ethnic clashes.

5. Conclusion

Based on the findings of this study, and their implications for language communication, the following conclusions are presented. Some signs observed in the languages of the ethnic group are similar, like the *shii!,* a vocal paralinguistic sign used to hush a child to stop making a noise. Also, the stretching out of the hand

and spreading the fingers at the other person (waka), a gesture to indicate displeasure at what the other person has done, is also found to be similar in the two cultures. There are also signs used by the ethnic groups that are different. There is a higher level of similarity (73%) than dissimilarity (27%) in the paralanguages of the ethnic groups under study which, when properly harnessed, can enhance inter-ethnic communication.

The findings of this study can help in engendering the communication between ethnic groups and also inform the production of paralinguistic charts that contain cues from major ethnic groups to be used in Nigerian Embassies all over the world to enhance communication.

References

Akujobi, O. (2005). Exploring the Semiotics and Praxis of Paralinguistic Signs between the Igbo and Hausa Extractions of Nigeria. *Research on Humanities and Social Sciences 5* (10).

Brown, G. (2017). Listening to Spoken English: Paralinguistic Features. London: Routledge. Retrieved on September 19 from http://www.taylorfrancis.com.

Bronckart, E. (2018). Pour une Approche Semiologique de l'Oral Illustrations a Partir des Figures d'Action. *Studia Universitatis Babes-Bolyai Philologia* 63 (2), 13-32.

Cooperrider, K., Natasha, A., & Susan G. (2018). The Palm-up Puzzle: Meanings and Origins of a Widespread Form in Gesture and Sign. *Frontiers in Communication 3* (23).

Kalin, S., Giampiero S., Dimosthenis, K., Hedvig, J. (2018). Analyses and Generation of Candidate Gaze Targets in Multiparty Open-world Dialogues. *Retrieved on* May 16 from http://www.divaportal.org.

Karpinski, M., Klessa K. (2018). Methods, Tools and Techniques for Multimodal Analysis of Accommodation in Intercultural Communication. *CMST*.eu 4 (1), 29-41.

Khalifa, M., Faddal, H. (2017). Impacts of Using Paralanguage on Teaching and Learning English Language to Convey Effective Meaning. *Studies in English Language Teaching 5* (2). Retrieved on May 17 fromhttp://www.scholink.org/ojs/index.php/selt.

Morris, C. (1938). *Foundations of the Theory of Signs*. Chicago: Oxford University Press.

Saussure, F. (1916). *Course in General Linguistics*. New York: Philosophical Library.

Zi, H. K., Lausberg, H. (2018). Koreans and Germans: Cultural differences in hand movement band gestural repertoire. *Journal Intercultural Communication Research*.

Appendix 1: Comparing Igbo and Yoruba Paralanguage

S/N	Signifier	Vocal Paralanguage	
		Signified (Igbo)	Signified (Yoruba)
1.	Shaa! /Taa!	Used to hush a child to be quiet.	Not Applicable
2.	Ohoo!	Used to indicate that 'l told you'	Not Applicable
3.	Kum	Sound made with the tongue and the upper palate, to indicate displeasure over something.	Not Applicable
4.	Shiii	Sound made with clenching the teeth, rounding the lip and exhaling air, used to stop people from making a noise.	Same
5.	M..m..m..m..!	Sound made in the glottis, used to indicate 'danger'	Ahhh!
6.	Mm!	Assent indicator	Same
7.	Mm..m!	Negative indicator	Same
8.	Ah!	Surprise	Applicable
9.	Ewooo!	A high-pitched sound indicating fear, pain, excitement or amusement.	Not Applicable
10.	Ehh!	Expressing surprise	Applicable
11.	Tsk tsk with shaking the head sideways.	Indicating disapproval	Not Applicable
12	Gasp	Used to indicate when somebody is shocked, afraid or when something suddenly happens.	Same
13.	Whistle	To make music or attract attention.	Same
14.	Cry	A loud inarticulate expression of pain, rage or surprise.	Same
15.	Laugh	To express amusement.	Same
16.	Groan	A long low cry expressing pain.	Same
17.	Rhythm	Moderately fast. The pattern of sound that characterizes a language or dialect of the ethnic group.	Fast

Table 1: Comparing some Igbo and Yoruba paralanguage using the Semiotic Theory

	Gestures		
1	Wagging the forefinger before somebody.	Be careful	Be careful
2	Swinging your whole palm backwards	Go	Go
3	Calling someone with the forefingers	Derogatory, for animals.	Derogatory, for animals.
4	Smile	Happy	Happy
5	Calling someone with your palm facing up or down and wagging your whole fingers.	Polite way of calling someone.	Polite way of calling someone.
6	Joining one's forefinger and third finger and touching one's lips.	An indication of a desire to smoke.	An indication of a desire to smoke.
7	When a woman rejects a man's handshake.	She is angry with the man.	She is angry with the man.
8	Opening Ones Lower Eyelids with One's hands.	Used to Indicate 'Serves you right'	Used to Indicate 'Serves you right'
9	Slanting one's mouth to one side.	Used to indicate 'Surprise'	Disrespect and to indicate when someone is telling a lie.
10	Turning ones back, opening the under garments, holding the buttocks in both hands, bending down and showing the other person the bare buttocks.	Used to indicate that the other person is despicable.	Not Applicable
11	Nodding	Yes	Yes
12	Shaking the head sideways	No	No
13	Holding and pulling both ears while talking with somebody.	Used to warn somebody.	Used to warn somebody.
14	Stretching out the hand and spreading one's fingers at the other person, when one is angry.	Used to indicate displeasure at one's action. (Waka)	Used to indicate displeasure at one's action. (Waka)
15	Turning your palm inside out with a raised eyebrow and looking pointedly at someone.	What is happening or Where are you going to or What is it?	What is happening or Where are you going to or What is it?
16	Opening one's lower eyelids with both hands and sticking out one's tongue at someone.	Used to indicate serves you right.	Used to indicate serves you right.
17	A man shakes a lady and scratches her palm softly.	Used to indicate a proposal of love.	Not Applicable
18	If the above-mentioned lady, removes her hand hastily and blinks deeply.	Used to indicate lack of interest in the proposal of love.	Not Applicable

Table 2: Comparing some Igbo and Yoruba paralanguage using the Semiotic Theory.

Appendix 2: Percentage Similarity and Percentage Difference Formula

Percentage Similarity:

$$\frac{No.\,of\,similarity \times 100}{63 \times 1} = \frac{46 \times 100}{63 \times 1} = 73\%$$

Percentage Difference:

$$\frac{No.\,of\,difference \times 100}{63 \times 1} = \frac{17 \times 100}{63 \times 1} = 27\%$$